Two all-new, all-Texas romances from
international bestsellers

DIANA PALMER

AND

LINDA LAEL MILLER

DIANA PALMER
LINDA LAEL MILLER

featuring

Merciless
&
McKettricks of Texas: Tate

MILLS & BOON

First published in Great Britain 2012
by Mills & Boon, an imprint of Harlequin (UK) Limited, Eton House, 18-24 Paradise Road, Richmond, Surrey TW9 1SR

UNTAMEABLE © Harlequin Enterprises II B.V./S.à.r.l. 2012

Merciless © Diana Palmer 2011
McKettricks of Texas: Tate © Linda Lael Miller 2010

ISBN: 978 0 263 89757 9

009-0412

Printed and bound by
CPI Group (UK) Ltd, Croydon, CR0 4YY

Merciless
DIANA PALMER

The prolific author of over one hundred books, **Diana Palmer** got her start as a newspaper reporter. One of the top ten romance writers in America, she has a gift for telling the most sensual tales with charm and humour. Diana lives with her family in Cornelia, Georgia.

To D.A. with much gratitude.

CHAPTER ONE

THE ATTRACTIVE BLONDE sitting on the chair beside Jon Blackhawk's desk in the San Antonio FBI office was as irritating as most of the prospective brides his well-meaning mother threw at his head. He was impatient and half out of humor already, with testimony on an upcoming court case awaiting him. This woman's fascination with the latest trend in hairstyles was leading him to think of bars. And he never took a drink.

"See, mine was done by Mr. James at Sherigan's," she continued, indicating her haircut, which looked quite frankly as if someone had put her head in a blender. He bit his tongue trying not to make the comment out loud. "He could do wonders for you. That long hair is *so* retro!"

There was a perfunctory knock at the door and his administrative assistant, Joceline Perry, stuck her head in the door. "Excuse me, Mr. Blackhawk, but you're due in court in ten minutes."

He nodded, forcing himself not to dance on the desk with glee. It would have been totally out of character, but the past thirty minutes of fashion information had left him feeling brainless.

He got to his feet. "It was good to see you, Charlene. Please give my love to my mother when you see her."

"I'll be seeing her tonight, since we're going to the theater together. It's a production of that romantic comedy that Shakespeare wrote, in a modern setting," she enthused. "Your mother has three tickets to it," she added with a hopeful smile.

He cleared his throat and tried desperately to think of an excuse.

Joceline, her blue eyes twinkling, interjected, "There's that meeting with your informer tonight at seven," she lied.

"Oh. Oh, yes, thank you," he said, trying not to sound as relieved as he felt. "Another time, perhaps," he told Charlene.

She shrugged. "I suppose your job requires you to do things at odd times," she said. "You might think about another profession," she said with a thoughtful frown. "I mean, if you get married, you won't have time for these evening job-related thingies."

His black eyes glittered. "I have no plans to marry."

She gave him an odd look. "Your mother said you were ready to start a family," she said blandly.

The glare darkened. "My mother has plans of her own. They are not mine," he added firmly.

Charlene gave him a charming smile and touched the sleeve of his gray suit jacket with a well-manicured hand. "Well, most men don't want to marry and have a family, until they realize how nice it is."

He didn't bend an inch.

Charlene sighed. "Rome wasn't built in a day," she ventured.

"It was, however, sacked by Charles V and his forces in one of the most violent attacks in military history," Joceline said with a sigh. "The Pope was forced to flee for his life." Her blue eyes went dreamy in their frame of short, straight black hair that just covered her small ears. "Charles V was the father-in-law of Mary Tudor, who was the sister of Elizabeth the First. Mary was in her thirties and Philip II was in his twenties when they married. It was a very strange match. But royalty in the sixteenth century was somewhat different in attitude." She smiled. "Do you study history?" she asked Charlene.

"Ugh," Charlene said, and shuddered dramatically. "What a sick and horrible subject. Old dead people."

Joceline's eyebrows arched. "The past determines the future," she said. "For instance, did you know that in seventeenth-century America, women were accused of witchcraft and hanged for any sort of misbehavior?" She cocked her head. "That blouse you're wearing would have landed you in a river in Massachusetts in no time. You see, there was a common belief that only witches floated when thrown into bodies of water," she added helpfully. She smiled again.

Charlene gave her a blank look. "This is the latest fashion," she pointed out. She glared at Joceline's neat black skirt, small-heeled black shoes and blue button-up blouse. "You might have been jailed for having such awful fashion sense," she countered with contempt.

"No, no, they didn't jail people for that," Joceline replied smoothly. "They put them in stocks, but not for being conservatively dressed." She cocked her head again. "However, women who cheated on their husbands were branded with a large letter A."

Charlene cleared her throat and glared even more. "I am separated from my husband and we are in the process of a divorce."

"Really?" Joceline asked, all eyes. "Well, isn't it lucky this is the twenty-first century?" she asked.

"I did not cheat on him!" Charlene raged.

Joceline's blue eyes were innocent. "I never insinuated such a thing!"

Charlene's face flushed. Beside her slender hips, against the expensive fabric of her slacks, her manicured hands were clenched. "The gentleman in question and I were merely having supper together after the theater! It was all lies!"

"I'm certain that it was," Joceline said with a bland smile.

Jon had been enjoying the repartee, but he quickly collected himself. "Ms. Perry, aren't you working on a case?" he asked deliberately.

She blinked. "A case, sir?" she asked.

"Follow-up interviews in my kidnapping court case?"

"The court case. Right." But she didn't leave.

Charlene was more irritated than ever. She grabbed her purse. "I see that it's an inconvenient time for us to talk," she told Jon. She went close to him, enveloping him in expensive perfume that made him cough. "I'll talk to you again later, in a more…personal environment, okay?"

He cleared his throat. He wished to goodness that she'd just leave. "KK," he said, using a gamer's abbreviation for "okay."

She glared at him. "Those abbreviations are silly. You play those stupid video games, too, like your brother, don't you?" she demanded. "Well, that's another thing you'll have to work on. No woman is going to tolerate a man who games in every free minute!"

"Unless she's a gamer, too," Joceline said, smiling sweetly. "So many of us women are, these days."

Jon gaped at her.

Charlene glared at her. "It figures," she said curtly.

Joceline kept smiling. She stared pointedly at the other woman's haircut. "My goodness, did your head get caught in a blender or something?"

Jon coughed enthusiastically, trying to conceal laughter.

"I'll have you know I paid a hundred dollars for this styling cut!" Charlene raged.

Joceline held out a hand. "Please lower your voice, ma'am," she urged. "This is a federal office. No verbal outbursts are allowed."

Charlene glanced from one of them to the other with exasperation. "I will never come here again! I'll see you at Cammy's house, when you have time for civilized conversation," she said haughtily.

Jon didn't answer her. Joceline pointedly held the door open and smiled vacantly.

"Have a nice day," she told the departing woman.

Charlene was muttering to herself as she reached the outer office.

Jon let out the laugh he'd been concealing. "That was rude," he told Joceline.

She gave him a blank stare. "Was it, really?" She glanced toward the door. "Should I call her back and apologize?" she asked innocently.

"You do, and you're really fired," he threatened.

She shrugged. "Jobs aren't that hard to get for a woman who knows how to type and give free video game advice," she said. She smiled.

He waved a hand. "Go work on that brief. And what meeting do I have with an informer tonight?" he added with a frown.

"I could arrange one, if you like."

He let out a rough laugh and went back around to sit at his desk. "Cammy's driving me nuts with these prospective brides," he muttered. "I don't want to get married!" he added firmly and glared at Joceline, in the doorway.

She held out both hands. "Don't look at me! I don't want to get married, either. So if you were thinking of asking me," she added outrageously, and with a haughty look, "don't bother. My son would be devastated if we had to try to fit a third person into our Super Mario battles," she added, naming one of the more popular games.

"No worries, there, I like military-themed games."

"And that MMORPG you play with your brother," she told him, referring to federal agent McKuen Kilraven.

"Massively multiplayer online role playing game," he translated and smiled. "I never would have suspected you of being a closet gamer."

She sighed. "Me, either," she replied. "But Markie loves them."

Her son. She had never married, but she'd been going out with a soldier who shipped out to the Middle East and never came back. It had surprised Jon that she'd had a child out of wedlock, when she was such a conservative, religious person. She never spoke of the child's father, and rarely of the child. She kept her personal life as private as Jon kept his own.

JOCELINE WAS AWARE of his curiosity about her. He was dishy, she thought, staring at him unconsciously, with that long, thick black hair in a ponytail down his back and that tall, lean, elegant physique. Women found him attractive, but he was standoffish. Gossip was that he'd never had a woman in his life. Both he and his brother were arch conservatives in just about everything, and neither of them had ever been known for licentious living.

Joceline put that thought out of her mind. She knew things about him that others didn't. In the five years she'd been with the office, watching him work in the field office's Violent Crimes Squad, she often held her breath when he went to work on the kidnapping cases that were his specialty. He had a special interest in human trafficking, particularly of children. He was a bulldog when he was working a case. It was one of many things Joceline admired about him.

Joceline wondered what Jon thought of her morals, knowing that she had a son and no husband. Markie had been a surprise; a shock, really. He was the one beautiful thing in her world, but news of his existence had not been good news at the time. She had told everyone that his father had been a good friend, home on leave from the military, and on the outs with a longtime girlfriend who'd dumped him. Joceline had commiserated with him. They frequently went out together in a platonic way, but that night they'd both had too much to drink. That was her story. But it wasn't quite true.

Joceline had been unsettled and uncertain about going through with the pregnancy at all. There were so many reasons why she should have ended it. But her love for the child's father, who would never know about him, made it impossible to go to a clinic. Such a dangerous, explosive secret she kept...

"I said," Jon repeated impatiently, "do you have the case files downloaded into my notebook computer for the court appearance?"

She blinked. "Sorry. What court appearance?"

He scowled. "The one you said I was going to be late for, the Rodriguez child abduction case. I thought it was next week."

"It is next week," she told him, with pursed lips.

He shook his head. "Just as well," he replied. "Another five minutes of discussion on new hairstyles and I think I'd have gone to the window and jumped out."

She gave him a bland look. "We're on the first floor," she reminded him.

"I meant, I'd have jumped out and hit the ground running," he amended.

"Isn't that what Detective Sergeant Rick Marquez did,

when a thief stole his laptop?" she recalled, chuckling. "And he got a citation for indecent exposure because he didn't put on any clothes when he went after the man?" She shook her head. "I understand the police department is still riding him high about it."

He chuckled, too. "Marquez is a conundrum. He'll make lieutenant one day, mark my words."

"I believe it."

The phone rang. She smiled, went out and closed the door.

THE NEXT MORNING, Joceline was almost half an hour late for work. When she came in, there were dark circles under her eyes and stress lines in her young face. She was only twenty-six, but she looked much older. She put her purse in her drawer and looked up as Jon appeared, impatiently, in his doorway.

"Sorry, sir," she said in a subdued tone. "I overslept."

His black eyes narrowed. "I haven't said much about it, but this is happening pretty often lately."

She flushed. "I realize that. I'm very sorry."

She was conscientious. She wouldn't do menial tasks, like bringing coffee, but she was the most competent paralegal he'd ever known. She did her job, she never goofed off and she did whatever the work required, even staying late without pay if it came down to it. It wasn't like her to party, so if she overslept, it had to be for another reason.

He came to stand in front of the desk. "What's wrong, Joceline?" he asked in a tone so gentle that tears stung her eyes.

She bit her lip to contain them. "Personal problems, sir," she said huskily. She held up a hand when he started to speak. "I can't...discuss them. I'm sorry. I'll try very hard to be on time from now on."

He wondered if her problem was a new man in her life. He

didn't like that thought. Then he was surprised that he was thinking it. Joceline was his assistant. Her private life was none of his business. Except that they'd been together for several years and he was concerned about her.

"If you need help," he began.

She smiled stiffly. "Thank you, sir, but I manage very well."

"What do I have on the agenda for today?" he asked, and cleared the way for business.

He was getting ready to leave for lunch with his brother, McKuen Kilraven, when Joceline came to the doorway. She wasn't smiling.

"What's up?" he asked.

She hesitated. "They cut Harold Monroe loose this morning."

He rolled his eyes. "Is my life insurance policy current?" he drawled.

She shook her head. "It isn't funny. I mean, Monroe manages to fumble everything he does, but he did attack a policeman with a Bowie knife when you had him arrested."

It was ironic that another man who'd made terrible threats to Jon earlier in the year had died of a heart attack in prison the day before he was due to be released. Joceline had thought her boss was safe, and had breathed a sigh of relief. But it didn't last. A few days later, Monroe was arrested for human trafficking and charged and swore vengeance against the people who had landed him in jail, including Jon.

"Monroe came at the policeman with a Bowie knife, tripped on the carpet, went head-over-heels and stuck the knife in his own leg," he reminded her with twinkling black eyes. "Then he tried to have the policeman prosecuted for assault."

"I understand some of the people in our legal system are still chuckling over that one," she agreed. "But even people who fumble sometimes manage to follow through on threats."

He waved a hand dismissively. "If he ever kills me, you can stand over my grave and say you told me so. I'm sure I'll hear you from wherever I am."

She didn't like that thought. She averted her eyes. "Anyway, the district attorney's office felt you should be aware of Monroe's parole status."

"I'm very grateful. You can pass that along to Mary Crawford at your leisure."

She grinned. Mary was one of their ablest assistant D.A.s and would probably win the big office one day.

Jon was reading her expressions. "Even if she gets to be D.A., you aren't going to work for her," he said firmly. "I'm too old to start breaking in new employees. The one we've got part-time is twisting my nerves raw."

"Phyllis Hicks is a nice girl," Joceline protested. "Just because she messed up one deposition..."

"Messed it up!" he exclaimed. "The woman can't even spell!"

"The spellchecker was malfunctioning," she said defensively.

"Joceline, she's in college part-time. They're supposed to teach you basic grammar in school before you even get to college, aren't they?" He threw up his hands. "Every time I go online, I see people using the contraction for 'it is' for the possessive form, using 'there' for 'their,' giving personal pronouns for inanimate objects...!"

She held up a hand. "Sir, we can't all be brilliantly literate. And there is the spellchecker function on all modern computers."

He glared at her. "Civilization will fail. You mark my words. If people can't spell, it's just a short jump to not being able to read instructions at all. Havoc will result."

It was his pet peeve. She just shook her head. "Havoc can't result from not reading instructions."

"Wait until some idiot strikes a match next to an oxygen tank and tell me that again."

Her eyes brightened. "There was this guy on the *Miami Vice* TV series—I have it on DVD—who walked into an illegal drug processing operation with a lit cigarette and blew up the whole building...!"

"Don't tell me. You still watch the *A-Team*, too." He rolled his eyes.

"They had to knock out B.A., Mr. T's character, every time they flew somewhere because he was terrified of airplanes," she chuckled.

"There are all sorts of programs on television," he began.

"Yes. How wonderful for people who can afford cable or satellite reception." She sighed dreamily. "It's wonderful to have a DVD player, even if it's old."

He was shocked. He'd never inquired about her finances. But now he took a closer look at her. Her clothing seemed serviceable, but quite old. Not that he cared much about women's fashions, but what she was wearing seemed several years out-of-date. Her shoes were nicely polished, but worn and scuffed.

She blushed when she noticed his intent scrutiny. "There's nothing wrong with dressing conservatively," she muttered.

His eyebrows arched. "God forbid they should put you in stocks," he commented.

"We don't live in Massachusetts and we aren't mucking about in the seventeenth century," she pointed out.

"Point taken." He sighed. "Is my brother going to pick me up for lunch?"

She put a finger to her forehead and closed her eyes. "I see a black SUV pulling into the parking lot as we speak." She opened one eye and looked past him out the window.

He threw up his hands and walked out the door.

Joceline grinned to herself. She liked winding him up. She did it often. He was far too somber. He needed to loosen up a little and stop taking life too seriously.

Then she thought about her own situation and sighed. It was just as well that she had a sense of humor, or she'd be dead herself. Her life was no bed of roses. However, it was just as well to smile as to cry. Neither would change anything.

"You're out of sorts again," Kilraven mused, eyeing the brother who resembled him so much. Well, they had the same hair color, but Kilraven kept his hair short, and Jon's eyes were very dark, where Kilraven's were pale gray and glittery. They were half brothers, but that didn't stop them from being close.

"Cammy's getting on my nerves," Jon said tersely. "It was another dizzy debutante yesterday morning. I had half an hour on fashion and hairstyles."

Kilraven glanced at him as he pulled into traffic. "You could use a little fashion sense. No offense." He chuckled.

"I dress quite well, thank you," Jon said, referring to his three-piece watered gray silk suit.

"You're elegant, all right," said Kilraven, dressed in khaki slacks and a white polo shirt. "But your hair's way out of style."

"I'm Lakota," he pointed out. "Nothing wrong with long hair."

"You're Cherokee, too," came the droll reply.

Jon sighed. "I like my roots and my culture."

Kilraven smiled. "So do I."

Jon glanced at him. "You don't show it."

He shrugged. "I'm not defined by my ancestry."

Jon glared. "Neither am I. But I prefer the Native American side of it."

"I wasn't making accusations," the older man said blithely. "You're just bent out of shape because Cammy wants you to get married yesterday and present her with a dozen grandkids."

"Aren't you and Winnie working on that?" Jon asked dryly, referring to Kilraven's new wife, Winnie Sinclair from Jacobsville.

Kilraven chuckled. "Yes, we are. I can't wait."

"I'm glad you can finally let go of the past," Jon said with affection. Kilraven's wife and child had been brutally murdered seven years earlier. He'd never dreamed that his older brother would ever get married again. It delighted him that Kilraven had found such a kind and loving partner.

"You ever going to get married?"

Jon grimaced. "Not to any of Cammy's idiot candidates."

He laughed. "This one wasn't from an escort service…?"

"I don't know." He pursed his lips. "I need to have Joceline run a background check on her, just to see."

"Illegal, unless she's applying for a job with the Bureau."

Jon lifted an eyebrow. "Aren't you a stickler for rules, when you're notorious for breaking them?"

"Hey, we all mature. Some of us just do it later than others."

"True."

"Have you bought the new Halo game?"

Jon smiled. "I bought it a long time ago, but it's still sitting on the shelf at home."

"You and World of Warcraft." Kilraven sighed, shaking his head. "My young brother-in-law, Matt, is crazy for it. When he's not in school, he's online, grouping with other people to kill monsters. His latest friend is a sixty-four-year-old grandmother of three. They do dungeons together."

Jon whistled. "Does she know his age?"

"Oh, yes. And he also plays with a group from a nursing home. They all have internet connections, and most of them play WoW. It's their sole entertainment now, since they're physically handicapped and can't socialize with the world at large." He smiled. "You know, that's not a bad thing. It keeps their hand and eye coordination going, and gives them a window into the whole world."

"I know. I play, too. What's Matt's WoW gamer handle?"

"One of his toons is an eightieth-level Death Knight named Kissofdeaths," Kilraven said.

Jon's eyes bulged. "That's Matt? I've been doing random dungeons with him! He tanks and I heal with my druid."

"I'll have to tell him. He'll roll on the floor laughing."

"Don't you dare," Jon warned. "Now that I know who he is, I'll ride him high."

Kilraven pulled into the parking lot of a local Mexican restaurant and turned off the vehicle. He looked at Jon. "They cut Harold Monroe loose," he said quietly.

"Don't you start. Joceline told me already. She's worried, too. Listen," he said with faint exasperation, "the guy is a total idiot. He can't even walk and chew gum at the same time!"

"He's had his finger in every illegal pie in San Antonio for years. He's been accused of petty theft, running a gambling operation, not to mention houses of prostitution, and now this latest charge, pimping immigrant girls. He sleazed out of the other charges, but you and Joceline tracked down witnesses to have him prosecuted for kidnapping the teen daughter of illegal immigrants for a local brothel," the older man said grimly. "He swore that he'd have the case dropped and he'd get even if he ever got out. He's been in jail for three months waiting trial and he's already spent more time in solitary confinement than any other prisoner they've got."

"Which only proves that he gets caught every time."

"That won't do you much good if he gets caught after he's offed you," Kilraven reminded him.

"I'm street smart," Jon said. "I have built-in radar when it comes to possible ambushes. You should remember that I've never had a speeding ticket."

"At the speeds you travel, I'm still amazed."

Jon grinned. "I always know where they're hiding to catch people."

That was true. It had dumbfounded Kilraven the first time Jon told him to slow down because there was a Department of Public Safety car sitting under a bridge over the next hill. Kilraven had just laughed, but he slowed down. Sure enough, when they topped the hill, there was the car, backed under a bridge out of sight.

"Some ability, and you a cop," Kilraven accused.

Jon shrugged. "It wouldn't do for a senior FBI agent to be caught for speeding in his own jurisdiction," he said.

"You shouldn't be speeding in the first place," Kilraven reminded him.

"Everybody speeds. I just don't get caught."

"There will come a day," his brother predicted.

"When it does, I'll pay the fine," Jon replied. "Are we going to eat or talk?"

Kilraven popped his seat belt and opened the door. "Okay, hide your head in the sand about Monroe. But please keep your doors locked at night and be aware of your surroundings when you're working late."

"You're worse than Cammy."

"I am not," Kilraven said huffily. "I haven't sent one single unattached woman to your office for nefarious purposes."

"I guess you haven't."

They walked toward the restaurant. "I don't suppose you've ever noticed what's right under your nose."

"What do you mean?"

"Joceline," Kilraven replied easily. "She's a fine young woman. Needs a helping hand with her fashion sense, but she's intelligent and quick-thinking."

"You just like her because she knows sixteenth-century Scottish history," Jon accused, because the subject was his brother's passion.

"She knows European history, as well. And seventeenth-century American history."

"Yes, she was spouting it to Cammy's candidate yesterday. She tied her up in knots. The woman was going on and on about fashion and Joceline cut her off at the ankles with historical references to dress codes."

"Told you she was smart."

"She is smart." He looked at Kilraven. "But I don't want to get married. Not for years yet. I'm just thirty!"

"Almost thirty-one, little brother," Kilraven said affectionately. "And you really don't know what you're missing."

"If I don't know, I can't miss it. Now let's get something to eat," he said quickly, cutting the other man off.

Kilraven chuckled as he followed him into the restaurant. Jon had actually taken Joceline on a date once, some years back. It had been a strange aftermath, including a hospital visit and some threats of legal charges. Jon never spoke of it. He kept secrets. But so did his brother. No doubt he didn't like remembering that his drink had been spiked right under his nose.

CHAPTER TWO

"BUT SHE'S SUCH a sweet girl," Cammy argued over the phone. "She's pretty and she knows all the right people!"

"She spent thirty minutes giving me news bulletins on the latest fashions and hairstyles," Jon muttered.

There was an exasperated sigh. "At least she's better dressed than that acid-tongued secretary of yours!"

"Administrative assistant," Jon corrected. "And Joceline at least manages within her budget. She doesn't have to borrow to buy clothes."

"It does show," came the sarcastic reply.

Jon frowned. "Cammy, don't you remember being poor?" he asked quietly.

"I do remember, and I'm your mother, so stop calling me by my first name."

"Sorry, force of habit. Mac does it all the time."

"Call him McKuen, if you please. I hate that nickname."

"So does he."

"Your secretary has a child out of wedlock," Cammy continued, unabated. "I hate having you associated with someone like that."

He felt himself bristling. "We live in the twenty-first century," he objected.

"Yes, and morality is all that separates us from savagery," she shot back. "We have rules of conduct to keep civilization from floundering. Just look around you at the outrageous things people are doing! Women don't raise children anymore, they run corporations! Do you wonder why the crime rates among juveniles are so high? Who's teaching them values? Who's…?"

He cleared his throat. "Cammy, I'm due in court."

She stopped short, still seething. "You should get another secretary."

"I'm so glad you called. Have a nice day. I'll phone you on the weekend."

"Come to the ranch for the weekend," she suggested.

Where her candidate would be waiting with glee.

"Afraid I can't, there's a stakeout."

"You're a senior agent, surely you can delegate!"

"Not on this one. Now I have to go. Really."

"I don't like it that you work on that violent crimes squad. You could work white collar crime! Jon…"

"Bye, Cammy!"

"Don't call me…!"

He put down the receiver and let out a puff of air. That was when he noticed Joceline, outside the door he'd forgotten to close. She was very pale and she didn't speak. She walked in, forced a smile and laid a document on his desk. While he was trying to find something to say, and worrying about how much of that conversation she'd overheard, she walked out and closed the door.

Joceline sat down at her desk heavily and tried to block out the sound of Jon's mother's voice, which had been audible even several feet away from the telephone. Most agents used cell phones, and eavesdropping wasn't really possible, but Jon used a landline in the office. And Cammy Black-hawk's voice carried. Joceline felt sick to her stomach as she registered the other woman's overt hostility toward her.

She knew that people talked about her. Gossip was un-avoidable in her situation, even in modern times, in a city. Cammy Blackhawk was a throwback to another generation, one just slightly less tolerant and open-minded than younger people today. It didn't help that Joceline was hopelessly in love with her attractive boss, or that she had uncomfortable dreams about him.

He enjoyed being single. He rarely dated, and even when he did, it was usually a professional woman, an attorney or a district court judge. Once it had been an attractive public defender. But it was usually only one date. Like the one he'd had with Joceline. She didn't dare think too much about that.

She was curious about why he didn't date. She couldn't ask him, of course. It was far too personal a question. But she'd overheard him talking to his brother once about how aggressive women could be. Knowing that his supposedly chaste reputation was like a red flag to a permissive female, she imagined that he'd been faced with imminent seduction more than once and didn't like it. As his mother was moral, so was he. They were both conservative to the back teeth, in fact.

Joceline looked at the photo of Markie that she kept in her wallet. He was a mix of his mother and father. He had his father's elegant straight nose and his black hair. His father was good-looking, and smart. She hoped that Markie would follow his father in that respect.

She sighed over the photograph. Her fascination with her pregnancy had grown by the day while she carried Markie. He was a beautiful child, blue-eyed and slender, with a mis-chievous expression that was characteristic of him. He loved to play hide-and-seek. He enjoyed video games, especially

Super Mario Brothers. He was constantly begging for a puppy or a kitten, but she'd explained gently that it was impossible. He was in day care while she worked, although now he was in preschool part of the day, and day care the rest, and they had no yard for a dog to play in. They had no room, either. It was a one-bedroom apartment, and Markie slept in a small bed near hers. It was wiser that way at night, due to medical problems that she'd never shared with her boss. She worried about her child constantly. There were good medications for his condition, but the ones she used didn't seem to work, especially in the spring and fall of the year. The leaves were just starting to fall in San Antonio as the weather turned cooler, and Markie was having more trouble than usual. It was no wonder that she had dark circles under her eyes and was late to work. Especially after a night like last night…

"…I said, did Riley Blake call?" Jon repeated.

Joceline jumped and dropped the small plastic photo insert she'd been holding.

Frowning, Jon picked it up. He stared at the child in the photograph with curiosity. "He looks like you," he said finally as he handed the insert back to her.

She put it away quickly. "Yes," she stammered. "Sorry, sir."

He shoved his hands in his pockets and stared at her with open curiosity. "We have those bring-your-child-to-work days here, but you never bring your son with you."

"It would be inconvenient," she said. "Markie is a bit of a pirate when he's in company. He'd be making hats out of files and standing on the desk," she added with a laugh.

His eyebrows arched. Cammy had said that Jon had been singularly mischievous as a young boy.

Joceline glanced at him. "They think he may have attention deficit disorder," she said. "They wanted to put him on drugs.…"

"What? At his age?" he exclaimed.

She shifted. "He's in preschool," she said. "He unsettles the other children because he's hyperactive."

"Are you going to let them medicate him?" he asked, with real interest.

She looked up, her blue eyes troubled. "I don't know," she said hesitantly. "It's a hard issue to deal with. I thought I'd discuss it with our family doctor and see what he thinks, first."

"Wise." He drew in a long breath. "That's a decision I'd have a hard time with, too."

She managed a smile. "Times have changed."

"Yes."

She searched his black eyes and her body tingled. She looked away quickly. This would never do. She fumbled her purse back under her desk. "I was going to print out that brief for you," she said, opening a file on the computer. "And you're having lunch with the deputy sheriff in that potential federal kidnapping case."

"Yes, we thought we'd discuss the case informally before lawyers become involved."

She gave him a droll look. "I thought you were a lawyer."

"I'm a federal agent."

"With a double major in law and Arabic studies and language."

He shrugged. His dark brows drew together. "How did you manage college?"

She blinked. "Excuse me?"

"You work endless hours and you have a small child," he said. He didn't add that he knew her finances must have been a problem, as well.

She laughed. "I went on the internet. Distance education. I even got a degree that way."

"Amazing."

"It really is," she agreed. "I wanted to know more about a lot of subjects." Her favorite was sixteenth-century Scotland. One of her other interests was Lakota history, but she wasn't telling him that. It might sound awkward, since that was his ancestry.

"Sixteenth-century Scottish history," he mused. He frowned. "You didn't have a case on my brother, did you? That's his passion."

She gave him a glowering look. "Your brother is terrible," she said flatly. "Winnie Sinclair must have the patience and tolerance of a saint to live with him."

He glared at her. "My brother is not terrible."

"Not to you, certainly," she agreed. "But then, you'll never have to marry him."

He chuckled.

"My mother was a MacLeod," she added. "Her people were highland Scots, some of whom fought for Mary Queen of Scots when she tried to regain the throne of Scotland after being deposed by her half brother, James Stuart, Earl of Moray."

"A loyalist."

She nodded. "But my father's family were Stewarts with the Anglicized, not the French, spelling, and they sided with Moray. So you might say they united warring clans."

"Did your parents fight?"

She nodded. "They married because I was on the way, and then divorced when I was about six." Her eyes became distant. "My father was career military. He remarried and moved to the West Coast. He died performing maneuvers in a jet with a flying group."

"Your mother?"

"She remarried, too. She has a daughter…a little younger than me. We…don't speak."

He frowned. "Why?" he asked without thinking.

"I had a child out of wedlock," she said. "When she found out, she disowned me. She's very religious."

He made a rough sound. "I thought the purpose of religion was to teach forgiveness and tolerance. Besides all that, didn't you just say she was pregnant with you when your father and she got married?"

"Well, it doesn't work out that way sometimes with religion, and the important point to her was that she was married when I was born. We were never really close," she added. "I loved my father very much." She cleared her throat and flushed. "Sorry, sir, I didn't mean to speak of such personal issues on the job."

"I was encouraging you to," he replied quietly. He studied her with open curiosity. "You love your son very much."

She nodded. "I'm glad I decided not to end the pregnancy…" She almost bit her tongue off. She grabbed the phone and pushed in numbers. "I forgot to make your lunch reservations!"

Which she never did, considering it a menial chore. But he didn't mention that. He'd upset her by asking personal questions. It hadn't been intentional. He wondered about her private life, about the child.

While she was talking, he went back into his office. He'd meant to apologize to her for Cammy's rudeness, which he was certain that she'd overheard. Then he'd been distracted by the photo of her child. She had thought of ending her pregnancy. Why? She seemed very maternal and conscientious to him, but perhaps she'd never wanted to be pregnant. Accidents did happen. It was just that his clearheaded administrative assistant didn't seem the sort to have amorous accidents, of any type. In the past four years, he didn't recall seeing her date anyone at all.

He sat down behind his desk and recalled her pregnancy. The Bureau didn't discriminate, although her condition hadn't gone down well with some people. But she'd been very quiet, very discreet, during the time she carried the child.

She'd almost died having the child, he recalled. It had disturbed him when he got his first look at her afterward. She'd been pale, listless, devastated by the ordeal.

He'd put that reaction down to pain and drugs following the caesarian section, but now he wondered even more about her history, about the shadowy father of her child.

The phone rang. He picked it up.

"It's Sergeant Marquez," Joceline said formally and put him through.

"Marquez," Jon said. "What are you up to?"

"If you're going to mention my run-in with the computer thief, don't you dare," came the dry reply. "I've already been the subject of extreme censure from everybody up to and including the mayor."

"Really? Perhaps they had a glimpse of you running nude down the street and were impressed."

"Get a life, Blackhawk, you're just jealous of the attention I got," Marquez scoffed. "I'll bet if you ran nude down a street, nobody would even notice you!"

Jon laughed uproariously. "We'll never know."

"Anyway, what I called to tell you is that Harold Monroe beat the human trafficking charges with a hotshot public defender and got cut loose after the parents suddenly refused to testify," he said. "I know the D.A.'s office probably notified you, but sometimes they're slow. I wanted to make sure you knew."

"You're not the first person to tell me. The guy's a total

loon and incompetent at that. He can't walk and chew gum at the same time."

"Even people who fumble can perform amazing feats," Marquez said. "You watch your back."

"I'll paint a target on it, so Monroe won't have so much trouble finding me." Jon chuckled. "Thanks for the concern, though. I appreciate it."

"No problem. You still following soccer?"

"Not so much. My video game is taking over my life."

"I heard." There was a pause. "You helped a tenth-level warrior get a bag to carry his loot in, over in the Barrens."

Jon's eyes popped. "Yes."

"It was one of my alts," Marquez chuckled. "See? You never know who you're playing with."

"Which reminds me, did you know that my brother's brother-in-law plays, too? He's got an 80 death knight." He gave the name.

"Good grief, he fought the Horde with me in Darkshore a few months ago on the pier, before it was destroyed when the expansion came out!"

"He's formidable."

"I'll say, he saved my butt. You just never know, do you?"

"That's what makes it so exciting." Jon hesitated. "You ever going to get married?"

"Look who's talking! Wasn't your last date that public defender who only went out with you to try to get information to save her client?"

Jon's face hardened. "Yes."

"She should have known better. I thought she was a little young for you."

"Twenty-two, to my thirty, almost thirty-one. That's not so much."

"It's a generation." Marquez chuckled. "But she had an agenda."

"It almost got her disbarred."

"At least you didn't have her taken out of your office in handcuffs."

"That woman was a call girl," Jon snapped. "I can't even tell you what she did, and in my own damned office! It was all my mother's fault."

"Cursing in a federal office is not correct behavior and could get you censured by the SAC, sir," Joceline's blithe tone came over the phone.

"Stop eavesdropping!" Jon railed at her.

"And raising your voice is another infraction of the rules of common courtesy," she reminded him.

"Joceline!" he growled.

"There's a public defender out here who wants to speak to you."

Jon hesitated. Marquez was chuckling softly.

"Oh, not that one," Joceline replied at once, with a laugh in her tone. "This one is male and quite handsome."

Why did that anger him? "I'll see him in a minute. Send him to the canteen and show him where the coffeepot is."

"That would be a menial chore, sir," Joceline replied blithely. "As you know, I don't perform menial chores. It's not in my job description." She hung up.

Jon slammed his hand on the desk. "One day I'll have you hung on the flagpole!" he growled.

"Temper, temper," Joceline said, sticking her head in the door. "You'll ruin the finish on your desk. I asked Agent Barry to show the visitor to the coffee." She gave him a smug look. "Apparently agents don't mind making coffee. Is that in your job description?"

He picked up a magazine and hefted it, with glittery black eyes.

She closed the door with a snap. "Assault with a deadly weapon...!" came through it.

"A gaming magazine isn't a deadly weapon!"

"Gaming magazines are against agency policy…"

Curses ensued.

"Sir!" Joceline exclaimed haughtily.

Jon actually groaned. Marquez was laughing outrageously.

"One day I'll pour my lunch over her head," Jon muttered.

"Make sure it's something delicious," Marquez suggested. "I'll let you get back to the wars. Just wanted to make sure you knew about Monroe."

"Thanks. I really mean it."

"Hey, what are friends for?" the other man asked. "See you."

He hung up.

Jon glared at the closed door before he got up and opened it.

Joceline was sitting at her desk, looking angelic. His indignant expression made her bite her lower lip. It would never do to laugh.

The public defender, a slender young man with his blond hair neatly trimmed, came down the hall carrying a plastic cup with black coffee in it. He made a face.

"Don't you have anybody here who can make a decent cup of coffee?" he complained. "You could take rust off old cars with this stuff."

"I make excellent coffee," Joceline said dryly.

The visitor looked at her. "Why aren't you making it, then?"

"It's not in my job description, sir," she said with a vacant smile. "I don't do menial tasks."

"You're his secretary, and you won't make him coffee?"

"I am not a secretary, I'm an administrative assistant and a paralegal," Joceline corrected. "And Mr. Blackhawk would faint on the floor if I ever did such an odd thing here."

"I wouldn't faint," Jon said indignantly. He paused. "I'd have heart failure."

"Fortunately I know CPR," Joceline said. "You're safe with me, sir."

Jon glared at her.

"Don't make an enemy of her," the public defender suggested. "If you drink coffee like this for long, you may have need of her medical training." He made a face and put the cup down on Joceline's desk.

"Please don't do that," she told him. "I'm not responsible for unsupervised beverages. If it spilled on a computer, the agency would have to ask you to replace it."

"How would it spill on a computer?" he asked.

Joceline's hand moved toward it. "It's sitting in a very bad place," she said, and indicated the laptop computer just inches away. "If my hand slipped…"

The public defender removed the coffee with a grimace. "I never," he began.

"Give me that." Jon took the cup of coffee, walked down the hall and dumped it into a potted ficus plant.

"How cruel!" Joceline accused when he returned and tossed the empty cup into the trash can beside her desk. "What did that poor plant ever do to you?"

"Nobody ever waters it," he muttered. "It won't complain. And don't you dare," he added narrowly.

She cleared her throat. "I don't even know anyone who has connections to plant abuse societies."

"With my luck you'd start one," Jon muttered. "Come in. Harris, isn't it?" he asked the public defender as he opened his office door.

"Bill Harris," the defender said, nodding.

"Have a seat. Now what is it you need to discuss?"

JOCELINE was late because she had to finish typing up three letters, and then print them out since Jon needed hard copies of them. The printer ran out of ink and it took her forever to find the cartridges. Then it ran out of paper and she had to open another carton. She was looking at her watch and grimacing when she finished. She only had ten minutes to get to the day care facility before it closed. The owner was going to be furious. She'd been warned about this once before.

"What is it?" Jon asked when he noticed her expression.

"I have ten minutes before the day care closes," she began.

"Get out of here," he said easily. "I'll finish up."

She hesitated.

"Go on!"

She grabbed her purse. "Thank you, sir."

"No problem."

She made it, but with only two minutes to spare. The taut expression on the owner's face when she arrived spoke volumes. Joceline was worried even more because there had been complaints about Markie's behavior at the day care.

"If this happens again…" the woman began.

"It won't," Joceline promised. "I'll arrange for someone to pick him up, if I'm ever asked to stay late again."

The owner sighed. "You work for a federal office. I suppose you can't keep regular hours."

"It's difficult," Joceline agreed. "I need the job too much to refuse overtime."

"My husband was a federal agent, many years ago," the woman said surprisingly. "He was always on call."

"I suppose it was rough for you, too."

The woman looked surprised.

"I know the wives of a couple of our agents, including our Special Agent in Charge. They bite their fingernails when we're on dangerous cases."

The woman smiled. "I had two children and I couldn't afford to put them in day care, so I stayed at home until they started school. Then I couldn't find day care I could afford afterward, so I started my own business."

Joceline smiled. "A wise solution."

The woman nodded. She drew in a breath. "If you have to be late like this again, just call me. I have a girl who left to raise her own children. She'd be happy to keep Markie and she'd pick him up for you. Would you like her phone number?"

"Yes," Joceline said at once, and wondered how she'd afford it.

She wrote the number down and gave it to Joceline. She smiled. "It won't cost you an arm and a leg."

"Your fees are unbelievably reasonable," she pointed out.

The older woman chuckled. "Because I had to afford day care myself," she replied. "I thought there should be a way to make it affordable to people on strangled budgets."

"I'm very grateful." Joceline grimaced. "My budget has gone past strangled to near homicide."

"You could ask that handsome boss of yours for a raise."

"How do you know he's handsome?" she asked.

"His picture was in the paper after he and another agent caught one of the human traffickers they were looking for. Makes me sick what some people can do to helpless poor people in the name of profit. Imagine, using little kids in brothels…" She smiled. "Sorry, I hate people who exploit children. I tend to stand on a soapbox on the subject. I'll get Markie for you."

She brought the little boy out a couple of minutes later.

"Mommy!" Markie laughed, holding out his arms to be taken. "I learned how to draw a bird. Miss Ellie taught me! She said I did it real good!"

"You'll have to show me. Tell Mrs. Norris good-night."

"Good night, Mrs. Norris," he said obediently, and smiled

at her before he did a nosedive with his face into his mother's throat and held on tight.

"Thanks," Joceline said.

The older woman shrugged. "Men have no idea how tough it is on women who work," she replied.

"None at all," was the quiet reply.

"I had fun!" Markie said when they went into the small, sparsely furnished apartment and Joceline put the three door locks in place. "I got to show you my pictures!"

He handed her a file folder.

She sat down, worn to the bone, and opened it with no real enthusiasm. What she saw shocked her.

"Markie!" she exclaimed. "You drew this?"

"Yes! I saw that bird outside and I drawed him."

"Drew him," she corrected absently.

"It's a…"

"…a goldfinch," she said for him, noting the bright yellow color of the small male bird and its subdued black markings. In the winter, the coat would turn from yellow to the dull green that characterized females.

"You like birds," he said, leaning on her knees while she looked through the drawings. "You got all sorts of books about them. And binoculars." He rubbed his head against her arm. "Couldn't I look through the binoculars again? I want to see if we got any of these birds at our house."

"We probably don't have goldfinches," she replied, because there was no room in her budget for the special seed that constituted the best finch feed. It was outrageously expensive.

"You could cook some bread for them," he said. "You cook real good."

"Thank you, sweetheart," she said, and bent to kiss his thick black hair.

"I like pancakes. Couldn't we have pancakes?"

She looked at his rosy cheeks, his big eyes, his sweet expression. He was her whole life. Amazing how he'd changed it, from the first time she looked at him. "Yes," she said, indulging him as she always did, probably too often. "Bacon and pancakes and syrup. But only because I'm so tired," she added.

He smiled. "Thanks, Mom!"

"You're welcome."

The other drawings were also of birds. Just sketches, but they showed great promise of a talent that could be developed. She needed to find him an art teacher if he continued to have interest in the subject.

But that would cost money and she had nothing left over at the end of the week. She sighed. At least she had Markie, she reminded herself. The rest was just superfluous.

CHAPTER THREE

THE PUBLIC DEFENDER, Harris, was trying to get his client a job. It wasn't really his concern, but the young man in question was just twenty years old and already had a wife and a small child. He'd been prosecuted on a bank robbery charge, which put him in the crosshairs of the FBI. He was arrested, charged, jailed, prosecuted and convicted. Now he was out on parole for good behavior after some spectacular legal footwork by this attorney. It had been one of Jon's cases.

"He got drunk one night with some friends, who knocked over a branch bank when it opened early one morning," Harris said. He toyed with his napkin in the restaurant where he'd invited Jon Blackhawk for dinner. "He drew five to ten, even though he was asleep in the backseat the whole time."

"Rough," Jon said.

"It's my first real case," the younger man said. "I want to do a good job." He glowered. "Substance abuse is responsible for so many problems in our society."

"They did try to ban alcohol once," Jon remarked.

Harris chuckled. "Yes, with interesting results. The only people who got rich during Prohibition were the gangsters."

"That's usually what happens when you declare something illegal. Is it a first offense for your client?"

Harris nodded. "He taught Sunday School, actually."

"I know a minister who was involved in a murder," Jon said, tongue-in-cheek.

Harris laughed. "I know what you mean. But this kid was straight from the time he was old enough to walk. I talked to every relative he had and several friends, not to mention educators who taught him, vouched for him."

"That's a lot of legwork."

"Yes, it is, and I did it on my own time. I believe in this kid. I want to help him. If I can get him a job, and make him understand that he has to stay away from his so-called friends, who are also out on parole, he might have a chance. He's got a three-year-old kid," he added heavily. "And a sweet young wife who adores him."

"Sad case." Jon was noncommittal. He'd heard this story so many times it was grating. It usually ended badly. But he wasn't going to tell this naive but passionate new attorney that. Ideals should be worth something.

"The boy lives in Jacobsville. I thought, since your brother worked in Jacobsville with Cash Grier he might be willing to talk to the local parole officer and put in a good word for him, mention the bad crowd that he got in with and see if there's some way he can be kept away from it," the public defender said hopefully. "A good talking-to at the outset of his parole might do some good."

Jon laughed. "It might at that. Okay. I'll ask him."

Harris brightened like a lightbulb turning on. "Thanks! I owe you one."

"None of us in law enforcement want to see a man fail for one mistake. However," he added solemnly, "if he steps out of line again, you'll be talking to a brick wall if you ask for help."

"I know that."

Jon smiled. He'd talk to Mac. But he knew how this was going to go down, all the same.

"The guy's a born loser," Mac said predictably when Jon phoned him. "If he's stupid enough to be led into crime, he'll stay there. He's a follower with no sense of judgment about other people."

"I don't doubt it. But I promised Harris I'd ask you to intervene. If the kid can be kept away from his old associates, it might help. You can say no. It's not my problem."

Mac sighed. "I suppose I could talk to Grier," he said grudgingly. "But if Harris's client gets into any more trouble, ever, I'll be his worst nightmare."

"I'll be his second worst. Thanks."

"Why are you making your own phone calls?" Kilraven asked suddenly. "Doesn't your AA do that for you?"

"She didn't come in this morning," Jon said, and the worry he felt was reflected in his tone. "Didn't call, either. That's not like her."

"Did you phone her apartment?"

"Yes. No answer."

"Curious. Does she have enemies?"

Jon laughed in spite of himself. "I'm not likely to find her in a sack in the river, if that's what you mean."

"Sorry. I guess I've been in law enforcement too long."

"Join the club. You and Winnie coming to dinner Friday night?"

"Yes, if Cammy isn't going to be there."

"Winnie likes Cammy!"

"I know, but we've both had the tirade from Cammy about her new candidate for your affections. She'll be on a roll and we don't want to spoil a perfect dinner with a lot of argument. If you get what I mean."

Jon chuckled. "I haven't invited her, if that's a help."

"Then you can expect us. Winnie will bring homemade rolls. I didn't ask. She offered."

"I'm amazed she can still manage to bend over the oven with her belly sticking out that far," Jon remarked. "Cammy's sure it's going to be a boy because she's big in front like that."

"Childbirth is a mystery to most people. Not to Cammy. We'll be over about six."

"See you then."

Jon hung up. He hadn't let it show in his tone, but he was worried about Joceline. It was the first time she'd ever missed work without calling first. Something big must be up. He immediately thought of her son.

He picked up the phone and started calling hospitals.

JOCELINE was pacing the waiting room floor. She'd brought her knitting bag with her, but even that chore hadn't diverted her. This had been a bad attack, the worst one yet. She'd tried to go into the cubicle with Markie, but the attending physician and a nurse had shooed her out in the kindest way possible. They needed to run tests, they explained.

It was hard to leave a child who sounded as if he were smothering to death. Joceline was beside herself. Markie was her whole life. What if he died this time? What if they couldn't save him...?

"Joceline?"

She jumped and gasped at the sound of her boss's voice behind her. She jerked around, astonished.

"It's not like you," he explained, "not to call, if you can't make it to work. I figured it had to be something catastrophic."

She bit her lower lip. "It's Markie," she said on a long breath. "A bad attack. The worst one he's had yet." She folded her arms over her small breasts. "They're running tests."

At least she had medical insurance, good insurance, from her job. But it wouldn't cover all of the expense, and she didn't know how she'd add another monthly payment to the bills she already had.

"What sort of attack?" Jon repeated. Her mind was busy. She hadn't even heard him.

"He has asthma," she said heavily. "In the spring and fall, colds go down into his chest. He has chest infections, sometimes pneumonia. There are new drugs, good ones, for his condition, and we use them. He has allergy shots every week, too. But his lungs are just weak. He's never had an attack come on so quickly, or be this bad. I didn't think I'd even get him here in time…" She bit her lip and turned away.

"Has he seen a specialist?"

"Yes. Lung specialists, allergists, the works." She sighed. "I don't even smoke," she said plaintively.

He wondered how she managed to pay specialists. It would be rough for anyone, but especially for a single mother on a limited budget. He didn't have to be told that a child with uncontrolled asthma was an expensive little person to treat. He'd had his own share of respiratory problems as a child, Cammy had once told him. He still had allergies, too.

Joceline looked worriedly at the door to the emergency room from which a white-coated physician with a stethoscope around his neck had just emerged.

"That's Dr. Wagner," she explained as she moved toward him. "He's our family doctor."

The tall, thin physician smiled as she approached. "It's all right, Joceline, he's doing very well. We'll have the test results for you very soon. You have to stop worrying so much," he added gently. "Odds are very good that he'll outgrow the asthma, and that the allergies will respond to the shots and diminish. It just needs time."

She let out a breath. "I try so hard to make him wear his jacket when it's cool and a raincoat when it's raining," she muttered. "He whips them off the minute he gets out of my sight. Then he catches cold. There was a cold rain yesterday morning, and he went outside during play period without a coat and didn't tell me until he woke up smothering this morning."

Dr. Wagner chuckled. "Don't blame yourself. He's very sorry that he did it, more because of how upset you were than how dangerous it was to him," he added. "He has a big heart for such a small child."

"He gets picked on a lot at school because he can't run like the other kids without getting out of breath," Joceline said heavily. "And because he has to take shots for the allergies. Why are kids so mean to each other?"

"Why are there bullies?" Dr. Wagner replied. "I don't know. I wish it was an issue that could be resolved. Now with cyberbullying so prevalent, a victimized child can see no peace even in his own home."

"There should be more lawsuits," Joceline muttered.

"I agree," Jon said quietly.

Dr. Wagner looked at Jon curiously.

"This is my boss," Joceline said quickly, so the doctor wouldn't get the wrong idea. "Senior Agent Jon Blackhawk."

Dr. Wagner shook hands. "I wanted to join the FBI myself when I was younger," the doctor said surprisingly, "but my father wanted me to study medicine." He laughed. "In the long run, I suppose he was right. We have four generations of physicians and surgeons in my family. I'd hate to be the one to break the tradition."

"It's lucky for us that you didn't," Joceline said. "Thank you for taking such good care of Markie."

He smiled. "I told you that one day you'd be glad you made the decision you made," he said enigmatically.

"I am, now, more than ever, despite the problems," she added with a weary smile.

"Why don't you go and get something to eat?" the doctor asked. "By the time you get back, Markie will be ready to go home."

"They won't have to keep him?" she worried.

"Oh, I don't think so," he replied. "We just want to make sure he's stabilized and get him started on the new antibiotic. There are new inhalers out also, Joceline, you should talk to his allergist about them. One is for pediatric patients and has shown good results."

She sighed heavily. The allergist had suggested one of the newer inhalers, which was over a hundred dollars a month. On her budget, even with good insurance, that was a fortune. But perhaps she could write to the drug company and request a reduced price. That had worked for her in the past. "Thank God he's going to be all right."

"Nice to meet you, Agent Blackhawk," Dr. Wagner added, smiling as he walked away.

"Nice guy," Jon remarked.

"Yes, we're very lucky to have him. He's taken great care of Markie."

Jon was studying her with narrowed eyes. The doctor's statement about the decision she'd made was puzzling.

She was tired and raw from lack of sleep or she might have reconsidered her words. "His father and I were very good friends. We had too much to drink and…there was Markie."

He stared at her. He didn't speak.

She averted her eyes. "I underestimated how—" she

started to say "drugged" and immediately caught herself "—drunk he was and he didn't realize that I was naive about men. We were both stupid." She hesitated. "I wasn't sure how I'd feel about a child who wasn't planned." She smiled. "But now he's my whole world." Her voice broke off.

"Your path hasn't been an easy one," Jon said quietly.

"Nobody's path is easy. We just do what we have to do, and go on living. I love my son," she added. "I have to live with the fact that Markie will always be illegitimate." She looked up at him. "It hurts me. I try to live a conservative life. But it's not Markie's fault."

"Of course not."

She picked up her purse from the seat she'd occupied. "I'll get some breakfast and see what they can do for Markie, but I don't know if I can come in today. I'm very sorry. I should have phoned."

"I was concerned," he replied. "Take the day off. If you can't make it in tomorrow, just let me know, it will be all right. The Bureau doesn't punish people for personal emergencies, you know," he offered with a kind smile.

She smiled back. "Thanks," she said.

"Markie's father, is he still alive?"

The question hit her unexpectedly. "I…I don't know," she stammered, desperate for a way out of the conversation.

"You said that he was in the military, stationed overseas," he began.

"Yes, I see," she faltered. She averted her eyes. "He was, uh, listed as missing in action."

"A tragedy."

She nodded. "Thanks for coming down here," she said, recovering her poise. "I don't know how you even found us…"

"Abuse of power," he quipped. He grinned. "I can pull strings when I want to."

"Unethical, sir," she pointed out.

He shrugged. "My brother is corrupting me."

She laughed. She glanced at the big clock in the waiting room. "You've got a meeting with the sheriff about that Oklahoma kidnapping in ten minutes at the courthouse," she exclaimed, referring to a case in which an agent in another field office had requested some help. FBI offices cooperated on cases from other jurisdictions that overlapped. "You'll never make it."

"I'll make sure I catch all the traffic lights when they're green." He chuckled.

"Thanks again."

"You're welcome. I'll see you tomorrow."

She nodded. She watched him walk away. It surprised her that he cared enough to hunt her down when she didn't show up for work. And he'd been really concerned. That made her feel warm inside. She fought it. His mother would be the worst enemy on earth to make. Joceline already knew how the woman felt about her. It gave her cold chills. But then she was worrying about things she might not ever have to consider. She had her son, and he was going to get better. That had to be her concern now. Only that.

"I'm really sorry about walking in the rain, Mommy," Markie apologized when they were back home in their small apartment. "I love rain," he added plaintively.

"I know you do, sweetheart, but your lungs don't," she said, trying to explain. "You don't like being sick."

He shook his head. "I don't like making you upset, too." He dived against her side and held on tight. "I love you so much, Mommy!"

"I love you, too, pumpkin," she replied and hugged him back, hard.

"I'll wear my coat next time."

They both knew he was lying. She'd just have to be more

careful. It wasn't the rain, the doctor had told her, but the fact that Markie was sensitive to viruses and he'd had one starting when he got wet. It wasn't dangerous for a healthy child, but then, Markie had never been really robust.

The specialist changed his allergy medicines. Joceline talked to the drug company and they agreed voluntarily to give her the inhalers for a fraction of the retail cost. The medication seemed to be working, too. Markie perked up. His valleys and peaks leveled off and he settled into school with resignation. Joceline had a long talk with Markie's teacher and the owner of the day care, and an attorney who was kind enough to help her *pro bono*. For the time being, the bullying was curtailed. But they did mention that Markie was distracting in the classroom and set a date for her to come back, alone, and discuss it with them.

Meanwhile, Markie got better and Joceline got her nerves back together. There was still the question of a diagnosis for Markie's behavioral problems. She didn't know what to do. There was really nobody who could help except their doctor. She'd asked him about Markie and he agreed that it was possible that the child had attention deficit disorder. He was researching the medications and considering a reply for her.

She was doing well until Cammy Blackhawk stormed into the office and glared at Joceline as if she was a hooker.

"I would like to see my son," she said haughtily.

Joceline, practiced at handling gruff and unpleasant individuals, gave her a vacant smile. "Of course, ma'am. Won't you have a seat in our modern and ergonomically designed waiting area?"

Cammy blinked.

Joceline picked up the phone. "Mrs. Blackhawk is here to see you, sir."

Jon came out the door at once, looking oddly protective as he glanced at Joceline and then at Cammy.

"Hi," he said.

Cammy stared at Joceline uncomfortably and then back at her son. "I want you to come to supper tonight," she said firmly. "I'm having a soiree…"

"Soiree?" Jon asked, surprised.

"It's a French word, sir," Joceline told him helpfully. "It means a small, informal dinner…"

"I know what it means!" he snapped.

She saluted him.

He rolled his eyes. "Cammy, I can't come. I'm having supper with Mac and Winnie," he said firmly.

"Don't call me Cammy! I'm your mother!" she grumbled.

"And I don't want to try to eat while I'm being regaled with the latest fashion information," he continued irritably.

"Many, many people buy specialized magazines to ferret out that information," Joceline began enthusiastically.

"Do you mind?" Cammy snapped at her. "I am trying to speak to my son!"

Joceline saluted her, too, smiled again and went back to typing on the computer.

"Come in here," Jon muttered, pulling Cammy into his office. He closed the door. "For the last time, I do not want to have supper with your matrimonial candidate!"

"She's a nice girl!"

His narrowed eyes glittered. "I don't want to get married! Winnie's pregnant. Why don't you go and overwhelm her with motherly advice?"

Cammy averted her eyes. "She's getting that from her own mother. I'm superfluous."

"Well, you can advise Mac on being a father," he countered.

"He's always being called away from the phone, and when I try to visit his office, he's always out," she said irritably.

"You're a bulldozer," he told her. "You don't think anyone can live if you're not telling them how to go about it."

"I'm just trying to help," she said, exasperated.

"You should have had more kids," he replied. "It's 'empty nest syndrome.' You're lonely and bored."

"You're all alone," she said miserably. "What will happen to you when I die?"

He was shocked by the question. "Are you planning to?"

She averted her eyes. "Don't be silly. I just want to see you happily married, like Mac is."

"If it had been up to you, Mac would never have married Winnie," he reminded her. "You thought she was after his money."

"So I made an error in judgment," she said, clearly uncomfortable. "But this nice girl is just what you need. She's outgoing and social, always dressed in the latest fashion and she knows many people in high places."

"So do I," he reminded her.

"You need a family. You don't even date anybody. Well," she amended thoughtfully, "there was that lawyer, but wasn't she just trying to get information out of you about a client?"

He didn't like being reminded of that. "I date when I feel like it."

"Yes, but you never feel like it!" she retorted. "You should have children to play with, now while you're still young enough to play with them and do things with them!"

"I'm not married, Cammy," he said patiently.

"I noticed!"

"I lead a hectic life," he continued. "Most women wouldn't be able to put up with the hours I keep."

"Charlene is beautiful and she's very tolerant of your lifestyle," Cammy began.

"She is not," Jon shot back. "She said that I'd have to give up video games."

"You play too many of them," Cammy agreed. "You should have children to take up your spare time."

"Don't you have anything else to do with your life besides trying to run mine for me?" Jon asked finally, exasperated.

"I am not trying to run your life. I want you to be happy."

"Harassing me about marriage isn't doing the job."

"It isn't harassment," she groaned. "Son, you don't even have a social life."

"I don't want one. I love my work."

"You always have," Cammy replied heavily. "You and McKuen, burying yourselves in dangerous occupations! The past has taken a heavy toll on both of you."

"And on you," Jon agreed. He kissed her forehead. "I know you miss Dad," he said gently. "So do all of us. But you're going overboard with plans for my future. You have to let life happen. You can't force people to do things they don't want to do."

"You'd like Charlene if you gave her a chance," she argued.

"She's the most opinionated woman I've met recently," he said gruffly.

"You're only upset because she said you'd have to stop playing so many video games," Cammy replied. "And she's right."

"She is not."

"We can agree to differ. You should get out more. You spend too much time in this office with that woman out there," she muttered.

"Joceline is my administrative assistant," Jon replied. "She's also a competent paralegal. Who do you think found the link that solved the murder of Mac's little girl?"

Cammy frowned. "I thought it was McKuen."

He shook his head. "Joceline dug out the information that broke the case."

Cammy was evidently surprised, and not pleasantly. She shifted her feet. "She's disrespectful."

"I haven't noticed that."

"And she's got a child. She's not married."

"She was going to be. Her fiancé died overseas in the military before he could marry her," he said with faint defensiveness.

"She told you that?"

He nodded.

"How do you know it's the truth?" she asked with a cold smile. "Women tell all sorts of stories."

"Why are you so antagonistic toward her?"

She didn't answer him. "If you won't come to supper, how about to lunch tomorrow?"

"It's a long drive to the ranch," he began.

"I'm staying at the apartment in town," she replied. "You'll come, won't you?"

He wanted a way out, but he was reluctant to refuse. Cammy was his mother. He didn't spend a lot of time with her, and he felt guilty.

"I suppose I could. If it's going to be just the two of us," he added firmly.

"Of course," she replied. She smiled. "Just us two."

"Now, I have work to do," he reminded her, opening the door.

"I'll have something nice for you to eat," she promised. She smiled at him and impulsively hugged him. "That's my good boy. I'll see you tomorrow." She kissed him, shot a cool look at Joceline and breezed out the front door.

"They do make Bengal tiger traps," Joceline said thoughtfully. "Although you would have to dig a deep hole in the office."

He wouldn't smile, he wouldn't smile...

She heard a muffled sound from behind his closed door, and she grinned.

THAT NIGHT SHE TOOK Markie to a local restaurant that featured a video game arcade. It was filled to capacity.

"Let's try this one," she said enthusiastically after they'd had chicken fingers and iced tea. "Here!"

"I like this one," Markie agreed with a grin.

It was piloting fighter planes and shooting at an enemy on a huge movie screen. Markie laughed uninhibitedly, and so did Joceline. She enjoyed the once-a-month outing as much as he did. They had little money for frivolous things like this, but she didn't want Markie to miss out on entertainment that other children had access to. For a four-year-old, he had an amazing dexterity and skill at the game.

She was aware of movement behind her. Suddenly there were three other people in the compartment, parked on either side of her and Markie, putting game cards into the slots.

"Think you're good, do you?" Mac Kilraven chided. "Let's see!"

"Don't let him bait you, Joceline," a very pregnant Winnie Sinclair said and laughed from beside him. "I can outshoot him! So can you!"

"A likely story," Jon Blackhawk scoffed as he manned the console next to Joceline's.

"I thought you were having dinner with them at home," she said to Jon, indicating his brother and sister-in-law.

"We did, but this is our favorite hangout," Jon said. "We like the games."

"If we had a bigger apartment, I'd import some like this." Mac chuckled. "It will be great for the kids."

"Your son seems to like it," Jon commented to Joceline as Markie took down another fighter.

"Look! I hit it!" He laughed.

"Good shot, there," Jon agreed, smiling at the child, who smiled back.

"Get in much practice in real life, do you?" Mac asked the boy with a wink.

"I don't get out much," Markie said in a very adult tone, and with rolled eyes at his mother.

Joceline laughed. "He's not allowed to carry antiaircraft weapons in public," she said, tongue-in-cheek.

"Aw, Mom." Markie sighed. "I never get to have any fun!"

"Tell you what, first enemy fighter jet that dives on you, I'll get you the best missile launcher I can find," Joceline told him.

"Wow," Markie said with pure worship in his eyes. "Thanks, Mom!"

She shrugged. "Nothing's too good for my boy," she said, and winked at him. She fought down her discomfort at having Markie around her boss. She didn't want any problems to crop up, and Jon Blackhawk's mother would be livid if she knew he was even playing video games with his administrative assistant outside work. But she wouldn't know. Hopefully.

CHAPTER FOUR

JOCELINE AND MARKIE walked toward the exit an hour later. They'd spent the balance on their game cards, although Mac and Jon had subsidized them, in a nice way.

"Thanks," she told Jon at the door. "Markie had so much fun. So did I," she added, but with averted eyes.

"It's all right to admit that you like something I do," he murmured dryly. "You so rarely approve of my actions."

"We wouldn't want you to get a superiority complex, would we, sir?" she asked.

"Why do you call him 'sir'?" Markie asked.

"He's my boss," she replied.

"Oh. Like those guys in the military call their bosses 'sir.'"

"Something like that," Joceline agreed.

"Does he put you in 'time-out' if you do something bad?" Markie persisted.

"I would never do such a thing," Jon assured him. "And your mother has never done anything bad." He hesitated. "Nothing really bad," he amended, giving her a speaking look.

"Menial tasks are not part of my job description, sir," she reminded him. She smiled.

"Making decent coffee isn't menial." He sighed.

"That depends on your definition," she retorted.

"You shoot real good," Markie told the tall man. He was looking pointedly at the bulge under Jon's jacket. "You got a gun."

"That's right," Jon told him. "I work for the FBI."

"I know. Mom talks about you all the time."

"We should go," Joceline said, a little flushed. "Thanks again," she added. "I'll see you Monday, sir."

"Mommy…" Markie protested as she rushed him out the door.

Mac had been listening. He glanced at his brother. "Talks about you all the time, huh?"

"I'm sure he meant in a work-related way," Jon said stiffly. "Joceline has worked for the agency for several years."

"So have you."

Jon glared at his older brother. "She works for me. Period."

Mac pursed his lips, but he didn't reply. He just chuckled and went back to the table where Winnie was waiting for him.

JON WAS OUT of humor when he walked into the office Monday morning. Joceline was still putting away her jacket and purse, having only just beaten him to work.

"You're late," he muttered.

She pointed to the clock over her desk. She was absolutely on time. It was eight on the dot.

He shrugged and went into his office to see what he had on his day planner. The phone rang while he was searching it.

His intercom buzzed. "Yes?" he replied.

There was a pause. "It's for you, sir. A Mr. Harold Monroe." She said the name pointedly.

He frowned and picked up the phone. "Blackhawk," he said.

"Hiya," he replied. "Remember me? I'm out now waiting for a new trial. I'll beat that trafficking charge. I got a great lawyer."

"Congratulations," Jon said. "I'll send over balloons."

There was a pause. "Balloons?"

"For the celebration."

"Cele...oh. Oh! Ha ha ha."

"Was there something else?"

"No, nothing else. I just wanted you to know I was out."

"Thank you."

Another pause. "You made a mistake."

"Did I?"

"Yeah. You want to be careful. My family gets even with people who hurt it. Always. I'll be seeing you, Agent Blackhawk."

He hung up.

Jon stared at the receiver before he replaced it. "It takes all kinds," he muttered.

He was on his way out the door when Joceline called to him.

"Rick Marquez wants you to stop by his office while you're out," she told him. "He says it's important."

"What is it about?" Jon asked, turning.

She put a finger to her forehead and closed her eyes. "I see mountains. Trees. Birds flying." She opened her eyes. "However, not being psychic, I have no idea."

"He didn't say?"

"Apparently not." She smiled vacantly. She cocked her head. "Would you like to know what the new skirt length is out of the Milan fashion shows...? Sir, it's not polite to turn your back on people who are talking to you!" she called after him.

"One day I'll strangle her," Jon muttered to Rick Marquez while they were sitting at the detective's desk, drinking coffee. He'd just related Joceline's latest verbal coup.

Marquez chuckled. "You'd never replace her," he commented. "I've seen paralegals come and go. Joceline is in a class all her own."

"I know." The other man sighed. "I wouldn't have half my cases solved without her. She can dig out information that I can't get. I have no idea how she pulls it off, either."

"She's psychic," Marquez said with big eyes.

"She is not. She's just very good with a telephone, and she can talk people into telling her things that they don't want to."

"She's a paralegal. Why isn't she working for a judge or at least a firm of attorneys?" Marquez asked with a curious frown.

"She started out as legal secretary to a firm of attorneys. But the senior partner retired, several more attorneys joined the firm and she was doing the work of three paralegals with the pay of one," Jon said. "We got her as a result. It was a good thing that Garon Grier didn't have her put on the rack when he started work at the office," he added thoughtfully.

Marquez burst out laughing. "What?"

"He was used to female workers making coffee for him. Joceline doesn't do menial tasks. Or what she considers menial tasks."

"Our administrative assistants make coffee," Rick said smugly. "Good coffee," he emphasized with a pointed look at Jon.

Jon sighed. "None of us can make drinkable coffee. On a bright note, our potted palm seems to thrive on caffeine."

"Excuse me?"

"Everybody dumps their coffee into it when we aren't looking." He chuckled.

Marquez sighed. "Oh, the adventure of working at a federal office."

"At least we have decent expense accounts," he replied. "We don't have to have a receipt for a cup of ice."

Marquez made a face. "It was a very hot day and our air conditioner wasn't working."

"You're from Mexico originally, and you live in southern Texas. You should be used to the heat," Jon commented.

"Yeah. Go figure." Marquez wasn't comfortable talking about his childhood. In fact, nobody except his adoptive mother, Barbara, in Jacobsville, even knew what his background was. And neither he nor Barbara knew the whole truth, but they were trying to find it. However, he had no plans to share that news with his visitor, even though he liked and respected the FBI agent.

"I didn't mean to offend," Jon said, sensitive to the expression that flashed just briefly across the other man's face. "I know about racial issues. You might have noticed that my ancestry includes feathered headdresses and mounted combat."

Marquez relaxed, and smiled. "So does mine, actually. One of my forebears was Comanche."

"Really? So was one of mine," he replied.

"No kidding? Small world."

"My mother has Cherokee, my father was full-blooded Lakota," Jon said.

Marquez's eyebrows arched. "Cherokees come from back East originally."

"Yes, they were relocated on the 'Trail of Tears.' Cherokees were rounded up in 1838 and removed to Oklahoma in late 1838 and early 1839, in the winter cold and snow without proper clothing, because of gold discoveries." He shook his head. "One of my ancestors said that we could never coexist with a materialist culture, because we shared everything and the conquerors wanted to own everything," he added.

"Interesting thought." He put down his coffee cup and became somber. "Harold Monroe's been hinting about retribution to one of my informants."

"I heard they cut him loose."

"Yes, they did. Like the rest of his family, he has something of a reputation for revenge." He looked pointedly at Jon. "He's been accused of racketeering, gambling, prostitution, you name it, but he's never spent more than a day in jail on any charge. One of the prosecutors in a murder case against his uncle-by-marriage died under mysterious circumstances, along with the only witness, and he was let go. Nothing was ever proven. You had Monroe in jail for several months while his lawyer worked to get the charges dropped."

"He should blame himself for putting little girls in the hands of pimps."

"That's not how he sees things. He said the kid was living in starvation-level poverty. He was just helping her find a better life. Simple."

"Yes. I saw the result of that better life," Jon said without elaborating, but the expression in his eyes was eloquent. "Well, they can drop charges, but I still have witnesses who'll testify. One was the man who sold his daughter to Monroe."

"That's the problem." Marquez grimaced. "The witness says he won't testify and he's withdrawn his statement."

"No problem," Jon said. "I know where we can find three more witnesses in the same family, two of whom are perfectly willing to testify despite any threats from Monroe."

"Give me their names and we'll help you locate them so you can get depositions, since it's a federal charge he was arrested on," Marquez replied. "Why didn't the witnesses come forward before?"

"Because they fell through the cracks," he said. "We had one witness, the father, who gave us a deposition, and the mother, as well as a sister. The federal prosecutor didn't think he needed more than a handful. Now we do." He shook his head. "I hope they don't go the way of the witness who was supposed to testify against Jay Copper at his trial about the death of that teenager in Senator Sanders's case. He accidentally fell off a ten-story building."

Marquez wrote down the names of the witnesses. "We do our best," he said defensively.

"So do we, and it wasn't a criticism. Unless you're really psychic, you can't foresee a murder in your city."

"It would be nice if we could." Marquez sighed. "I just hope Monroe doesn't walk on this one."

"With the federal charges dropped on a technicality," Jon said, grinding his teeth at the so-called technicality, which involved a slipped link in the evidence chain, "and new charges pending, the ball may be in your court if we can't make ours stick. You can still get him for trafficking, though. We'll help."

"He won't walk. I promise." He narrowed his eyes. "But you watch yourself."

"You're giving Monroe too much credit," Jon said. "He's a beer short of a six-pack." He pursed his lips. "Maybe two beers short of a six-pack."

"He may be, but he's dangerous. You got him on a trafficking charge. But he's worked his way out of numerous other charges including one daylight robbery. That one was committed as a juvy—" which meant a juvenile offender "—and he only drew a few days in detention before he turned eighteen."

"Yes, he managed to get first offender status and kept his nose clean until his record was wiped," Jon said. "But he was twenty-five when he was accused the next time, and he got a good attorney, courtesy of his boss, Hank Sanders, the racketeer brother of Senator Will Sanders who's up on murder charges." He smiled. "Hank turned out to be a good guy. He saved my brother's butt in the standoff with Jay Copper, just after Mac and Winnie came back from their honeymoon."

"Some honeymoon, trying to convince Senator Will Sanders's wife, Pat, to tell what she knew about the murder of Kilraven's wife and little girl," Marquez amended.

"Which she did, but Copper ordered the murder of Mac's wife," Jon said somberly. "He said that the perp, the late Dan Jones, wasn't ordered to kill Melly, Mac's little girl, but I never believed him. One of his idiot goons turned state's evidence and verified that Copper told Jones to get both the wife and child. He'll pay for Melly's death, and Monica's. The D.A. has asked for the death penalty."

"Good luck to him," the other man said cynically. "Juries don't like to order it."

Jon nodded. "I had to sit in a death-penalty case once. You think, this guy should die for the crime he committed. But when you put your vote to it, and realize that you're ordering the guy's death, well that's a whole other thing."

"A matter of personal conscience," Marquez agreed. "A very hard decision to make, for any human being." He studied Jon. "But it's you I'm worried about. Monroe may be an idiot, but he has an uncle who's knee-deep in the local mob, Jay Copper, and a brother-in-law who's been in and out of prison for years, Bart Hancock. Hancock walked on accessory charges linked to Jay Copper's arrest, because the tape Winnie got of Copper telling the story of the murders went mysteriously missing. Hancock has been implicated in two murder-for-hire plots and never got much past arraignment. He makes sure there are no witnesses."

"There's something in the back of my mind about Hancock. Wait! Now I remember," Jon said. "Joceline dug up some information on him that was supposedly classified. Don't ask—" he held up a hand "—she has sources. Anyway, Hancock was in spec ops in Iraq during the 2003 invasion."

"That's right. He worked with a private contractor. There was a big stink about civilian casualties, and Hancock was in it up to his neck. His buddy was an officer in the private corporation that ran the coverts, and he cleaned up Hancock's record so he wasn't prosecuted." He sighed heavily. "They say he killed children and enjoyed it."

Jon's jaw set. "What a sweetheart."

"Isn't he, though?"

"Yes."

Jon's mind was busy. The man who died linked to Melly's murder, Dan Jones, was a bit of a mystery. Jon had always wondered if the man was really going to confess that he'd done it. He didn't seem the sort to kill children. But Jay Copper's spec ops nephew, he had been friends with the perp, and the accomplice who'd gone with the perp to commit the murders was never found. What if…?

"You've remembered something, haven't you?" the other man asked, noting the facial expression of his visitor.

Jon nodded. "Yes, that there were two shooters at Mac's house that night. We only identified one. The tape had Jay Copper talking about his nephew, Peppy, who helped Dan Jones kill Monica. He said the child got in the way. Peppy was questioned but he suddenly had a supposedly airtight alibi for that night. Then the tape where Jay Copper told about Peppy's part in the murder went missing from the evidence room…"

"I'd forgotten that." Marquez opened a file on his computer and his dark eyes narrowed as he read what was on the screen. "Peppy. His full name is Bartholomew Richard Hancock. And his brother-in-law is Harold Monroe, which makes Monroe Jay Copper's nephew by marriage. I don't have to tell you Copper's reputation for getting back at anyone who works against his family." He glanced at Jon, whose face wore a look of utter astonishment. "You never made the connection, did you?"

It had been four months ago, the end of the trail when all the suspects in Dan Jones's death, and at the same time the Kilraven murders, were fingered. Only Senator Will Sanders and Jay Copper had been arrested and sent to jail pending trial. But the man, Peppy, had slipped out of the noose with the help of a slick attorney and had never been charged even as an accessory, thanks to that missing tape, which, through an unfortunate lapse, had not been copied or transcribed before it was stolen. Jay Copper denied he'd ever implicated Peppy. The fact that Kilraven, and Winnie, were closely involved helped to discount their testimony about it. Pat Sanders had suddenly backtracked on her own testimony, despite the efforts of Hank Sanders, the senator's brother, to coax her to repeat it.

Harold Monroe had been arrested by Jon on the human trafficking charge not a week after Peppy Hancock had slipped out of the accessory murder charge in the Kilraven case. Jon and Joceline had worked tirelessly to find the evidence to connect him with the trafficking, which they'd been investigating prior to his most recent arrest. But no, Jon had never made the connection.

"So Harold Monroe may be an idiot," Marquez agreed, "but Hancock isn't. You want to watch your back. He might target anyone close to you, but especially Joceline, since she helped you get evidence on him. His uncle Jay would know she helped. He has somebody in law enforcement feeding him information. We've never been able to identify who."

Jon sighed. "Why is life so complicated?"

Marquez indicated the office they were sitting in. "This is

a police precinct. If you want answers to philosophical questions, you should consult a psychologist."

Jon glared at him. "Thanks a lot."

Marquez grinned. "You're welcome. More coffee?"

Knowing that Peppy, alias Bart Hancock, had possibly been involved in the murder of Mac's daughter, Melly, was like carrying live dynamite to Jon. He didn't know if he should tell his brother at all, at least not until he could do some more checking. If Marquez was right, and he usually was, that meant the murder of Mac's wife and child hadn't been completely solved at all. Mac had thought Jay Copper, having ordered the hit, had been brought to justice and would pay for the child's death. But if Peppy had helped the late Dan Jones with the hit—that was another whole can of worms. And Peppy was married to Harold Monroe's sister. What a mess. A threat Jon had laughed off suddenly became a real possibility, and not just a danger to himself.

He went back to his office and sat down heavily at his desk, staring at the wall opposite. Joceline called him on the intercom and he didn't even hear it. He was sick at his stomach.

She poked her head in the door and frowned when she saw his expression. "Something wrong?"

He nodded. He glanced at her. His black eyes were glittery. "Come in and close the door. Do I have anything urgent pending?"

"No." She closed the door and sat down on the uncomfortable straight chair in front of his desk. No comfortable seats for this boss; he didn't like people overstaying their welcome. She was uncomfortable, too, and not just from the chair. Was he going to fire her? She was a bundle of nerves lately. She had a meeting pending with both Markie's teacher and the owner of the preschool about his behavior. They were going to recommend drugs, she just knew it. She had no money, no option to change his school for a more expensive one. She was in the hot seat and she didn't like it.

"Am I being fired due to budget cuts?" she asked bluntly.

He noted her worried expression. Joceline was a single parent with only the bare necessities and even though she had great prospects, it might take time for her to find a new job.

"Of course not," he said at once.

She relaxed, just a bit. A jerky little smile passed her lips. "Sorry. I worry."

"The talk about budget cuts involves travel, not personnel. At least for now. We all worry, but until they come up with robots who won't mind working our hours, I think we're probably safe as far as employment goes," he said with an attempt at humor. "I need someone to talk to."

"There's your brother," she said. She frowned. "I think we have a psychology consultant in an office somewhere…?"

"Not that kind of talk," he said stiffly. "I don't discuss personal issues except with family."

"Of course you don't, sir." She smiled vacantly.

He hated that damned smile. He averted his eyes. "It's about the murder of Mac's wife and child."

"Jay Copper ordered it and he's been arraigned for it."

"There's a hiccup."

"Sir?"

He leaned back in his chair with a grimace. "Copper has a nephew who he possibly sent along with Dan Jones on the hit." He also recalled that Copper had admitted to helping Peppy kill Dan Jones for his defection, not that they could prove it without that missing tape.

"I'm not surprised," she replied. "He has a lot of idiot relations. Most of them are doing hard time."

He glanced at her. "Bart Hancock isn't. And he's Harold Monroe's brother-in-law."

She was very still. The man had threatened her boss, but she hadn't connected him with the Kilraven case. "Bart Hancock."

"He's Jay Copper's nephew. His nickname is Peppy."

She let out a breath. "Oh, my God," she said, with reverence. She knew the name and the connection immediately, and it put another meaning on Monroe's warning that his family would get back at Jon Blackhawk. If Peppy had killed a child…

"I can't talk to Mac about this, he'd go crazy," he told her. "And Winnie's very pregnant," he added, alluding to his sister-in-law's pregnancy.

"What are you going to do?" she asked.

"I don't know. Unless we can play connect-the-dots and find somebody, anybody, tied to the case who's willing to testify against him, I don't know what we can do. Most of the witnesses were killed, including Dan Jones and even his girlfriend."

"Her minister spoke to Dan Jones," she recalled at once.

"Yes, but he didn't actually speak to Dan Jones confidentially," he reminded her. "So he doesn't know anything. It's probably the only reason he's still alive."

She felt uneasy. "Harold Monroe wants revenge for his arrest."

He nodded. "He's a notorious fumbler."

"He's managed to avoid jail for the most part, until the kidnapping charge."

"Only because of Jay Copper, who's a master of intimidation," he replied. "But Copper's still in jail, awaiting trial, and even he can't do much intimidating from his present domicile. Not that he can't hire it done," he added heavily.

"Your brother has a friend in covert ops who watched out for Winnie Sinclair's mother when she was in danger investigating the Kilraven murders," she reminded him. "Perhaps he could tag along with you."

He glared at her. "I'm a senior FBI agent," he reminded her coldly. "I do not require a bodyguard!"

She held up both hands. "No offense, but you can't watch your back all the time."

"Yes, I can."

She glowered at him. "There's the matter of kryptonite turning up in unusual places, Superman," she said with faint sarcasm.

"I didn't invite you in here to insult me," he pointed out.

"You wanted advice. I'm flattered that you value mine. Here it is. Don't tell your brother anything until you can find a witness who knows what Bart Hancock did—if he really was involved in the murder of Kilraven's family."

He sat back in the chair. It was a leather chair, old and not really cushy, but very comfortable. It was odd, she thought, for such a rigid, Spartan sort of man to like a comfortable chair at his desk when he provided hard chairs for visitors. But then, he was something of an anachronism himself.

"I suppose you're right," he replied quietly. Privately he was thinking how hard a job that was going to be, finding anybody connected to the case who was willing to risk his life to testify against a child murderer. Even civilians knew what happened to men who went to prison for that particular crime. They didn't last a long time incarcerated. The other inmates didn't appreciate child killers.

"You might involve Rick Marquez and Gail Sinclair," she advised, referring to two of the best homicide detectives on San Antonio's police force. "They're both familiar with the case, and Gail really is psychic. She might come up with some witness you haven't even considered."

He brightened a little. "That's good advice."

"Yes, it is," she mused, smiling.

He glared at her. "No reason to become conceited."

"But, sir, I have so much to be conceited about," she said haughtily. Her blue eyes twinkled. "Want to know what the stylists are doing for the holiday season this year? How about the latest fashion buzz from Paris?"

He was looking more irritable by the second. "When I want to know those things, I'll call Cammy and have her send her matrimonial prospect right over to enlighten me," he said sarcastically.

Her eyes widened. "I can call her for you. Right now, if you like."

"If you do, you'll really be out looking for a new job," he returned.

She shrugged. "Okay. But you don't know what you're missing. All those color predictions, skirt length changes…"

He stood up. "Out!" he said, pointing to the door.

She stood up, too. "Ingrate," she muttered.

He came around the desk. He was really tall, she thought, when he stopped less than an arm's length away from her. "You're a fountain of wisdom from time to time, Joceline," he said very softly. "We have our differences, but you're a real asset here."

She flushed. "Thanks."

He looked down into her eyes for longer than he meant to, and was suddenly aware of a new tension, a new electricity that arced between them.

Joceline felt her heart bounce up into her throat at the intensity of his gaze. She couldn't seem to tear her eyes away, and a huge shock surged up inside her like an almost tangible joy.

His eyes narrowed as he felt the same impact of pleasure. His jaw tautened noticeably.

"Your eyes are the oddest shade of blue I've ever seen," he remarked quietly. "Almost a royal blue."

"Yours are black," she replied, searching them.

"Yes." Involuntarily his lean, beautiful hand came up and touched her flushed cheek. "This is very dangerous," he said in a deep, velvety tone. "I might think of it as an invitation."

"I might point out that you're the one inviting trouble," she retorted and stepped back. There were reasons why she could never allow him closer than arm's length. "My legions of male admirers would set upon you like flies on honey and sunder you limb from limb. Not only that, there's this famous gorgeous movie star who calls me three times daily...and there he is, on the phone again!" she exclaimed, and almost ran from the office to answer the phone on her desk.

He was still laughing when he closed the door.

It HAD BEEN a narrow escape. Joceline's knees were weak for the rest of the day every time she gazed at her gorgeous boss. She avoided looking directly at him, because she was afraid that he was right: she had been inviting trouble.

On the other hand, he'd touched her cheek. He was the one who'd come so very close to her. It was only the second time in their years together that he'd ever approached her in an intimate way—although it wasn't actually intimate. And he didn't remember the first time. She hoped, she prayed, that he never would.

An hour later, still dreaming of her boss, Joceline was feeding information into the computer when the part-timer, Phyllis Hicks, stopped by her desk with a question.

"These forms are so boring," she complained. "My dad works in the homicide department at San Antonio P.D. and I get to look at crime scene photos." Her eyes gleamed oddly. "Murder is such an exciting thing, don't you think?"

"Murder?"

Phyllis shifted. "The investigation, I mean. You get to catch criminals. My daddy's real good at it."

"Who is your dad?"

"His name's Dave Hicks, he works with Marquez." She made a face. "I don't like Marquez at all."

That was a surprise. Most people did. Most women found him attractive.

"Of course, he's not my real dad," she added. "My real dad is special. He thinks outside the box. He's not afraid of anything." She laughed. "He lets me do stuff with him. It's very exciting." She caught herself and gave Joceline a beaming smile. "Sorry, I get carried away. Now about this form, do I have to fill in every single space?"

Joceline told her how to input the information, but long after Phyllis went back to her typing chores, Joceline sat quietly in her chair. She felt vaguely uneasy about the young woman. Was it normal to enjoy looking at crime scene photos? They made Joceline very ill. Once she'd even thrown up when she saw one in a file that involved the vicious killing of a young woman who'd threatened Senator Will Sanders. The woman had been brutally killed, a crime for which Jay Copper was charged. But Phyllis liked them?

There was no accounting for taste, she supposed, and there was the notorious forensic investigator, Alice Mayfield Jones Fowler, who really got into her work at crime scenes and never seemed to be bothered by what she had to see. On the other hand, Alice didn't find murder scenes exciting, either.

"I'll never fit in this modern society," Joceline muttered to herself. She didn't understand the fascination with death, with zombies, with vampires...

Well, she loved the very popular vampire movie trilogy, so that wasn't quite true. Perhaps Phyllis was just exaggerating. She might have never seen a crime scene photo. She was working in an office that dealt with violent crime, so perhaps she felt being excited by the process of crime-solving was expected.

Joceline shook her head and went back to work.

When quitting time came, she grabbed her purse, called good-night through the closed door and almost ran out of the building. She'd had enough for the day, after Phyllis's strange questions.

Even the fact that she had a worrisome meeting with school officials next was less disturbing than her boss's odd behavior. Joceline kept dark secrets. She had no wish to ever display them, least of all to Jon Blackhawk.

CHAPTER FIVE

THE HEAD OF the school, Mr. Morrison, and Markie's teacher, Ms. Rawles, were very nice about it. But they were emphatic that Markie's antics were disruptive and that he needed medication to prevent him from being a distraction to the other students.

Joceline just looked at them. She didn't agree or disagree.

"We would like your assurance that this matter will be resolved," Mr. Morrison said kindly. "Your pediatrician can put Markie on a medication to control his outbursts."

She smiled blankly. "In other words, you want me to go to my doctor and order him to put my four-year-old son on drugs?"

There were shocked, indignant looks.

She stood up, still smiling. "I'll have a long talk with my son. I'll also speak with our family physician. We don't have the funds to afford a pediatrician, I'm sorry to tell you. Markie's hospital visits are expensive, and we have an allergist in addition to a family physician, but we're rather limited in our budget. I have to have medical care for both of us, and a family practitioner is the best we can do right now."

They were still speechless.

"I will, however, speak with my family doctor about your insistence that Markie needs to become drug dependent. And if my physician agrees with you," she added sweetly, "then I will find another family physician."

"Uh, Mrs., that is, Miss, I mean Ms. Perry," Mr. Morrison stammered.

"I believe the politically correct designation is Ms.," she said helpfully.

"We only think Markie, being so young, requires some help with his difficulty in focusing…"

"That's right, sir, make sure that every child obeys without question so that teachers don't have to deal with any behavioral problems."

He glared at her. "Ms. Perry…!"

"In our defense," Ms. Rawles said gently, "our class has thirty-five students. We're much in the same boat as many other schools where teachers have to manage classrooms with thirty to forty students. We do the best we can. We really care about our students. But it's so hard to teach when we have children who simply can't pay attention. Markie is disruptive. He can't sit still, he talks out of turn, he gets into things…"

Joceline studied her. "Do you have children, Ms. Rawles?"

"I'm not married. I certainly wouldn't put the stigma of illegitimacy on my child," the other woman said at once, and then flushed, because she realized that Joceline had a child out of wedlock.

Joceline smiled, but she wasn't happy with the remark.

The principal cleared his throat. "I'm sure that whatever you and your physician decide will be fine with us."

"Of course," Ms. Rawles said, obviously distressed. "I'm very sorry. I never should have said such a thing to you!"

Their attitude took the edge off her temper. She could see their side of the issue, as well. "Actually Markie likes you very much, and so do I," Joceline cut her off. "It's all right. A lot of people have said worse things to me. His father was a very good man. We had too much to drink and did something out of character for both of us. He went missing in action overseas on duty before we could get married," she added gently, telling the falsehood with the confidence of years of secret keeping.

The two school officials looked guilty.

"A tragedy," Ms. Rawles spoke for both of them. "The world is changing very quickly. Sometimes new concepts are difficult."

"I go to church, and take Markie, every Sunday," she told them with a quiet smile. "Everybody makes mistakes. Some are more difficult to live with than others. But I love my son. I feel blessed to have him."

They both brightened. "He's a smart little boy."

"That's why he's into everything, he's curious," Joceline replied. "And I have already discussed this with our doctor. He's researching medicines, but he says that discipline might be a better choice than drugs in Markie's case. I don't mean hitting him with a bat to get his attention," she added. "The doctor says that overactive children need consistency and routine and a limit to the number of toys they play with to keep them from being overstimulated. There are many new studies on both sides of the issue, but I would prefer to at least try the least drastic measure first. If it doesn't get results, then I'll have to consider other options. Compromise," she added with a smile, "is the foundation of civilization."

"It is," Mr. Morrison agreed, rising. He seemed to relax a little.

Ms. Rawles stood up, too. She smiled. "I apologize again for my remarks."

"It's all right," Joceline said again. "You'll let me know if the situation doesn't improve?" she asked the teacher.

Ms. Rawles nodded. "Yes, I will. And thank you for coming in to talk to us. I know your job requires long hours."

"Your job?" Mr. Morrison asked curiously.

"She works for the FBI," Ms. Rawles said with a grin, glancing at Mr. Morrison's shocked face.

"My goodness!" he blurted out. "I had no idea."

"I'm not involved in enforcement of federal laws," she said. "I only do the paperwork that helps get criminals convicted. I keep the gears oiled."

He chuckled. "How interesting! We're having a Career Day here in November. Perhaps you might like to speak about your duties?"

"I would," she said, "but my boss is very strict. He might not like it."

"We wouldn't want to get you in trouble with him," he replied. "But think about it."

"I will. Thank you both for being so understanding."

"I have two daughters in high school," Mr. Morrison said. "I do know how children can be." He was very quiet. "One of my daughters took Ritalin for ADD," he added, referring to attention deficit disorder.

Joceline wanted to ask, very badly, how that had turned out. But there was something in the man's face that deterred her. She thanked them again, said her goodbyes and went to pick up Markie at day care.

The next day she mentioned the principal's remark in passing to Agent Blackhawk.

"Morrison. Yes, the school principal. Sad story."

"Sir?"

"His eldest daughter is a senior in high school. She was

arrested for possession of a Class I controlled substance and convicted of intent to distribute. She's on probation as a first offender. Her mother died of an overdose."

Joceline was shocked.

"You didn't hear that from me," he added. "We don't discuss cases brought by other agencies. In this case, San Antonio P.D."

"Yes, sir."

He cocked his head. "She was placed on drugs in grammar school for ADD."

"That would have been my next question until you said you wouldn't discuss it," she said demurely. She sighed. "They wanted me to get my doctor to put Markie on those drugs." She looked up quickly and grimaced. "That was uncalled for. I'm very sorry, sir. Personal matters should remain personal, especially on the job."

His black eyes were steady and quiet. "Are you going to do it?"

She moved uncomfortably. She didn't answer.

He moved closer. So close, in fact, that she could feel the heat of his powerful body and smell the spicy cologne he wore. She looked up at him and felt her heart jump.

"Are you going to do it?" he repeated, in a softer tone.

She swallowed. "I told them I'd talk to my family physician about giving Markie drugs for behavioral modification and that, if my family physician agreed, I'd get another family physician," she murmured dryly. "I didn't really mean it. I want to do what's best for Markie."

A chuckle escaped him. "I imagine that's not all you said."

Her blue eyes twinkled. "Well, Markie's teacher made a remark that hit me on the raw but I kept my cool. I can't help that everything I think appears on my face, though…"

He shook his head. "Ms. Perry, you are an anachronism."

"Sir?"

"It would take longer than I've got to explain," he replied, checking his watch. "I'm overdue for a meeting in the SAC's office."

"And I have work to do."

He pursed his lips. "Some people would consider making coffee 'work.'"

She smiled what he'd come to think of as her trademark expression. "Some people would consider a tomato a fruit."

"A tomato is a fruit."

She made a face and went back to her desk.

MARKIE wanted to play his video game. He grimaced when his mother started talking about his acting out in class and his inability to sit still.

"Nobody likes me," he muttered.

"Yes, they do. But when you won't stay at your desk, you make a lot of problems for your teacher. You aren't the only student she has."

He sighed. "It's so boring in there," he told her. "I already know all that stuff. But I'm younger than the other kids, and they make fun of me when I can't run like they can, on account of my lungs."

She felt that pain all the way to her shoes, but she knew from long and hard experience that bullies were a fact of life at any age. Unless the bullying was taking a dangerous toll, she found it best to let Markie handle those problems himself. Which he did. Once, when an older child tried to force him to give up his pocket money, he yelled "Thief!" at the top of his lungs until the owner came. He was reprimanded, but the bully got in trouble, too. He never tried to extort money again. For a sickly little boy, Joceline thought proudly, Markie had a stout and brave spirit. He wasn't afraid of anything.

"Why are you smiling?" he asked.

"I'm very proud of you," she said. "Your father would be proud of you, too, for the way you handle yourself when people try to pick on you."

"My dad was brave, wasn't he?"

"Very brave," she replied.

"Don't we have any pictures of him?" he asked.

This question was disturbing. She knew it would only get more difficult as time went by. "No, I don't," she said honestly. "I'm really sorry, Markie."

"Did he look like me?"

She studied him with a sad smile. "Only a little," she said, and hid her relief.

"Most of the other kids have daddies to take them places. I wish I knew him," he told her.

She picked him up and hugged him close. "I wish you did, too."

"You like your boss, don't you?" he asked when she put him down.

She felt flushed. "He's very nice."

"He plays video games just like us," he said.

"His brother plays them, too."

"You don't play much," he accused.

She bent and kissed his forehead. "I have housework to do. Mothers are busy people. But I play with you on the weekends, don't I?"

"Yeah. You do." He grinned at her. "And I beat you."

"Every time," she agreed with a laugh.

"I might let you win next time," he said thoughtfully.

"You might?"

He started to answer her playful reply when the phone rang.

Joceline picked up the receiver, still laughing from Markie's teasing. "Hello?"

There was a pause. It was cold and unnerving.

"Hello?" she asked again.

"Your boss is first," a gruff voice said. "Then you."

"What?" she exclaimed.

A dial tone was the only response she got. She wanted to think it was a mistake, a wrong number. But she knew it wasn't. She felt cold chills at the threatening words.

"Who was it, Mommy?"

"Just a wrong number, baby," she said, and forced a smile. "I have to get your clothes ready for school tomorrow. I'll be in the laundry room."

"Okay," he said absently, already lost in his video game.

Joceline closed the door of the playroom and leaned back against the wall with her eyes closed. She couldn't remember ever feeling so afraid.

She almost called her boss to tell him about the threat, but she thought she'd involved him too much already in her private life. It wasn't a good policy, to bring domestic problems to work. She didn't want to jeopardize his job, or her own. She didn't want him around Markie, either.

On the other hand, she had a sneaking hunch about the identity of her caller. She couldn't prove it. She'd only heard Harold Monroe's voice once, when he'd called brazenly to tell her boss he was out of jail. Strange, though, the voice seemed deeper than Monroe's. But he could be disguising it.

THE CALL BOTHERED HER. So after she reminded Mr. Blackhawk about his day's schedule and noted that he had ten minutes free before he was due in federal court to testify on a case, she walked into his office and closed the door.

He gave her a surprised look.

She sat down in front of the desk. "I'm sorry, but I had a phone call last night, and although I can't swear to the identity of the caller, I think it might have been Harold Monroe."

He sat up straighter. His black eyes narrowed. "What did he say?"

"That you were first, and I was next."

His expression was hard to read. "Do you have an answering machine on your phone?"

She nodded enthusiastically. "Oh, yes, sir, and a ham radio and a plasma TV, a couple of sports cars…!"

"Ms. Perry," he said curtly.

"Sorry, sir. I forgot myself. Won't happen again." She crossed her heart.

He shook his head. "It's not a laughing matter."

"I wasn't laughing. It's just that I don't have the budget for that type of equipment," she said with a straight face.

"I should have known that."

Probably so, but, then, he and his brother—not to mention his seethingly rabid mother—were worth millions, if the gossip was true. She didn't doubt that he could walk into the nearest electronics store and purchase the highest-ticket item it contained without blinking an eye. Joceline was on a much stricter budget.

"You live in an unsecured apartment house," he said, thinking aloud.

"We have locks on the doors and a telephone."

He glared at her. "Locks keep honest people out. That's all they do."

She folded her hands in her lap. "Over the years that I've worked here," she began, "I've heard a lot of people make threats. I don't know of a single one that actually turned into an incident."

"Yes, well I do," he said curtly. "I won't take chances with your life, or your son's."

"It was your life I was thinking about," she said quietly. "He has a reason for wanting to harm you."

His eyebrows arched. "Are you actually expressing concern for my welfare, Ms. Perry?" he asked with mock astonishment.

"Yes, sir," she said calmly. "It's very difficult to train a boss not to expect impossible menial tasks," she added with a gleam in her blue eyes. "I'm not anxious to break in somebody new."

He laughed faintly. "Touché." He glanced at his watch and got to his feet. "I'll talk to a few people and see what sort of arrangements I can make for someone to keep an eye on you after work."

"On our budget, sir, we can probably afford a ten-year-old boy in a trench coat with one of those Junior Spy kits."

He really glared at her then. "My brother has all sorts of shadowy contacts that we don't talk about. I'm sure at least one of them owes him a favor. Rourke comes to mind."

"No," she said at once. "No, absolutely not. I will not have that one-eyed lunatic anywhere near me!"

His eyebrows arched. She'd rarely been so outspoken about any of the people who came through the office. "He's very good at private security."

Her jaw set so tightly that it bulged.

"Out with it," he ordered.

She shifted restlessly. "He said I should be gagged and locked in a closet."

He had to stifle a laugh. "May I ask what prompted him to make such a remark?"

Her eyes avoided his. "He was making fun of my shoes."

He looked down. She was wearing the ballet slippers she usually wore to work, bad for the instep but extremely comfortable—and affordable.

"Some of us can't manage Neiman Marcus even on a good government salary," she said, still ruffled months after the remark was made.

"Rourke pops off and thinks he's being amusing."

"He'll get popped off if he makes another such remark to me," she said curtly.

He chuckled. "I'll see if anybody else owes Mac a favor."

"It sounded like Harold Monroe, but I couldn't prove it. He was probably just fishing, to see if he could frighten me. And he knew I'd tell you what he said," she added. She hesitated. "Sir, you really could use someone to watch your back. Monroe may be a certifiable idiot, but he has family connections who aren't."

"I'm aware of that."

"Don't get insulted," she added when he looked annoyed. "You FBI types always think you're the biggest, meanest dogs on the block and usually you're right. I don't like funerals," she added firmly.

"Or breaking in new bosses."

Her eyes twinkled. "Exactly."

"I'll do my best to stay alive." He started out the door and hesitated. "If my brother calls, tell him I want to talk to him. I'll be back after two."

"I did notice that, sir," she added pleasantly, "having noted it on your calendar."

His jaw clenched.

"Won't you be late for court?" she asked. "It's Judge Cummings sitting today, too, isn't it, and he doesn't like the FBI." She smiled angelically. "Do be polite, sir."

He muttered something under his breath.

"Sir!" she exclaimed. "This is a government office...!"

He was out the door before she could finish the sentence.

BETTY RIMES was constantly amused by Joceline's ongoing verbal attacks on her boss.

"He could just fire you," Betty pointed out.

"He wouldn't dare. There are very few paralegals working outside the judicial system, where would he ever find someone to replace me?" Joceline asked, amused.

"We have a part-time administrative assistant," she was reminded grimly. "And Phyllis Hicks does offer to make coffee for the boss."

"I don't do menial chores," Joceline reiterated. "It isn't in my job description."

Betty sipped her coffee. "Yes, but, dear, she'd work for half what they pay you," she added worriedly. "It's a flat economy. So many people are out of work."

Joceline didn't let her uneasiness show. She just smiled. "Mr. Blackhawk is used to me and he doesn't like strangers."

"That's true. It's just that he doesn't make the major budgetary decisions."

Joceline stared at her. "What do you know that you're not telling me?"

Betty bit her lip. "It's probably nothing…"

"Tell me."

"I overheard one of the senior agents discussing something Mr. Grier said at lunch." Garon Grier was now the Special Agent in Charge for the Jacobsville satellite office, and he frequently showed up at the San Antonio office to have lunch with the San Antonio SAC. "Mr. Grier was disturbed at talk that they were going to reduce his office staff, and our own SAC apparently wondered out loud if we could make do with one administrative assistant for the Violent Crimes Squad here, with a part-time assistant."

Joceline didn't move. She stared at the other woman with dawning horror. Betty had been with the Bureau for a long time, over ten years, and she had seniority.

"I said it was probably just talk. He might have even been joking. Please don't worry," Betty said gently. "Probably they'll come up with some other idea for saving money by cutting our travel budget. I just didn't want it to come at you out of the blue. You're a great paralegal. I know Judge Cummings would snap you up in a second for his office, or the assistant D.A. would for hers."

That was true. But no matter how good the working conditions, or how great the pay, those offices wouldn't contain Jon Blackhawk. While that might be a good thing, in some respects, it was devastating in another.

"Joceline, you're not going to lose your job," Betty said, her tone reassuring. "The SAC and Mr. Blackhawk would both fight for you."

They would. She knew that. Despite her insistence on the parameters of her duties, she was good at what she did, and she never slacked or avoided work. There were those unavoidable times when she was late for work...

She looked up at Betty worriedly. "I've been late sometimes."

The older woman was sympathetic. "Everybody knows why," she said surprisingly.

"What?"

"We know your son has medical problems," the older woman replied with a smile.

"But I never told anyone," she stammered. "I mean, Mr. Blackhawk came by when I had to bring Markie to the hospital," she began.

"And he told all of us," she said. "He didn't want anyone assuming that you missed work for some frivolous reason. He's quite fond of you, in his way. Although watching him react to you is funny. You do put his back up, as they say."

"Keeps him on his toes." Joceline laughed. "He really does tend to brood."

"Oh, coffee!" Phyllis said, smiling. "Can I have some, too?"

"Sure, sit down," Joceline invited. She noted the younger woman's clothing; it looked like the sort of thing Cammy

Blackhawk would wear. But Phyllis had said her father worked as a police detective and Phyllis was in college part-time. Where would she get the money for expensive clothes? Maybe Joceline was just tired and getting irritated over minor matters.

"We were talking about our workload," Betty commented.

"It's so boring," Phyllis said. "I wish I could be a detective, like my dad, and get to go to crime scenes."

"You watch too many crime television shows, Phyllis." Betty chuckled.

Phyllis gave her a blank stare.

"You know, those forensic programs that deal with trace evidence solving big cases," Joceline said helpfully. "They call it fiction."

"So many people don't know the difference." Betty sighed. "Now juries are so clued up that they argue with attorneys about trace evidence in murder trials. They watch a television show a few times and think they're qualified to rule on pathological evidence."

"Yes, it's nothing like what they show on television," Phyllis said. "Bodies are so clean and tidy. In real life, the blood is everywhere. It splashes around like paint..." She stopped because they were staring at her silently. "Oh, my dad lets me look at file photos sometimes," she said quickly. "To teach me how evidence is really gathered."

"I see," Betty said, but she was visibly uncomfortable.

"Some of those shows are just a little too graphic for me, especially when my son might walk in and see something that would give him nightmares," Joceline said with a smile.

"I was never squeamish, even when I was little," Phyllis scoffed. "That murder case we worked on with Mr. Blackhawk was really fascinating, the one that Jay Copper got arrested for," she added suddenly. "Aren't you working with a file about that Hancock man? Digging out information about his past?"

"I'm trying to run down stuff. I got some rap sheets from San Antonio P.D. this morning. They're on my desk. I haven't had time to input the information. I may have to sign them out and do it at home."

"I guess it's a long rap sheet," Phyllis said.

"Very."

"Such a sad case, the Kilraven murders," Betty said. "Imagine, someone killing a child like that."

"Kids, adults, a life is a life." Phyllis shrugged. "They all die the same."

"You have a different outlook when you have a child," Joceline said tautly.

Phyllis assumed a smile. "Well, of course you do."

Betty sipped more coffee. "I worry about Monroe's threats," she said somberly. "Mr. Blackhawk seems to think it's a joke, but the man is dangerous. His wife's uncle taught him how to be a monster, and his brother-in-law is a terror."

Joceline nodded. "Jay Copper is going to do some very hard time, if he manages to avoid the needle," she added meaningfully. "Imagine ordering the death of a woman and a small child!"

"And I'm sure that he did order it, despite all his denials," Betty said grimly. "Dan Jones may have done the actual killing, but Jay Copper was behind it. If they can just convict him, is the thing. I hope they do."

"Mr. Blackhawk is supposed to meet an informant tonight at seven," Joceline said heavily. "He refuses to have a bodyguard. He doesn't think Monroe is a threat."

"That's foolhardy," Betty said. "Look what happened to Detective Marquez when he went to meet some shadowy informant."

Marquez had been blindsided and hospitalized. Joceline

was uneasy about the meeting tonight. "Mr. Blackhawk takes chances."

"Oh, I'm sure he'll be all right," Phyllis said airily. She glanced at her watch—a very expensive one. "Gosh, I have to get back to work. Thanks for the coffee."

She left without putting change in the kitty that helped pay for renewing the canteen supplies. Without a word, Betty took a bill out of her pocket and placed it in the container.

"Young people." She sighed.

Joceline smiled. "You're nice."

"Thanks. So are you."

"I do hope they can convict Jay Copper of little Melly Kilraven's murder," Joceline said quietly. "Kilraven still isn't over it," she added gently, "although he and his wife, Winnie, are expecting around the new year." She smiled. "What a Christmas present they're going to have this year if she goes into labor early!"

"Christmas!" Betty exclaimed. "I haven't even started shopping!"

"It isn't even Thanksgiving yet," she was reminded.

"Yes, but I usually have everything bought by August." She laughed. "I'm efficient on the job. I wish I could be that efficient off it."

Joceline laughed, too. "Well, we all do what we can."

The phone rang. Joceline got to her feet. "Back to work. Thanks for the heads-up," she added in a soft tone. "At least if I get the ax, I'll be somewhat prepared. Perhaps I should start working up a résumé."

"Wait," Betty advised. "A lot of this is all talk. I don't think the office can operate with just me taking a workload from the squad, and only a part-timer for Mr. Blackhawk all at once. I'd have a nervous breakdown. And I can't persuade people to talk to me like you can. You're marvelous at digging out information."

Joceline pursed her lips. "I can do that," she agreed. "Maybe there's work for a skip tracer," she added, indicating a line of work that involved digging out information for detectives. "I might look good in a trench coat."

Betty laughed again.

JUST BEFORE quitting time, the phone rang as Joceline was gathering things into her bag to take home, including the long file on Bart Hancock.

Joceline picked up the phone. "Hello?"

"My love! It's been so long!"

She knew that voice. Its South African accent was unmistakable. She pictured a rugged, tanned face with an eye patch and blond hair in a long ponytail. "Rourke," she muttered.

"You know you're happy to have me around again," he drawled. "Guess what? I'm going to be your shadow for a few weeks. Until the would-be perp stops making threats, at least."

"I can't wait," she replied. "Do you have body armor?"

He hesitated. "Excuse me?"

"Body armor," she emphasized. "Riot gear."

"No. But I can borrow some. Why will I need it?"

"If you attempt to shadow me, I'll rub bear grease all over you and open the lion cage at the zoo," she said sweetly.

There was a slow, deep chuckle. "Joceline, my love, I have two tame lions who live with me back home in South Africa. I'm not intimidated by big cats. However, if you'd like to rub me all over with bear grease," he added in a deep, velvety tone, "I can be in your office in two minutes flat. I'll even run red lights!"

She slammed the receiver down, her lips making a thin line. She muttered under her breath.

A minute later, the phone rang again. She jerked it up

and, without thinking, said, "If you call here one more time, Rourke, I'll have you up for harassment!"

There was a faint pause, as if she'd shocked the listener. Then Kilraven's voice came over the line, deep and very somber.

"Joceline, I've got some bad news."

"Winnie...?" she began worriedly, because she was fond of his wife. They often went shopping together.

He swallowed. "Not Winnie. My brother..."

"Jon? Something's happened to Jon?" She sounded almost hysterical and she didn't care. Harold Monroe's phone call came back to her in a flash of anguish. She gripped the phone, hard. "What happened?"

"He's been shot. Critically. He's at the Hal Marshall Memorial Medical Center... Hello? Joceline?"

He was talking to himself. Joceline had her purse over her shoulder. She ran to Betty's small office and told her what had happened.

"I'm on my way to the hospital. I'll call you the minute I know something!"

Betty started to mention that Jon's family was certainly gathered around him, and would relay any news. But the look on Joceline's face stopped the words in her mouth. She wondered if Joceline was even aware of her feelings for Jon Blackhawk, which were blatant on her drawn, worried face.

CHAPTER SIX

KILRAVEN WAS SITTING in an uncomfortable chair in the emergency room waiting area, with Winnie beside him. He looked up when Joceline walked in. His expression, usually unreadable, was as concerned as hers.

"Have you heard anything new?" she asked, pausing to greet Winnie with a hug.

"They've taken him into surgery," Kilraven replied grimly. "They said they'll know more when they operate. He was shot in the back. In the back!"

Joceline's face flamed. "I hope they find Harold Monroe and hang him."

Kilraven nodded. "I can't prove it, but I'm sure he's the one who did it. And I'll find the proof, no matter how long it takes me!"

"I'll help," Joceline agreed harshly.

"Want some coffee?" Winnie asked her husband, who nodded.

"I'll go get it," he said, starting to rise.

She pushed him back down. "I need the exercise. The

doctor says it's good for me to move around. But thanks, sweetheart." She bent to kiss him. "Would you like a cup, Joceline?" she added.

"Yes, please." Joceline dug for a dollar bill and handed it to her insistently. "You're not buying me coffee," she said stubbornly. "I'm an employee of a federal agency and I won't be the subject of a bribery scandal," she added with mock hauteur.

Winnie chuckled. "Have it your way, Elliott Ness."

Kilraven frowned. "He headed up the FBI in Chicago during racketeering days. He was incorruptible."

"The history professor," Winnie teased, and kissed him again.

"I'm not up on American history unless it has Scots connections." His area of expertise was seventeenth-century Scottish history.

"Was Elliott Ness a Scot?" Joceline wondered aloud.

"I'll look into it," Kilraven promised.

Winnie went to get coffee. Kilraven and Joceline sat rigidly, watching the doors open and close as medical personnel in green scrubs went to and fro, occasionally flanked by white-coated physicians with stethoscopes draped around their necks.

"Busy place," Kilraven ventured.

"Yes." She turned over her purse. "Have you called your mother?"

"She's on her way here," he said. "I made her promise not to drive." He grimaced. "She's wrapped two cars around telephone poles in the past five years."

"Oh. She drives like you, then," Joceline said with a pleasant smile.

He glared at her. "I have never wrecked a car."

"Sorry. I forgot. They were blown out from under you. Major difference." She was nodding.

He shifted. "Everybody gets bomb threats."

"Yours aren't threats, and how lucky that you weren't in the cars at the time they exploded."

"Can I help it if I inspire passion in people?"

"People in black ops do that, I'm told." She chuckled.

He shrugged. "I'm trying to walk the straight and narrow, especially now," he said with a smile. "I'm doing the most boring job the company could find for me. Surveillance."

"It's safer than what you used to do," she said. She frowned. "Did you send Rourke after me?"

"Yes, I did," he said, "and stop trying to run him off. Monroe is deadly serious, as you might have noticed today. Jon told me that Monroe said you're next. You have a small child and the two of you live in an apartment building with no security to speak of. Rourke will protect you."

"Who's going to protect him from me?" she wondered aloud.

"That is a good question."

They paused to stare at the door leading to the surgical wing. A surgeon in green scrubs came out it, looked toward Kilraven and motioned for him to join him. Joceline went, too, ignoring the surgeon's obvious surprise. Under other circumstances, Kilraven would have chuckled at her concern for a boss she constantly drove nuts.

Joceline could hear her own heart beating and hoped Kilraven wouldn't notice. She was scared to death. If Jon Blackhawk died, it would be like the sun going out forever. She refused to even entertain the possibility. But she knew that he could die. And might. She gripped her purse like a lifeline, hoping, praying…*let him live, please, I'll go to church more, I'll give to charity more, I'll be a better person, be kinder, more tolerant…* She closed her eyes. *You can't bargain with God,* she told herself.

"I'm cautiously optimistic," the surgeon said, glancing

at Joceline when her explosion of soft breath diverted him. "The bullet missed the major organs and lodged in the wall of his chest. It did some damage to a lung, and of course filled the pleural cavity with blood. We've removed the bullet and inserted a tube to drain the excess fluid and reinflate the lung. The damage to his lung is minimal. Apparently he was shot from a distance, and with a nonfragmenting bullet, thank God. The damage will heal. It helps that he's young and in great physical shape."

"Can I see him?" Kilraven asked quietly.

He hesitated. But he was a kindly man, and these two people loved his patient. He wondered if the woman was a girlfriend. She was certainly concerned.

"In a few minutes," he told them. "We'll move him into recovery temporarily, then he'll go to ICU for a day or two. Just as a precaution," he emphasized when he noted his two listeners going pale. "We want to make sure complications don't develop that might retard his progress. We'll keep him for three or four days after that, again, to make sure he's progressing as we think he should. But I think he'll be fine," he added gently.

"They'll come to get us, when we can see him?" Kilraven asked, glancing at Joceline as if it were a given that she'd go in, too.

"I'll send a nurse," he promised. "He's an FBI agent, isn't he?"

"Yes," Kilraven replied. "One of the best."

"We do a big business in gunshot wounds in our emergency room," the doctor said with a heavy sigh. "Sadly there are more guns than trauma surgeons in this area."

"One day that will change," Kilraven said.

The doctor only smiled. "Not in my lifetime, I'm afraid. I'll get back to work. They just brought in a child of seven, victim of a drive-by shooting." He shook his head. "In my day, drugs were only whispered about. There was no wide-scale distribution, no gangs with guns, no…" He shrugged. "It was a less tolerant world, but far less violent."

"They did this experiment," Kilraven said quietly. "I read about it. They put rats in a confined area until they were so crowded that they could barely move. They became aggressive and began attacking the others and even cannibalizing them."

The doctor nodded. "We are too many, with too few resources, in too little space in cities on this planet. Nature has a way of thinning the population without any help from us." He glanced toward the emergency room. "However, I must add that I prefer nature's approach. Guns and knives are messy."

"I agree," Kilraven said. "I've seen my share of the results."

Nobody added that he'd helped a few criminals into emergency rooms.

The surgeon smiled reassuringly and went back to work.

Joceline was trying to avoid letting Kilraven see her tears.

"Hey, now," he said in a teasing tone. "Don't do that. Never let them see you cry."

She laughed with a hiccup and brushed at her eyes. "He's an awful boss," she muttered. "Keeps me working late, throws things, insults me…"

"Jon insults you?" he asked, shocked.

"He asks me to make coffee," she scoffed. She brushed away another tear. "Imagine that!"

"He's just tired of threatened lawsuits from visiting attorneys who have to drink the coffee the agents make," Kilraven explained.

"Then they should stop letting Murdock make coffee," she pointed out.

"That's been suggested," he replied. "At the same time, they mentioned dirt and shovels..."

"There's a large potted plant in our office that could use a jolt of fertilizer," she mused. "However, Agent Murdock is far too large to plant in it."

"We could..." he began enthusiastically.

She held up a hand and glowered at him. "Please! This is a hospital!"

"Just a thought." He sighed. "I bring my own coffee now when I visit Jon at his office, though."

At the sound of her boss's name, she relaxed a little. "I'm glad he'll be all right." She hesitated. "I guess I should get going."

"You can see him first."

She was uncertain. "You and Winnie should go in."

"Winnie will say that you should," he said with a gentle smile.

"Thanks," she murmured huskily and wouldn't look up.

Kilraven didn't say what he was thinking. Joceline and Jon had been antagonistic toward each other for a long time. But there was one night when they'd actually gone to a party together, about four years ago. The Bureau had been providing protection for a young woman who was dating a foreign dignitary's son, and avoided a kidnapping. She'd insisted that Jon, the agent in charge of the case, come to her birthday party and bring a date. So Jon had made Joceline go with him. He hated parties. He hated socializing. So did Joceline. But she went.

Funny, Joceline had acted oddly afterward and tried to quit her job. Jon had talked her into staying. He hadn't said much about the incident, just that he'd had way too much to drink and Joceline had been forced to drive him to the hospital. It turned out that someone had spiked Jon's drink with a hallucinogenic drug, trying to be funny. The culprit, a foreign dignitary's son, had fled the country shortly there-after and never returned.

He hadn't thought about that for a long time. His brother never drank as a rule. He was very straitlaced. Today, it had hurt terribly to see Jon lying on a gurney with blood seeping from the wound on his back. He loved his brother. Cammy was going to go ballistic. She'd lived in fear of this all during Jon's career in law enforcement. She kept rosaries every-where, even in the glove compartment of her car, and she prayed constantly for his safety. At least she wasn't driv-ing herself to the hospital or there might be two tragedies. Kilraven would have gone to get her, but he'd been afraid to leave Jon—as if by his own physical presence he could keep Jon alive.

The nurse beckoned to them a nerve-racking few minutes later. Neither Kilraven nor Joceline really believed that Jon wasn't going to die. They had to see him for themselves, to be sure.

He was in a hospital gown, but his chest was bare. He was white as a sheet. There was dried blood on his firm, chis-eled mouth. He was laboring to breathe, even with the tube that ran out of his chest to drain off the fluid. There was a drip feeding from a tube on a pole into his arm. There were oxygen tubes in his nostrils and he was hooked up to half a dozen monitors. His long, jet-black hair was tangled on the pillow. His eyes were closed.

Besides the beep of the monitors and the electronic sounds, there was only the sudden jerk of Joceline's breath, almost a sob, which she quickly smothered.

"He'd hate having his hair tangled," she said quietly.

"Yes."

He glanced at her, noting that she didn't have much more color in her face than Jon did in his. She was gripping her purse as if she feared it might escape.

"He's one tough customer," Kilraven told her comfortingly. "And I do know something about gunshot wounds. I'm sure he's in a lot of pain, and it will take time for him to recover. But he's going to live, Joceline."

She swallowed her fear and nodded slowly. "Yes," she agreed.

"Tomorrow he'll be telling the nurses how to do the drip and threatening the doctor to try to get out of the hospital."

She nodded again. It was so painful to see him like that. He was such a strong, vital man…

Kilraven was watching her covertly. It surprised him to see her at a loss for words, to see her so frightened. Perhaps she was thinking about the shadowy man in her life who went missing overseas. Markie's father.

Markie. He felt a sudden sinking worry. "Going to step out for just a sec," he told her, and moved out of the ICU unit to make a quick phone call.

Joceline barely noticed. Her hand went out to smooth the thick, long, tangled black hair on the pillow. She recalled another time when she'd touched it, felt its cool silkiness, clung to it as feelings rose so high that she thought she might die of them. He didn't remember. It was a good thing. She didn't want him to remember.

"Don't touch my son!"

She froze, jerking her hand back, as Cammy Blackhawk came into the room. She glared at the younger woman as she moved to the bed, her back to Joceline.

"Jon," she whispered. "My poor, poor boy!"

She bent to kiss his forehead, and fought tears. She smoothed back his hair and stared at him for a long moment. Then she turned to Joceline, all cold dignity and hostility.

"You have no right to be in here," she snapped.

Joceline didn't argue. She looked one last time at Jon before she turned and left the cubicle.

"Where are you going?" Kilraven asked, surprised to meet her in the hall.

"I'm leaving," Joceline said, very pale but composed. "Life goes on. Your mother is in there," she added stiffly.

"Oh, God, now the real torment begins," he groaned. "She'll stand the staff on its ear and they'll threaten to hang her from a window by a sheet!"

She laughed suddenly.

"Don't let her worry you," Kilraven said in a low tone. "She's not what she seems. Honest."

Joceline didn't reply. "I hope he does well."

"He will. I'll call you myself if there's any change."

She nodded. "Thanks, Kilraven."

His eyes narrowed. "Joceline, I've had Rourke stake out your son's preschool."

"What?" she exclaimed, going white.

"Monroe made threats," he reminded her. "We can't prove it so we can't have him arrested. He's being watched, that's all I can say. But your son may be on the firing line. He has to have protection. So do you."

It was horrifying to think that Markie might end up in a hospital bed, victim of some deranged criminal. "Surely, not! He's just a child!"

"So was Melly," Kilraven reminded her with a grim expression, speaking of his daughter who had been killed. "She was barely three, when—" His voice broke.

"I'm sorry," she told him. "Truly sorry."

"Sorry doesn't bring her back, and it won't protect your son, either," he added. "Rourke will. So tolerate him."

She grimaced.

"You don't have to like him. I know he's a pain. But he's the best private security I know."

"All right."

He studied her for a moment. "You never bring your son to

work. You don't have a photo of him on your desk. But you obviously love him very much."

"Don't speculate," she bit off.

He was just staring at her. Not even blinking. "I'm not speculating."

"I keep my work life and my home life separate," she said stiffly. "I'm somewhat defensive about my status," she added, and averted her eyes.

"So you don't draw attention to it."

"Yes," she said quickly, anxious for an answer that would shut him up.

"I get it." He didn't press her. But he was getting some very interesting vibrations running underneath the casual conversation. "Don't worry about your boss," he added gently. "He's in great hands."

She looked toward the glass cubicle, where Cammy Blackhawk was still smoothing her son's hair and talking to him. "I noticed."

"I meant the doctor," he mused.

"Oh."

"You don't know about Cammy's past, and I won't tell it to you," he said surprisingly. "But there's a reason she's the way she is. Try not to take her attitude too seriously."

"She loves her son. There's nothing wrong with that."

"She does, but she's micromanaging his life. Or she's trying to."

"She wants the best for him." She pursed her lips and her blue eyes twinkled suddenly. "She wants him to have the best fashion advice money can buy."

"He'd do a lot better with a woman who could play video games with him."

"Don't look at me," Joceline said firmly. "I have one man in my life. I don't need another."

"Your son's father went missing in action, you said."

"Yes."

"I still have contacts in active military circles," he said, watching her with uncanny closeness. "I could have them do some checking."

She dropped her purse. She bent and picked it up. "Sorry, it's been an unsettling day," she said. "I'm clumsy. No, thanks, it's already been checked out. He disappeared in those mountains where they think the remnants of Al-Qaeda were hiding in a secret base. They were certain that he was killed, they just were reluctant to tell me."

She hadn't looked up once.

"I see," he said.

She was hoping for an interruption when Winnie Sinclair came up with two cups of coffee. She handed one to her husband. "You've had a long day, you should go."

"Yes," Joceline said gratefully. "You'll call me, if there's any change?" she added worriedly.

"Of course we will," Winnie assured her.

"The assistant D.A. asked about you," Kilraven said. "She's still hoping you might jump ship and go to work for her," he added, teasing.

"There might be a real possibility of that," Joceline said on a heavy sigh. "They're talking about cutting staff in my office. Betty has seniority, so if one of us is cut, it will be me." She shook her head. "This has been a bummer of a day."

Kilraven frowned. "They'd never let you go."

She smiled sadly. "They'll let anybody go, if they have to. I don't have any illusions about being the best administrative assistant on earth." She sighed. "Now I have to worry about that and my boss, and my son…"

"Not about Markie," Kilraven assured her. "Rourke will make sure no harm comes to him. Or to you."

Joceline ground her teeth together. "Okay."

"And Jon will be all right," he added.

She bit her lip. "He had blood on his mouth."

"Joceline, he was shot in a lung," he reminded her. "He would have been spitting up blood when they found him. Thank God he was in sight of a main street when it happened!"

"Yes," she whispered, hurting as she considered how frightening and how painful it would have been, to have experienced what her boss had—to be shot in the back.

"Now go home to your son," Winnie said gently. "He will keep you from brooding too much."

"The chief brooder is in there." She indicated the cubicle where Cammy was still sitting with Jon. "He does it much better than I do."

"He'll be fine. Just keep the office together until he recovers," Kilraven told her.

She smiled. That was optimistic. She had to be optimistic, too. "Okay. Do you know any really good defense attorneys, by the way?"

Kilraven blinked. "Not really, but I can ask around. Why do you need one?"

"I don't, yet. As long as Rourke stays out of sight."

Kilraven chuckled. "He is a piece of work, isn't he?"

"Saved your butt, my darling," Winnie reminded him with a hug.

He returned it and kissed her hair. "Yes, but he was being obnoxious."

"It's what he does best."

"He'll keep Markie safe," Kilraven reminded Joceline. "He's good at what he does."

"Which would be what, exactly, when he isn't returning favors for you?" Joceline asked curiously.

"Never you mind," he said firmly. "That's need to know, and you don't."

"Spoilsport."

She smiled at both of them and sent one last, worried glance toward where Jon Blackhawk lay, so quiet and still, before she left the waiting room.

"Something's fishy," Kilraven murmured.

"About what?" Winnie asked.

He didn't tell her. He had his suspicions, all wrapped up in mystery and Joceline's reticence. But he was going to do some digging, when he had time.

He and Winnie went back to ICU to join Cammy.

"Has she gone, that awful girl?" Cammy asked angrily.

"She's his right arm at work," Kilraven reminded her firmly. "She's stood by him when half a dozen other women would have run screaming out the door."

"I don't like her. She's not a moral person."

"What if she'd ended the pregnancy, would that make her any more moral in your eyes, Cammy?" Kilraven asked coldly. "What if it had been you, pregnant with Jon?"

Cammy swallowed, hard, and averted her eyes. Her jaw tightened. He was provoking nightmares and she couldn't even tell him. She couldn't tell anyone. She smoothed Jon's hair. "He looks so pale."

"His system has been through a shock," Kilraven reminded her. "Been there, done that."

"Yes, I know, my dear," she said gently, and she hugged him. "I'm sorry. I'm being terrible. I was so worried…" Tears stung her eyes.

He hugged her. "Jon's going to be fine."

"Yes."

He sighed. "I thought the murders were neatly wrapped up. But there's a new trail emerging. I just found out that the guy we think did this," he indicated Jon, "has a brother-in-law who may also have been involved in Melly's death."

"What?" Cammy exclaimed, horrified.

"That's not all. Now he's after Joceline's little boy." He wasn't certain of that, but it was a good guess.

Cammy was conflicted. She didn't like that Joceline person. But she loved children. Anybody's children. "That's too bad."

"It is."

"She doesn't have a live-in boyfriend or someone who could protect him?"

"Joceline lives alone. But I sent Rourke to watch the boy."

"Rourke." She rolled her eyes. "Well, on the other hand, he is a bachelor and of an age to marry." She was thoughtful. If Joceline married Rourke, she'd move to South Africa, far from Jon. She smiled. "Perhaps they might like each other."

Kilraven didn't reply. He could see wheels turning in Cammy's mind, and suddenly he felt sorry for Rourke.

JOCELINE dropped her things off at her apartment. She was going to be late getting Markie, but she'd phoned and the owner, especially under the circumstances, told her to take her time that she'd be glad to wait. She'd heard about Jon's shooting on the news. She was very sorry. Not nearly as sorry as Joceline, who was sick and worried out of her mind.

If he died, how would she live with the secret she kept? It gnawed at her like a dog with a bone. She was so upset that her hands shook as she locked her door and went out to get into her car. She thought she saw a shadow move, but she was certain it was her imagination. She was so much on edge, she was seeing things.

She tried to put Jon's condition in the back of her mind. She didn't want to upset Markie. She thanked the owner profusely when she picked up Markie at the day care center. He had new drawings to show her. "This is my teacher," he said, showing her a sketch he'd done, which was crude but recognizable. "And this is a dog that came to the playground.

A man came in a truck and took him away," he added sadly. "Will they kill him?"

"No! They'll just find his owner. That's all." She smiled and hoped that it was the truth.

"I wish we could have a dog," he said.

She fastened him into the backseat and got in behind the steering wheel. Of all the things about modern life that she disliked, this was her pet peeve. A child should sit beside its parent, not isolated in the backseat. Yes, air bags saved lives and they were dangerous and could kill a small child. But when she had been small, Joceline had ridden in the front seat of her father's pickup truck, strapped in like a miniature adult, happy and laughing. Someone should figure out a child seat that could withstand the air bags going off, and allow kids to be closer to their parents.

She sighed as she pulled out into traffic. Her boss was going to be all right. He was going to be all right. She had to believe that, to save her own sanity. Markie would be all right, too. Rourke would watch out for him. She didn't have to like Rourke to know that he was good at his job—whatever it was, when he wasn't doing favors for Kilraven. She started looking around to see if she could recognize the one-eyed lunatic in any passing cars.

"Mommy, are you looking for somebody?" Markie asked curiously.

She cleared her throat. "I'm just checking traffic, that's all."

"Isn't your boss named Mr. Blackhawk? Somebody said he was shot. Is he dead?"

"No! He's just wounded and in the hospital. He's not dead," she said at once.

"I'm glad. We played video games with him that night. I like him."

She smiled sadly. "I like him, too."

"Could we go and see him?" he asked.

Joceline, surprised, just stammered. "There's an age limit, Markie," she foundered. Well, there used to be. She wasn't sure of modern hospital policy. It had been several years since she herself had been in one, when she'd had Markie.

"You mean I can't see him?"

"Yes. That's what I mean. His mother is with him."

"Oh, that's okay, then."

Joceline had other thoughts about that, but she didn't share them. "How about an ice-cream cone?" she asked.

"Wow! Could we?"

"Yes." It was the little things, she considered, that made life bearable. Even the hard times were smoothed over by something simple and comforting.

She stopped at an ice-cream parlor and ordered two cones, strawberry for herself and butter pecan for Markie. She handed his to him with a smile.

He licked it and laughed up at her with sparkling eyes. He was going to be handsome when he was older, she thought. She thanked God every day that he looked more like her than his father.

When they got home, just after dark, the front door was standing open.

"Stay here," Joceline told Markie firmly.

"What is it, Mommy?"

She didn't answer. She went to a point where she could see the front door. Nothing was visible inside it. She knew better than to walk into the apartment. Someone had broken in. Someone who might still be in there, might be armed, might want to kill Joceline and Markie just for their closeness to Jon Blackhawk…!

"Well!" came a deeply accented voice from inside the apartment. "It's a good thing you didn't come home sooner."

And Rourke appeared in the doorway, big and handsome and smiling.

CHAPTER SEVEN

"ROURKE!" JOCELINE EXCLAIMED. "You idiot! You scared me to death!"

He strode down the steps, his hands in his pockets, whistling. He was tall and lean and muscular, with long blond hair in a ponytail down his back. He had one light brown eye. The other was hidden under a rakish black eye patch. "Now, darlin', if I hadn't come along when I did, you'd have had a very bad shock when you opened that front door. Hi, little feller. How are you?" he asked the small boy in the backseat in a very pronounced South African accent.

"I'm good," Markie said. "Who are you?"

"Rourke," was the amused reply.

"You only got one eye."

"I noticed," Rourke told him, not taking offense.

"I'm sorry."

The man looked at the boy with a visible softening. "Nice of you to say that."

"Did some mean man hurt you?"

"You might say that," Rourke replied.

"I like your eye patch. You could be a pirate on Hallow-
een."

Rourke burst out laughing. "You know, I've been called a
pirate a time or two." He looked pointedly at Joceline.

"Why are you here, and what's wrong with the apartment?" she asked worriedly.

"Nothing major. Step over here a bit." He smiled reassuringly at Markie. But when he turned back to Joceline, his
hard face was solemn. "Someone had a go at your desk. At a
guess, they were looking for something. Any idea what?"

Her heart stopped. She had no important papers, nothing
that would interest an outsider. There was only the usual
things, bank deposit records, tax information, Markie's birth
certificate and her own, nothing…nothing… There was her
diary!

She brushed past Rourke and ran into the apartment in
a panic. She kept the diary in her bedside table, but it was
under a mass of other objects, like paperbacks and a pad
and pen, over-the-counter analgesics, booklets and instructions for electronic things like her clock. She fumbled in the
drawer, horrified at some of the things she'd written down.
It had never occurred to her than anyone would rob her!

She pulled out books, scattering them, scared to death.
But then, there it was, at the bottom of the drawer, its small
lock intact. It hadn't been opened. She clutched it to her
breast and shivered with reaction.

"Something damaging in there, I presume?" Rourke asked
gently.

She looked at him with sick fear. "People write things that
they never should."

He nodded solemnly. "Yes."

She drew in a harsh breath. "I'd better burn it, I think."

"Put it in the bank, in a safe-deposit box," he suggested.

She stared at him. "Along with my diamond collection and my gold bars."

He laughed.

"Listen, I can barely pay the rent. There's no money for extras. It's better to destroy it. No good could come of keeping it, anyway."

"Keeping what, Mommy?" Markie asked as he joined them. Rourke had brought him inside the minute Joceline vanished into the apartment.

She grimaced at her lack of instinct, leaving Markie alone in the car.

"It's all right, I've got your back," Rourke assured her with a smile.

"It's just a diary, Markie," Joceline told him. "I wanted to make sure I knew where it was, that's all."

"Can I read it?"

She swallowed. "When you're older."

"Okay."

Rourke was watching her through a narrowed pale brown eye. Something in that diary was enough to make her panic. He wondered what it was.

THE REST of the apartment was seemingly untouched, at first glance. Joceline was nervous. Someone had touched her things, invaded her privacy. She felt violated. Now she wondered if she needed new locks.

"Yes, you do," Rourke said when she mentioned it. "I'll install dead bolts tomorrow. Do you need permission from the landlord?"

She shook her head. "I asked once before and the manager approved it, in writing. I just didn't get around to it."

Rourke nodded.

Her expression was briefly unguarded as she looked up at him. "I wasn't scared before," she said unsteadily.

His one eye narrowed, and his lean face hardened. "Any normal human being would be afraid for a child," he said quietly, so that Markie didn't hear.

She turned on the small television. "Time for someone's favorite show, I believe?" she teased, putting Markie in his little beanbag chair in front of the TV.

He giggled. "I love this one," he told her, and immediately became entranced by the cartoon characters on the screen.

"He can already pick out certain characters in Japanese just by watching that cartoon," Joceline told Rourke. "I think he may have a flair for languages."

"Do you speak any?" he asked without appearing to care.

She laughed. "I can barely speak my own language."

"Then he must get it from his father or someone else in his family," he said easily.

Joceline went pale. "You think so? I'd better check and make sure nothing was taken." Which brought back the enormity of having her apartment ransacked. She was terrified and trying not to show it, because she didn't want to upset Markie

She went quickly from room to room and found that though she'd thought nothing else had been touched, she was wrong. There were papers scattered, drawers askew, even chair cushions upended.

"What in the world could they have been looking for?" she wondered uneasily.

"What sort of important papers do you keep here, besides that diary?" Rourke asked, nodding toward the diary that she was holding so tightly in one hand.

She pushed back her hair and looked around worriedly. "Nothing much. The usual bills and important papers. Birth certificates."

"Are they all here?"

She went to the folder where she kept her personal documents, in a cheap cardboard filing cabinet, and pulled out the file folder. There was nothing that would prove anything. She'd been very careful about that.

She opened the folder and looked inside, and sighed with helpless relief. "Everything's right here," she said, and laughed unsteadily.

Rourke's eyes were narrow and thoughtful. He wasn't going to tell her that there were ways to collect documents without physically removing them. Any good agent carried a tiny camera, often disguised as a cigarette lighter or pen. A lock on a diary was so simple to open that a beginner could do it with ease, and without leaving any telltale mark of tampering. She was unusually worried about that diary and some of her important papers. Why?

She saw his mind working and her face tautened. "Don't pry."

"Was I prying?" he exclaimed, and grinned.

"You were thinking about it," she accused.

"Pretty and smart and reads minds, too," he teased.

She flushed. "Let's leave it at 'smart.'"

"And doesn't like flattery. I'm taking notes," he added. He smiled at her. "How would you feel about living in Africa?"

"I am not leaving the country with you," she said firmly.

"I have a nice little place there in Kenya, with a pet lion."

"A lion? You got a lion?" Markie was out of his chair in a flash, looking up at the tall blond man. "Could I pet it?"

"You could even ride him," Rourke assured him with a big smile. "He's very tame. I raised him from a cub. Poachers got his mum."

"Oh, that's very sad," Markie said. "I would feed him hamburgers, if I had a lion."

"I don't think they'd like it if you tried to keep him in your apartment," Rourke assured him.

"These two guys in England did just that." Joceline chuckled. "It was viral on the web about two years ago. Two boys bought a lion cub and kept it in their apartment, then they had to let it go to a preserve in Africa because it got so big. They went to see it, despite people warning that it was wild and would attack them. But it ran right up to them and put its paws on their shoulders and started rubbing its head against them. It even took them to see its mate." She sighed. "I cried like a baby, watching it. They had the story on the news. Afterward, I sent a little check to the foundation that took in the boys' pet."

"Wild animals aren't so very wild after all," Rourke agreed. "Pity so many people see them as a way to quick profits."

"Oh, I do agree," Joceline said.

"See how much we have in common?" he asked.

"I want to go to Africa and see his lion," Markie announced. "Can we go now?"

"Logistics aside," Joceline told him gently, "I do have a job and you have to go to school tomorrow."

"Oh." He thought about that for a minute. "Can we go Saturday, then?"

Both adults laughed.

"Children make impossible things seem so uncomplicated," Rourke remarked when Markie had gone back to his program and Joceline was serving up cups of strong black coffee. He wondered if her budget would stretch to giving free coffee to visitors, and decided that he'd bring her a pound of his special South African coffee next time he came over.

"Yes. Markie's had a hard time of it," she remarked with a sigh. "He has asthma and his lungs aren't strong. We spend a lot of time in doctors' offices."

"There are allergy shots," he said helpfully.

"He takes them," she said. "And they help. But if he's

stressed or exposed to viruses, he gets sick easier than most kids do."

"He's a fine little boy," he remarked, glancing at him. "You've done well."

"Thanks."

The diary was lying beside her right hand. She hadn't let it out of her sight since they'd been in the apartment. It wasn't really his business, but he was quite curious about what dark secrets she was keeping.

"What are you going to do with that?" he asked, indicating it.

"Tear it up and burn it," she said at once. "It must never be read by anyone except me. Ever."

His eyes narrowed.

"Stop speculating."

His eyebrows arched.

"My, you can say a lot without opening your mouth," she muttered.

"Facial expressions 101," he replied.

"Will they come back, you think?" she asked worriedly.

He shook his head. "Either they found what they were looking for, or it wasn't here."

"Found…?" She was staring at him with stark horror. She looked again at the diary. It was locked. Then she remembered something she'd heard from a visitor from a covert agency, about how easy it was to pick a lock and photograph a document. Her face went pale.

"Joceline," he said gently, reading her horror, "what do you have in there that's so frightening?"

"A great source of blackmail if I were rich," she said heavily. She smoothed her hand over the diary. "But I'm not rich. And I can't imagine what use anyone else would have for it." That wasn't quite true. The right person could do a lot of damage with the information in that little book. She shuddered to think what a criminal like Monroe could do with it.

"You mustn't worry," Rourke said gently. "I'll check around and see what I can dig out. I have all sorts of sources."

She searched his expression worriedly. "I'm not afraid for myself. I don't want anyone else hurt."

"You think someone else could be?"

She swallowed. "Yes."

"What tangled webs we weave," he murmured, alluding to a poem about deception.

"Indeed." She sipped rapidly cooling coffee. "We make choices. Then we live with them."

"Do you think you made the right one?" he asked.

She smiled. "I made the only one I could." She looked toward her son, who was oblivious to everything except the Japanese manga on the television. "I've never regretted it."

"He's quite a boy."

"Thanks."

"His dad died in the service, I understand?" He didn't look at her as he said it.

"Overseas. In the military."

"Sad."

"Very." She got up. "More coffee?"

He chuckled. "No, thanks. I tend to be wired even at good times. Too much caffeine can be a real killer, in my case."

"I drink too much of it," she confessed.

He got to his feet. "I'll get working on those locks. Do you go back to the office tomorrow?"

She hesitated. "Well, I don't know," she said suddenly. "My boss won't be there, and the only cases I'm working are his…"

Just as she said it, the phone rang.

She got up to answer it, hesitated, with her hand outstretched as if she were about to put it into fire.

She jerked it up. "Hello?"

There was a long silence.

Her blood felt as if it froze. "Hello?" she repeated.

The line went dead.

She turned and looked at Rourke with absolute horror.

He took the receiver from her, punched in some numbers, listened and then spoke. "Yeah," he said to someone. "Do it quick. I want to know what brand of liquor he drinks in ten minutes or less. Just do it." He hung up. Joceline was amazed at how authoritative, and how businesslike, he could be when he wasn't clowning around.

"You have it tapped," she whispered.

"Yes," he replied curtly. "The minute I pulled into the driveway."

She bit her lower lip. "I'm glad you came over."

His eyebrows arched. His one eye twinkled. "You are? I can have a marriage license drawn up in less than an hour…!"

"Stop that," she muttered. "I'm not going to get married."

"But I have my own teeth," he protested. "And I don't even have a gray hair yet."

"That has nothing to do with it."

"A man with good teeth and no gray hair is a fine matrimonial prospect. I can also speak six impossibly difficult languages, including Afrikaans," he added.

She went to clean the coffeepot, shaking her head the whole way.

ROURKE installed dead bolts and window locks. He also brought thermal curtains, heavy ones, for the windows. He didn't tell her that a sniper would have a field day with the block of apartments overlooking hers. She wouldn't have thought that anyone would be crazy enough to shoot at her or the boy.

That diary really puzzled him. He went out to get something to eat, and while he was out, he made two more telephone calls. Joceline would have had a heart attack if she'd heard the topic of discussion.

JOCELINE DIDN'T SLEEP WELL. She was certainly safe enough. Rourke had kipped down on the sofa in the living room, despite her protests, fully dressed. She was uncomfortable with a man in her apartment, but she couldn't say much. That phone call with just heavy breathing had terrified her. She wasn't afraid for herself, but she was afraid for Markie. There were good reasons that she didn't advertise anything about his beginnings. Now they could serve to end his young life.

She tossed and turned. Jon would be all right, Kilraven had told her he was certain of it. But she couldn't get the picture of his white face and closed eyes and bloodstained lips out of her mind. He was such a strong, lively man that it was more disturbing to see him helpless. If he died, she didn't know what she'd do. She'd made decisions that had come back to haunt her. Perhaps she shouldn't have kept secrets. It had seemed the only possibility at the time. But, now…

She got up just before daylight and went into the kitchen to make breakfast, bleary-eyed and sleepy.

Rourke glanced into the kitchen. She was already fully dressed, in jeans and a T-shirt. She wouldn't wear that rig to work, of course, but she wasn't making food in her nightgown with a strange man in her apartment.

"Hungry?" she asked, smiling as he joined her in the doorway.

"I could eat. Cereal?" he asked.

"Oh, no. I make biscuits and eggs and bacon for Markie. I want to send him to school with a good breakfast."

"Biscuits? Real biscuits?" he asked, surprised.

"Yes." She got out a wrought-iron skillet. "I make them in this," she said, running her fingers lightly over the coal-black surface. "It belonged to my great-grandmother. It's the only real heirloom I have."

"Impressive," he said, and meant it. "I haven't seen one of these since I was a kid myself."

She smiled. "It brings back a lot of memories."

"Did you know your great-grandmother?"

"Oh, no, she died before I was even born. But my grandmother talked about her all the time."

He frowned. "What about your parents?"

She swallowed. "My father died, years ago. My mother and I don't speak."

"Sorry."

"Me, too. It would have been nice if Markie had some grandparents of his own."

He pursed his lips and watched her deft hands make the dough and roll it out and cut it.

"You do that very well," he said.

She laughed. "I've had lots of practice."

"You can cook. But you won't make coffee at the office."

"It's a matter of principle," she replied. "If I start doing menial tasks, I won't ever stop. My job is demanding. I spend most of the day on the phone trying to track down information, talking to people, making contacts. There's a rhythm. If I break it to go make coffee or start serving it to visitors, I lose my concentration."

"I see."

"My boss doesn't," she said with a wicked little grin. "But over the years he's learned to accept it." She put the biscuits in the preheated oven. "He looked terrible," she said, her expression far away.

"Gunshot victims mostly do," he said. "But his injuries were slight, compared to what they could have been, I assure you."

She turned to look at him. "You think he'll really be all right?" she asked, concerned.

"Of course."

She studied him intently for a moment. "You've been shot," she said.

He nodded, and he didn't smile. "Twice. Once in the chest, once in the leg. Neither occasion was pleasant."

"They say Africa is a very dangerous place."

"It is," he agreed. "It depends on where you go. But violence is international. You find it in a lot of places."

"I guess so."

"I am South African, but I have a place in Kenya, near a game preserve," he told her, and his expression was wistful. "I have a manager there to oversee it, but I miss being able to do that myself. I spend a lot of time traveling. More than I like."

"You work in a dangerous profession."

He pursed his lips. "Dear girl, you don't know what my profession is."

"Oh, I think I could make an educated guess," she retorted.

"Which would be wrong. I don't work outside the law."

"Well!"

He nodded. "You remember that."

She laughed and shook her head.

SHE TOOK Markie to school. She took time to talk to Mr. Morrison about the break-in and the threat by Monroe. He was furious that someone would threaten a child. He promised to keep a careful eye on Markie and make sure his teacher knew the situation.

Then she drove to the hospital. She knew she was going to have a war trying to get past Cammy Blackhawk, but she was going anyway. She couldn't go on with her job and her life without knowing for herself how Jon was.

She walked into the lobby and up to the desk, to ask which room in ICU he was in and if she could see him. But they'd already moved him out of ICU into a room, she was told. Her heart lifted. He couldn't be dying if they'd done that!

It turned out to be a private room on the second floor, very clean and bright. She stopped in the doorway, gripping her purse, waiting for Cammy to explode out into the hall and tell her to go away.

Jon turned his head on the pillow and spotted her. His dark eyes brightened. "Come in."

She looked around warily.

"She's not here." His voice was strained. "She's gone shopping with the fashion adviser."

She laughed then walked to the bed and looked down at him quietly. "I'm glad you're better."

"I'm better?" he asked with a grimace.

"You must be, or you'd still be occupying a cubicle in ICU," she assured him. "I called the office but they said I didn't have to go in today. I told them I was coming to see you," she added. "Everyone sends their regards and some of the other agents in your squad are coming to see you as soon as visitors are allowed."

"I work with a great group of people." He drew in a painful breath. "I'm going home to Oklahoma, to the ranch, when they release me. I won't be able to work at the office for a couple of weeks, and the scenery is better there. So is the security," he added grimly. He looked at her pointedly. "You're coming with me."

Her heart flipped over. "I...I...what?"

"You and the child," he said curtly. "Rourke told my brother what happened. You're not going to be killed because I made an enemy."

Her legs felt wobbly. "I can't go to Oklahoma," she said quickly. "I'd have to take a leave of absence and take Markie out of school...!"

"Details that can be worked out quite easily. I sent Mac to deal with all that." He waved an elegant hand and winced at the movement.

"But...!"

"Don't argue," he said heavily. "I'm in no condition for a fight."

She bit her lower lip. There were a dozen good reasons why she shouldn't let Markie be anywhere around this man, ever. She couldn't find an argument that would work without telling the truth, which would never do.

"It's a nice ranch," he said curtly. "Your son loves animals. He can even ride a horse."

"No!"

"Joceline, both Mac and I were riding ponies at the age of three," he told her. "I wouldn't let him get hurt. We have cowboys trained to work with disabled children who come to the ranch to ride our horses."

"You do?" She was surprised. She'd never thought that disabled people could ride.

"Yes." He shifted and grimaced. He was sore and sick. He hated being confined to a bed, being hospitalized. It was the first time in his law enforcement career that he'd suffered a bullet wound. He could remember vividly the sense of sudden slowing when the bullet hit. He'd not felt the pain at first, just a hard blow, like a fist in his back. Then everything slowed down and he saw the sidewalk coming up to hit him, and felt blood in his mouth. It had been an absolute shock.

"You shouldn't be moving around," Joceline said, concerned. "You might reopen the wound."

He glared at her. "I have my mother to harass me about such things. I don't need you to help her!"

She bit her lip again. Faint color touched her cheeks. "Sorry. Slip of the tongue. Won't happen again." She crossed her heart.

He laughed despite himself and then groaned, because it hurt.

"Another slip. Very sorry," she said quickly. "I just wanted to see you, to make sure that you were all right."

"I got shot," he said icily. "I'm not all right!"

"You're not dead, either," she reminded him.

He sank back on the pillows and fiddled with the lightweight sheet and blanket that covered him. The hospital gown was barely visible above it. "I'm freezing to death," he muttered. "I want a real blanket and a comforter. And I want to go home!"

The nurse stuck her head around the door and grimaced. "Sir, could you complain in a little quieter manner?" she asked gently. "There's a gentleman next door recuperating from a knife wound. He's trying to sleep."

Jon glared at her.

She cleared her throat, and walked back out.

Jon muttered unspeakable things under his breath.

"Your mother will have kittens if you even suggest taking me to Oklahoma," Joceline told him firmly. "I cannot work in a combat zone."

He sighed. "Neither can I, really, but what sort of choice do we have?" he asked. His black eyes narrowed. "Rourke told me that you had a break-in at your apartment and that there was a harassing phone call."

She looked as tired as she felt. "Yes. We had to call the police and have them investigate. Markie was scared to death until one of the investigators gave him a piece of chewing gum and enthused over his Diego toys," she added, alluding to a children's program on TV.

Jon was surprised. "Not your typical investigator."

"It was Rick Marquez," she said, laughing. "He's sort of in a class all his own. He knows Rourke, too, apparently."

"Most people in law enforcement know Rourke, or know about him," he added. He shifted and grimaced again. "I don't want you alone in your apartment until we get the case wrapped up. Peppy may have been involved in my niece's murder. If that's the case, and he's helping Monroe get even with me, he'd have no problem shooting another child," he added meaningfully. He didn't say that he was convinced that Monroe would never have been able to carry out the shooting without flubbing it.

She knew what he was referring to. It made her pale. "That being said, I would feel safer at your ranch. I understand you have at least one retired federal agent on your payroll."

"We have three," he corrected, "plus a former hit man for the mob."

She stared at him without blinking.

He laughed. "He was very young and desperate when he did his first job. He was tricked into it and he didn't fire the fatal shot. He did go to prison and he was able to redeem himself before he became a hardened criminal. He did his time and paid the price. It was twenty-five years ago. He needed a job when he got out and he'd worked with livestock at the prison where he served his time. I talked to him there several times when I was interviewing convicts on current cases."

She was still leery.

"You'll understand when you meet him. I'll have our private jet fly you and Markie up there tomorrow."

"Your mother…"

"She's on her way to Paris tonight, with the fashion consultant, to see the new spring lines," he said in a droll tone. "I promised to call her daily about my progress. She'll never know you were there."

"You should tell her," she said worriedly.

"If I do, you'll never arrive. She'll commandeer the plane and land you on a desert island somewhere."

She laughed. "Okay."

"It's only for a few days. When you come home, we'll have to make some sort of security arrangements to keep you and Markie safe. I've already talked to the SAC about giving you time off to help me work on cases at the ranch."

She hated her financial inability to do anything about that, but she had no choice except to accept help. She couldn't put Markie at risk.

"It will be all right," he assured her.

"Nothing ever really is," she mused. She smiled. "I'm glad you're getting better." She looked at her watch. "I have to go."

"I'll have the pilot phone you tonight," he told her. "Is Rourke staying?"

She glowered at him. "Yes. He won't leave and I'm not strong enough to pick him up and toss him out the door."

He smiled. "He's the best at what he does. Don't argue."

"Okay."

His eyes searched hers and held them. It was like a mild electric shock. "I'll see you tomorrow, Joceline." His deep voice was almost purring.

She drew in a steadying breath. Her heart was turning cartwheels. "Okay."

He smiled. "Thanks for coming to see about me."

She shifted. "It's in my job description. Take dictation, run down leads, keep a neat filing system online and come see the boss when some idiot shoots him." She glanced at him. "But I don't make coffee."

He just shook his head. But there was a light in his dark eyes that was puzzling. She thought about it all the way home.

CHAPTER EIGHT

THE PLANE WAS a small jet. Joceline was surprised at the luxury inside. The plane had a cabin that was more luxurious than the best hotel she'd ever seen. It had everything from thick blankets to wrap around Markie to beverage service, and even meals.

"We try to make sure that our bosses have everything they need when we fly." The steward chuckled.

"It's very nice of Mr. Blackhawk to let us fly up," Joceline told him. "My car would never make it to Dallas, much less Oklahoma," she added with a laugh.

He laughed. "I know what you mean. Until I landed this job, I considered any vehicle with less than a hundred thousand miles on it as brand-new."

She leaned forward. "Mine just turned over on a hundred thousand. But it's one of those little Japanese imports and in great mechanical shape. It should go for a few more miles."

"I agree. They're great cars for people on budgets. Hey, sport," he told Markie, "you ever seen the inside of a cockpit?"

"No," Markie replied from inside the blanket.

"Want to?"

He sat up. "You mean it?"

"I do."

He pushed off the blanket. "Sure!"

"Come on, then," the steward said with a grin, and held out his hand.

"It's okay?" Markie asked his mother.

"Certainly," she assured him, smiling.

He went with the steward and Joceline sat back in her seat, worrying again. So much turmoil in her life, in such a short time. She was sick with fear and she couldn't let it show because it would upset Markie. She was afraid to be in the apartment, but even more afraid to go to the Blackhawk family ranch. She'd kept Markie separate from her work all his life, away from her boss and his family. It was awkward and difficult, this trip. But she comforted herself with the knowledge that it was only for a couple of days. Surely in that short length of time, nobody would pry.

She closed her eyes. She hadn't been sleeping well. She kept seeing Jon's pale face and bloodstained lips the night they'd taken him to the hospital. He could have died without ever knowing…

She bit down hard on that thought. He could never know. She'd made a hard decision and now she had to live with it. She closed her eyes and was suddenly asleep before she knew it.

"MA'AM?"

She heard the voice through a fog. She'd been riding an elephant and carrying a buffalo rifle, dressed in buckskins and a floppy hat yelling "Lay on, McDuff!" to someone in the distance.

She opened her eyes and blurted out the dream, laughing.

"Something you ate, maybe?" the steward asked with twinkling eyes.

"Must have been something awful," she agreed, sitting up straight. "An elephant of all things, and carrying a Sharps buffalo rifle, .50 caliber." She shook her head. "I guess it was that first-person account of a fight Quanah Parker was in that I've been reading."

"The one they call the fight of Adobe Walls, where Comanches led by Quanah Parker, outnumbered them something like five-to-one, got into it with a handful of buffalo hunters armed with those rifles and they fought him off?"

She grinned. "The very one. Quanah Parker was quite a guy."

The steward nodded. "His mother was white, a captive who was married to the chief of that particular Comanche tribe," he added. "The whites traded for her and took her, forcibly, back home. She tried over and over to escape and go back, but she couldn't. She just died."

She shook her head. "She loved her Comanche husband. And he never remarried. People are always trying to make other people do what they want," she said with a quiet smile. "Nothing ever changes much."

"Never does. We're about to land," the steward said. "Your son went to sleep when he came back in here," he added, nodding toward Markie, covered up in blankets and sound asleep.

"We've had a fraught couple of days," she said without elaborating. "I don't think he's slept much, and I certainly haven't."

"The ranch is a nice place for sleeping," the steward told her. "It's out in the country. No city noises, no traffic sounds. Just cattle bellowing occasionally and dogs barking."

"They have dogs?" Markie asked suddenly, sitting up to throw off the blankets.

"Oh, yes," the steward told him with a smile. "They raise champion German shepherds."

"Oh, dear," Joceline said. The animals had a bad reputation for being aggressive.

The steward laughed. "I can almost tell what you're thinking, but these babies wouldn't hurt a fly—not unless someone in the family was attacked. You'll see what I mean when we get there."

"I wish we could have a dog," Markie said with a pointed look at his mother.

"Just as soon as we buy that mansion in France, I'll buy you one," she told him with a straight face.

"We're gonna live in France?" the child exclaimed. "When?"

Joceline sighed and explained the concept of sarcasm to him.

A big Lincoln SUV met them at the small airstrip on the ranch. It was driven by a grizzled old cowboy with bright blue eyes and a big grin under his reddish-gold and gray whiskers.

"Miss Perry? I'm Sloane Callum. I'm sort of the chauffeur and odd job man around here. Mr. Blackhawk sent me to fetch you and the boy."

"Nice to meet you," she said, shaking hands and smiling.

"So you're that secretary we hear so much about!" he exclaimed as he loaded her small suitcase and Markie's duffel bag into the vehicle.

She didn't correct him. In his day, administrative assistants were referred to as secretaries. She smiled. "I hope what you heard wasn't too bad."

He made a face. "I hate making coffee, too," he told her as he watched her strap Markie in the backseat. "Damned shame, that, sticking kids as far away from their parents as possible even in a vehicle."

She stared at him with surprise.

He shrugged. "I had a little boy down in Mexico, many years ago," he said quietly. "He always rode up in the front of the truck with me, so I could ruffle his hair and point out things to him without getting a crick in my neck."

"That was before air bags," she reminded him gently. "It's too dangerous to let a child sit up front now."

"If you want my opinion, and not many people do—" he grinned "—I think the government pushes its way into our lives way too much. You can't legislate morality or safety, but they're sure trying to. We actually have cowboys around here who wear helmets to ride a damned horse!"

She muffled a giggle. He had a way of expressing things that was more amusing than disturbing. He grimaced. "Don't mind me. I'm a throwback to prehistoric times. I don't fit in anywhere." He opened the door for her. "See? Neanderthal manners, I still open doors for ladies."

She smiled at him. "I like it. You remind me of Jack Palance in that movie he won an Oscar for. I thought it was delightful, the way he protected that young woman."

His eyebrows arched and he grinned more widely.

She buckled her seat belt while he went around and got in under the steering wheel. He looked at a note pasted to the visor and glared at it, but he buckled his own seat belt. He noticed Joceline's puzzled stare and turned the visor so that she could read the note.

It read, "Put on the damned seat belt and shut up about government regulations on private industry."

She burst out laughing. "Do I want to know who wrote that?"

"Your boss," he said, and not surprisingly, as he started the SUV and drove off. "We had a big row about it when I first came to work here. I lost."

"Most people do when they get in arguments with him."

He drew in a long breath. "I'm sorry about your trouble," he told her, with a glance in the rearview mirror at Markie, who was glued to the window, looking at cattle and open country in the distance. "Sick so-and-so who'd target a child."

"Yes," she said heavily. "It's been something of a shock that we've become involved in this. Not that I'm not worried about the boss. He got shot, after all."

"If he'd been here, never would have happened," the cowboy said shortly. "I track him when he's on the ranch. He don't know it, but he's never alone. I know how federal agents get threatened. Nobody's taking out the boss on my watch."

"That makes me feel better," she said. She smiled. "I'll bet you hunt."

"Sure do. Animals, too," he added enigmatically.

She caught her breath as the hacienda-style ranch house came into view. It was enormous, most assuredly a mansion with no excuses or apologies. There were electronic gates made of black wrought iron and everything else was thick, sand-colored adobe. It was mid-November, so nothing was blooming, but Joceline saw dozens of trees lining the long driveway and dotted around the Spanish patio with its big fountain. There was a stone floor on the patio and when she looked up, she was surprised to see a man with a high-powered rifle on the balcony upstairs.

"Sharpshooter," the cowboy told her. "We have three who work shifts. Used to be just one, randomly up there, but since the boss got shot, we're more cautious."

"Not a bad idea," she agreed.

"You'll be safe here, Ms. Perry," he told her gently. "Nothing to worry about. Nothing at all," he added, jerking his eyes toward the oblivious child in the backseat. "You'll both be safe."

She smiled. "Thanks."

He parked at the door, where the semicircular driveway flanked another large, working fountain. He got out and came around to help Joceline and Markie out of the SUV.

"Look at the fountain!" Markie exclaimed, running to perch himself on the stone bench. "And it's got fish! Gold-fish!"

"Chinese goldfish," the cowboy told him with a smile. "There's a big Japanese koi pond out back with enormous fish of all sorts of colors. There's even a yellow one with blue eyes."

"Can I see?" Markie exclaimed.

"Not right now," Joceline said firmly. "First we go see the boss and get settled in our room," she added.

"Come along, young feller," the old cowboy told him with a grin as he picked up the luggage and carried it through the open wrought-iron gate.

"It's so pretty!" Markie enthused. "Look at all the trees! We don't got even one tree at our apartment!"

"Don't have," Joceline corrected automatically.

"There's a doggie!" he exclaimed, and started running toward an enormous, black-faced German shepherd dog.

"Markie, no!" Joceline almost screamed. "Don't…!"

"Dieter, freund!" the cowboy called in fluent German. *"Ja, Ja, freund. Das ist ein braver hund!"*

Joceline spared him a shocked glance before she rushed to Markie's side.

But the dog wasn't hostile. On the contrary, he went right up to Markie with a slow, loping gait, and sat down just in front of him, leaning forward so that the child could pet him.

"He loves kids," the cowboy told her. "Dieter is an old man, like me," he added on a chuckle. "He came over from Germany. Notice his hocks. They almost touch the ground.

American-bred German shepherds' hind legs are joined higher up."

She did notice. The dog's build kept him very close to the ground. He was beautiful, with a thick shiny black coat and pale brown markings. He seemed very happy to sit and let Markie hug and pet him.

"You speak German to him," Joceline said, curious.

"Yes. All our dogs are trained to respond to it." He didn't add that there was a secret attack command in German known only to the handler and a few of the most trusted cowboys. The code was never to be used unless in the gravest of emergencies. Activated, the dogs were quite capable of attacking and bringing down a human intruder. Considering Jon's line of work, not to mention his brother's, they couldn't take chances. At least once, a would-be killer had tried to force his way in. He'd been taken off to jail, with a stop by the local hospital to stitch his wounds.

"What if an intruder also spoke German?" she wondered.

"They'd ignore him. They respond to our voices."

She shook her head. "I can't believe he's that tolerant."

He smiled. "Considering their size and strength, it would be insane not to have them gentle around family and friends."

"I totally agree."

"Come on inside."

He led them through the house. Markie protested until the dog, Dieter, was allowed to come inside, as well. He walked right beside Markie, as if an attachment had already been formed there.

"My goodness," Joceline exclaimed, noticing the dog's actions.

"He likes you," the old cowboy told Markie with a grin.

"I like him, too. He's cool!" Markie said excitedly, petting the dog's head.

The inside of the house was open and dotted with comfortable chairs and plants and paintings. The color scheme was mostly shades of tan and brown, with some green and even a little gold in the upholstery and curtains. There was a huge stone fireplace, in which a fire was already roaring. It was cold.

"They got a fireplace!" Markie exclaimed. "Can I go sit by it?"

"Not without me," Joceline said firmly. "Come on, sport, let's get our bags unpacked before we worry people to death trying to explore, okay?"

Markie sighed. "Okay."

The old cowboy's blue eyes twinkled. He led them into a room the size of Joceline's whole apartment.

"This is the main guest suite," he told her. "There's a smaller room through the bathroom, if you want the boy to have his own, but there are two king-size beds in here."

Joceline was still gaping. "My whole apartment would fit in here," she murmured.

He laughed out loud. "So would my cabin," he told her. "But I like cozy places. You might say I've grown accustomed to them over the years," he added enigmatically.

She smiled as he put the bags down. "Thanks for bringing us here."

"Oh, I enjoyed it." He looked at Markie wistfully. "Nice to have a kid around the place again."

She frowned. "Again?"

"Kilraven's little girl spent some time here." His face went hard. "There's gossip that one of the shooters weaseled out of being charged with her death—the one that shot the boss and threatened you. He won't get in here, and he won't get away if I find out the rumor is true. I know people all over who could put a stick in his spokes. She was a precious little child—" He broke off and turned away. Just for a few seconds, the expression in his eyes had been frightening.

"The boss's room is two doors down, that way," he added when he was in the hall, pointing in the direction. "He's expecting you." He smiled. "Nice to have you here, ma'am. And you, young feller," he added to Markie. "Later, when you're settled in, I'll show you the horses if your mom don't mind."

"I don't," she assured him.

He gave her a quizzical glance. "You might, later. Don't worry about offending me, you won't," he added with a gentle smile. "You don't know me."

He tipped his hat and walked off, his spurs jingling as he went out the door. Dieter got up and followed him.

"Dieter," Markie called.

"Let him go," Joceline said. "He may be a working dog," she added.

"Oh. Okay then." He looked up at her. "We going to see Mr. Blackhawk now?"

"Yes."

She led the way down the hall and paused at the door. It was standing open.

"Joceline?"

That was Jon's deep voice. Odd, the way the word rippled along her nerves, bringing the oddest sweet sensations. She smiled self-consciously. "Yes, it's me."

She walked in, holding Markie's hand more for her own comfort than his. Jon was propped up on pillows, wearing a burgundy silk pajama top that was unbuttoned over his broad chest. His long hair was loose around his shoulders, a little tousled, as if he'd been sleeping.

He looked at Markie and smiled. "Hello."

"Hello," Markie said. He moved to the bed and leaned on it. "I'm sorry you got shot."

"Yes. Me, too."

"You got nice dogs," Markie said. "And I like your fish, too."

"Thanks."

"Dieter likes me."

"I'm not surprised," Jon said. "He's very fond of children. We got him from a family in Germany. He was our first breeding dog. He's sired several generations of wonderful pets."

"He's gorgeous," Joceline agreed. "I was surprised at how gentle he is."

Jon smiled at her and winced when he shifted position. "He's gentle until he needs to be aggressive."

"I guess you have to have good security here," she said.

"I've had a few threats over the years. At least I don't have to check the underside of my vehicles for bombs, though," he added flatly.

She shook her head. "Your brother attracts trouble."

"Yes, and it's contagious, apparently." He reached beside him and touched a button. "Megs, would you come in here, please?"

There was a soft, female voice that answered. A couple of minutes later, a small, dark woman with long black hair and brown eyes came into the room, wiping her hands on her spotless white apron. She stopped when she saw the visitors and broke into a wide smile.

"Welcome," she said in her softly accented English. "I knew you were coming, so I have prepared something very special for dinner. You like sushi, I am told."

Joceline gasped. "How did you know?" It was her secret passion and she couldn't afford to have it very often.

"I told her," Jon said with a smile. "You came out to eat with Mac and me once, a few months ago. I've never seen anyone enjoy a dish so much."

"I love it," she confessed, but didn't add that her budget wouldn't stand much of it. Sushi was frightfully expensive.

"We have a guy on the payroll who was a sushi chef before he decided he wanted to be a cowboy," Jon explained. "I sent

Megs to fetch him. We have fresh seafood flown here from California, so he can slice and dice to his heart's content."

"Thank you," she said with genuine appreciation.

"My pleasure," he replied. "It's a small repayment for the inconvenience of you having to come up here to do my work."

"I didn't mind," she protested.

"Sushi is raw fish," Markie said with his blunt honesty, and made a face.

"Yes, but our chef can also make fish sticks and home-made French fries," Jon murmured with twinkling black eyes. "I hear somebody really loves those."

"Me!" Markie exclaimed. "And lots of ketchup on!"

The adults laughed.

"I am making cookies, also," Megs said. "Would your son like to come into the kitchen and help me? He can test the cookies, if you don't mind," she added dryly.

"Oh, please, can I?" Markie asked his mom, hugging her legs and looking up at her with melting blue eyes. "Please?"

"Go on," Joceline said and lifted him up to kiss his rosy cheek.

"Aww, Mom," he protested, wiggling to be put down.

"Have fun," she called as he followed a laughing Megs out the door.

"Megs?" she asked Jon when they were alone.

"A private joke," he said warmly. "She overdid the nutmeg in eggnog one Christmas and I started calling her Megs. It stuck."

She smiled. "She's very nice. Everybody here is nice, especially that cowboy you sent to the airstrip to drive us here. The one with red whiskers. Sloane Callum."

"Oh, yes. You liked him?" he asked.

"Very much. He offered to teach Markie how to ride

later." She frowned. "He said an odd thing, that he wouldn't be offended if I didn't want him to, later."

He chuckled. "Some people don't like to have him around. He knows it and doesn't take offense. He and Cammy get into it once in a while. He's very opinionated. So is she, of course."

"He hunts, he said, and then he added that he hunted animals, too."

"Callum spent some time in prison for hunting men," he said abruptly.

Her eyes widened. "That was him? The hit man you told me about?" she exclaimed.

He nodded. "He was very young and his mother was dying of cancer. He fell in with a bad crowd, but they took him in after and slowly led him into doing things he should never have done. He wound up in prison. He got out, went into a rehabilitation program and ended up here. He's been with us for over ten years now."

She was impressed. "And no blemishes on his record in all that time?"

He pursed his lips. "He did try to go after Jay Copper, when it came out that he'd ordered the hit on Mac's wife that also led to the murder of Mac's daughter, Melly. He was very fond of Melly. He had a son of his own, an illegitimate one. When he went to prison, and his profession became public knowledge, his girlfriend left him."

"What happened to his son?" she wondered.

"God knows. He tried to find him, but I don't think he ever did. He was concerned that the boy probably wouldn't want to know him."

She didn't say anything. She was trying to decide how she'd feel if she'd found out that her father was a hired killer. She really didn't know.

"This house is huge," she said, for something to talk about that wasn't controversial.

"Too big," he mused. "My mother doesn't socialize much, except when she's trying to get me married. She gives parties and invites her candidate of the week."

"Sorry."

"You have no idea how hard it is to find places to hide on this ranch," he said wistfully. "She's getting familiar with all the ones I've found, so now I have to stay in San Antonio most of the time to escape her."

"She probably wants more grandchildren," she told him and averted her eyes.

"She's rather pushy," he said gently. "I'm sorry she was rude to you. She was rude to Mac's wife, too, but Winnie took her down a few pegs," he added. "She still calls her the 'little blonde chainsaw,' but she says it with affection now."

"Winnie's nice."

"Very nice." He studied her with narrowed black eyes. "You're pretty nice yourself," he said quietly. "Coming all this way, inconveniencing yourself, just to work."

"You couldn't come to the office," she pointed out.

"No, I couldn't. I'm sorry you had to take the child out of school."

"I spoke to his teacher. They understand the situation. It will be all right. He'll catch up. He's very bright."

"He'll like it here, I think. There's a lot for a child to do. He seems to love animals."

"He does. He's always begging me for a dog. But we live in an apartment, and it's not allowed."

She thought of her apartment, and then of the break-in, and shivered.

"We talked about the attempted burglary," he said suddenly. His jaw tautened. "And the phone call that came after it. They are part of the reason I insisted on bringing you up here, where we can keep you and your son safe. I hate that you're mixed up in this."

She was surprised, and touched. "Thanks," she said softly, "but we both work for a highly visible law enforcement agency. It's unrealistic to think there would never be a risk involved in it."

"It shouldn't involve your son," he said bluntly.

"I used to be naive enough to think that no human being would ever harm a child."

"Wishful thinking."

"Yes, it is, isn't it?" she asked. She drew in a long breath. "That's what scared me about having my apartment broken into, the fact that someone might hurt Markie. He's all I have in the world."

He frowned. "You said your...Markie's father," he corrected, "was killed overseas."

She averted her eyes. "Yes."

"Did you care for him?"

She bit her lip. "Very much."

An odd expression touched his handsome face. "I'm sorry."

She turned away. "It was a tragedy, in many ways."

"Would you have married him, you think?"

Unseen, her hands dug into the fabric of her jeans. "He didn't have those sort of feelings for me," she managed to say.

"He had some sort, or you wouldn't have Markie," he said, and then groaned silently at the slip of the tongue.

She swallowed, hard, and turned back to him. Her face was pale. "Please. It's difficult to talk about something so personal," she said heavily. "Could we change the subject?"

He lifted an eyebrow. "I hear that the Chinese have a restaurant where robots deliver meals to the table."

A surprised laugh escaped her tight throat. "What?"

He chuckled. "I read it on a virtual news site."

"The internet has revolutionized the way we share information," she replied.

"So it has. What was your boyfriend's name?" he added suddenly.

"Mr. Blackhawk…!"

"Jon. We're not at the office." His gaze slid over her with a strange intensity. "What do people call you?"

"Sir?"

"What do people call you? Surely you have friends, family…"

"All my family is dead, except my mother, and we don't have any contact now," she blurted out. "I lost touch with my high school friends. I had a friend when I was training as a paralegal, but she married and moved to California."

"You must have a nickname," he persisted.

She bit her lip.

"Come on. Tell me."

She shifted, took a deep breath and said, "Rocky."

He blinked. "I beg your pardon?"

"Rocky."

"Would you like to explain how you came by such a, shall we say, unique nickname?"

"I sort of punched another girl at school for pouring grape juice all over my new white skirt."

His black eyes twinkled. "Rocky. I like it."

"I'd better go find Markie. When do you want to start working?"

"In the morning," he said. "You need a little time to get over the trip and settle in."

She moved toward the door. "Then I'll see you later."

He smiled. "Sure thing. Rocky."

She flushed and dived out the door.

CHAPTER NINE

MARKIE WAS ALREADY in love with Megs. He followed her around, rambling on about her wonderful cookies and how big the house was, and how many animals the Blackhawk family seemed to have. There was a big white Persian cat curled up near the fireplace. It let Markie pick it up and hold it in his lap. There was another cat, a tortoiseshell one, that kept its distance.

Joceline was delighted at the friendliness of the people who worked for Jon. She didn't expect it. Her idea of wealthy people was undergoing a reversion of late. Not that she thought Cammy Blackhawk would be friendly if she knew Jon's "secretary" was living here, even temporarily.

"Markie loves the kitchen," Joceline told Jon while she was taking dictation for emails that would be sent to various agencies about current cases.

He chuckled. He was still in some pain, and he slept a lot, but he was improving daily. "She despairs over my eating habits. I don't like heavy meals, but she loves to cook."

She studied him over her laptop. "You're still pale."

He shrugged, and then winced, because it hurt. "You get shot and you'll understand why."

"I'm glad you're going to be okay." She smiled at him, and her eyes lit up. "I'd hate having to break in a new boss."

He smiled back. His eyes narrowed on her face. She was pretty when she smiled. He liked the color of her hair, and the thickness of it. He liked her long neck and the pert, firm little breasts that stretched the front of her pale blue sweater. He frowned. In a flash of memory, he pictured something he shouldn't even have seen.

"You have a mole," he said unexpectedly. "On your rib cage..."

She gasped and went red.

He cleared his throat and shook his head. "Good God, I must be out of my mind. How would I know such a thing?"

She fumbled with the keyboard and almost dropped the small notebook computer.

"Sorry," he added. "I'm really sorry. I don't know why I said that."

"It's okay, no problem," she stammered. She forced a laugh. "Probably an aftereffect of the anesthesia, it makes you do and say all sorts of weird things."

"Yes. They said it might." But he wasn't smiling now. And as he looked at her, he felt a pang of conscience. He didn't understand why...

JOCELINE always read Markie a bedtime story. Usually it was Dr. Seuss. His favorite was "Green Eggs and Ham."

She laughed as he made a face.

"I wouldn't eat green eggs," he muttered.

"Just between us, I wouldn't, either," she whispered.

He grinned at her. "I like it here," he told her. "Megs makes good cookies."

"Yes, she does. Megs makes everything good."

"I wish we could stay here." He sighed. "They got horses. I want to ride a horse."

"We're going to talk about that. But not tonight, young man," she added. "Now let's finish the book. You have to go to sleep so you can get up early in the morning and help Megs set the table for breakfast!"

"She's going to make biscuits."

"I heard."

"I like it when you make biscuits. You don't cook much except for breakfast."

"I don't have time, baby," she said gently. It was hard to describe her hectic job to a child. She was usually so tired when she got home in the evenings that she just thawed out food she'd frozen earlier. She had a cooking day on the weekend, when she made large amounts of a dish, separated it into portions and froze it. Then she could serve the entrée with vegetables and fruit during the week. It ensured that Markie had balanced meals, and that she did, too.

"I like your biscuits."

"Thanks." She bent and kissed him.

"I'm sorry your boss got shot," he said. "I like him a lot."

"So do I. Now let's finish reading," she said firmly.

She tucked Markie in, kissed him good-night and turned out the light. She left the door cracked so she could hear him. Sometimes he had night terrors. She didn't like having him out of her sight, even if others thought her overprotective. He did have health problems.

She went back into her own bedroom and sat down heavily in a chair. She'd been kept so busy that she hadn't had time to worry about the break-in at her apartment, but in the darkness she couldn't forget it. She'd burned the diary, as she'd threatened to. It served no purpose other than to remind her of an episode that was both painful and poignant. It contained information that could be devastating not only to herself but to innocent people if it were ever revealed. Far better to have it destroyed than risk that.

But Jon's outburst today had shocked and frightened her. She'd read enough on psychotropic drugs to know that flashbacks could occur, but she was less informed on memory. He shouldn't have remembered anything. And perhaps he didn't, consciously, but the intimacy of being here, in his home, in his bedroom with her had triggered some wisp of memory. It disturbed her. She should never have overreacted, either. But it had been impossible not to.

She locked her arms over her breasts and closed her eyes with a long sigh. She'd promised herself that she would never reveal the truth, not even under torture. But what if he remembered other things? What if it wasn't a fluke and he was regaining lost time?

She sat up, leaning over. Surely life couldn't be so cruel. After all she'd been through, it couldn't end like this.

She got up and paced. What would she do if he remembered? It would be a nightmare. And what about his family… how would they…?

"Stop it," she told herself in a husky whisper. "Stop it! You're making mountains of molehills."

The sound of her own voice startled her. She laughed self-consciously, got into her pajamas and climbed into bed. Surprisingly, she slept.

"YOU SHOULD eat more than that for breakfast," Jon scolded as she finished the last delicious piece of a homemade croissant just before she sat down in the chair beside his bed and rested her coffee cup on the table, on a doily.

"I usually cook breakfast for Markie, but I never eat much," she said apologetically. "I don't have time."

"Megs says the boy eats like a horse." He chuckled.

She smiled. "He's always starving, to hear him tell it."

"He drew a sketch of Megs. She showed it to me. You should have him taught," he added gently. "He has great natural talent."

"I think so, too," she said. "I've considered it."

His eyes narrowed. "I can take care of the tuition."

She fumbled with her notebook and almost dropped it. "I can manage," she said abruptly.

"Why are you so nervous with me?" he asked suddenly. "You're not like this at work."

She swallowed. "I'm not used to being around you away from work."

"No, that's not it," he said somberly. "It's something else."

She felt butterflies wobbling around in her stomach. "Mr. Blackhawk…"

"Jon," he corrected gently.

She bit her lower lip. "I can't…"

His black eyes narrowed on her face. He held out a big hand. "Come here, Joceline." His voice was gentle, tender. It sent ripples of sensation over her skin.

She should have ignored it. She should have pretended not to hear him…

She put the notebook computer carefully on the table by her chair and went to sit beside him on the bed.

His arm slid around her. He studied her with unnerving curiosity. "We've danced around the subject for several years. You would never tell me what happened that night we went to the diplomat's daughter's party."

She bit her lip again. "You were under the influence of a very powerful psychotropic drug," she began.

"Yes, I know all that," he said impatiently. "But what happened?"

"You…you got very sick and I drove you to the emergency room," she stammered.

"We came to the apartment first," he said doggedly. "I do

remember that much. I remember you helping me into bed. The rest is very blurry, but there has to be a reason that I know about that mole, Joceline."

She tried to move away. His arm tightened. "You...got a little out of hand," she confessed with a nervous smile.

One eyebrow lifted. "Amorously out of hand?"

She cleared her throat. "Just a little..."

He tugged. She landed on his broad, bare chest, her hands going on each side of his head on the pillow.

"Don't! You'll open the wound!"

"Not a chance," he mused. Her eyes had flecks of green in them. He was fascinated by this view of her, very close. Her mouth was soft and pretty, with a natural bow shape. Her nose was straight, with a tiny line of freckles over it. There was a faint red tinge in her hair, which was thick and soft. He smoothed his hand over it.

"You're pretty," he said in a deep, soft tone.

"I...am not." She laughed.

"Pretty," he repeated. His eyes darkened. His hand speared into the hair at her nape and his fingers contracted. He pulled her face down to his. "Don't worry...it's just the anesthetic making me goofy a few days down the line...."

His wide, firm mouth covered hers, brushing at the tightness of her lips until he teased them apart. His arms contracted gently, enveloping her. The kiss was slow, soft, insistent.

She loved the way he kissed her. She moaned softly, help-lessly, and went limp against him. He turned, and a gruff sound escaped his throat as it hurt, but he kept turning until she was lying on her back. His mouth never left hers. His big hand smoothed under her sweater, over her pert breast and down, to touch the mole he knew about, the mole he was certain he'd never seen.

His thumb eased up under the band of her bra and teased

around the softness of her breast, while his mouth crushed
onto hers in the heated silence of the room.

"Dear...God," he whispered hoarsely, fumbling at the
catch behind her back.

He found it and unsnapped it. His hand smoothed over her
firm, soft little breast. His eyes were blazing as he looked at
her, registering the helpless attraction, the utter delight in
his touch. He touched the hard nipple, heard her gasp at the
pleasure it kindled.

"Unbelievable," he said huskily.

He pushed up the sweater and the bra and looked at her
firm, dusky-tipped breasts. "Beautiful," he whispered as his
head bent.

His lips smoothed over the hard rise, his tongue caressed
it. She moaned again and arched up to ease his access to her
body. She loved what he was doing. She couldn't even pretend to protest.

His hand smoothed under her back, feeling the soft, bare
skin, which was like warm silk to his touch. His mouth
opened on her breast and suckled it, hard. She cried out.

He lifted his head to look down at her flushed, shocked
face. His nostrils flared. He'd never felt anything so powerful, so erotic, in all his thirty years.

"They gossip about me at work," he said gruffly. "They
speculate. You can't pretend you haven't heard the rumors."

She managed a nod.

"They're true," he said, his eyes black and glittery. "I've
dated. I've even had petting sessions over the years. But I've
never gone all the way with a woman."

She averted her eyes.

He turned her head back, so that he could see her face.
"Cammy and my father raised us very strictly," he told her.
"We were taught that sex outside the sanctity of marriage is
a sin. It was such a powerful lesson that we were prisoners

of our own beliefs. At first, I had so many hang-ups that I couldn't do it. Then as I got older, I was embarrassed that I'd never done it."

"We're all prisoners of our upbringing," she agreed.

He smoothed his hand over her breast, enjoying the view of it, of her instant reaction. "You're as religious as any woman I've ever known, yet you have a child out of wed-lock."

"Yes," she said tautly. "I made a decision…"

"A wonderful decision," he corrected tenderly. "He's a great little person. You've done well with him."

"Thanks."

"The point is you've had sex." His thumb and forefinger contracted on a taut nipple, producing a helpless moan from her. "What does it feel like?" he asked in almost a whisper.

Her lips parted. "I…don't really know," she confessed. "It was so quick…"

"He was in a hurry?"

She swallowed. "We were just kissing. And then all of a sudden, it was so urgent…" She averted her eyes. "It just happened. It hurt a little, and then it was over."

"Damn him!"

"He was…drunk," she said, defending him even now. "He isn't, wasn't," she corrected quickly, "the sort of person who ever lost control."

It went without saying that she was the same sort. He didn't say it. "You think he was killed overseas?"

"Yes, I'm sure that he was," she replied, but she didn't look at him. "He was very sorry."

"Did he want you to keep the child?"

"He…didn't know about the child," she replied. "I couldn't tell him. It was too late."

His hand stilled on her body. He didn't like the idea that she'd had someone else. It ate at him like an acid. He bent and brushed his mouth over her taut breast, enjoying the sounds of pleasure that she emitted when he did it. He could erase the bad memory. He could pleasure her, like this, but more. Much more.

His mouth became insistent. She shivered. The pleasure was quickly becoming unmanageable.

She felt his hand at the fastening of her slacks and she caught his wrist.

"No," she whispered urgently. "We can't!"

He was almost too far gone to stop. He fought with his own instincts, visibly, trying to backtrack.

His eyes went to the door, which was standing half open. He laughed in spite of himself.

She followed his gaze and colored even more. "Oh, dear."

He pulled her sweater down. "Do you want me to apologize?" he asked.

She searched his eyes. "You're not sorry," she replied, trying to make a joke of it.

"No, I'm not," he replied, and his black eyes twinkled. "You taste like honey."

She flushed and scrambled to her feet. She fumbled the catch of her bra back into place, pulled down her sweater and tried to smooth her hair with her hands.

"There's a brush on the dresser," he said helpfully. He was lying with his face propped on a hand, watching her with obvious pleasure.

She went to get it. She smoothed it over her hair and then noticed his. Without thinking, she went and sat down on the bed beside him and ran the brush over his long, thick hair. He sat up to give her access.

"Your hair is beautiful," she said while she brushed it. "Your brother and I saw it all tangled when you were shot. We said you'd hate having it out of place."

"I would." He watched her face, smiling. "I've never let a woman brush it."

She smiled. "I'm flattered."

When she finished, he took the brush from her and brushed her own hair. "Mutual grooming. A predictable behavior in primate society."

She laughed. "Is it?"

His fingers touched her swollen mouth. "How long have we been together?" he asked.

"A long time. Almost five years."

"And we didn't know each other at all."

She nodded silently. Reality was working its way into her mind. She'd let her boss kiss her. More than kiss her. He had a mother who ate live rattlesnakes and who hated her guts. She had a child who would complicate everything.

"Stop thinking," he told her firmly. "We'll take it one step at a time. No pressure."

She met his eyes worriedly. "Your mother hates me," she stated.

"Cammy is a puff adder."

She blinked. "Excuse me?"

"It's a snake. Friend of mine from Georgia told me about them. They're nonpoisonous, but they can raise up on their tails and spread their cheeks and hiss like a cobra. But if someone goes at them with a stick, they faint from fear."

She burst out laughing. "A defensive behavior."

"Yes. Cammy's like that. She's all marshmallow inside. But she's learned to hide it from people by being obnoxious."

Joceline didn't think that was the case. But it was so new, and wonderful, to have Jon looking at her this way that she didn't voice her opinion.

She stood up. "We should get back to work."

He smiled. "Yes. We probably should."

She put up the brush and sat back down with the notebook computer in her lap. He stared at her warmly for a long moment before he began dictating again.

Joceline didn't know how to handle the new situation. She was afraid that Jon was going to want more from her than she could give. She had grave misgivings about her place in his life, and a real fear of his mother's reaction if they became involved. Then, too, there was Markie. How he was going to fit into this scenario was the most frightening part of it.

And into this worry came, quite suddenly, two new complications. There was a call. It came into the main phone line at the ranch, and picked up by the message machine. The caller was brief, and blunt, and threatening.

"You're all dead, now," he said. "The kid goes first. You don't hurt my family and live to tell about it."

Jon heard it before the others did. He had a trace put on the call, but it came from a cell tower miles away, and they couldn't get beyond that. He called the local FBI office. They sent out a couple of men with electronic equipment to set up a network.

Then Joceline made some phone calls and discovered to her utter shock that Harold Monroe had been formally charged with the murder of McKuen Kilraven's little girl, Melly. There was a witness who had come forward to offer testimony, a man who had been in the cell with Monroe and who had heard him brag about his part in the killing during his weeks in jail waiting for trial on the human trafficking charge that was dropped. Monroe had been stupid enough to tell the man about the murder weapon and his ingenuity in hiding it in a public place. The police, led by Rick Marquez, on a tip from Jon, who'd spoken to a contact, had subsequently searched the culvert right outside the San Antonio Police Department and found the shotgun—the murder weapon—tucked in a garbage bag with Monroe's fingerprints on the stock of the gun, they said. A stupid mistake. A very stupid mistake, by a stupid man who thought the police were too dumb to ever catch and convict him.

Jon was in shock, as well. None of them had ever thought that Harold Monroe, the idiot nephew-by-marriage of Jay Copper, was even smart enough to use a shotgun, much less kill a child with it. All the evidence had pointed to Copper's nephew Peppy Hancock. It was the most convoluted set of circumstances Jon had ever seen in his years of law enforcement, and it went against the odds in every way. It was almost as if the charge had been contrived, for some inexplicable purpose.

Jon was worried about what his brother might do. Mac had loved his child very much. They were certain that a dead man, Dan Jones, had been involved in her murder, and Jay Copper had been arrested and prosecuted for engineering it. Mac had even heard Copper say that Peppy had been sent to assure that the hit went down. But now it seemed there was another shooter, in fact, the main shooter, whom no one had suspected and who was just being charged. Monroe blamed Jon and even his "secretary" and her child for his getting caught.

Jay Copper had dangerous contacts. The voice on the phone, which had to have been Monroe's, had promised retribution and Jon couldn't afford to underestimate the caller's intent.

So he called his brother, reluctantly, and asked him to get Rourke to come to the ranch and provide extra backup.

"I thought you liked him," Joceline said curiously when he told her about it.

"I do." But he didn't look as if he did. He was remembering his mother's comment that Rourke was unmarried and apparently interested in Joceline. He didn't want the competition, especially right now, in the beginning stages of a new, breathlessly romantic relationship between them.

"Do you like him?" Jon asked her with faint antagonism.

"Well, yes, but only as a friend," she said at once.

He seemed less rigid after that.

But Joceline was remembering something that the trip had knocked out of her mind. Someone had broken into her apartment. She'd burned the diary, but what if someone had photographed it?

She was still brooding about the break-in when Kilraven showed up at the ranch without Winnie, and in a cold and threatening mood.

"They've got Harold Monroe in jail again," Jon said at once. "But this time he won't slip through the cracks, with or without some hotshot attorney paid for by his wife's uncle Jay."

"You think so?" Kilraven asked in an icy tone. "He just made bail."

Jon sat straight up in bed, wincing from the movement. "He what?"

"He has contacts," Kilraven said icily. "Those contacts have contacts. They found a judge who released him on a half-million-dollar bond. His attorney assured the judge that he was no flight risk."

"Which judge?" Jon wanted to know.

Kilraven named a young judge just elected to the bench the previous year.

"Him," Jon said irritably. "He'd sign off on a serial killer's bond, on humanitarian grounds."

Kilraven's eyebrows arched. It was unusual, to say the least, to have his somber and politically correct younger brother sound off about a judge or anyone connected to the judicial system.

"He's naive for someone that intelligent."

Jon's black eyes glittered. "Somebody, probably Harold

Monroe, called here and made threats," he told his brother. "Most significantly, he's threatening Joceline's son."

Kilraven studied him quietly. "Like the boy, don't you?"

"Yes," Jon said at once. He smiled. "He's intelligent and quite talented with an art pencil. I told Joceline he should have lessons."

"Melly liked to draw," Kilraven replied, his eyes somber as he recalled his daughter's last drawing before her tragic death.

"She had talent," Jon agreed. "I'm sorry," he added gently. "I know it must sting to have another hand in Melly's murder revealed. But he won't get away with it, in spite of the judge's little faux pas."

"I'm not so sure. Jay Copper has property down in the Caribbean. Monroe could fly down there and hide out forever."

Kilraven just smiled.

"What do you know that I don't?" Jon demanded.

"Monroe has his own personal shadow," he said complacently. "And no, I will not tell you who it is."

"Rourke," Jon said at once, glowering.

Kilraven's eyebrows arched. "I've got Rourke watching Joceline and her son."

"He's here?" Jon exclaimed, and sat up straighter, wincing again, as he looked around as if he expected to find the man in his room.

"He's been here since they arrived," Kilraven informed him. "He keeps a low profile, so that nobody knows he's around until they need to know."

"If my employees missed him, several of them will be looking for new jobs," he said flatly.

Kilraven chuckled. "That old-timer of yours spotted him immediately and stuck a .45 revolver in his back. Rourke said he almost had to change pants, it was such a shock."

Jon smiled in spite of himself. "You know who that old-timer is."

"Of course I do." He grinned.

"I feel better, knowing that. I don't like people walking around here under the radar."

"It has to be that way," Kilraven said gently. "We can't put Joceline's child at risk."

"No. We certainly can't."

"I need to talk to her. About the break-in at her apartment."

Jon frowned. "Do they have a suspect?"

"Not unless you mean Harold Monroe," he said, "or one of his cronies. No, it's about something in the apartment that they might have been looking for. Rick Marquez can't get an expense voucher to fly up here and question her, so I'm standing in for him." The way he said it was just a little too casual.

"Really?" Jon murmured, unconvinced.

"Really." Kilraven had a straight face. "Why are you so suspicious?"

"It's not like you to do favors for the police."

He shrugged. "Rick isn't your typical detective."

Jon thought about that, and then relaxed. "No," he replied after a minute. "He's not. She'll be in the kitchen, I imagine. She sees to Markie's meal before she has hers."

"I'll just pop in and have a word with her," Kilraven said.

"You sound like him."

"Him?"

"Rourke," he said, and made the man's name sound like a snarl.

Kilraven had to fight back a grin. It was quite obvious to him that his brother was jealous of Rourke, and not because of the sort of work he did.

"I'll work on my accent," he replied. "You doing better?" he added with genuine concern.

"Yes. It's just slower than I'd like. I want to get back to my office and make sure Harold Monroe doesn't leave the country before his trial."

"I'm going to make sure of that," Kilraven said quietly. "If he had a hand in Melly's death, and I think he did, he'll never escape justice."

"Just make sure you aren't dishing it out," Jon replied firmly. "I don't want to lose the only brother I've got. And you have a child on the way. Any day."

"I know that." Kilraven sighed heavily. "It's just hard, dealing with this. I thought it was all wrapped up when we knew Dan Jones had done the killings on orders from Jay Copper. I never dreamed there was another shooter. Then we were so sure it was Peppy Hancock, but he had an airtight alibi from a young woman for the night in question. How the hell did Monroe pull off something so involved without blabbing before this? He can't keep his mouth shut."

"I don't know. It's odd, isn't it?"

"Jay Copper said he sent Peppy to help make sure Dan Jones did what he was told. We couldn't prove it because without the missing tape it was just hearsay evidence, so Peppy couldn't be formally charged for involvement. And now it's Hancock's idiot brother-in-law Harold Monroe, of all people, who's been arrested for the murder of my wife and child."

"After weaseling out of a human trafficking charge." He frowned. "Why did he target Joceline and the boy? Was it because she works for me?"

"Why else?" Kilraven asked with a bland expression.

Jon laid back down with a long sigh. "I hate having her in danger, having the boy under a threat."

"We'll take care of both of them," Kilraven assured him. "You just concentrate on getting well. Okay?"

Jon smiled. "Okay."

Kilraven shrugged. "I'm glad you're going to be all right."

Jon's eyes twinkled. "Thanks."

Kilraven chuckled. "You're the only brother I've got, even if your hang-ups are an ongoing embarrassment to me."

"Look who's talking!"

"And on that note, I'm leaving," Kilraven said with a grin. "I'll see you again before I leave."

"I'll count on that."

CHAPTER TEN

KILRAVEN FOUND JOCELINE in the kitchen, just mopping up Markie's face. He was laughing as she tickled his nose with the napkin.

They both looked up when he entered the room.

"Well, that must have been a good lunch," he told the boy with a smile.

"It was great!" Markie said.

"Megs is putting that new cartoon movie on for you to watch in the living room," he told the child. "I hear you really want to see it."

"Oh, I do! Thanks!"

"Our pleasure."

Megs came to the door and motioned to the boy, smiling at the adults as she did so.

"See you later, Mom," Markie called as he ran toward Megs.

"He's a really fine youngster," Kilraven said quietly.

"Thanks. I think so."

He turned back to her, and he wasn't smiling. "Ever hear of the Locard Exchange Principle?"

She searched his eyes. "Of course. Every criminal who steals something leaves some trace of his presence behind."

"Rourke has few peers in evidence gathering. He found a partial fingerprint on the table by your bed. It's consistent with prints on file."

She bit her lower lip. "Whose prints?"

"A former cat burglar who did odd jobs for Jay Copper."

Her face grew taut. "Why was he in my apartment? I don't have anything worth stealing."

"You kept a diary, Rourke said," he replied.

She bit her lower lip, hard. "I burned it."

"Any decent burglar can make a photographic copy of a document without taking the original."

She swallowed her fear. "That would indicate a blackmail attempt. But I don't know anything that could hurt anyone else."

"Come in here a minute, will you?"

He opened the door to the library. She hesitated, but he looked so somber that she went inside and let him close the door behind them.

"You went to a party with Jon a little over four years ago," he said without preamble. "He was given a psychotropic drug, without his knowledge, and he wound up in the hospital. You drove him there."

"Yes. It was a sick joke by the boyfriend of the girl he rescued from a kidnapping," she said.

"Soon after that, you tried to quit your job. And very soon after that, you became pregnant."

She averted her eyes. "I went out with a friend and we had too much to drink…" she began.

"My brother is the father of your child. Here, look out…!"

He caught her as she started to fall. He put her on the sofa and pushed her head down, gently, until the wave of nausea passed.

"Damn," he exclaimed softly. "I'm sorry. I should have been more careful."

She swallowed, and then swallowed again. Tears welled up in her eyes. "You're just guessing," she bit off.

"I'm not," he replied quietly. He sat down beside her. "Your son's blood type is A positive. So is Jon's. I checked dates. According to the police report, you went to the party with Jon almost exactly nine months before Markie was born."

"Dates can be coincidental. And a lot of people share the same blood type," she began helplessly.

"I don't know what was in that diary, but I can guess," he continued. "You have to tell Jon, before he finds it out from Harold Monroe or someone in his organization."

She looked up with tortured eyes. "And you think he'd believe me?" she asked, incredulously. "Why do you think I kept it to myself all this time?"

"You were the only woman he ever took to a party," he said.

"Yes, and he's rich and I could barely pay my rent," she said coldly. "He didn't even know me that well. He'd have thought that I was blaming him to make a nice little secure nest egg for myself."

"That's cynical."

"Sure it is," she replied. "But it would have been his first thought. It would probably still be your mother's. We all know how she feels about her son."

He searched her tormented eyes. "Would you rather he heard it on the six o'clock news? That's the sort of thing Monroe would consider good fun."

She sat up straight. "You're assuming that Harold Monroe is the one who sent the burglar to my apartment. You're also assuming that he photographed my diary."

"They're good assumptions. Why else would he have been there?"

She frowned. "How would he even have known about the diary?"

He was frowning now, also. "Then why go into your apartment?"

"Exactly. He was looking for something he thought I had." Her eyes narrowed in concentration, then suddenly she sat up abruptly "Wait a minute... I'd forgotten something... There was a file detailing personal and criminal information about Bart Hancock. I was going to transcribe it, but the day Jon was shot I took the file home to work on it. It was the day of the robbery at my apartment...!"

"Did you take it back?"

"I couldn't find it," she said, flushing. "I was going to tell the boss, but then after Jon got shot and the robbery at my place, I was so upset that I forgot all about it. Oh, boy, am I in trouble! They'll fire me for incompetence...!"

"They won't. But the D.A. needs to know about that file. I'll talk to him."

She was almost prostrate with relief. Until she realized that she'd spilled the beans to Kilraven. She looked at him with horror.

"I'm not going to tell Jon about Markie," he assured her gently. "But you have to. You know that."

"I'm not telling him," she said stubbornly. "And you're not telling him. He'd never believe it. He'd only think I was lying out of greed. I've told people for years that Markie's father was in the military and he died overseas. I'm not changing that story now."

He looked at the stubborn set of her features. "How do you think Jon is going to feel if he knows that he has a child he was never told about?"

"He's never going to know," she said flatly. "If he wanted

to be married by now, he would be. And it wouldn't be to a low-class nobody like me. My parents were farm people. My father was the first person in his entire family to ever get a college degree. My mother never even graduated from high school. She works as a waitress and her husband works as a night watchman. We're the sort of people your mother would never voluntarily invite into her home!"

"Cammy's not like that," he said softly. "You don't really know her."

"I know that she wants the best for her son," she said, avoiding his eyes. "Just as I'd want the best for my own. It's not a bad thing to leave some secrets unsolved, Kilraven."

"You're not going to bend an inch, are you?"

She shook her head. "I had to decide whether or not to keep my child," she said softly. "I made the only decision I could, but I also had to consider what would happen to Jon if he was presented with the consequences of an accident he doesn't even remember happening." She looked up at him. "I couldn't make him responsible for something he did in a drugged state of mind, something he'll never really remember. I could have stopped. I didn't. It's my fault. I was only a little tipsy. He wasn't."

"And you love him."

She swallowed again. "Yes." She looked up. "You won't tell him?"

He shook his head. "No. But I think you're wrong. About telling him the truth, and about his reaction. He's furious that I had to bring Rourke up here."

"Rourke is here?" she asked, stunned.

"He's been here ever since you arrived. I couldn't take the chance that Monroe might make good on his threat. He's a fumble-fingered idiot, but he has friends who aren't."

"You really think he was only after the file?"

He smiled. "Yes."

She relaxed a little. "I'll still be in trouble about that."

"I don't think so. But tell Jon about the file, just to be on the safe side."

She nodded.

"And think about what I've said. Just think about it?"

She grimaced. "I will. But I won't change my mind."

"Fair enough."

ROURKE walked into the room with Kilraven a few minutes later.

"Joceline, my angel!" he exclaimed, opening both arms wide. "We can be married in ten minutes, if you'll just agree. I can bribe a judge...!"

"I work for the government," she said stiffly, and she didn't smile.

He threw up his hands. "Are they all like that?" he asked Kilraven. "So full of business and puffed up with maintaining the law?"

"Most of us are, yes," Kilraven said with pursed lips.

"Don't take her side," Rourke pleaded. "I'm dying of unrequited love, and you're not helping me a bit."

"You're supposed to be protecting her, not trying to marry her," Kilraven pointed out.

"Damned straight," Jon said from the doorway of his bedroom. He was haphazardly wrapped in a blue toweling robe, with striped pajama bottoms below and bare feet lower, and a bare broad chest visible in the opening. He was glaring at Rourke.

"You shouldn't be out of bed!" Joceline fussed.

Jon lifted an eyebrow. "I'm tired of lying down."

"You'll tear open the wound!"

He glared even more darkly at her. "Cut it out."

She glared back. "Blood is hard to get out of beige carpet," she said gruffly.

He burst out laughing and winced as it pulled the stitches.

"See there? That's why you shouldn't be out of bed! Kilraven, make him lie down," she told his brother.

"I had to have stitches the last time I tried to make him do anything," Kilraven told her patiently.

She sighed with pure exasperation. "He's going to pull something loose!"

Jon ignored them both and was now glaring at Rourke. "You're here to keep her and the boy safe, not to make a spectacle of yourself with mock marriage proposals. We clear?"

Rourke's eyebrows met over his eye and eye patch. His one pale brown eye twinkled amusedly. "Oh, yes, sir," he agreed.

Jon's black eyes narrowed. "And you're not to let the child out of your sight, ever."

Rourke chuckled softly.

"Something funny?" Jon asked belligerently.

"Well, considering that the boy shares a suite with his mother, and you want me to watch him around the clock..."

"You know what I mean!"

"Jon, you're tottering," Kilraven said, moving to his brother's side. "Now get back in bed and stop trying to micromanage everything and everyone around you."

"I'm not tottering!"

Kilraven caught him as he pitched forward.

"Told you so," he muttered. "Now come on. Back to bed!"

He half lifted the younger man back into his room, and into the huge bed. "Now stay there," he said firmly.

Joceline peered around the door. "Is he all right?" she asked worriedly.

Jon's dark eyes smiled into hers. "Just a little weakness," he assured her. "Nothing to worry about."

"Okay," she replied, and relaxed. "If you're sure."

"Did you check with Betty at the office about that court date for Jacob Rand's preliminary hearing, the one I'm supposed to testify at?" he asked.

"Forgot. I'll do it right now."

He watched her walk away with soft, quiet eyes.

Kilraven pursed his lips and his eyes smiled. "She's nice," he said.

Jon nodded. "I'm lucky to have her. Even if she won't make coffee."

Kilraven didn't reply to that. He was busy worrying about other complications. Ones that were going to be inevitable when the truth came out.

Joceline had Jon's work caught up in three days. She was uncertain about whether or not to remain. He was healing well, but there were things she could do at the office and needed to do, to prevent a pileup when he returned. But he was reluctant to have her leave.

They'd gotten into the habit of having a bedtime snack together after Markie went to sleep. Of course, it led inevitably to hot sessions in his bed that were growing more passionate and harder to stop as time went on. Her reaction to him was instantly, helplessly responsive. He knew it and became even more insistent.

But she was able to pull back. Barely.

"We can't," she said huskily when he became even more insistent about undressing her.

"Why can't we?" he murmured against her soft breasts. "Everyone else does it."

She pulled his head back. "Because we aren't everyone else," she insisted. "And because I already have one child out of wedlock."

He took a sobering breath. "Yes."

She sat up, rearranging her clothing and got to her feet. "I should leave."

"No!"

She turned and looked down at him. "It's only going to get worse," she said miserably. "It's just because you know me and this is a new experience. You don't even like me usually."

He was looking at her with hungry eyes. "I've always liked you."

"Oh, really?" she asked in a teasing tone. "Was that before or after you threw a law book at me?"

"I threw it at the wall," he pointed out. "And it wasn't a law book, it was a gaming magazine."

He made a face.

She grinned at him. "I really do have to get back to the office. And I...need some space. Just for a few days."

He cocked his head and studied her. "Then what? After the few days?"

She drew in a long breath. "Can't we talk about that later?"

His face grew tight. "You're looking for an exit sign."

"My whole life has been a series of exit signs," she murmured.

"You don't think I'm serious."

"You don't know me," she replied. "You don't know a thing about me."

He frowned. "What do I need to know?"

"More than I'm willing to tell you, at the moment. And I do need some sleep."

He grimaced. He laid back down with a sigh. "I suppose you're right. Maybe it wouldn't hurt us to slow down a little."

"I'm glad you agree."

"I'm being forced to," he pointed out. But he smiled.

She shrugged. "I want you to get well."

"Me, too." He gave her a long look. "But Rourke is going

back with you. I don't like it," he confessed. "But I have to agree that he'll take care of you."

She felt insecure. "You don't think someone would really try to hurt Markie?"

"They killed my niece."

She swallowed a rush of panic. "Yes."

"They won't get Markie. I promise you they won't," he said.

She let herself relax, just a little. "Thanks."

"And we'll talk some more. Tomorrow."

She hesitated. But his smile was intoxicating. Her heart jumped. She smiled back and nodded. "Tomorrow."

JOCELINE jumped out of bed, aglow with the newness of her relationship with Jon and hope that there might really be a future for them. She was herding Markie toward the kitchen when she opened the door and ran into a nightmare.

Cammy Blackhawk gave her and the child a glare that would have stopped a rampaging horde.

"What are you doing in my home?" she asked coldly.

Joceline wasn't usually lost for words, but she had reason to fear this woman and her reactions. She hesitated. "Working."

"Not for me," Cammy said haughtily. "I have never invited you here! I never would! And to bring that...that child here! How dare you!"

Joceline bent and lifted Markie into her arms. He was looking upset already. He stared at the dark-haired woman with wide, shocked eyes.

"Please lower your voice," Joceline said stiffly. "You're upsetting Markie!"

"As if I care," the other woman replied haughtily. "You had your fun and he's the living proof of it, proof that you have no morals whatsoever!"

Joceline bit her lower lip. "You don't know a thing about me," she said huskily.

"I know all I need to. You're here trying to turn my son's head, to make yourself attractive to him! You're chasing him because he has money and you're poor!"

"You stop yelling at my mommy, you bad old girl!" Markie said angrily.

Cammy was momentarily diverted by the child, which gave Joceline enough time to turn on her heel and go back the way she'd come.

"Where are we going, Mommy?" Markie asked.

"Home, baby, as soon as I can pack." Her heart was beating overtime. She was almost in panic mode, she, who rarely panicked. She'd never seen such hatred in another human's eyes.

"Good," he muttered, and buried his face in her neck. "I don't like her. She's mean!"

"You stay away from my son!" Cammy added haughtily. "I've brought my young friend here to take care of him while he's recuperating. We don't need you!"

Well, that meant he wouldn't miss out on any exciting fashion news, but it was beyond Joceline's whirling mind to vocalize the thought.

She put Markie down and started putting things into her ragged old suitcase. Cammy stood in the doorway, waiting, her arms folded tight over her chest. It outraged her that the woman had been here, with Jon, alone in her own house while she was in Europe!

"Make sure you don't take one thing that isn't yours," Cammy snapped.

Joceline ignored her.

Markie clung to his mother's legs. "I don't like it here," he told her. "I want to leave."

"We're going in just a minute, baby," Joceline told him.

The child's voice was husky and he was breathing oddly.

Joceline went down on one knee. "Breathe. Breathe. Look at me. Just breathe, okay? Don't think about it. Just breathe. Here—" she grabbed the rescue inhaler "—breathe in. Again. Yes. Better?"

He nodded. His chest rose and fell rapidly, but with less force. His breathing regulated, just a little, as the medicine started to work.

"What's wrong with him?" Cammy asked, reluctantly.

"Nothing at all. Get your toys, sweetheart."

Markie picked up a worn bear and a ragged cowboy doll and hugged them to his chest. He was still a little shaky. Joceline was worried sick but she didn't dare show it. She finished putting their few articles of clothing in the suitcase, stuffed Markie into his jacket and put on her own. She picked up her purse and the suitcase.

"You're welcome to check my luggage," she told Cammy.

The older woman was looking at them with eyes that saw more than they wanted to. They saw poverty and hopelessness and reluctant acquiescence to an unreasonable demand.

"We'll go now," Joceline said. She took Markie's hand and led him out the door. She stopped and turned, her chin lifting with quiet pride. "Can you please ask someone to drive us to the bus station in town? It's too far for Markie to walk."

"You don't have a car?"

"My car wouldn't make it past downtown San Antonio, Mrs. Blackhawk," Joceline said with painful pride. "Mr. Blackhawk flew us up here."

"I'll have one of the hands drive you to town."

"Thank you. We'll wait on the porch." She tugged Markie along with her.

Cammy picked up the in-house phone. "Have one of the men drive Miss Thingy to the bus station with her...son," she spoke into it. "She's on the porch."

"I'll drive her myself, you raging old bat," came an Afrikaans-accented tone over the phone. "And you can take your prejudices and your old-world attitudes and go straight to hell with them."

The phone on the other end was slammed down. "I never!" she exclaimed, outraged.

She stormed into Jon's bedroom. Her protégée was trying to puff up his pillows while he glared at her.

"That terrible man told me to go to hell!" she told Jon, fuming. "What sort of people do you have working here?"

"Who told you that?" he asked, furious.

"That Rourke person," she said angrily. "I only asked someone to take your secretary to town to catch a bus…"

"Joceline? Catch a bus?" He sat straight up in bed. "Damn it!"

"Now, Jon…"

He reached for the phone. "Get me Rourke. I'll wait!" He glared at Cammy. "Rourke, what's going…she did what?" He listened. "Yes. You go with them. Take her to the airstrip… I'll send the pilot down. Tell her…hell, never mind, I'll tell her myself."

He hung up. He got up. "I'm going back to San Antonio. Get the hell out of my bedroom!" he told the blonde and his mother.

"Jon," Cammy said gently, "I'm sorry. Please. Don't get up. You're ill…"

"I was getting better until you decided to destroy my life!"

Cammy bit her lip. Tears were forming in her eyes. "Jon, that woman has designs on you. I don't think you really understand…"

"You're the one who doesn't understand," Jon shot back. He was furious. "You're not going to manage my life for me. You're not going to tell me whom I can marry, or what I can do. You're my mother, not my owner!"

Cammy shifted her stance. "You're sick and now I've upset you. I'm very sorry. I'll apologize to what's-her-name later..."

"Her name is Joceline," he said in a tone that threatened.

"Yes, of course, Joceline..." She straightened. "She had a child out of wedlock," she began.

"So did you," Jon shot back furiously.

Cammy's face went white as a sheet. "Wh-what?"

"Except that you chose termination over delivery, isn't that right?" Jon persisted, while the blonde stood by in total shock and without saying a word. "You were afraid that my father wouldn't want the child, since you weren't married to him at the time, and you had a termination. It wasn't until he proposed that you realized what you'd done, but it was too late then, wasn't it?"

She leaned back against the wall, shattered. "I never told anybody!"

"Dad drank," he said coldly. "When he drank, he talked. He'd have married you, he said, if you'd only told him in time. He grieved for the child. He grieved for you, for a decision you'd made that he thought would tear you apart." His eyes were cold. "But it didn't hurt you, did it, Cammy, since you can sit in judgment on a woman who had more courage than you did."

She closed her eyes and shivered.

"Uh, this is obviously a very private conversation. I think I'll just wait outside," the blonde said, tiptoeing out of the room.

"You can wait with her," Jon told his mother. "I'm leaving, as soon as I can get dressed."

Cammy opened her eyes. They were dark and troubled. "I thought it was the only thing I could do," she said in a distant tone. "I never thought about how it would be, after..." She looked up at him. "I never wanted you to know."

"My father wished that he didn't know," he returned. "You're so self-righteous, Cammy. You're right, everybody else is wrong. You know just what other people should do, how they should live, who they should marry," he added coldly, nodding toward the closed door. "But who are you to make those decisions?"

Cammy folded her arms over her breasts. "I want you to be happy."

"And you think living with your Vogue-obsessed candidate would make me happy?" he asked incredulously.

She swallowed. "Maybe…maybe I've been a little overboard."

"A little." He glared more. "Let me tell you something. If I had to marry a woman like that—" he nodded toward the door "—to get a child, I'd be a bachelor forever. Looks don't matter to me. There are qualities far more important."

She shifted again. She looked guilty. "That little boy. He doesn't breathe right."

"He has asthma," he said coldly. "He has violent attacks that land him in hospital. Especially when he's upset!"

Cammy grimaced.

"Joceline isn't going to have an easy time of it, thanks to you, and I'm going back to San Antonio with…with…!" He grimaced and almost fell.

Cammy rushed forward and caught him. She helped him back to the bed, fighting tears. "I'm sorry. I'm so sorry."

"Damn it!" he ground out as he lay back down. He was too weak to carry out the threat.

She smoothed back his clean, dark hair as she had when he was a sick little boy. "It's all right. I'll make everything all right. Don't you worry. You just get well." She bit her lip, hard. "I'm sorry!" Tears were rolling down her cheeks.

Jon didn't reply. He was so angry he couldn't even manage words.

JOCELINE FOUGHT TEARS all the way to San Antonio. She was upset, but Markie was even more upset. She knew already that his agitation meant a hospital visit. He was building to an attack even with the medicines he used.

"I'm sorry, love," Rourke said gently. "I mean it. Cammy can be a…" He grimaced as he glanced at the child. "Well, she can be a pill."

"Not her fault," Joceline replied with a tight smile. "She doesn't know me."

"Her loss," he replied, and the tenderness in his tone brought a muffled sob from her throat.

"Now, now." He sat down beside her and pulled her close, rocking her. "Not to worry, the world's still going around. Right, me boy?" he asked Markie with a grin.

Markie was worried about his mother. She was crying. That mean old woman had upset her. But the big man sitting with them made him feel comforted, as if it would be all right. He smiled back. Sure. It would be all right. If he could just breathe…!

CHAPTER ELEVEN

BUT IT WASN'T all right. Joceline went home with Markie, and they'd no sooner gotten inside the apartment when he started choking.

She called Rourke, who rushed them to the emergency room. They waited outside for news while the doctor saw Markie.

"He'll be all right," Rourke promised her.

His phone rang. He got up and answered it, moving off a little. He looked worried. He said something, hung up and went back to Joceline.

"I have to go," he said quietly. "I can't explain. I've been working on a case with some other people and they've come up with a strategy that I think, I hope, will work! I'll get one of my men to watch out for you. I promise, you won't know he's around. I don't want to leave. I have no choice."

"It's okay," she told him. "Thanks for getting us here."

He pulled a bill out of his pocket and stuffed it into her coat. "Don't fuss," he said firmly. "You'll have to get a cab home. I'll make this up to you, I promise. Call me when you know how the boy is. Okay?"

He jotted down his phone number and handed it to her on a slip of paper. "Okay," she said.

He winked at her and went out the door, obviously distracted.

Joceline bent over her lap, taking deep breaths. She'd been through so much. Now she was faced with a bigger hurdle. Jon's mother had shot her right out of his life. Cammy wanted Jon to fire her and get another "secretary." She was the most possessive, rabid mother on earth and Joceline's faint dream of a future with Jon had been nipped in the bud.

It was probably for the best, she told herself. After all, she was keeping dire secrets. But what else could she have done? She'd made the only possible decision. Now she had to pay for it. And go on paying for it.

She burst into tears. It was just too much: the robbery, Jon getting shot, that horrible man threatening to kill her little boy, the possible loss of her job and now Jon's awful mother bulldozing her right out of the house. She hadn't even been allowed to say goodbye. It was just too much!

"Oh, no, you mustn't. You mustn't cry so!"

She heard the voice as if in a dream, and felt arms close around her and hug her close and rock her. "It will be all right. You'll see."

She must be dreaming, she told herself. Probably she'd been hit in the head and was in a coma. Because unless her senses were truly deceiving her, this was Cammy Blackhawk hugging her tight and assuring her that everything was going to be all right. Hallucinations, she told herself firmly. She was having hallucinations....

Cammy produced a handkerchief and wiped her eyes. "I spent many nights in emergency rooms with Jon, when he was so small," she said in a conciliatory tone. "I know how frightening it is. But Jon outgrew his asthma. Your son will, too. You'll see."

Joceline bit her lip. She didn't know what to say, what to do. It was incredible, that the woman had followed her here. Why was she being kind?

"You don't trust me," Cammy said, and nodded. "Sit down. Let me tell you a story."

Joceline sat on the chair beside her, the hardest sort of chairs in the world that they seemed to love to put in hospitals.

"When I was very young, my grandfather liked to have parties with his friends. They drank and passed out. So I could sneak out of the house and nobody noticed. I liked this older man a lot. He worked for the reservation police in those days..." She smiled at the other woman's surprise. "Yes, I lived on the reservation in Kyle, South Dakota, because my grandfather was there. My mother had married very young and died having me. My father, well, he just disappeared and left me with my grandparents in South Dakota. When my grandmother died one winter, it was just me and Grandpa." She sighed. "To make a long story short, I was in love and I went too far. I...was afraid he wouldn't want the child. He was very religious, you see." She averted her eyes. "I did what I thought I should do. Then he married me and I realized..." She swallowed. "He never spoke of it again. He already had McKuen, and then I had Jon. So we had our two sons and we raised them to be moral and socially conscious and to never do anything they would be ashamed to announce in church."

Joceline was listening, shocked.

"I judged you," Cammy said quietly. "I had no right. I didn't have your courage. You kept your baby."

Joceline averted her eyes. "I made a decision. I never knew if it would be the right one. I knew that Markie would never know his father."

"That is a tragedy."

"A big one."

Cammy took the younger woman's cold hands in hers. "I am sorry for what I said to you. For the way I acted. I am most sorry for the difficulty it has caused for your son. But he will be all right. Jon had such attacks. They were always terrifying, but they always ended and he was fine."

"Markie has weak lungs."

"So did Jon. It was one reason I was very strict about not letting him smoke." She sighed. "Alas, I could never stop his father, and I did try. Then McKuen took up those awful cigars…!"

Joceline smiled. She bit her lip. "Is Jon all right?"

"Yes. He tried to come back to his apartment here. He was very angry. It was my fault." She lowered her eyes. "I worry about him so much. I don't want him to be left alone." She bit her lip and lifted her dark eyes to Joceline's. "They say I have high blood pressure. They want me to take pills for it. I don't want to. I hate medicine."

"But you must," Joceline said gently. "You don't want to have a stroke. Dying is not the worst thing that could happen to you. You could be paralyzed. When I was little, my grandmother had one. She was paralyzed on one side and laid in her bed that way for two years before she died. It was so sad. You must take the medicine!"

Cammy drew in a long breath. "I could die anyway."

"No. You're going to be a grandmother," she said and managed a smile even through her misery. "Very soon, too."

Cammy brightened. "I'd forgotten. My second grandchild."

Joceline nodded. Her eyes were curiously sad. "Yes. Your second one."

"I suppose I should think about that and stop trying to force Jon to marry girls I like," she said, grimacing. She studied Joceline. "Rourke wants to marry you. It makes Jon furious," she added with a soft chuckle.

"Markie likes Rourke," Joceline said noncommittally. "He has lions on his farm in South Africa."

"Africa is a very dangerous place—you should not take a child there," Cammy said firmly. "And Rourke is no mother's idea of a suitable husband for her daughter!"

Incredible. Cammy was actually trying to discourage her from marrying Rourke?

Before she could say anything else, the emergency room physician found her. He smiled. "Not to worry," he said in a British accent, "the boy's going to be fine. We had to give him several treatments, but we've cleared his lungs. I think it's safe for you to take him home now."

"Will he need antibiotics?"

"No. Just the preventive inhaler. Do you have one?"

"Yes."

"And the rescue inhaler, if you need it," he added. He smiled. "He's quite a bright little boy. He was worried about you. There had been a quarrel, I gather?"

"Yes, and my fault." Cammy stepped forward. "But it's all over now."

The doctor seemed surprised. "Then I'll take you to Markie."

Joceline and, to her surprise, Cammy fell in behind him.

Markie looked horrified when he saw the older woman walk in with his mother.

Cammy went forward before Joceline could speak and lifted the child in her arms. "I am very sorry," she said softly, and she smiled. "I am a mean old woman, but I think I can get over it. Would you like an ice cream?"

Markie seemed torn between indignation at the woman's treatment of his mother and the promise of a rare and special treat. He looked at Joceline for guidance.

She actually chuckled. "I think the offer of ice cream is going to save the day."

Cammy smiled back.

They took Markie to the hospital cafeteria and he did get ice cream, but only after a suitable meal, for which Cammy paid and accepted no argument.

She sipped black coffee and refused dessert. "I never eat sweets," she told them. "An old habit. When I was a child, we were told that sugar was the foundation of all health problems and we were only allowed candy or cake on very special occasions."

"Are you a Native American?" Markie asked curiously. "We study them in school."

Cammy nodded. "My blood is mostly Cherokee, but I have grandparents who were Lakota Sioux and a grandfather who was Comanche."

"Can you speak it?"

"I can speak a little Cherokee," she said, smiling. "We lose the native languages if they aren't spoken. I try to remember what my parents taught me."

"Jon's father was Lakota, wasn't he?" Joceline asked.

"Yes. His blood was full." She laughed. "His mother thought I was unsuitable, because my blood was mixed."

Joceline was shocked.

"As you see, prejudice has no home," she added. "I married him anyway. They did not speak to us for two years. When Jon was born, they softened."

"Children do that."

"Indeed."

Joceline felt so worn. She was burned out, from the trauma of Jon's shooting and their changed relationship, not to mention the flight from Oklahoma with a furious Cammy at their backs. And now, here she was, Joceline's worst enemy, buying them ice cream. Jon had been right: Cammy wasn't who she seemed to be.

She spooned ice cream into her mouth and frowned. Something suddenly occurred to her, something she'd been far too upset to consider. "How did he know?"

Cammy blinked. "Excuse me?"

"Somebody broke into my apartment," she explained. "Kilraven and I think it was to get a file that I took home with me. How did the burglar know I'd taken the file home?"

"Did you tell someone?" Cammy asked.

"Just Betty, at our office, when we were having coffee." The spoon paused in midair. "No." She dismissed that thought at once. "She's been there longer than I have. She's one of our most trusted employees."

"Someone else in the office?"

"There are so many people who work there," Joceline said uneasily. "Not only the agents and clerical staff, but we have a lot of part-timers who come in to help. We have linguists and information specialists, computer programmers, pay-roll…" She frowned. "Well, one of our part-timers was at the table, but it couldn't have been her. You see, her father is a homicide detective for the local police department." She laughed. "I suppose someone could have overheard us and mentioned it to another person, you know how that goes. It's a busy office." She sighed. "It's been a very hectic week."

"I know what you mean. I have spent the past few years certain that one of my sons would be killed by some crimi-nal," she said heavily. "They work at such dangerous jobs, like my late husband."

"They're very good at what they do," Joceline said gently. "And very careful."

"Yes. You're right." She smiled. "I worry too much." She looked down at her coffee. "I made a decision. I hope it was the right one." She looked up. "Jon will need you, very much."

Joceline wondered at the phrasing, but Cammy quickly changed the subject.

Cammy took them home in a cab and paid for it, ignoring Joceline's protests. "It was my fault, all of it," she said gently. "This is the least I can do."

"Thank you."

Cammy studied her quietly. "You love my son."

Joceline clammed up. "He's my boss. Of course I'm... fond of him."

Cammy's dark eyes had narrowed. The little boy holding Joceline's hand was suddenly so familiar to her that she felt a pang of terrible conscience. He did act so much like Jon, at that age...

She was adding up facts. Jon's date with Joceline years ago at a party where he'd been drugged, about nine months before Markie was born; her seemingly out of character behavior to give birth to a child out of wedlock when she was such a religious person; did that add up to something that Cammy hadn't seen?

She felt a pang of conscience for the things she'd said to and about this brave young woman. She had another secret of her own that she couldn't share with anyone. She was walking into a very great danger that she hadn't confided even to her own sons. She hoped she was doing the right thing. She'd been reluctant at the time; she hadn't been too well-disposed toward this young woman and her child. Now she felt better about the decision. It was going to be painful for other people, as well. But if it would save a life...

She didn't let on about her suspicions. She simply smiled, and waved, with one last, lingering look at Markie, and let the cabdriver take her to a hotel room she'd reserved. She leaned her head back against the seat, thinking silently.

When she got to the hotel, she had company just briefly. She was told what to do, and when. But before she followed the instructions, she called McKuen.

"What do you know about Joceline's son?" she asked bluntly.

"Nothing I'd ever tell you, Cammy," he replied with equal bluntness.

"I went to see her. She had to take her little boy to the hospital because of me," she added with some shame. "I never felt so guilty about anything."

McKuen relaxed a little. "That was nice."

"Jon threw me out of the house," she added sadly. "He wasn't even speaking to me when I left. I sent my young friend home, Charlene, you know. I remembered the little boy trying to breathe because I upset him so much. I was sorry for what I did. I wanted to try to make it up to Joceline and her child, so I called her apartment and when she wasn't there, I figured out what must have happened, so I called hospitals until I found them. That man made threats. Will she and the child be safe in her apartment?"

"Men are watching her every minute."

"Not Rourke," she said firmly. "He should not be her guardian. He lives in Africa."

"You wanted her to marry him and go there…"

"That was before," she said. "Markie acts and if you look closely, he resembles…Jon," she said hesitantly. "Except for the color of his eyes and his skin—but he would tan very well in the sun, I expect."

"You're reaching, Cammy."

"Am I? Jon went to a party with Joceline and his drink was spiked. He was very drugged. All I have to do is find out the exact date of the party and the exact date of Markie's birth," she added doggedly. "I can hire a private detective."

He drew in a breath. "You think too much like me."

He didn't mention that he'd already done what she was suggesting.

"He's my grandson." She almost choked on the word. "Markie is my grandson!"

He hesitated. Then he let out a breath. "Yes. She was afraid that Jon wouldn't believe the boy was his, that he'd think she was trying to blackmail him for money. He didn't know her very well then. She did what she thought was best. She couldn't give up the baby. She loved him, and his father, too much."

Cammy closed her eyes. Tears ran out of them. "I've been horrible to her."

"We noticed."

She sniffed and opened her eyes. She straightened. "Never again. I'm going to see to it that the child has everything he needs, and Joceline, too. And Jon should marry her, at once!"

"Cammy, you're forgetting one little complication."

"What?"

"Jon doesn't know that Markie is his child."

Cammy sat down in a chair. Hard.

Kilraven noted the silence on the other end of the phone. "Joceline won't tell him. She's still afraid he won't believe it. The child has A positive blood type, so does Jon. A DNA test would be conclusive."

"We'd have to make Joceline do it. She wouldn't. She's stubborn, like me."

Kilraven chuckled. "Yes."

Cammy drew a breath. "Well, you'll have to tell him."

"Oh, no. I'm not telling him."

"Then I will."

"You can't, either. Now don't go trying to manage things again. Look how you've already messed up."

She bit her lip. "Jon's furious at me. I deserve it, but I'm so scared. I didn't want to leave him alone at a time like this. I shouldn't have upset him." She didn't add that she had another reason for feeling very guilty about the way they'd parted. It would be devastating. She felt sick inside. She still wasn't sure she was doing the right thing.

"He'll cool off. I'll go see him, if you like."

"Would you?" she asked hopefully. "It would ease my mind. You can tell him how sorry I am, and that I took Joceline and the boy home from the hospital."

"I'll tell him. You know Jon. He just has to cool off."

She hesitated again. "I have high blood pressure. If it kills me, what will the two of you do? At least you have Winnie. Jon has nobody. Well, he has a child and a woman who loves him, but he doesn't know. What if I die?"

"You won't die. Didn't the doctor give you medicine?"

She fiddled with her lap. "Yes."

"Then take it, Cammy. You have a grandson, and another one almost ready to make an appearance."

"Yes." She brightened.

"You can't die yet."

She drew in another breath. She couldn't say anything, but maybe, just maybe, she could prepare them. "I feel it, you know. I have this awful cold sense that something terrible is going to happen. I had it before the shooting, but it didn't go away. Listen, I love you very, very much. I love your brother. You tell him. If anything happens…"

"Nothing's going to happen!"

She sighed. "You're sure?"

She sounded so worried. "I know these feelings of yours sometimes pay off," he replied. "But you're not on the spot with this one. You're going to live a long time."

She stared at an odd shadow on the wall. So soon? She gripped the phone, hard. "Of course I am."

"Now stop worrying and…Cammy? Cammy!"

There had been a sound. A gunshot. Two gunshots. Then

a final, horrible one. Kilraven left the phone line open, grabbed a spare cell phone he always carried and started punching in numbers. His hands were shaking.

A HOMICIDE detective outside, Rick Marquez in fact, told Kilraven at the door of Cammy's hotel room that they'd found Cammy Blackhawk on the sofa, sitting up, stone dead, with bullet wounds in her chest and stomach. The phone was in her lap. Evidence teams were all over the room, photographers, the coroner's assistant, the coroner's investigator and homicide detectives. Outside, a reporter was trying his best to gain entrance, to no avail.

Kilraven absolutely wasn't allowed inside. Rick Marquez embraced him tightly, feeling the other man's resistance at first and then helpless shudders as the reality hit him.

"It's all right," Rick said gently. "It's all right. You'll snap back and do what you have to do."

"I'll find the man who did this. I'll hunt him to the ends of the earth," Kilraven said harshly as he drew away, a little flushed.

"We'll find him," Rick said. "I've got every law enforcement agency in town on alert and looking for the shooter."

"Harold Monroe made the threats against my family."

"Yes, and he's out on bond, I'll give you that. But you know Monroe screws up everything he does," Rick reminded him grimly. "Odd thing about him knowing where the murder weapon was in your family's case. That was a professional hit. Very clean. Very structured. Not a hair out of place. The guy knew what he was doing. That just doesn't seem like goof-up Harold Monroe to me."

Kilraven didn't reply. He was too shocked and hurt. He swallowed. He and Cammy had their differences, but he'd always loved her. How was he going to tell Jon? And was Cammy likely to be the only casualty?

"I've got someone watching your wife," Rick said somberly. "Rourke's got a man on Joceline and her son. We're even watching you, Kilraven," he added. "Whoever did this, and I'm not convinced it's Monroe, is dealing out revenge. It could be Jay Copper. Even in jail, he can call for help. We'll check everyone who's phoned him or seen him, or Harold Monroe, since their arrests. We'll find the perp."

"Find him in time, won't you?" Kilraven asked. "First my wife and child, then my brother, now my mother…" He turned away. "Damn him!"

"I know how you feel," Rick said.

Kilraven turned back to him, narrow-eyed.

"Okay, I don't," Rick conceded. "I really don't. But I promise you, on my mother's soul, I will find the killer."

Kilraven softened, just a little. "Watch your own back. You've been targeted in the past, too, and so has my wife's mother."

"My best detective colleague, Gail Rogers," Rick agreed. He smiled. "You should tell your brother. There's a reporter outside. He'll have it on the wire in no time. No way should Jon see this on CNN."

Kilraven nodded.

Marquez watched him go with great misgivings. Marquez had been maneuvered into doing something he wasn't sure about, on the word of a man he really shouldn't even have trusted. But the Blackhawks trusted him. And some traps required strong bait. He hoped his health insurance would cover the damage when certain facts were known.

KILRAVEN flew up to Oklahoma on the jet and phoned to have Sloane Callum meet him at the airstrip, but it was one of the hands who showed up.

"Sloane's really sorry, he got drunk and locked himself

in his room," the cowboy said with a grimace. "He doesn't drink, you know. But he said we all slip sometimes."

"I guess." Kilraven didn't say anything more. He didn't even tell the man why he'd rushed home.

He walked into Jon's bedroom, grim and dreading the conversation. Jon looked sick and weak, and pale, and he was still smarting from Joceline's abrupt departure on his mother's orders.

"Cammy and I had a row," he told Kilraven. "Did she send you to try to make it up?"

Kilraven went and sat down on the bed next to his brother. It was going to be so much harder because of the argument. "I have some news. It's not good."

Jon studied him. "Not like you to beat around the bush," he said with a faint smile. His expression froze. "Not Joceline or the boy?"

He shook his head. "No. Not them." It was so hard. He remembered his wife and child, the way they looked. He remembered Jon, in the emergency room. This was…

"Cammy. Cammy?"

Kilraven closed his eyes.

Jon was speechless. He just looked at his older brother with shock and disbelief.

"She was talking to me on the phone. There were three shots."

Jon couldn't wrap his mind around it. His mother was dead. Jay Copper had been arrested for conspiracy in the murder of Mac's wife and child, and Harold Monroe had been charged with helping kill Monica and Melly Kilraven. Now Monroe had targeted Jon's family for revenge. The bastard had killed Cammy, had killed his mother, the one person they'd never expected to need protection!

"No!" he ground out.

Kilraven gathered the younger man carefully against his

broad chest and wrapped him up as tight as he dared. "No!" Jon groaned in anguish, and his eyes grew wet against his brother's broad shoulder.

Two brothers, closer in grief than ever before, were silent and still for a very long time.

"We had men watching everybody," Kilraven said a few minutes later. "Everybody except Cammy. God knows why, it never occurred to me that he'd try for her. Why? She never hurt a soul!"

"She was part of my family," Jon replied coldly. "Family is a big thing to Jay Copper. He killed a young underage girl to protect his own illegitimate son, the senator, remember? Monroe may only be his nephew by marriage, but you remember Jay Copper's sister committed suicide when Bart Hancock was briefly charged with participating in the murders."

"Monroe may be out on bail, but we'll tie him to this as well as to Melly's murder. He'll do hard time, even if he doesn't get the damned needle!" Kilraven replied. "He won't get out of this with a team of lawyers. It's a done deal. He cooked himself with his own big mouth and he was taped," he added. "One of the detectives had an inmate wired with a promise of a deal with the D.A.—everybody wanted the man who put the hit on my daughter, even the inmate who volunteered to get the evidence. The inmate had a daughter of his own about the same age."

"Does Monroe have kids?" Jon asked bitterly.

"No, it's just him and his wife. He had a father who was in jail for a murder years ago, at least, that's what we heard, but we didn't check back that far."

"How is the senator's brother, Hank Sanders, tied into this?" he asked, naming a former decorated SEAL team member, who'd help them save Kilraven and the woman who was now his wife.

"He isn't. Jay Copper had two sisters. One had Bart Hancock, the other had Harold Monroe's wife. The sisters are both dead. Bart Hancock's mother died when her son's involvement in the murder of your family came out."

"Sad. For her, not for her son."

"Yes."

Kilraven turned back to Jon. "We need to get you out of here, now."

"We have to plan a funeral," the younger man said grimly.

"We do, but we're having it in San Antonio. It was where Cammy lived for many years. She'd be...happier there, anyway, near us."

"I'd rather bury her in Jacobsville," Jon said surprisingly. "Don't ask me why. It just seems more her sort of place than an impersonal city cemetery."

Kilraven nodded. "Yes. It does."

There was a tap on the door. Sloane Callum peered around it. "Sorry to hear about Mrs. Blackhawk," he said somberly. "We had our differences but she was a good person. And sorry I was under the weather. I won't take another drink, I swear!"

"Everybody slips once in a while," Jon replied. "It's all right."

"I can put on more men to watch out for you," Callum said.

"No need. I'm going back to San Antonio with my brother," Jon said. "We have to see to arrangements about Cammy. We're going to bury her in Jacobsville."

"You're leaving?" Callum looked worried. "You'd be safer here, boss, I'd never let nobody hurt you...!"

"I know that. Thanks. But I'm going to do what I have to."

Callum hesitated. "Okay, then." He seemed deep in thought. "Well, sorry again."

"Thanks."

Callum left the room.

"He watches me like a hawk," Jon said. "He's a better watchdog than the German shepherds are."

"I guess he feels he owes it to us," Kilraven replied. "Better get moving."

Jon got out of bed, a little wobbly. "Yes." The shock was starting to wear off and he felt a cold, sharp pain that was unrelated to his wound. "I yelled at her, before…"

"She had this feeling," Kilraven said at once. "She was talking about having high blood pressure and taking meds for it, then she said to tell you that she loved you, loved us, very much. I was just thinking how odd that was to say when I heard the shots."

Jon's teeth clenched. "Thanks. It makes it a little easier."

"I don't know how the killer knew where to find her, unless he's watching us," Kilraven said suddenly.

"Time for a little detective work, I think," Jon replied. "We need some answers, quickly."

"I couldn't agree more. In fact, you work for one of the best agencies in the world, and I'm sure at least one agent has free time and would be willing to ferret out a few facts on the recent movements of anybody who's related to Jay Copper!"

CHAPTER TWELVE

JON CALLED JOCELINE with the news the minute he was settled into his San Antonio apartment. He barely got the first words out when she asked where he was and hung up.

Markie was in school, with one of Rourke's men watching him. Joceline had to argue her way out of her apartment and, in the end, accept a ride from her own unfamiliar watchdog just to get to Jon's apartment. But she made it.

She walked in when he opened the door, closed it behind her, locked it and went right into his arms.

He held her close, rocked her, buried his face in her warm throat.

"I know, you're a big tough guy," she said, her voice muffled by his shoulder. "But losing a parent hurts. There's nothing wrong with grief."

"No." His mouth burrowed into her warm throat, opened, pressed hard. "Joceline…!"

His hands went under her blouse, up to the fastening of her bra. She didn't protest, not even when he removed every inch of clothing from her pretty body and started kissing his way down it.

He couldn't lift her; the wound was too fresh. But he tugged her into the bedroom, closed the door, smoothed her down on the bed and stripped off his pajamas without a second thought.

She opened her arms to him, welcoming, comforting, and let him pin her to the bed with his weight.

"I shouldn't," he began.

She pulled his mouth down to hers and held it there, shifting to make way for his long legs and the sudden, sweet thrust of him inside her.

He gasped at the sensation he'd never felt. At least, he didn't think he'd felt it. But the rhythm of his body on hers was oddly familiar, like the sound of her soft gasps of pleasure as he shifted and twisted.

He lifted his head and looked down at her, saw the hard, dusky pink tips of her breasts, the shivering of her body, the wide-eyed fascination of her eyes as she looked down to where they were joined.

He lifted his hips to let her watch. He watched, too. It was the most intense sensation, like plunging into molten heat, sheathing himself in the moist darkness of her with a slow, steady rhythm.

He groaned, shocked, as pleasure shuddered through him in slow waves every time he moved.

She watched his face, fascinated. She was feeling those sensations, too. It was nothing like the quick, almost frantic pace of the first time. It was glorious. She lifted, moaning as it increased the pleasure they were sharing.

He whispered to her, shocking things, loving things, smiling at her reactions, her responses. His hand slid under her hips and moved them to his rhythm. He was aware of pain from the wound, discomfort in other areas, but the delicious pleasure dwarfed them.

He closed his eyes, shuddering, as it became suddenly urgent. He pushed down hard, deep, pinning her wrists, looking straight into her wide, helpless eyes as he buffeted her with his weight.

"It's coming," he whispered hoarsely. "It's coming…!"

"Jon," she cried out, arching. "Oh, Jon…!"

He ground down into her, clenching his teeth, driving for satisfaction, frantic for release. "I'm sorry, it's too quick…!"

"No…it's…not!" she bit off. She matched his rhythm with quick, sharp movements of her hips, shifting so that he was there, right there, right there…!

He heard her hoarse cry, followed by a moan so descriptive of what he was feeling that he moaned with her, shuddering with each penetration as the joy rose to such heights that he felt himself explode inside her.

He arched over her, his face contorted, shuddering, shuddering. He thought it would never end. He said so.

But finally, inevitably, his damp body collapsed on hers and they lay together, still intimately locked, intimately close, with their heartbeats shaking the bed.

He stretched, wincing, and lifted his head to look at her. "Joceline," he whispered. "Why does this seem familiar?"

She hesitated. Her heart was still pounding, and she was too emotionally spent to guard her expression.

"I have had sex, haven't I?" he asked gently. "I had it with you."

She swallowed, hard. She wanted to deny it, but he looked at her as if he already knew the truth. And he did. He was making mental notations, doing sums, finding answers to questions he'd never asked.

His lips parted on a rush of breath. "Markie. He's mine. He's my son!"

She bit down on her lower lip. "I didn't think you'd believe me, that anyone would believe me," she whispered tearfully. "You didn't know me. I could have been after you for your wealth, your position…" She closed her eyes. "I didn't know what to do."

"So you had my child, thinking I wouldn't want him or you." He bent and crushed his mouth down on hers. "You fool," he whispered. "You sweet little fool…oh, God!" he groaned as his movements brought the heat and urgency back. "I can't stop. I don't want to stop…!"

"It's all right," she whispered, lifting to the harsh, deep thrust of his body. "I don't, either." She arched up to the mouth closing on her breasts with aching delight. "I love you…so much!"

It was like pulling a trigger. There was no stopping then. He groaned as he drove into her, drowning in the joy of being loved and wanted. His mouth ground into hers as the rhythm grew faster and more urgent.

"Dear…God, it's…like dying…!" he groaned hoarsely as he shuddered again and again. "So sweet!"

"Sweet," she whispered. She moaned. Her body shivered under the driving thrusts. She wrapped her long legs around his hips and lifted, lifted, arched, dying to end the tension, to make it like it was before, to know utter ecstasy.

She cried out, sobbing, as the tension suddenly broke for them both and they lay straining together, shuddering, as the climax shook the bed.

He moved lazily afterward, his body teasing hers in a caress that was beyond her dreams of closeness.

"This is how it should have been, how it would have been, if I hadn't been drugged," he said at her ear, his voice drowsy with satisfaction. "I would have loved you like this, slow and sweet, until you dug those short nails into my hips and bit me." He laughed softly. "I didn't know women really did things like that. I thought it was fiction. When I heard you cry, the first time, I thought I was hurting you, until I looked down into your face."

Her arms slid around his neck and she sighed with exhaustion. "I wanted you so much that night. It was really sweet, most of it. Just at the last, you were out of control and I was very naive. It hurt, and there was no time afterward to do it again. I had to get you to the hospital. Then when I knew Markie was going to grow in my body, I had to make a decision."

He lifted his head and looked at her. "You made the right one. He's a wonderful boy." His eyes darkened. "My son."

"Yes. Your son." She smoothed back his long hair. "You don't have to marry me...."

He chuckled. "It will look better if we're married. I won't be able to stay out of your bed."

She sighed as she looked into his eyes. Her own were bright with tears of joy.

He smoothed his cheek against hers. "Now we have to face unpleasant things," he said quietly. He drew away from her, fascinated by the process of intimacy, more fascinated with how they both looked afterward. He smiled.

She flushed, gazing at him. That made his smile broader. He slid into his pajamas and pulled the sheet over her. She was looking decidedly embarrassed.

He sat down beside her. "We decided to bury my mother, Cammy, in Jacobsville," he said. "But first we have to find a way to flush out the killer. He's going to pay for what he's done."

"Some of those men you're paying must have been watching Harold Monroe since he made bail," she said. "That's our starting point."

He nodded. He brushed her hair away from her cheeks. He looked very possessive. "But first we have lunch. Then we go and pick up our son from school. I have things to tell him," he added with a secretive smile.

Joceline smiled back. Even through the tragedy, she had the first hope of a happy future.

JON AND KILRAVEN went alone to the funeral home in Jacobsville to make the arrangements. There were two men in suits there, very official-looking, who went into one of the viewing rooms when the brothers came in.

The funeral home director seemed unsettled when they asked about making arrangements. He hesitated, smiled with a little embarrassment, showed them into his office and then left for a minute.

The door was open. The brothers noted that he went into the same room where the men in suits had gone. He was back in a minute.

"Yes, now where were we?" he asked as he sat down at his desk and pulled up a file on the computer. "Yes, the funeral. You do realize that your mother requested a closed casket and that she wanted no one, especially her sons, to view her?" he asked solemnly.

That was news to both of them. They said so.

"How do you know that?" Kilraven asked suspiciously.

The funeral home director, Mr. Adams, flushed. He looked back at the screen. "She came to see me earlier in the week," he said quickly. "She had a premonition, she said." He glanced at them. "She made the arrangements herself."

Kilraven looked at Jon. The funeral home director was oddly stiff. "Well, she had these moods," Kilraven said at last, and the director relaxed visibly. "I guess it makes sense."

"She wouldn't want people staring at her," Jon said quietly. "I'd feel like that, too. It's okay. I understand," he told the director.

"So do I," Kilraven added. "We'll need to contact her minister and we'll need pallbearers..."

"We'll have no end of offers from both our agencies," Jon reminded his brother. "Not a problem."

"We'll contact her minister," the director offered, "and take care of all the other arrangements. You'd like an arrangement for the casket?"

"Yes."

"I'll call the florist," the director added.

"Have you had any calls about Cammy?" Jon asked suddenly.

"In fact, we have," he replied. "Several newspapers, a television journalist and some man who never identified himself," he said, reading notes he'd made on the computer. "I thought it was very odd."

"No chance you recorded it." Jon sighed.

The man cleared his throat. "Well, we've never had any need to," he began.

"Of course not," Kilraven agreed.

The director outlined the service and they set a date for the funeral and arranged with a company to open the gravesite Cammy had already paid for in a memorial garden in, of all places, Jacobsville. The brothers had wanted to bury her there, but she'd already anticipated it and bought a plot. They smiled at her efficiency, through the sorrow.

JON HAD SUPPER with Joceline and Markie. He was sad about Cammy, and it showed. He was going back into work the next day, despite the protests from everybody.

"I'm perfectly able to work," he argued.

Joceline glowered at him. "You're just out of the hospital and your mother has been..."

"Yes, I know," he said, intercepting the word before it could upset him. "But life goes on. You have to come in, too." He smiled at Markie. "Not you, I'm afraid," he said with a smile. "You'll have school."

Markie sighed. "Okay, Dad," he said.

Jon actually flushed when he heard the word. "That sounds very nice," he said gently.

Markie grinned. "My daddy works for the FBI. The other kids are going to be soooo jealous!"

Jon and Joceline both laughed.

"Another thing we have to plan is a wedding, and quickly," Jon added.

"Can I be the flower boy?" Markie asked.

They burst out laughing again.

"No, but you can carry the rings. How about that?" Jon asked.

"That would be okay, I guess," he said, and dug into his spaghetti.

JON WAS UNEASY. He'd been so full of grief, and too fascinated with Joceline and his new status as Markie's father, to start to make sense of all that had happened. But now he was trying to put all the pieces of the puzzle together.

Jay Copper had said that he sent his nephew Peppy to help Dan Jones murder McKuen's first wife, Monica, and their daughter, Melly. But Peppy, alias Bart Hancock, had escaped the charges, thanks to a missing tape and only hearsay evidence to carry to court. Hearsay, especially from the family of the deceased, would not convince a jury of guilt.

Subsequently, Jon had arrested Harold Monroe for human trafficking and the less-than-brilliant career criminal had managed to have the charge dismissed thanks to the retraction of the charge by the main witness. Joceline's apartment had been broken into. A file involving Bart Hancock had gone missing. Jon had been shot.

Then a witness had come forward who'd been planted in

Monroe's cell during his confinement awaiting trial on the trafficking charges. The inmate was wired. He gave evidence that Monroe had bragged about helping to kill three-year-old Melly Kilraven and had even told the inmate the location of the hidden shotgun that he'd used on her. That had led to his rearrest on a murder charge. Incredibly, he was allowed bail at the hearing and soon after, Cammy Blackhawk had been murdered.

But there was something wrong here. Joceline had mentioned it. How had anyone known that she'd taken the file home? How did someone know where Cammy Blackhawk would be so that he could kill her? How had Harold Monroe, of all people, managed to pull off Jon's shooting, Cammy's shooting and, further back in time, the murder of Kilraven's wife and child? The man could barely talk on the phone and think at the same time.

Jay Copper's sister, Bart Hancock's mother, had committed suicide when she was told that her brother and her son had been implicated in the murder of a child. Bart Hancock had been charged with the murder of children in Iraq years before, but was never brought to trial. Harold Monroe was notorious for fumbling whatever crime he attempted. He was always being rescued by his vicious uncle.

But Monroe had apparently bragged about being Melly Kilraven's killer, and even blabbed about the location of the murder weapon. Was that in character? And the inmate who just happened to be in the cell with Monroe, and offered to collect evidence, was just a little too convenient to suit Jon's sense of logic.

He leaned back in his chair and his black eyes narrowed. He was fitting puzzle pieces together. He took a sip of cold coffee, grimaced and regained his train of thought.

Joceline had taken home a file on Bart Hancock. She hadn't told anyone, except Betty at the office. And a part-time secretarial worker had overheard, but her dad was a homicide detective. Unlikely that she'd be involved in a robbery.

And Betty had no reason to want to hurt coworkers. Perhaps Joceline's phone line had been tapped. No. Rourke had put equipment on her phone for a trace; he'd have found evidence of a wiretap. That ruled out the possibility that someone had listened in on her conversation. Which took the ball right back to the office, where Betty worked.

He picked up the phone and punched in Betty's extension.

"Yes?" she answered in her sweet tone.

"Hi," he replied. "Could you come in here, please?"

"Sure thing."

A couple of minutes later, she tapped on the door, opened it and walked in. She closed it behind her and sat down in front of the desk.

"Something wrong?" she asked.

"Joceline brought a file home with her…"

"Oh, yes," she said, shaking her head. "She was so upset! I told her they wouldn't fire her over one mistake," she chuckled. "And we still had an earlier version on the computer's hard drive, anyway. It was just a paper copy."

He turned his computer around. "Can you bring it up on the screen?"

"Sure."

She punched in the information, waited, waited, frowned. "That's very odd. It isn't here. I know I scanned those documents into the computer."

"What exactly was in them?" he asked.

She sat back down, still frowning, and pushed back her short, curly blond hair with a nervous hand. "I'm not absolutely sure," she said. "There was no really sensitive information in it, just some remarks by the arresting officer about Bart Hancock's mother making threats when they took him in for questioning in a local murder case. Oh, and his daughter being under suspicion for an assault that proved fatal, but that she was never charged. She was a juvenile at the time."

Jon sat up. "His daughter?"

"I believe it was his daughter. I don't remember anything else." She grimaced. "Now I'm going to be in trouble, too. I don't know how that information went missing!"

"I'll talk to the SAC," Jon said gently. "Nobody's going to blame you. But we are going to want to know how that file was removed."

"We do background checks on all the people we hire," Betty said worriedly. "There's no way we could have anybody here with a criminal background."

"Not all people who commit crimes have criminal backgrounds."

"Yes, some people never get caught." She studied him. "I hope they catch whoever shot you," she said bluntly, "and also the person who killed your brother's wife and child, and Mrs. Blackhawk." She shook her head. "It seems they planned to wipe out your whole family. But why would they threaten Joceline and her little boy? It makes no sense. She isn't part of your family."

But she was. So was Markie. Nobody outside of the family knew. But obviously, somebody else did. He'd asked Joceline about Markie's birth certificate, but she hadn't listed a name under "Father." On the other hand, there was the record on Jon's brush with hallucinogenic drugs the night Markie had been conceived, and the record of Markie's birth nine months later. Both those events were on records that could be accessed. Someone could have connected those dates and checked them out. His brother had done that, and had told him after the fact. It wasn't too far-fetched to think someone else could have done the same investigative work. Perhaps a law enforcement person with access to computer records. And they knew Jay Copper had somebody on the inside, somebody with a badge. They'd never found out who it was. Such a person would have access to databases of crimes that civilians couldn't access.

"You've connected something," Betty guessed.

"Yes. All of this ties into computer records that only someone in law enforcement could get access to. Well, legally, I mean."

She pursed her lips and frowned. "Anyone in this office with the right clearance could get to them. And the offices aren't locked during lunch hours."

"They should be. I'll bring it up with the SAC."

"Good idea."

"That part-time girl we've got working for you," he began slowly. "What do we know about her background?"

She laughed. "Phyllis? Her dad's a homicide cop at San Antonio P.D.," she said. She pulled the computer keyboard into her lap, punched in codes and brought up Phyllis Hicks's file. She turned the screen back to Jon.

"She's working on a degree in computer programming. Her specialty is going to be cybercrime, and she wants to work here as an agent. She got the entry-level position part-time so that she could continue her college studies."

He was looking at her photograph and wondering why it seemed so familiar. "Who's her father?"

"You know him, he worked with Gail at one time," she added, naming Kilraven's mother-in-law. "His name is Dave Hicks. He's a police detective."

"I remember. Mac said Hicks was at the hospital with Marquez when Rogers got shot." He hesitated. "We never found out who shot her, either."

"Another mystery." She shook her head. "So many shootings. Marquez got blindsided, you recall, when he and Gail were working on the Senator Will Sanders case."

"Everything goes back to Sanders's arrest for murder," he mused. "Not everyone knows that he's Jay Copper's illegitimate son, and Copper is a maniac about protecting his family. All these shootings happened when the investigations began into the case that Copper was finally arrested for, the murder of a young girl who'd been to Sanders's house. But he was also charged with conspiring to murder Dan Jones, who'd been involved in silencing the witnesses, and he was charged with masterminding the murder of Mac's wife and child."

Betty nodded. "Wasn't there some talk about Jay Copper's sister, Bart Hancock's mother, being a mental patient? I know she spent some time in institutions before Copper started making big money as the senator's right-hand man."

"She did. Hancock has never been normal. But I didn't think he had children."

"If memory serves, Hancock only had one child, a daughter. He wasn't married to the child's mother, because she found out what he was doing overseas just after she had the child. Hancock's daughter would be the granddaughter of Hancock's mother, who committed suicide."

Jon was frowning. "Do we know her name?"

"I believe it was in the missing file," Betty said. "But I'll bet Joceline could dig that information up in a heartbeat," she added with a grin.

"I won't take that bet," he replied, chuckling. He picked up the phone. "Hey, Rocky, how about digging up the name of Bart Hancock's daughter for me? Yes. That's the one. You bet." His voice had dropped to a purr. "Yes. Thanks."

"Rocky?" Betty mused.

"It's an in-joke," he replied. He sighed. "And you'll hear some gossip, so I'll be the first to tell you. Joceline's little boy is my son. I didn't know until a few days ago," he added, noting Betty's shock.

"That party, where you were drugged," Betty said at once.
"Yes."

"I wondered. You see, Joceline is such an upright person,"
she added gently. She smiled. "Better marry her."

"The license is already applied for," he said, and smiled.
The smile faded. "First, we have to get through a funeral,
though."

"I'm so sorry," Betty said. "I know your mother got on
your nerves, but she was a good person."

His face tautened. It was painful to discuss Cammy's
death. "Yes. She was a good person."

Betty got up. "I'll file a report about the missing information," she said.

"Good idea."

She paused at the door. "Glad to have you back," she said,
then smiled and left.

Joceline came into the office a minute later, looking very
disconcerted.

He got up and took her by the shoulders. "What is it?"

"I found out who Bart Hancock's daughter is."

He blinked. "Excuse me?"

"You see, he didn't marry her mother. But her mother
married a policeman a few years later, who adopted her
daughter and gave her his name. The policeman is now a
detective with San Antonio P.D. His name is Dave Hicks."

"Yes, Betty and I were just talking about him." He sat
up straighter. "Phyllis Hicks is our part-time clerical worker
who's in college part-time, but can't spell. And she's Bart
Hancock's daughter? Does she know?"

"That's something we'll have to find out, I'm afraid."

Bart Hancock's daughter worked in their office. She had
access to computer records, telephone conversations and just
about any other sort of information she might care to dig out.
And what she didn't know, her adoptive father could find out

in a heartbeat through his police contacts. He might not even know why she was asking for the information, if she was the person who'd relayed Joceline's movements, and Cammy's, to a shooter.

Jon's breath caught. "Right under our noses!"

"We can't prove anything," she added quickly. "We don't even have a reason to charge her."

"Plus, we can't let on that we know her background," he replied. "And her adoptive dad works for San Antonio P.D., with access to all sorts of records."

"Yes."

"Well, at least now we have the beginnings of a real investigation. And some possible suspects."

She nodded. "Life just got a lot more complicated."

His hands were absently caressing her arms. "We were planning a graveside service, but Cammy's arrangements call for a public one." His eyes narrowed. "I think we might want to pay very close attention to who shows up."

"I was thinking the very same thing," she agreed.

CHAPTER THIRTEEN

THE FUNERAL HOME'S chapel was very crowded. Almost all the employees of the San Antonio FBI field office who knew Jon showed up. Half the Jacobsville, Texas, police department was on hand and so were members of various other federal agencies who knew the very popular brothers.

"I hadn't counted on so many people," Jon told Kilraven as they sat in the front pew with Winnie and Joceline.

"Not to worry, I've got several people watching. And I've gotten court-ordered wiretaps, as well," Kilraven replied quietly. "Now that we have some solid leads, we're going to blow the case wide-open."

Joceline was looking over her shoulder. Her eyes almost popped. "I don't believe it!"

The others followed her wide-eyed stare. Harold Monroe was just walking in the door.

"Son of a…!" Kilraven muttered and started to get up. His expression was homicidal.

Jon pulled him back down. "Don't you dare," he said sternly. "Cammy would come back and haunt us both!"

"He killed my baby girl," Kilraven gritted.

"He's only been accused. Not convicted," Jon reminded him. "You're an officer of the law. You can't touch him. Get a grip."

Kilraven subsided, but not happily.

And then the oddest thing happened. Harold Monroe, shifty-eyed and uncomfortable, but determined, walked down the aisle to where the family was sitting and stopped in front of Kilraven.

"I didn't kill her," he said in a low tone, glancing around to make sure he wasn't overheard.

Jon scowled. "What?"

Monroe went down on one knee. He was flushed and nervous, constantly looking around the room. "I know, you think I done it all. I ain't smart. I help some poor kids get work and you think it's bad the way I do it, but listen, I ain't never killed nobody! Especially not no little kid."

The brothers were just staring at him, dumbfounded.

"And no ladies, either," he added gruffly, glancing at the casket.

"You bragged to another jailbird that you killed my daughter," Kilraven said, barely restraining the urge to throttle the man in front of witnesses. "You even fingered the murder weapon."

Monroe lowered his voice. "Yeah. So they'd find it. I put it where I was told to. I was scared. But you tell them smart guys to look at the prints on the shells that was in it. I didn't take the shells out, you see. I left them. I figured, when I got a chance, I'd make it right. That little girl. That poor little kid…!"

A monster with a conscience? The spellbound audience was exchanging puzzled glances.

"He said he'd kill my wife. She's all I got. She's smart. She works in a library. She never hurt nobody!"

"He who?" Jon asked curtly.

"You look at them prints on those shells. You'll see who. And he's got a kid. She's crazy like him," he added huskily. "He took her along with him, when..." He swallowed. "She wasn't seen. He didn't want her stepdad to find out. She could get information from him, see. But you check them prints, then you find out where she was the night your little girl got shot. You check where she was when..." He glanced at the casket again, and grimaced. "Well, you'll see who. You'll see a lot."

"You confessed on tape," Kilraven said.

"Yeah, I did. I knew the guy was wired."

"How?"

Monroe shifted. "I can't say. I said enough already. I set it up so I could be accused, then maybe they wouldn't think I'd told on them. I could say, you know, that I was willing to take the rap for it, if they'd leave my wife alone." He lowered his voice. "They'll kill me in a heartbeat if they find out I told you this."

"Like hell they will." Kilraven motioned to a man in a suit in the aisle. He came forward. "This is Harold Monroe," he told the man. "If he dies, we come after you in a pickup truck at night wearing ninja gear. Get the picture?"

The man chuckled. "Yeah."

Monroe's eyes bulged. "You're protecting me? I'm out on bond on a murder charge! I even confessed!"

"We'll get the charges dropped," Jon said quietly. "You testify to what you know, we'll see what we can do for you on the other charges. If you stop trying to exploit kids."

Monroe sighed. "I ain't smart enough to make money any other way. But, hey, I guess I could move to Vegas and become a pimp." He grinned, showing a missing tooth.

Jon shook his head.

Monroe leaned forward. "You want to do some checking

with San Antonio P.D.," he added in a whisper. "The guy whose fingerprints are on the shells in that shotgun, he's related to Jay Copper. But I never told you that. You found it out."

Kilraven nodded. "God, Monroe, this is going to ruin your rep in local criminal circles if it ever gets out."

"You ain't telling nobody," he said coldly. "Got that?"

Kilraven smiled.

"We'll do what we can for you," Jon said. His eyes narrowed. "Why come forward now?"

"I was gonna let the evidence on that shotgun turn the trick, but I was afraid it might fall through the cracks, especially when Mrs. Blackhawk got killed. Then I knew I had to say something. She was a great lady," he said, nodding toward the casket. "See, my dad got sent to prison for murder a long time ago. He was young and his mom had cancer, and needed medicine he couldn't pay for. When he got out, your family hired him, gave him a job, trusted him when nobody else would."

"Sloane Callum is your father?" Jon exclaimed, shocked.

"Yeah, but he never married my mom," Monroe said. "He wanted to, but she didn't believe in that stuff. Kind of a hippie, see. Anyway, I made sure nobody knew, 'cause I didn't want him to lose his job if you knew about me."

"He's a good man," Jon said quietly. He was still reeling from the inefficiency of the detectives who'd done the background check on Sloane Callum and missed this connection.

"Yes, and she was a good woman," Monroe said, nodding toward the casket again. "She made you hire him. She didn't know about me, either, but she was good to my dad." He closed his eyes. "If I'd known they were gonna do that, I'd have told my dad, and he'd have watched her."

"You made threatening phone calls," Jon began.

"Not me," Monroe replied, and with evident sincerity.

"You were just doing your job when you arrested me. No call to kill a man for that. I don't hold grudges. That's why I called you, to show you I didn't hold it against you. I just wanted you to know I was out."

"Then who…?"

"Check the prints on them shells," Monroe said again. "That's all I'm…oh, God."

He was looking toward the back of the church. A young blonde woman had walked in and was looking at him with cold eyes. He got to his feet, flushed.

"Get him out of here," Jon told the undercover agent, who herded a worried Monroe out the back door of the chapel. "Quick!"

"He told us nothing," Kilraven cautioned the others.

The blonde came up to the family, looking compassionate and sincere. "I'm so sorry about your mother," she said, and seemed really honest.

"Thanks, Phyllis," Jon said with a subdued smile. "We appreciate your coming to the service."

"A lot," Kilraven added. Winnie nodded.

"Yes," Joceline agreed, and smiled warmly.

The woman gave them a shrewd appraisal. "Wasn't that the Monroe man who was arrested for trafficking?" she wondered. "What was he saying to you?"

"Gloating," Jon said coldly.

"Kilraven was going to punch him, but Jon wouldn't let him," Joceline added curtly. "After all he's done, the nerve to show up here!"

The young woman shrugged, but she couldn't hide the gleam of relief in her eyes. "Well, I just wanted to say sorry, about Mrs. Blackhawk," she added. "Such a pity. Gosh, your family has had some real tragedies, hasn't it?"

"Some real tragedies," Kilraven said quietly. "And now one more to add to it." He indicated the casket.

"It must have been devastating," she agreed. "Do they have any idea who might have done it? I mean, that Monroe man made threats, didn't he? Betty told me about the phone calls," she added quickly.

"Lots of threats," Jon said coldly. "And he's going to pay for them very soon."

She smiled. "Good. I hope he does. I'll see you all at the office, then."

"Yes," Jon replied. "Thanks for coming."

"You're very welcome." She looked at the casket with an odd curiosity, smiled at them and walked back to have a seat in the back of the chapel.

The Blackhawks looked at each other, but said nothing. Jon gripped Joceline's hand tightly in his own as the music began and a clear, sweet voice began to sing Cammy's favorite gospel song, "Amazing Grace." Despite all his best efforts to keep his emotions under control, Jon's eyes were wet as the last strong note ended on the song. But so were those of everyone else in the chapel.

THE CRIME LAB was far ahead of Jon when he spoke to Alice Mayfield Jones Fowler, their chief investigator, about the prints on the murder weapon.

"Sure, we got those prints first thing. Criminals always overlook something obvious. Monroe's prints were on the barrel, but someone else's prints were on the shells. Not too smart, to put them back in the gun after they'd been fired."

"Alice, you always put empty shells in the chamber when you store a shotgun," Jon said gently.

"Yes, I know that. I meant that he put back the same shells he'd used, with his fingerprints all over them." She whistled. "I was just checking to make sure you knew that."

"Alice…"

"Anyway, yes, there were prints, and they belong to Bart Hancock."

It was what Jon had thought all along. Harold Monroe was an idiot. He'd never killed anyone or even been connected with murders. Most criminals didn't step outside their comfort zones. Monroe bought and sold children, which was reprehensible, but he wasn't a killer.

"Now what?" Jon asked, thinking aloud.

"Now you get a search warrant…" she began.

"Alice!"

"Hey, I was just thinking aloud, honest, I know the FBI doesn't need to be led by the hand in a murder investigation—" She chuckled, then sobered. "Sorry about your mother, by the way. That was such a shock. I mean, it never occurred to any of us that she'd be a target."

"It should have. I feel guilty."

"You're human, Blackhawk," she said gently. "Don't beat yourself over the head."

"Yes. I guess so."

"If you can connect the murder weapon to Hancock, you've got a pretty good case on circumstantial evidence. Odd thing, there were other fingerprints on the shells, just a partial. But when we ran them through the database, we didn't get even one hit."

"That is odd," Jon agreed, curious. "Any ideas?"

"None. If you can make Hancock talk, he might tell you. I ruled out Dan Jones, by the way. His prints weren't on the shells."

"Even odder."

Jon was thinking, weighing clues. "I may have something even better to cinch the case."

"What?"

"Oh, no. I'm not telling you. Next thing I know, you'll be in Hollywood pitching a murder mystery to some producer."

"Dang. Foiled again!"

"Are you working my mother's case?" he asked.

"Well, I thought I was, but they wouldn't let me into the hotel room," she said. "Marquez said they had another investigator working it."

Odd, he thought again. Marquez usually asked for Jones. Or Fowler, which was her married name. She'd married Harley Fowler, the son of a U.S. senator.

"I guess I was late on the scene." She sighed.

"I guess."

"But if you need help…"

"I'll call. And thanks."

"No problem."

He was now certain that Hancock was responsible for Melly's death and also for Cammy Blackhawk's. What Hancock's daughter had to do with either case was still nebulous, but Jon was going to make sure the man didn't sleaze out of the new charges.

So when he phoned Rick Marquez to request copies of the police report on his mother's death, he was shocked to run into a brick wall.

"No," Rick said at once.

"No?" Jon was taken aback.

"Not yet."

"All I want is the preliminary report…"

"Not yet." Rick hesitated. "I know this case is personal with you. That's why I'm not giving you anything, especially crime scene photos."

"I could get a warrant…"

"Yes, you could, and I'd find a judge to deny it. Maybe the same judge who let Monroe out on bail. Speaking of Monroe, we can't find him anywhere. Would you know anything about that?"

"Who, me?" Jon asked. "Why would I know?"

"He was speaking to you at the funeral home and then he vanished."

"Strange," Jon said evenly.

"Isn't it?"

Jon drew in a long breath. "I spoke to Alice Jones."

"Alice Fowler."

"Yes. She said they checked fingerprints on the shells in the murder weapon in the murder of my niece."

"That's true. We're compiling evidence right now for a warrant to arrest Bart Hancock."

"Good luck getting to him," Jon said coldly. "Isn't he at his uncle's place in the Bahamas?"

"We heard he was."

"Extradition is going to be a lengthy process, even with evidence."

There was a long pause. "Yes."

Jon felt alarm bells going off in the back of his mind. "What's going on, Marquez?" he asked suddenly.

"Why do you think something's going on?"

"Just a feeling."

"I can't tell you anything."

"Can't or won't?"

"Both." There was a pause. "What?" There was muffled conversation. "Sorry, got to go. I'll keep you posted on the investigation. And I'm sorry about your mother."

"Yes, so are we," Jon said heavily.

"I'll be in touch." He hung up.

Jon was slow putting down the phone. There was a click. With a slow smile, he reached for a button and pushed it. Things were beginning to look up.

"I ABSOLUTELY can't believe Harold Monroe, coming up to us at the funeral and denying he was responsible," Joceline told

Jon that evening at her apartment, while they watched their son draw a picture of a camel he'd seen on a news program.

"I can't, either," Jon replied. "But I'm glad."

"Me, too."

"I think we may solve more than one murder, when all the evidence is collected." He shook his head. "I work for the FBI. So does my brother, intermittently. And neither of us knew that Monroe's father worked at the ranch. If we had known, with his record, I'm sure we'd have blamed him for Cammy's murder."

"I can understand why."

"I suppose even criminals have some odd sense of honor." She brushed her hand over Markie's black hair. "You really can draw, my baby."

"Yes, you can." Jon took the pencil away from him, picked him up and placed him on his lap. "You look somewhat like me," he said in a deep, affectionate tone. "Amazing, that I never noticed before."

"You're a lot bigger than me," Markie said, and giggled when Jon tickled him.

Jon hugged the boy warmly. "I love being a father."

"Ouch, Dad, you're squeezing me!" Markie complained.

Jon chuckled and let him escape, back to the table where his pencil and paper were lying. "Of all the surprises of my life, this was the nicest," he said, sighing. He looked at Joceline, loving the sweetness of her expression, the familiarity of her. "You should have told me," he added, but in a tender tone.

"You know why I didn't." She caught his big hand in hers. "I thought it would destroy your life and hurt your career. And I knew your mother would do everything in her power to keep us away from you." She grimaced. "She really was a kind person, under that gruff attitude. I was only just getting to know her. I'm so sorry I didn't have the time."

"So am I." His eyes were sad. "There's a hole in the world."

"And in your heart," she added. She sat down in his lap and hugged him. "Time will help it heal."

He held her close, burying his face in her throat. "Yes."

"Are you sad, Daddy?" Markie asked, coming up on one side. "It's because my grandma died, isn't it?"

"Yes." Jon smiled at him. "It hurts."

"She was mean at first, but then she bought us ice cream." He sighed. "Now I won't have a grandma anymore."

"She would have spoiled him rotten," Jon said when Markie had gone back to his drawing.

"Yes."

He shifted her on his lap with a sigh. "I wonder what Rick Marquez is up to?" he murmured.

"Why do you think he's up to something?"

"He won't let me see the police report on Cammy's death." She blinked. "He won't?"

He eyed her. "You could get it."

"Now, those are protected files behind firewalls," she began.

"And you can hack anything."

She pursed her lips. His eyes were twinkling. "Most anything," she agreed.

"Will you?"

"If you'll bring Markie to visit me in prison," she said under her breath, tongue-in-cheek.

"I'll get you the best criminal lawyer in San Antonio," he promised.

She got up. "Okay. I'll use a false identity and cross my fingers." She went to the computer on the dining room table and sat down to turn on the power.

Ten minutes later, she went back to Jon, frowning.

"What's wrong?" he asked.

"There are no files."

He blinked. "What?"

"No files at all. No photos, no evidence forms, nothing."

"That's not possible," he said curtly. "It's a murder case."

"I know. But nothing has been filed."

He was thinking, working in his mind. "It's only been a few days," he rationalized. "Perhaps they haven't had time to upload photos or other evidence."

She didn't answer him.

He took out his cell phone and called his brother. "Mac," he said. "There are no files on Cammy's murder."

"Have you led Joceline into a life of cybercrime trying to hack protected police files?" came the reply.

"Yes."

"No files, you say."

"Exactly."

"I'll dig around and let you know what I find." He hung up.

"Mac's going to try," he told Joceline. "This is confusing."

Joceline was chewing on the facts herself. Kilraven hadn't been allowed into the hotel room where Cammy died. There had been two strange men at the funeral home, and Jon said the funeral director had been disconcerted when they mentioned an open casket at the service. Now there were no files on the case. She added up those facts and produced a conclusion that she didn't dare voice.

Jon had reached the same conclusion. They looked at each other without speaking.

"There would have been no reason to stage it," she said for both of them.

"Unless they had knowledge of a plot to kill her and set it up to save her," he replied. "Maybe to get evidence that could be used against the would-be shooter and give them time to do more checking."

"Exactly."

His heart lifted suddenly. It might not be the tragedy he'd expected. Cammy might still be alive, in hiding, and Marquez had forbidden any knowledge of it to Jon or Joceline because he suspected someone working with them, someone who might accidentally find out that it was a setup.

Joceline gripped Jon's hand tight. "We could be wrong," she said. "There are plenty of circumstantial things that we're concocting into a theory."

"I know that."

"Is my apartment bugged, you think?" she wondered.

"If it is, we both know who bugged it," he replied. "And the killer can't have planted any listening devices here. They'd have been removed."

Jon's cell phone rang. He answered it.

"Yes, it's bugged, yes, someone did plant listening devices but I found them all," a deep voice with a curt South African accent replied. There was a chuckle. "Your conclusions are very interesting, but I'll say nothing to affirm or deny their correctness. You'll have to sit back and wait for results, like the rest of us."

"Where is Sloane Callum?" Jon asked.

"In a safe place. He put his own life on the line to help us with a project."

"There's a very dangerous person out there," Jon said quietly.

"You have no idea," Rourke replied tersely. "We've made some disturbing discoveries. I can't say any more."

"You've got somebody watching my brother and his wife?"

"Yes, also you and Joceline and the boy."

"All right. But I'd remind you that I do work for the premier law enforcement agency in the country."

"Which would get you carte blanche in this investigation

except that you have one or more suspects in your very own office."

"One or more?" Jon burst out.

"I can't say any more. And don't try to pump Marquez," he added. "I trained him in counterespionage myself. He's incorruptible."

"Damn," Jon muttered.

"You'll like the result. Be patient."

Jon sighed. "Very well. Thanks, Rourke."

"Some odd things may happen tomorrow," Rourke added quietly. "Be on your guard, don't go anywhere alone. Make sure Joceline doesn't leave the building without you."

"What about my son?" Jon asked.

"We have two agents at the school," he replied. "He'll be safe. I give you my word, and I don't give it lightly."

"He'd better be."

"One other thing," he added.

"Yes?"

There was a pause. Jon heard someone else speaking, in a taut, firm tone. Rourke came back on the line. "I can't say anything else. Trust me. I have your best interests at heart."

"Didn't Napoleon make such a statement just before Waterloo?" Jon wondered aloud.

"That's your brother's thing, military history, not yours," he was reminded tongue-in-cheek. "Get a good night's sleep. You're going to need it." He hung up.

Jon looked at Joceline and then at his son with real worry. He didn't know what or how much to tell Joceline. He only hoped whoever was orchestrating this developing plot knew what they were doing. He wished he knew what it was.

CHAPTER FOURTEEN

THE NEXT DAY, Joceline sat at her desk, typing up reports on the computer, with her mind totally not on what she was doing. She was upset because of a hint Jon had given her about today. He'd said to be on her toes, and nothing more. She wondered what he meant. He was unusually protective, and tense, as if he was expecting danger.

Their part-time worker, Phyllis Hicks, had shown up for work, mingling with the other office workers on their floor. Joceline tried not to pay too much attention to her, but she was nervous. The woman had a look in her eyes, on her face, that was disconcerting. She didn't seem quite normal. Especially today.

Joceline averted her gaze to her work and tried not to notice that Phyllis was staring at her pointedly. But when the woman stopped beside her desk, she was forced to look up and smile, as if she knew nothing of the woman's background.

"Hi, Phyllis, how's school going?" she asked.

Phyllis raised an eyebrow. "You have a reputation in the

office for being able to get information that nobody else can find," she said, lowering her voice. "So it's a safe bet that you've checked me out and found something that all the agents who investigated my background missed. I thought I'd covered it up very well," she added with a cold smile. "But I must have missed one little link somewhere."

"Excuse me?" Joceline said carelessly and with a feigned vacant smile.

"You know who my real father is."

"I do?" She smiled again.

"Stop it," Phyllis said, and her eyes took on an odd, feral sort of gleam. "No more games. They've been watching me, Marquez and his friends. My dad told me. He tells me everything. All I have to do is flatter him and make a fuss over him, and he'll dig into files for me. I say it's helping me to learn my job. He buys it, every time."

"He does?"

Phyllis placed her hands on the desk and leaned forward, so that her voice didn't carry. "My dad says they've got a file on me. It shocked him. He thinks they're trying to railroad me on an attempted murder charge, because I told him it was all lies. He was shocked that a good detective like Marquez would target a sweet, helpless little thing like me."

"Are cobras helpless?" Joceline asked.

"They'll never get enough evidence to convict me," she whispered. She smiled and seemed proud of herself, in a sick way. She started talking quickly, as if she couldn't stop. "I persuaded my real daddy into letting me go with him, to make sure Dan Jones did the job on Kilraven's daughter. I was just seventeen, but I was already a dead shot. My daddy taught me. Dan Jones was such a wimp. He couldn't shoot a child. He even cried. I took the shotgun away and killed the little girl with it. It was easy. Really easy. It didn't bother me at all. My daddy said I was a natural." Her eyes gleamed with an insane light while Joceline tried not to gag. "So he talked Jay Copper into letting me do some wet work for them. I could get in places they couldn't. My stepdad knew all sorts of things I could use, and he didn't have a clue he was feeding me information I gave to my real dad. I could even get weapons out of the evidence room and put them back, nobody ever suspected me. Imagine, hiding a murder weapon in an evidence room." She laughed. Her face clenched. "Then that stupid Monroe had to go and claim credit for my kill, mine! He blabbed about the shotgun. I should never have told my real daddy where I put it. You can't tell people anything these days. Nobody can keep his mouth shut!"

"You killed a child," Joceline said, horrified.

"What's one less kid in the world?" she asked blankly. "I was going to do yours, but they wouldn't let me. They said killing his secretary's kid wouldn't hurt him nearly as much as doing his mother." She laughed again, coldly. "So I found out where she was staying, listening in on her conversations with her son, and I took a wheel gun with the serial number filed off and did her, right in her hotel room, while she was on the phone with Kilraven." She laughed harder. "That was so funny. Imagine how he felt when he heard her die and couldn't do a thing!"

Joceline's mouth was half open. The woman was confessing to two murders, in an FBI office, to Joceline and she wasn't wired and the office wasn't bugged. It would be hearsay evidence, no matter what oaths Joceline swore to tell the truth.

"You really are out of your mind," Joceline said tautly.

"Don't say that!" she snapped at the older woman. "They said that about my grandmother because she killed herself. My real daddy told her what I did. She couldn't take it. She overdosed on some pills." She straightened. "She was really weak. But I'm strong. I can do anything, just like my real daddy. He killed Dan Jones. He wouldn't let me go with him that time, but he told me all about it. It was so exciting!" she whispered, her eyes gleaming. "He said Jones cried and begged him and Jay Copper not to kill him. The idiot got religion. He was going to sell out Jay Copper and my real daddy. Well, they got Copper, but they didn't get my daddy and they won't get me, either. And Harold Monroe is going to die. He isn't part of our family anyway—he's just married to my aunt!"

"You can't think they won't find evidence to convict you," Joceline said quietly. "You won't get away with it."

"Who's going to arrest me?" she chided. "And on what evidence—your word? Kilraven and his new wife told them they heard Jay Copper say that my daddy helped him kill that girl, but once the tape was gone, they couldn't prosecute daddy. It was just their word against his."

"How did that tape disappear?"

"I took it out of the evidence room." She smirked. "And we had a friend get in your apartment and take the records that proved I was daddy's illegitimate daughter," she added coldly. "I took the files out of the mainframe computer, here. It's handy, working for the FBI," she added.

"You can't think you'll get away with it," Joceline said.

"Why not?" the other woman asked with a careless laugh. "I've never even been under suspicion." Her eyes narrowed. "Your kid's been lucky so far. Hasn't he?"

Joceline got to her feet. Her blue eyes were glittering as she moved toward the other woman. "If you touch my son, if you even think of touching him, you won't be able to hide anywhere on earth."

"You think you could stop me?" Phyllis replied.

"I think someone has to," Joceline said quietly, "before you hurt someone else's child. You're absolutely insane."

"Don't…say…that!" Phyllis lunged at her, lightning-fast,

pushing her back across the desk. "I'm not crazy!" She had her hands around Joceline's throat, her nails biting in, and Joceline could hardly breathe. If they didn't hurry…!

"And that's enough of that, lady." A gruff voice came from over Phyllis's shoulder. She was pulled upright, turned around and handcuffed in a fluid, easy motion.

"What the hell…?" Phyllis exclaimed.

Joceline got to her feet, a little shaky. Jon put his arm around her, examined her throat and grimaced. She only smiled at him, safe and relieved.

"It may take us a little time to wrap up all the loose ends," Detective Marquez told the furious, red-faced killer, "but we get there." He motioned to the two uniformed officers he'd brought with him, one of whom had Phyllis by the arm. "And notice that I'm reading you your rights. I wouldn't want to leave one single loophole for a defense attorney." He read her the Miranda rights.

"You set me up!" Phyllis exclaimed, glaring furiously at a shell-shocked Joceline.

"Actually Rourke set you up," Jon said coldly, "with a little help from Detectives Marquez here, and Gail Rogers. This time the tapes won't go missing, I promise you. Your stepfather is down at police headquarters trying to explain how he helped you get into the evidence room."

"He won't tell them anything!" she spat.

"Oh, he's up for retirement in six months. I expect he'll tell them whatever they want to know," Jon added. His eyes were cold as ice. "You killed my niece, and my mother. I'll be at every parole hearing until I die. You'll never get out of prison."

"First they have to convict me," she said sweetly, "and they have no evidence."

Jon gave her a quiet stare. "I suppose it didn't occur to you that shotgun shells need to be wiped of prints as well as the barrel of the gun?"

She stared back at him blankly, and then with dawning realization. "Monroe!" she burst out. "That stupid, stupid idiot told them where the murder weapon was hidden!"

"He took the blame for it," Jon lied, "to save you."

She shifted, surprised. "He doesn't even like me."

"You're part of his family, aren't you?" he asked, and surprised himself defending Monroe.

"I guess so." She sighed angrily. "But the idiot put a noose around my neck all the same. My real daddy will take care of him!"

"Oh, I don't think so," Kilraven said, joining them. He smiled coldly at the woman who'd killed his three-year-old daughter. He had to fight the instinct that was telling him to snap her neck before she could even get to jail. "Your real daddy has been arrested and charged with complicity in the murder of my wife and child. You see, there were two sets of fingerprints on those shotgun shells." He didn't add that they wouldn't be able to identify those prints officially until she was arrested and booked and fingerprinted. He was hedging his bets.

She was absolutely at a loss for words. Her face went red, and not from embarrassment. She let out a barrage of curses, some of which had Jon lifting his eyebrows.

"Get her out of here," Jon advised the policemen. He was still afraid that Kilraven might do something regrettable.

"Good idea," Kilraven said icily.

They removed her. Kilraven, Jon and Joceline watched her go with the same expressions.

"What a shock," Jon said heavily.

Detective Marquez came closer, his hands in his pockets. He grimaced. "I'm afraid the shocks aren't over for the day."

"What?" Jon asked hesitantly.

"You have to promise not to hit me," he told the brothers. "It was the only thing I could think of to save her, especially after your employee Sloane Callum phoned me, all upset, and told me that he'd heard what was going down once Cammy Blackhawk got to the hotel. I got an earful about Jay Copper's family tree in the process. So I came up with this idea, to let the killer think she'd scored a direct hit. I had no idea that Rourke had some knowledge of Hollywood-style special effects," he added thoughtfully.

"Special effects?" Jon asked.

Marquez shifted. "Sorry, I was thinking out loud about the guy's background. Yes. Sloane called Monroe and had him pay Phyllis a visit. He knew what sort of gun she carried. While she was out of the room, he switched clips. She fired blanks from a concealed position and thanks to some carefully rigged explosive charges over a Kevlar vest, it looked as if real bullets had caused major damage to Cammy's chest. Phyllis left without checking closer, thank God. It would have ruined the setup and we'd have blown the case."

"Wait a minute," Jon faltered. "Cammy's not dead?"

"She's alive?" Kilraven echoed, dumbfounded.

"Alive and still cursing me for putting the two of you through a mock murder." Marquez sighed. "My medical insurance is paid up, so if you want to punch me…!"

Both brothers grabbed him at the same time and hugged him, even Jon, who was notorious for avoiding displays of public affection.

Joceline laughed, delighted. "What a trick! No wonder you wouldn't let Kilraven or Alice Fowler into the crime scene or give them access to the police report on the 'murder'!"

Marquez glared at her. "Yes, despite your best efforts to hack my computer."

"Oooops!" she said, red-faced.

"About which, fortunately for you, I know nothing," he added.

"Thank goodness!" she said. "I look terrible in orange jumpsuits!"

"Where is she?" Jon asked.

"At the ranch," he replied, chuckling at their surprise. "Sloane said it was the safest place, because he'd kill anything that came near her. He was indignant that a cousin of his was responsible for this mess, even if she was only related to his son by marriage."

"Harold Monroe is his son," Jon reminded Marquez.

"I know. I wired his inmate-friend to record his so-called confession." He laughed. "This has been one incredible case. In all my years with the force, I've never come across anything similar. Well, except for this one case, in my days as a police officer, when a state senator's wife was involved in a grisly murder and went to prison for it. Judd Dunn was involved in that one. So was Cash Grier."

"I remember. The senator was Dunn's best friend. Tragic case. Didn't the senator marry his secretary?" Kilraven asked.

"Yes, they have two little boys now. He's retired from politics and spends his time pushing legislation to help farmers."

"Happy endings."

"Very. I want to see Cammy," Jon said.

"Me, too," his brother seconded.

"We'll all go," Joceline said. "Can you go ask the SAC if we can have the rest of the day off?" she asked Jon.

He grinned. "On my way."

"I'll get back to work before the shock and relief wear off and they start looking for blunt instruments of violence," Marquez mused, glancing from one brother to the other.

"We wouldn't hit you," Jon protested.

"Well, we wouldn't hit you hard," Kilraven amended. And he grinned.

CAMMY was waiting at the front door when the five of them arrived. She grabbed her sons and hugged and hugged them and cried and hugged them some more. They were doing much the same.

Eventually she let them go and embraced Joceline and Winnie and bent to pick up little Markie, who was unsettled by all the emotion.

"It's okay," Joceline told her son, "these are happy tears. We thought your grandmother was...well, that we wouldn't see her again."

"I know. There was a funeral and I couldn't go." He looked at his grandmother and touched her silver-threaded black hair in its high, elegant bun. "I'm so glad you didn't die, Granny."

Her eyes teared up again and she hugged him closer. "Me, too. Oh, I'm so happy!"

"So are we," Winnie murmured, and she hugged Cammy, as well.

A FEW DAYS LATER, they sat around the huge, open fireplace in the living room and talked over the shattering events of the past months.

Sloane Callum started into the room, his cowboy hat gripped in one big hand, but he hesitated when he saw all the people.

Jon got up and went to him, his eyes black and quiet as they met the other man's.

"I know, I'm fired," Callum said heavily. "I should have told you about my own son, and my family connections, long ago. But I thought you wouldn't want to trust me..."

Jon hugged him, hard. "You saved Cammy's life. And because we hired you, your son helped us find the killer of my niece, Melly, and Mac's first wife." He took the other man by the shoulders. "Don't even think about quitting. We owe you."

"All of us," Kilraven agreed quietly.

"Especially me," Cammy added, and smiled at Callum. "I knew you'd be a wonderful addition to the ranch staff. I was right." She looked at her sons and glared. "I'm always right, so you should listen to me when I tell you things for your own good."

"You wanted me to marry Charlene," Jon reminded her.

"And you wanted me to stop seeing Winnie," Kilraven reminded her.

She threw up her hands. "Two little mistakes!" She sighed. They laughed.

"I will try to reform," she said in a gentle tone. "From now on, I'm going to keep out of your business and mind my own." She sat down beside Joceline. "There are just one or two things. Small things. You should take Markie to a lung specialist and let them do tests, and I'll pay for it. You should have a pretty wedding gown. We can go to Neiman Marcus and pick one out. And we should do something about the color scheme in Jon's apartment—there should be bright colors…"

Jon and Kilraven got up. "We're going to buy Callum a beer," they said, then spoiled their exit by bursting into laughter just outside the living room door.

"Now what in the world are they laughing at?" Cammy wondered aloud. "Never mind, about Jon's apartment…" she continued, unabashed.

Joceline and Winnie exchanged amused glances, but they paid rapt attention.

EPILOGUE

PHYLLIS HICKS WAS charged with the murder of Kilraven's first wife and his daughter, as well as the attempted murder of Cammy Blackhawk, and many other charges. She would be put away for a long time, and there would be no other children who would be hurt by her madness.

The murder charges against Harold Monroe were quietly dropped. He vanished out of sight, amidst rumors that he was in some sort of federal protection program. They were only rumors, of course.

Jon and Joceline were married in the interdenominational church in San Antonio that Joceline had attended for years, with flower girls and Markie as ring bearer, and Winnie and Cammy as dual matrons of honor. Many of the San Antonio FBI agents found a way to attend, though some had to watch the ceremony on a DVD later.

Joceline and Markie moved in with Jon, but she kept her job at the office. Cammy argued that she should stay home with Markie, but Jon argued that he'd go nuts if he had to break in a new assistant. He won, too.

Markie's behavior improved to such a degree that any decisions about medication were left for future discussion, perhaps the result of a much more settled home life.

Winnie Kilraven was rushed to the hospital with labor pains just a week before Christmas. She produced a tiny little boy with a thick head of black hair, and big tough McKuen Kilraven cried as he held his son in his arms.

Jon and Joceline put up a Christmas tree in his apartment with ornaments that had been handed down for generations in his family, and some of the small ones she and Markie had accumulated from Christmases past in her apartment. Cammy had contributed a beautiful Swarovski crystal one for their first Christmas together as a family. She and the Kilravens were going to join Jon and Joceline and Markie at the ranch for the yearly mealfest. Joceline was looking forward to it. So was Markie. In view of the near-tragedies, it was going to be a marvelous celebration of life.

The tree was tall and round and tapered and beautiful. Markie just stared at it in awe when Joceline brought him home from day care to find it already set up with the lights blaring in the living room.

"Oh, it's like magic!" he exclaimed, touching it almost reverently.

Jon's arm went around Joceline and pulled her close. He looked down into her soft, loving eyes with absolute wonder. "Yes. It is like magic."

"Daddy, do you love Mommy?" Markie asked him suddenly, looking up at him with big, wide blue eyes.

Joceline was embarrassed. Jon had never said the words, not even when he was the most passionate. "Markie," she began, in protest.

Jon cupped Joceline's face in his big, warm hands. "I love her more than anything or anyone in the world," he said softly, and smiled at her surprise as he bent to kiss her with breathless tenderness.

"More than you love me?" Markie asked plaintively.

Jon chuckled. He picked the boy up in his arms and kissed his hair. "I love both of you more than anything in the world," he amended.

"I love you, too, Daddy." Markie sighed, and hugged the tall man warmly. "I was just thinking," he added thoughtfully. "Wouldn't it be nice if I had a brother like you do?"

Jon looked at Joceline with a wicked smile. "Wouldn't it?" he mused.

Joceline laughed and colored prettily. They hadn't used precautions at all, so much in love that the addition of a child to the family would be a wonder, not a worry. In fact, she was already late on her monthly.

Jon knew. His eyes twinkled.

"Or a sister, I guess," Markie told them. "I could teach her how to draw."

"Truly," Joceline agreed.

Markie looked past them at the majestic Christmas tree. "It's going to be the best Christmas we ever had, Mommy!" he burst out.

She looked at her husband and her child, and her blue eyes were overflowing with joy. "Yes, my darling," she told him. "The best Christmas ever!"

* * * * *

McKettricks
of Texas: Tate

LINDA LAEL MILLER

The daughter of a town marshal, **Linda Lael Miller** is a *New York Times* bestselling author of more than eighty historical and contemporary novels that reflect her love of the West. Raised in Northport, Washington, the self-confessed barn goddess now lives in Spokane, Washington. Her most recent *New York Times* bestsellers include *The Bridegroom* and *The Montana Creeds* trilogy. Dedicated to helping others, Linda personally finances her Linda Lael Miller Scholarships for Women, awarded annually to women seeking to improve their lot in life through education. More information about Linda, her novels and her scholarships is available at www.lindalaelmiller.com. She also loves to hear from readers by mail at PO Box 19461, Spokane, WA 99219, USA.

For Leslee Borger, my fellow cowgirl,
with love and appreciation.

PROLOGUE

Silver Spur Ranch
Blue River, Texas

SPRING THUNDER EXPLODED overhead, fit to cleave the roof right down the middle and blow out every window on all three floors.

Tate McKettrick swore under his breath, while rain pelted the venerable walls like machine-gun fire.

Like as not, the creek would be over the road by now, and he'd have to travel overland to get to town. He was running late—again. And Cheryl, his ex-wife, would blister his ears with the usual accusations, for sure.

He didn't give a damn, she'd say, about their delicate twin daughters, because he'd wanted boys, as rough-and-tumble as he and his brothers had been. That was her favorite dig. She'd never know—because he wasn't about to let on—how that particular remark never failed to sear a few layers off his heart. He would literally have died for Audrey and Ava—the twins were the only redeeming features of a marriage that should never have taken place in the first place.

Since one good jab was never enough for Cheryl, she'd most likely go on to say that being late for their daughters' dance recital was his way of spiting *her,* their mother. He'd *used* his own children, she'd insist—he *knew* she hated it when he was late—yada, yada, yada.

Blah, blah, blah.

Tate didn't have to "use" the twins to get under Cheryl's hide—he'd done that in spades after the divorce by forcing her to live in Blue River, so they could share custody. Audrey and Ava alternated between their mother's place in town and the ranch, a week there, a week here, with the occasional scheduling variation. As soon as he picked them up on the prescribed days, Cheryl was off to some hot spot to hobnob with her fancy friends and all but melt her credit cards.

Tight-jawed with resignation, Tate plunked down on the edge of his bed and reached for the boots he'd polished before shedding his rain-soaked range clothes to take a hasty shower. Clad in stiff new jeans and the requisite long-sleeved white Western shirt, the cowboy version of a tux, he listened with half an ear to the rodeo announcer's voice, a laconic drone spilling from the speakers of the big flat-screen TV mounted on the wall above the fireplace.

He was reaching for the remote to shut it off when he caught his brother's name.

The hairs on Tate's nape bristled, and something coiled in the pit of his stomach, snakelike, fixing to spring.

"...Austin McKettrick up next, riding a bull named Buzz-saw..."

Tate's gaze—indeed, the whole of his consciousness—swung to the TV screen. Sure enough, there was his kid brother, in high-definition, living color, standing on the cat-walk behind the chute, pacing a little, then shifting from one foot to the other, eager for his turn to ride.

The shot couldn't have lasted more than a second or two—another cowboy had just finished a ride and his score was about to be posted on the mega-screen high overhead—but it was long enough to send a chill down Tate's spine.

The other cowboy's score was good, the crowd cheered, and the camera swung back to Austin. He'd always loved cameras, the damn fool, and they'd always loved him right back.

The same went for women, kids, dogs and horses.

He crouched on the catwalk, Austin did, while down in the chute, the bull was ominously still, staring out between the rails, biding his time. The calm ones were always the worst, Tate reflected—Buzzsaw was a volcano, waiting to blow, saving all his whup-ass for the arena, where he'd have room to do what he'd been bred to do: wreak havoc.

Break bones, crush vital organs.

A former rodeo competitor himself, though his event had been bareback bronc riding, Tate knew this bull wasn't just mean; it was two-thousand pounds of cowboy misery, ready to bust loose.

Austin had to have picked up on all that and more. He'd begun his career as a mutton-buster when he was three, riding sheep for gold-stamped ribbons at the county fair, progressed to Little Britches Rodeo and stayed with it from then on. He'd taken several championships at the National High School Rodeo Finals and been a star during his college years, too.

It wasn't as if he didn't know bulls.

Austin looked more cocky than tense; in any dangerous situation, his mantra was "Bring it on."

Tate watched as his brother adjusted his hat again, lowered himself onto the bull's back, looped his hand under the leather rigging and secured it in a "suicide wrap," essentially tying himself to the animal. A moment later, he nodded to the gate men.

Tate stared, unable to look away. He felt an uncanny sensation like the one he'd experienced the night their mom and dad had been killed; he'd awakened, still thrashing to tear free of the last clammy tendrils of a nightmare, his flesh drenched in an icy sweat, the echo of the crash as real as if he'd witnessed the distant accident in person.

He'd known Jim and Sally McKettrick were both gone long before the call came—and he felt the same soul-numbing combination of shock and dread now.

A single, raspy word scraped past his throat. *"No."*

Of course, Austin couldn't hear him, wouldn't have paid any heed if he had.

The bull went eerily still, primal forces gathering within it like a storm, but as the chute gate swung open, the animal erupted from confinement like a rocket from a launchpad, headed skyward.

Buzzsaw dove and then spun, elemental violence unleashed.

Austin stayed with him, spurring with the heels of his boots, right hand high in the air, looking as cool as if he were idling in the old tire-swing that dangled over the deepest part of the swimming hole. Four long seconds passed before he even lost his hat.

Tate wanted to close his eyes, but the message still wasn't making it from his brain to the tiny muscles created for that purpose. He'd had differences with his youngest brother—and some of them were serious—but none of that mattered now.

The clock on the screen seemed to move in slow motion; eight seconds, as all cowboys know, can be an eternity. For Tate, the scene unfolded frame by frame, in a hollow, echoing void, as though taking place one dimension removed.

Finally, the bull made his move and arched above the ground like a trout springing from a lake and then rolling as if determined to turn his belly to the ceiling of that arena, and sent Austin hurtling to one side, but not clear.

The pickup men moved in, ready to cut Austin free, but that bull was a hurricane with hooves, spinning and kicking in all directions.

The bullfighters—referred to as clowns in the old days—were normally called on to distract a bull or a horse, lead it away from the cowboy so he'd have time to get to the fence and scramble over it, to safety.

Under these circumstances, there wasn't much anybody could do.

Austin bounced off one side of that bull and then the other, still bound to it, his body limp. Possibly lifeless.

Fear slashed at Tate's insides.

Finally, one of the pickup men got close enough to cut Austin free of the rigging, curve an arm around him before he fell, and wrench him off the bull. Austin didn't move as the pickup man rode away from Buzzsaw, while the bull-fighters and several riders drove the animal out of the arena.

Tate's cell phone, tucked into the pocket of the sodden denim jacket he'd worn to work cattle on the range that day, jangled. He ignored its shrill insistence.

Paramedics were waiting to lower Austin onto a stretcher. The announcer murmured something, but Tate didn't hear what it was because of the blood pounding in his ears.

The TV cameras covered the place in dizzying sweeps. In the stands, the fans were on their feet, pale and worried, and most of the men took their hats off, held them to their chests, the way they did for the Stars and Stripes.

Or when a hearse rolled by.

Behind the chutes, other cowboys watched intently, a few lowering their heads, their lips moving in private prayer.

Tate stood stock-still in the middle of his bedroom floor, bile scalding the back of his throat. His heart had surged up into his windpipe and swollen there, beating hard, fit to choke him.

Both phones were ringing now—the cell and the extension on the table beside his bed.

He endured the tangle of sound, the way it scraped at his nerves, but made no move to answer.

Onscreen, the rodeo faded away, almost instantly replaced by a commercial for aftershave.

That broke Tate's paralysis; he turned, picked up his discarded jacket off the floor, ferreted through its several pockets for his briefly silent cell phone. It rang in his hand, and he flipped it open.

"Tate McKettrick," he said automatically.

"Holy Christ," his brother Garrett shot back, "I thought you'd never answer! Listen, Austin just tangled with a bull, and it looks to me like he's hurt bad—"

"I know," Tate ground out, trying in vain to recall what city Austin had been competing in that week. "I was watching."

"Meet me at the airstrip," Garrett ordered. "I have to make some calls. I'll be there as soon as I can."

"Garrett, the weather—"

"Screw the weather," Garrett snapped. Nothing scared him—except commitment to one woman. "If you're too chicken-shit to go up in a piss-ant rainstorm like this one, just say so right now and save me a trip to the Spur, okay? *I'm* going to find out where they're taking our kid brother and get there any way I have to, because, goddamn it, this might be goodbye. Do you *get* that, cowboy?"

"I get it," Tate said, after unlocking his jawbones. "I'll be waiting when you hit the tarmac, Top Gun."

Garrett, calling on a landline, had the advantage of hanging up with a crash. Tate retrieved his wallet from the dresser top and his battered leather bomber jacket from the walk-in closet, shrugging into it as he headed for the double doors separating the suite from the broad corridor beyond.

With generations of McKettricks adding wings to the house as the family fortune doubled and redoubled, the place was ridiculously large, over eighteen thousand square feet.

Tate descended one of the three main staircases trisecting the house, the heels of his dress boots making no sound on the hand-loomed runner, probably fashioned for some sultan before the first McKettrick ever set foot in the New World.

Hitting the marble-floored entryway, he cast a glance at the antique grandfather's clock—he hadn't worn a watch since his job with McKettrickCo had evaporated in the wake of the IPO of the century—and shook his head when he saw the time.

Four-thirty.

Audrey and Ava's dance recital had started half an hour ago.

Striding along a glassed-in gallery edging the Olympic-size pool, with its retractable roof and floating bar, he opened his cell phone again and speed-dialed Cheryl.

She didn't say "Hello." She said, *"Where the hell are you,* Tate? Audrey and Ava's big number is *next,* and they keep peeking around the curtain, hoping to see you in the audience and—"

"Austin's been hurt," Tate broke in, aching as he imagined his daughters in their sequins and tutus, watching for his arrival. "I can't make it tonight."

"But it's your week and I have plans…."

"Cheryl," Tate bit out, "did you hear what I said? Austin's hurt."

He could just see her, curling her lip, arching one perfectly plucked raven eyebrow.

"So help me God, Tate, if this is an excuse—"

"It's no excuse. Tell the kids there's been an emergency,

and I'll call them as soon as I can. *Don't* mention Austin, though. I don't want them worrying."

"Austin is hurt?" For a lawyer, Cheryl could be pretty slow on the uptake at times. "What happened?"

Tate reached the kitchen, with its miles of glistening granite counters and multiple glass-fronted refrigerators. Cheryl's question speared him in a vital place, and not just because he wasn't sure he'd ever see Austin alive again.

Suppose it was too late to straighten things out?

What if, when he and Garrett flew back from wherever their crazy brother was, Austin was riding in the cargo hold, in a box?

Tate's eyes burned like acid as he jerked open the door leading to the ten-car garage.

"He drew a bad bull," he finally said, forcing the words out, as spiky-sharp as a rusty coil of barbed wire.

Cheryl drew in a breath. "Oh, my God," she whispered. "He isn't going to—to die?"

"I don't know," Tate said.

Austin's beat-up red truck, one of several vehicles with his name on the title, was parked in its usual place, next to the black Porsche Garrett drove when he was home. The sight gave Tate a pang as he jerked open the door of his mud-splattered extended-cab Silverado and climbed behind the wheel, then pushed the button to roll up the garage door behind him.

"Call when you know anything," Cheryl urged. "Anything at all."

Tate ground the keys in the ignition, and backed out into the rain with such speed that he nearly collided with one of the ranch work-trucks parked broadside behind him.

The elderly cowpuncher at the wheel got out of the way, pronto.

Tate didn't stop to explain.

"I'll call," he told Cheryl, cranking the steering wheel.

He begrudged her that promise, but he couldn't reach his daughters except through his ex-wife.

Cheryl was crying. "Okay," she said. "Don't forget."

Tate shut the phone without saying goodbye.

At the airstrip, he waited forty-five agonizing minutes in his truck, watching torrents of rain wash down the windshield, remembering his kid brother at every stage of his life—the new baby he and Garrett had soon wanted to put up for adoption, the mutton-buster, the high school and college heartthrob.

The man Cheryl swore had seduced her one night in Vegas, when she was legally still Tate's wife.

When the jet, a former member of the McKettrickCo fleet, landed, he waited for it to come to a stop before shoving open the truck's door and making a run for the airplane.

Garrett stood in the open doorway, having lowered the steps with a hydraulic whir.

"He's in Houston," he said. "They're going to operate as soon as he's stable."

Tate pushed past him, dripping rainwater. "What's his condition?"

Garrett raised the steps again, shouldered the door shut and set the latch. "Critical," he said. "According to the surgeon I spoke to, his chances aren't too good."

Tate moved toward the cockpit, using the time his back was turned to Garrett to rub his burning eyes with a thumb and forefinger. "Let's go."

Minutes later, they were in the air, the plane bucking stormy air currents as it fought for every foot of altitude. Lightning flashed, seeming to pass within inches of the wings, the nose, the tail.

Eventually, though, the skies cleared.

When they landed at a private field outside of Houston, an SUV Garrett had rented before leaving the capital waited on the hot, dry asphalt. The key was in the ignition; Garrett took the wheel, and they raced into the city.

They were all too familiar with the route to the best private hospital in Texas. Their parents had died there, a decade before, after an eighteen-wheeler jumped the median and crashed head-on into their car.

A nurse and two administrators met Tate and Garrett in the lobby, all unwilling to meet their eyes, let alone answer their questions.

When they reached the surgical unit, they found Austin lying on a gurney outside a state-of-the-art operating suite, surrounded by a sea of people clad in green scrubs.

Tate and Garrett pushed their way through, then stood on either side of their brother.

Austin's face was so swollen and discolored they wouldn't have recognized him if he hadn't crooked up one side of his mouth in a grin that could only have belonged to him.

"That was one bad-ass bull," he said.

"You're going to be all right," Garrett told Austin, his face grim.

"Hell, yes, I'm going to be all right," Austin croaked out. His eyes, sunken behind folds of purple flesh, arched to Tate. "Just in case, though, there's one thing I need you to know for sure, big brother," he added laboriously, his voice so low that Tate had to bend down to hear him. "I never slept with your wife."

CHAPTER ONE

Three months later

CHERYL'S RELATIVELY SMALL backyard was festooned with streamers and balloons and crowded with yelling kids. Portable tables sagged under custom-made cakes and piles of brightly wrapped presents, while two clowns and a slightly ratty Cinderella mingled with miniature guests, all of them sugar-jazzed. Austin's childhood pony, Bamboozle, trucked in from the Silver Spur especially for the birthday party, provided rides with saintlike equanimity.

Keeping one eye on the horse and the other on his daughters, six years old as of 7:52 that sunny June morning, Tate counted himself a lucky man, for all the rocky roads he'd traveled. Born almost two months before full term, the babies had weighed less than six pounds put together, and their survival had been by no means a sure thing. Although the twins were fraternal, they looked so much alike that strangers usually thought they were identical. Both had the striking blue eyes that ran in the McKettrick bloodline, and their long glossy hair was nearly black, like Cheryl's and his own. His girls were healthy now, thank God, but Tate still worried plenty about them, on general principle. They seemed so fragile to him, too thin, with their long, skinny legs, and Ava wore glasses and a hearing aid that was all but invisible.

Cheryl startled Tate out of his reflections by jabbing him in the ribs with a clipboard. Today, her waist-length hair was wound into a braided knot at the back of her neck. "Sign this," she ordered, sotto voce.

Tate had promised himself he'd be civil to his ex-wife, for the twins' sake. Looking down into Cheryl's green eyes— she'd been a beauty queen in her day—he wondered what he'd been drinking the night they met.

Gorgeous as Cheryl was, she flat-out wasn't his type, and she never had been.

He glanced at the paper affixed to the clipboard and frowned, then gave all the legalese a second look. It was basically a permission slip, allowing Audrey and Ava to participate in something called the Pixie Pageant, to be held around the time school started, out at the Blue River Country Club. Under the terms of their custody agreement, Cheryl needed his approval for any extracurricular activity the children took part in. It had cost him plenty to get her to sign off on that one.

"No," he said succinctly, tucking the clipboard under one arm, since Cheryl didn't look like she intended to take it back.

The former Mrs. McKettrick, once again using her maiden name, Darbrey, rolled her eyes, patted her sleek and elegant hair. "Oh, for God's sake," she complained, though he had to give her points for keeping her voice down. "It's just a harmless little pageant, to raise money for the new tennis court at the community center—"

Tate's mind flashed on the disturbing film clips he'd seen of kids dolled up in false eyelashes, blusher and lipstick, like Las Vegas showgirls, prancing around some stage. He leaned in, matching his tone to hers. "They're *six,* Cheryl," he reminded her. "Let them be little girls while they can."

His former wife folded her tanned, gym-toned arms. She looked good in her expensive daffodil-yellow sundress, but the mean glint in her eyes spoiled the effect. "*I* was in pageants from the time I was five," she pointed out tersely, "and I turned out okay." Realizing too late that she'd opened an emotional pothole and then stepped right into it, she made a slight huffing sound.

"Debatable," Tate drawled, plastering a smile onto his mouth because some of the moms and nannies were looking in their direction, and they'd stirred up enough gossip as it was.

Cheryl flushed, toyed with one tasteful gold earring. "Bastard," she whispered, peevish. "Why do you have to be so damn pigheaded about things like this?"

He laughed. Hooked his thumbs through the belt loops of his jeans. Dug in his heels a little—both literally and figuratively. "If other people want to let their kids play Miss This-That-and-the-Other-Thing, that's their business. It's probably harmless fun, but *mine* aren't going to—not before they're old enough to make the choice on their own, anyhow. By that time, I hope Audrey and Ava will have more in their heads than makeup tips and the cosmetic uses of duct tape."

Eyes flashing, Cheryl looked as though she wanted to put out both hands and shove him backward into the koi pond—or jerk the clipboard from under his arm and bash him over the head with it. She did neither of those things—she didn't want a scene any more than he did, though her reasons were different. Tate cared about one thing and one thing only: that his daughters had a good time at their birthday party. Cheryl, on the other hand, knew a public dustup would make the rounds of the country club and the Junior League before sundown.

She had her image to consider.

Tate, by contrast, didn't give a rat's ass what anybody thought—except for his daughters, that is, and a few close friends.

So they glared at each other, he and this woman he'd married years ago, squaring off like two gunfighters on a dusty street. And then Ava slipped between them.

"Don't fight, okay?" she pleaded anxiously, the hot Texas sunlight glinting on the smudged lenses of her glasses. "It's our *birthday,* remember?"

Tate felt his neck pulse with the singular heat of shame. So much for keeping the ongoing hostilities between Mommy and Daddy under wraps.

Cheryl smiled wickedly and rested a manicured hand on Ava's shoulder, left all but bare by the spaghetti strap holding up her dress—a miniature version of her mother's outfit. Audrey's getup was the same, except blue.

"Your daddy," Cheryl told the child sweetly, "doesn't want you and Audrey to compete in the Pixie Pageant. I was trying to change his mind."

Good luck with that, Tate thought, forcibly relaxing the muscles in his jaws. He tried for a smile, for Ava's sake, but the effort was a bust.

"That stuff is dumb anyway," Ava said.

Audrey appeared on the scene, as though magnetized by an opinion at variance with her own. "No, it *isn't,*" she protested, with her customary spirit. "Pageants are good for building self-confidence and making friends, and if you win, you get a banner and a trophy *and* a tiara."

"I see you've been coaching them to take the party line," Tate told Cheryl.

Cheryl's smile was dazzling. He'd spent a fortune on those pearly whites of hers. Through them, she said, "Shut up, Tate."

Ava, always sensitive to the changing moods of the parental units, started to cry, making a soft, sniffly sound that tore at Tate's heart. "We're only going to be six *once*," she said. "And everybody's looking!"

"Thank heaven we're only going to be six once," Audrey interjected sagely, folding her arms Cheryl-style. "I'd rather be forty."

Tate bent his knees, scooped up Ava in the crook of one arm and tugged lightly at Audrey's long braid with his free hand. Ava buried her face in his shoulder, bumping her glasses askew. He felt tears and mucus moisten the fabric of his pale blue shirt.

"Forty?" she said, voice muffled. "Even *Daddy* isn't that old!"

"You're such a baby," Audrey replied.

"Enough," Tate told both children, but he was looking at Cheryl as he spoke. "When is this shindig supposed to be over?"

They'd opened presents, devoured everything but the cakes and competed for prizes a person would expect to see on a TV game show. What else was there to do?

"Why can't you just stop fighting?" Ava blurted.

"We're *not* fighting, darling," Cheryl pointed out quietly, before turning to sweep her watchful friends and the nannies up in a benign smile. "And stop carrying on, Ava. It isn't becoming—or ladylike."

"Can we go out to the ranch, Daddy?" Ava asked him plaintively, ignoring her mother's comment. "I like it better there, because nobody fights."

"Me, too," Tate agreed. It was his turn to take the kids, and he'd been looking forward to it since their last visit. Giving them back was always a wrench.

"Nobody fights at the ranch?" Audrey argued, sounding way too bored and way too sophisticated for a six-year-old. Yeah, she was a prime candidate for the Pixie Pageant, all right, Tate thought bitterly—bring on the mascara and enough hairspray to rip a new hole in the ozone layer, and don't forget the feather boas and the fishnet stockings.

Audrey drew a breath and went right on talking. "I guess you don't remember the day Uncle Austin came home from the hospital after that bull hurt him so bad, before he started rehab in Dallas, and how he told Daddy and Uncle Garrett to stay out of his part of the house unless they wanted a belly full of buckshot."

Cheryl arched one eyebrow, triumphant. For all their land, cattle, oil shares and cold, hard cash, the McKettricks were just a bunch of Texas rednecks, as far as she was concerned. She'd grown up in a Park Avenue high-rise, a cherished only child, after all, her mother an heiress to a legendary but rapidly dwindling fortune, her father a famous novelist, of the literary variety.

But, please, nobody mention that dear old Mom snorted coke and would sleep with anything in pants, and Dad ran through the last of his wife's money and then his surprisingly modest earnings as the new Ernest Hemingway.

Cheryl had never gotten over the humiliation of having to wait tables and take out student loans to put herself through college and law school.

"I wonder what my attorney would say," Cheryl intoned, "if I told him the children are exposed to *guns,* out there on the wild and wooly Silver Spur."

While Tate couldn't argue that there weren't firearms on the ranch—between the snakes and all the other dangers inherent to the land, firepower might well prove to be a necessity at any time—it was a stretch to say the girls were "exposed" to them. Every weapon was locked up in one of several safes, and the combinations changed regularly.

"I wonder what *mine* would say," Tate retorted evenly, the

fake smile aching on his face, "if he knew about your plans for this week."

"Stop," Ava begged.

Tate sighed, kissed his daughter smartly on the forehead, and set her on her feet again. "Sorry, sweetheart," he said. "Say goodbye and thanks to your friends. The party's over."

"They haven't even sung the song I taught them," Cheryl said.

Ava leaned against Tate's hip. "We're not good singers at all," she confided.

Somewhat to Tate's surprise, it was Audrey, the performer in the family, who turned on one sandaled heel, faced the assemblage and announced cheerfully, "You can all go home now—my dad says the party's over."

Cheryl winced.

The kids—and the pony—seemed relieved. So did the nannies, though the proper term, according to Cheryl, was *au pairs.* The mothers, many of whom Tate had known since kindergarten and dated in high school between all-too-frequent breakups with Libby Remington, the great love of his youth, if not his entire life, hid bitchy little smiles with varying degrees of success.

"The girls are a little tired," Cheryl explained, with convincing sincerity. "All this excitement—"

"Can we ride horses when we get to the ranch?" Audrey called, from halfway across the yard. "Can we swim in the pool?"

Tate made damn sure he didn't smile at this indication of how "tired" his daughters were, but it was hard.

Ava remained at his side, both arms clenched around his waist now.

"Their suitcases," Cheryl said tightly, "are in the hall."

"Let's load Bamboozle in the trailer," Tate told Ava, gently easing out of her embrace. "Then we'll get your stuff and head for the ranch."

Ava peeled herself away from Tate, walked over and took Bamboozle by the bridle strap, patiently waiting to lead the elderly animal to the trailer hitched to the back of Tate's truck. Audrey had disappeared into the house, on some mission all her own.

"Don't help," Cheryl snapped, out of one side of her mouth. "You've already done enough, Tate McKettrick."

"I live to delight you in every possible way, Cheryl."

Audrey poked her head out between the French doors standing a little ajar between the living room and the patio. "Can we stop at the Perk Up on the way out of town, Dad?" she wanted to know, as calmly as if the backyard weren't full of dismissed guests. "Get some of those orange smoothie things, like before?"

Tate grinned. "Sure," he told his daughter, even though the thought of stopping at Libby's coffee shop made the pit of his stomach tighten. He'd only gone in there the last time because he'd known Libby was out of town, and her sister, Julie, was running the show.

Which was ridiculous. They'd managed to avoid each other for years now, no mean trick in such a small town, but it was getting to be too damn much work.

"Just what they need—more sugar," Cheryl muttered, shaking her head as she walked away, her arms still crossed in front of her chest, only more tightly now.

Tate held his tongue. *He* hadn't been the one to serve cake and ice cream and fruit punch by the wheelbarrow load all afternoon.

Cheryl kept walking.

Tate and Ava led the pony into the horse trailer, which, along with his truck, took up at least three parking spaces on the shady street in front of Cheryl's house. He'd bought the place for her as a part—a *small* part—of their divorce settlement.

"Boozle might get lonely riding in this big trailer all by himself," Ava fretted, standing beside the pony while he slurped up water from a bucket. "Maybe I should ride back here with him, so he'd have some company."

"Not a chance," Tate said affably, dumping a flake of hay into the feeder for the pony to munch on, going home. "Too dangerous."

Ava adjusted her glasses. "Audrey really wants to be in that Pixie Pageant," she said, her voice small. "She's going to nag you three ways from Sunday about it, too."

Tate bit back a grin. "I think I can handle a little nagging," he said lightly. "Let's go get your stuff and hit the road, Shortstop."

"I probably wouldn't win anyway," Ava mused wistfully, stopping her father cold.

"Win what?" Tate asked.

Ava giggled, but it was a strained sound, like she was forcing it. "The *Pixie Pageant,* Dad. Keep up, will you?"

Tate's throat went tight, but he managed a chuckle. "Sure, you'd win," he said. "And that's another reason I won't let you enter in the first place. Just think how bad all those other little girls would feel."

"Audrey could be Miss Pixie," Ava speculated thoughtfully, a small, light-rimmed shadow standing there in the horse trailer. "She can twirl a baton and everything. I keep on dropping mine."

"Audrey isn't entering," Tate said. Bamboozle was between them; he removed the pony's saddle and blanket, ran a hand along his sweaty back. "She'll just have to content herself with being Miss *McKettrick,* at least for the foreseeable future."

Ava mulled that over for a few moments, chewing her lower lip. "Do you think I'll be pretty when I grow up, Dad?"

Tate moved to the back of the trailer, jumped down, turned and held out his arms for Ava, even though she could have walked down the ramp. "No," he said, as she came within reach. "I think you'll be beautiful, like you are right now."

Ava felt featherlight as he swung her to the ground, and it gave him a pang. Was it his fault that the girls had been born too soon? Was there something he could have done to prevent all the struggles they'd faced just getting through infancy?

"You're only saying that because you're my dad."

"I'm saying it because it's true," Tate said.

Ava stepped back while he slid the ramp into place under the trailer, then shut and latched the doors. "Mommy says it's never too soon to think about becoming a woman," she ventured. "Things we do now could affect our whole, *entire* lives, you know."

Tate kept his back to the child, so she wouldn't see the fury in his face. He spoke in the most normal tone he could summon. "You'll only be a little girl for a few years," he answered carefully. "Just concentrate on that for now, okay? Because 'becoming a woman' will take care of itself."

Wasn't it only yesterday that the twins were newborns, making a peeping sound instead of squalling, like most babies, hooked up to tubes and wires, dwarfed by their incubators at the hospital in Houston? Now, suddenly, they were six. He'd be walking them down the aisle at their weddings before he knew what hit him, he thought bleakly.

He shoved one hand through his hair, longing to get back to the ranch and pull on battered jeans that had never known the heat of an iron. Shed the spiffy shirt, so fresh from the box that the starch in the fabric chafed his skin.

On the ranch, he could breathe, although he'd seriously considered moving out of the mansion, taking up residence in the old bunkhouse or a simple single-wide down by one of the bends in the creek.

Mothers and nannies streamed past, herding grouchy children toward various cars and minivans. A few of the women spoke to Tate, most of them cordial, while a few others wished Ava a happy birthday in subdued tones and ignored him completely.

Tate wasn't much for chatting, but he was friendly enough. When somebody spoke to him, he spoke back.

A scraping sound alerted him to Audrey, dragging her suitcase down the front walk on its wheels. He went to take the bag from her, stowed it in the front seat, on the passenger side, where his dog, Crockett, used to ride. Crockett had died of old age more than a year before, but Tate still forgot he wasn't around sometimes and stood with the truck door open, waiting to hoist his sidekick aboard.

"You got your bag packed?" he asked Ava, when she scrambled into the back seat, with Audrey. They both had those special safety rigs, booster chairs with straps and hooks.

"I've got plenty of clothes at the ranch," Ava responded, with a shake of her head. One of the pink barrettes holding her bangs out of her face had sprung loose, and her braid was coming undone. "Let's go before Mom makes us come back and sing."

Tate laughed, rounded the front of the truck and got behind the wheel.

"Beauty-Shop Betsey," Audrey scoffed. "What possessed Jeffrey's mom to buy us doll heads with curlers?" She'd been talking like a grown-up since she was two.

"Hey," Tate said, starting up the engine, waiting for the flock of departing vans and Volvos to thin out a little. God only knew when Blue River, official population 8,472, had last seen a traffic snarl like this. "If somebody goes to all the trouble of buying you a birthday present, you ought to appreciate it."

"Mom said we could exchange the stuff we don't want,"

Audrey informed him, with a touch of so-there in her tone. "Everybody included gift receipts."

Tate figured it was high time to change the subject. "How about those orange smoothies?" he asked.

TATE MCKETTRICK, LIBBY REMINGTON thought, watching as he drew his truck and horse trailer to a stop in front of her shop, got out and strode purposefully toward the door.

It bothered her that after all this time the sight of him still made her heart flutter and her stomach jump. Damn the man, with his dark, longish hair, ink-blue eyes, and that confident, rolling way he moved, as though he'd greased his hip sockets.

Although it was growing, with a population now of almost 9,000, Blue River wasn't exactly a metropolis, and that meant she and Tate ran into each other from time to time. Whenever they did, they'd nod and quickly head in separate directions, but they'd *never* sought each other out.

Poised to turn the "Open" sign to "Closed," Libby closed her eyes for a moment, hoping he was a mirage. A figment of her fevered imagination.

He wasn't, of course.

When she looked again, he was standing just on the other side of the glass door, peering through the loop in the *P* in *Perk Up,* grinning.

A McKettrick—a pedigree in that part of the country— Tate was used to getting what he wanted, including service on a Sunday afternoon, when the store closed early.

Libby sighed, turned the dead bolt, and opened the door.

"Two orange smoothies," he said, without preamble. "To go."

Libby looked past him, saw his twin daughters in the back seat of his fancy truck. An old grief rose up within her, one she'd worked hard to lay to rest. From the time she'd fallen for Tate, back in second grade, she'd planned on marrying him when they both grew up, been bone-certain *she'd* be the one to have his babies.

"Where's Crockett?" she asked, without intending to.

Sadness moved in Tate's impossibly blue eyes. "Had to have him put down a while back," he said. "He was pretty old, and then he got sick."

"I'm sorry," Libby said, because she was. For the dog.

"Thanks," he answered.

She stepped back to let Tate in, against her better judgment. "I'm fostering a couple of mixed breeds, because the shelter is full again. Want one—or, better yet, both?"

Tate shook his head. Light caught in his ebony hair, where the comb ridges still showed. "Just a couple of those smoothie things. Orange. Light on the sugar, if that's an option."

Libby stepped behind the counter, more because she wanted to put some kind of solid barrier between herself and Tate than to mix the drinks he'd requested. Her gaze strayed to the kids waiting in the truck again. They both looked like their father. "Will there be anything else?"

"No," Tate said, taking out his beat-up wallet. "How much?"

Libby told him the price of two orange smoothies, with tax, and he laid the money on the countertop. There were at least three drive-through restaurants on the outskirts of town; he'd pass them coming and going from the Silver Spur. So why had he stopped at her store, on Blue River's narrow main street, with a horse trailer hitched to his huge phallic symbol of a truck?

"You're sure you don't want something for yourself?" she asked lightly, and then wished she'd kept her mouth shut.

Tate's grin tilted to one side. He smelled of sun-dried laundry and aftershave and pure *man*. A look of mischief danced in his eyes.

When he spoke, though, he said, "It's their birthday,"

accompanied by a rise and fall of his powerful shoulders. His blue shirt was open at the throat, and she could see too much—and not quite enough—of his chest.

Libby whipped up the drinks, filling two biodegradable cups from a pitcher, attached the lids and set them next to the cash register. "Then maybe you'd like to give them a dog or two," she replied, with an ease she didn't feel. Being in such close proximity to Tate rattled her, but it probably didn't show. "Since it's their birthday."

"Their mother would have a fit," he said, reaching for the cups. His hands were strong, calloused from range work. Despite all that McKettrick money, he wasn't afraid to wade into a mudhole to free a stuck cow, set fence posts in the ground, buck bales or shovel out stalls.

It was one of the reasons the locals liked him so much, made them willing to overlook the oil wells, now capped, and the ridiculously big house and nearly a hundred thousand acres of prime grassland, complete with springs and creeks and even a small river.

He was one of them.

Of course, the *locals* hadn't been dumped because he'd gotten some other woman pregnant just a few months after he'd started law school.

No, that had happened to *her*.

She realized he was waiting for her to respond to his comment about his ex-wife. *Their mother would have a fit.*

Can't have that, Libby thought, tightening her lips.

"The ice is melting in those smoothies," she finally said. Translation: *Get out. It hurts to look at you. It hurts to remember how things were between us before you hooked up with somebody you didn't even love.*

Tate grinned again, though his eyes looked sad, and then he turned sideways, ready to leave. "Maybe we'll stop by your place and have a look at those dogs after all," he said. "Would tomorrow be good?"

He'd stayed with Cheryl-the-lawyer for less than a year after the twins were born. As soon as the babies began to thrive, he'd moved Cheryl and his infant daughters into the two-story colonial on Oak Street.

The gossip had burned like a brush fire for months.

"That would be fine," Libby said, back from her mental wanderings. Tate McKettrick might have broken her heart, but he'd loved his ancient, arthritic dog, Davy Crockett. And she needed to find homes for the pair of pups.

Hildie, her adopted black Lab, normally the soul of charity, was starting to resent the canine roommates, growling at them when they got too near her food dish, baring her teeth when they tried to join her on the special fluffy rug at the foot of Libby's bed at night. The newcomers, neither more than a year old, seemed baffled by this reception, wagging their tails uncertainly whenever they ran afoul of Hildie, then launching right back into trouble.

They would be very happy out there on the Silver Spur, with all that room to run, Libby thought.

A rush of hope made the backs of her eyes burn as she watched Tate move toward the door.

"Six?" she said.

Tate, shifting the cups around so he could open the door, looked back at her curiously, as though he'd already forgotten the conversation about the dogs, if not Libby herself.

"I close at six," Libby said, fanning herself with a plastic-coated price list even though the secondhand swamp cooler in the back was working fine, for once. She didn't want him thinking the heat in her face had anything to do with him, even though it did. "The shop," she clarified. "I close the shop at six tomorrow. You could stop by the house and see the dogs then."

Tate looked regretful for a moment, as though he'd already changed his mind about meeting the potential adoptees. But then he smiled in that way that made her blink. "Okay," he said. "See you a little after six tomorrow night, then."

Libby swallowed hard and then nodded.

He left.

She hurried to lock the door again, turned the "Closed" sign to the street, and stood there, watching Tate stride toward his truck, so broad-shouldered and strong and confident.

What was it like, Libby wondered, to live as though you owned the whole world?

On the off chance that Tate might glance in her direction again, once he'd finished handing the cups through the window of his truck to the girls, Libby quickly turned away.

She took the day's profits from the till—such as they were—and tucked the bills and checks into a bank deposit bag. She'd hide them in the usual place at home, and stop by First Cattleman's in the morning, during one of the increasingly long lulls in business.

The house she'd lived in all her life was just across the alley, and Hildie and the pups were in the backyard when she approached the gate, Hildie lying in the shade of the only tree on the property, the foster dogs playing tug-of-war with Libby's favorite blouse, which had either fallen or been pulled from the clothesline.

Seeing her, the pups dropped the blouse in the grass—the lawn was in need of mowing, as usual—and yipped in gleefully innocent greeting. Libby didn't have the heart to scold them, and they wouldn't have understood anyway.

With a sigh, she retrieved the blouse from the ground and stayed bent long enough to acknowledge each of the happy-eyed renegades with a pat on the head. "You," she said sweetly, "are very, *very* bad dogs."

They were ecstatic at the news. A matched set, they both had golden coats and floppy ears and big feet. While Hildie looked on, nonplussed, they barked with joy and took a fren-

zied run around the yard, knocking over the recycling bin
in the process.

Hildie finally rose from her nest under the oak, stretched
and ambled slowly toward her mistress.

Libby leaned to ruffle Hildie's ears and whisper, "Hang in
there, sweet girl. With any luck at all, those two will be living
the high life out on the Silver Spur by tomorrow night."

Hildie's gaze was liquid with adoration as she looked up
at Libby, panting and swinging her plume of a tail.

"Suppertime," Libby announced, to all and sundry,
straightening again. She led the way to the back door, the
three dogs trailing along behind her, single file, Hildie in the
lead.

The blouse proved unsalvageable. Libby flinched a little,
tossing it into the rag bag. The blue fabric had flattered her,
accentuating the color of her eyes and giving her golden
brown hair some sparkle.

Easy come, easy go, she thought philosophically, although, in truth, nothing in her life had *ever* been easy.

The litany unrolled in her head.

She'd paid $50 for that blouse, *on sale.*

The economy had taken a downturn and her business reflected that.

Marva was back, and she was more demanding every day.

And as if all that weren't enough, Libby had two dogs in
dire need of good homes—she simply couldn't afford to keep
them—and she'd already pitched the pair to practically every
other suitable candidate in Blue River with no luck. Jimmy-
Roy Holter was eager to take them, but he wanted to name
them Killer and Ripper, *plus* he lived in a camper behind his
mother's house, surrounded by junked cars, and had bred pit
bulls to sell out of the back of his truck, along a busy stretch
of highway, until an animal protection group in Austin had
forced him to close down the operation.

Libby washed her hands at the sink, rubbed her work-chafed hands down the thighs of her blue jeans since she was out of paper towels and all the cloth ones were in the wash.

No, as far as placing the pups in a good home was concerned, Tate McKettrick was her only hope. She'd have to deal with him.

Damn her lousy-assed luck.

CHAPTER TWO

BY THE TIME they got to the ranch, Audrey and Ava were streaked pale orange from the smoothie spills and had developed dispositions too reminiscent of their mother's for Tate's comfort. The minute he brought the truck to a stop alongside the barn, they were out of their buckles and car seats and hitting the ground like storm troopers on a mission, pretty much set on pitching a catfight, right there in the dirt.

Tate stepped between them before the small fists started flying and loudly cleared his throat. The eldest of three brothers, he'd had some practice at keeping the peace—though he'd been an instigator now and again himself. "One punch," he warned, "*just one,* and nobody rides horseback or uses the pool for the whole time you're here."

"What about kicks?" Audrey demanded, knuckles resting on her nonexistent hips. "Is kicking allowed?"

Tate bit back a grin. "Kicks are as bad as punches," he said. "Equal punishment."

Both girls looked deflated—he guessed they had that McKettrick penchant for a good brawl. If their features and coloring hadn't told the story, he'd have known they were his just by their tempers.

"Let's put Bamboozle back in his stall and make sure the other horses are taken care of," Tate said, when neither of his daughters spoke. "Then you can shower—in separate parts of the house—and we'll hit the pool."

"I'd rather hit Ava," Audrey said.

Ava started for her sister, mad all over again, and once more, Tate interceded deftly. How many times had he hauled Garrett and Austin apart, in the same way, when *they* were kids?

"You couldn't take me anyhow," Audrey taunted Ava, and then she stuck out her tongue and the battle was on again. The girls skirted him and went for each other like a pair of starving cats after the same fat canary.

Tate felt as if he were trying to herd a swarm of bees back into a hive, and he might not have untangled the girls before they did each other some harm if Garrett hadn't sprinted out of the barn and come to his aid.

He got Audrey around the waist from behind and hoisted her off her feet, and Tate did the same with Ava. And both brothers got the hell kicked out of their knees, shins and thighs before the twin-fit finally subsided.

There was a grin in Garrett's eyes, which were the same shade of blue as Tate's and Audrey's and Ava's, as he looked at his elder brother over the top of his niece's head. "Well," he drawled, as the twins gasped in delight at his mere presence, "*this* is a fine how-do-you-do. And after I drove all the way from Austin to be here, too. Why, I have half a mind to send your birthday present right back to Neiman Marcus and pretend this is just any old day of the week, nothing special."

Simultaneously, Tate and Garrett set their separate charges back on their sandaled feet.

Audrey smoothed her crumpled sundress and her hair— females of all ages tended to preen when Garrett was around—and asked, with hard-won dignity, "What did you get us, Uncle Garrett?"

Last year, Tate remembered with a tightening along his jawline, it had been life-size porcelain dolls, custom-made by some artist in Austria, perfect replicas of the twins themselves. He was glad the things were at Cheryl's—they gave him the creeps, staring blankly into space. He'd have sworn he'd seen them breathe.

"Why don't you go around to the kitchen patio and find out?" Garrett suggested mysteriously. "Then you'll know whether it's worth behaving yourselves for or not."

Hostilities forgotten—for the time being anyway—the girls ran squealing for the wide sidewalk that encircled the gigantic house.

Whatever Garrett had bought for Audrey and Ava, it was sure to make Tate's offering—a croquet set from Wal-Mart—look puny and ill-thought-out by comparison.

Not that he put a lot of stock in comparison.

"I thought you were in the capital, fetching and carrying for the senator," Tate said, taking his brother's measure in a sidelong glance.

Garrett chuckled and slapped him—a little too hard—on one shoulder. "Sorry I missed the shindig in town," he said, ignoring the remark about his employer. "But I managed to get here, in spite of meetings, a press conference and at least one budding scandal neatly avoided. That's pretty good."

Tate sucked in a breath, let it out. Jabbed at the dirt with the heel of one boot. Garrett was a generous uncle and a good brother, for the most part, but he was living the wrong kind of life for a Texas McKettrick, and he didn't seem to know it. "I don't know what gets into those two," Tate said, shoving a hand through his hair. As far as he knew, he hadn't been in smoothie-range on the ride home, but he felt sticky all over just the same.

Whoops of delight echoed from the distant patio and Esperanza, the middle-aged housekeeper who had worked in that house since their parents' wedding day, could be heard chattering in happy Spanish.

"They'll be fine," Garrett said lightly. Easy for an uncle to say, not so simple for a father.

"What the hell did you get them this time?" Tate asked, starting in the direction of the hoopla. His mood was shifting again, souring a little. He kept thinking about that damn croquet set. "Thoroughbred racehorses?"

Garrett kept pace, grinning. He usually enjoyed Tate's discomfort—unless someone else was causing it. He was no fan of Cheryl's, that was for sure. "Now, why didn't I think of that?"

"Garrett," Tate warned, "I'm serious. Audrey and Ava are six years old. They have more toys than they could use in ten lifetimes, and I'm trying not to raise them like heiresses—"

"They *are* heiresses," Garrett pointed out, just as, a beat late, Tate had realized he would. "Over and above their trust funds."

"That doesn't mean they ought to be spoiled, Garrett."

"You're just too damn serious about everything," Garrett replied.

Just then, Ava ran to meet them, glasses sticky-lensed and askew, her grubby face flushed with excitement. "It's our very own *castle!*" she whooped. "Esperanza says some men brought it on a flatbed truck and it took them *all day* to put the pieces together!"

"Christ," Tate muttered.

"A crew will be here next week sometime, to dig the moat," Garrett told Ava. He might have been promising her a dress for one of her dolls, the way he made it sound.

"The *moat?*" Tate growled. "You're kidding, right?"

Garrett laughed. Would have given Tate another whack on the back if Tate hadn't sidestepped him in time. "What's a castle without a moat?"

Ava danced with excitement, as spindly legged as a spring deer. "There are *turrets,* Dad, and each one has a banner flying from the top. One says 'Audrey' and one says 'Ava'! There are stairs and rooms and there's even a plastic fireplace that lights up when you flip a hidden switch—"

Man, Tate thought grimly, that croquet set was going to be the clinker gift of the century. Damned if he was about to shop again, though, and he hadn't set foot in Neiman Marcus since he was sixteen, when his mother dragged him there to pick out a suit for the junior prom.

He'd endured that only because Libby Remington was his date, and he'd wanted to impress her.

Tate rustled up a grin for his daughter, but his swift glance at Garrett was about as friendly as a splash of battery acid. "A castle with turrets and flags and a prospective moat," he drawled. "Every kid in America ought to have one."

"You think *I* overdid it?" Garrett teased. "Austin had a line on a retired circus elephant—rehab is boring him out of his ever-lovin' mind, so he cruises the Internet on his laptop a lot—until I talked him out of it. Trust me, you could have done a lot worse than a *castle,* big brother."

Right up until he rounded the last corner of the house before the kitchen patio and the acre of lawn abutting it, Tate hoped the thing would turn out to be no bigger than your average dollhouse.

No such luck. It dwarfed the equipment shed where he kept the field tractor, a couple of horse trailers, several riding lawn mowers and four spare pickup trucks. Set on rock slabs, the castle itself was made of some resin-type material, resembling chiseled stone, and stood so tall that it blotted out part of the sky.

Audrey, wearing a pointed princess hat with glittered-on stars and moons and a tinsel tassel trailing from it, waved happily from an upper window.

Tate turned to Garrett, one eyebrow raised. "What? No drawbridge?"

"That would have been a little over the top," Garrett said modestly.

"Ya think?" Tate mocked.

Esperanza, beaming, flapped her apron, resembling a portly bird with only one wing as she inspected the monstrosity from all sides.

Tate waited until Princess Audrey had descended from the tower to fling herself at Garrett in a fit of gratitude—soon to be joined by Ava—before giving one wall a hard shove with the flat of his right hand.

The structure seemed sound, though he'd want to inspect every inch of it, inside and out, to make sure.

"Am I the only one who thinks this is ridiculous?" he asked. "An obscene display of conspicuous consumption?"

"The plastic is all recycled," Garrett avowed, all but reaching around to pat himself on the back.

Tate rolled his eyes and walked away, leaving Garrett and Esperanza and the girls to admire McKettrick Court and returning to the trailer to unload poor old Bamboozle. He settled the pony in his stall, gave him hay and a little grain, and moved to the corral fence to look out over the land, where the horses and cattle grazed in their separate pastures.

At least there was one consolation, he thought; Austin hadn't sent the elephant.

The sound of an arriving rig made him turn around, look toward the driveway. It was a truck, pulling a gleaming trailer behind it.

A headache thrummed between Tate's temples. Maybe he'd been too quick to dismiss the pachyderm possibility.

Audrey and Ava, having heard the arrival, came bounding around the house, their shiny tassels trailing in the blue beginnings of twilight. Both of them were glitter-dappled from the pointed hats.

Tate and his daughters collided just as the driver was getting down out of the truck cab. A stocky older man, balding, the fella grinned and consulted his clipboard with a ceremonious flourish bordering on the theatrical.

"I'm looking for Miss Audrey and Miss Ava McKettrick," he announced. Tate almost expected him to unfurl a scroll or blow a long brass horn with a velvet flag hanging from it.

Tate was already heading for the back of the trailer, his headache getting steadily worse.

Somehow, despite his bulk, the driver beat him there, blocked him bodily from opening the door and taking a look inside.

By God, Tate thought, *if Austin had sent his kids an elephant...*

"If you wouldn't mind, Mr.—?" the driver said. His name, stitched on his khaki workshirt, was "George."

"McKettrick," Tate replied, through his teeth.

"The order specifically says I'm to deliver the contents of this trailer to the recipients and no one else."

Tate swore under his breath, stepped back and, with a sweeping motion of one arm, invited George to do the honors.

"Who placed this order," Tate asked, with exaggerated politeness, "if that information isn't privileged or anything?"

George lowered a ramp, then climbed it to fling up the trailer's rolling door.

No elephant appeared in the gap.

The suspense heightened—Audrey and Ava were huddled close to Tate on either side by then, fascinated—as George duly checked his clipboard.

"Says here, it was an A. McKettrick. Internet order. We don't get many of those, given the nature of the—er—items."

The twins were practically jumping up and down now, and Esperanza and Garrett had come up behind, hovering, to watch the latest drama unfold.

George disappeared into the shadowy depths, and a familiar clomping sound solved the mystery before two matching Palomino ponies materialized out of the darkness, shining like a pair of golden flames. Their manes and tails were cream-colored, brushed to a blinding shimmer, and each sported a bridle, a saddle and a bright pink bow the size of a basketball.

"Damn," Garrett muttered, "the bastard one-upped me."

"Yeah?" Tate replied, after pulling the girls back out of the way so George could unload the wonder horses. "Wait till you see what *I* got them."

LIBBY HAD EATEN SUPPER—salad and soup—watched the evening news, checked her e-mail, brought the newspaper in from its plastic box by the front gate and done two loads of laundry when the telephone rang.

Damn, she hoped it wasn't the manager at Poplar Bend, the town's one and only condominium complex, calling to complain that Marva was playing her CDs at top volume again, and refused to turn down the music.

In the six months since their mother had suddenly turned up in Blue River in a chauffeur-driven limo and taken up residence in a prime unit at Poplar Bend, Libby and her two younger sisters, Julie and Paige, had gotten all sorts of negative feedback about Marva's behavior.

None of them knew precisely what to do about Marva.

Picking up the receiver, she almost blurted out what she was thinking—"It's not my week to watch her. Call Julie or Paige"—and by the time she had a proper "Hello" ready, Tate had already spoken.

No one else's voice affected her in the visceral way his did.

"I need those dogs," he said, almost furtively. "Tonight."

Libby blinked. "I beg your pardon."

"I need the dogs," Tate repeated. Then, after a long pause that probably cost him, he added, "Please?"

"Tate, what on earth—? Do you realize what time it is?" She squinted at the kitchen clock, but the room was dark and since she'd just been passing through with a basket of towels from the dryer, she hadn't bothered to flip on a light switch.

"Eight?" Tate said.

"Oh," Libby said, mildly embarrassed. The hours since she'd left the Perk Up had dragged so that she thought surely it must be at least eleven.

"You know I'll give them a good home," Tate went on. "The dogs, I mean."

Libby suppressed a sigh. The pups were curled up together on the hooked rug in the living room, sound asleep. Faced with the prospect of actually giving them up, she knew she was going to miss them—a lot.

"Yes," she agreed. "I know. You can pick them up anytime tomorrow. Just stop by the shop and I'll—"

"It has to be tonight, and—well—if you could deliver them—"

"Deliver them?"

"Look, it's a lot to ask, I know that," Tate said, "and I can't explain right now, and I can't leave, either, even though Garrett and Esperanza are both here, because it's the girls' birthday and everything."

"And you want to give them the dogs for a present after all?"

"Something like that. Lib, I know it's an imposition, but I'd really appreciate it if you could bring them out here right about now."

"But you haven't even seen them—"

"Dogs are dogs," Tate said. "They're all great. And I figure you wouldn't have suggested I adopt them if they weren't good around kids."

"It's normally not the best idea to give pets as gifts, Tate. Too much fuss and excitement isn't good for the animal or the child." What was she *saying?*

She'd been the one to suggest the adoption in the first place, and with good reason—the poor creatures needed the kind of home Tate could give them. With him, they would have the best of everything, and, more important, Tate was a dog person. He'd proved that with Crockett and a lot of other animals, too.

"We're not talking about dyed chicks and rabbits at Easter here, Lib," Tate replied. He was nearly whispering.

"What about kibble—and, well—things they'll need?"

"They can survive on ground sirloin until I can get to the store and pick up dog chow tomorrow," Tate reasoned. "I'm in a fix, Libby. I need your help."

The pups had risen from the hooked rug and stood shoulder to shoulder in the doorway now, ears perked, tails wagging. Her heart sank a little at the sight.

"Okay," Libby heard herself say. "We'll be there as soon as I can load them into my car and make the drive."

Tate let out a long breath. "Great," he said. "I owe you, big-time."

You can say that again, buster, Libby thought. *How about fixing me up with a new heart, since you broke the one I've got?*

The call ended.

"You're going to be McKettrick dogs now," Libby told the guys, with a sniffle in her voice. "Best of the best. You'll probably have your own bedrooms and separate nannies."

They wagged harder. It was impossible, of course, but Libby would have sworn they knew they were headed for a place where they could settle in and belong, for good.

"Heck," she added, on a roll, "you'll even get names."

More wagging.

Libby found her purse and, after considerably more effort, her car keys. Since she lived across the alley from her café and walked everywhere but to the supermarket, she tended to misplace them.

If her aging, primer-splotched Impala would start, they were on their way.

"Want to come along for the ride?" she asked Hildie, resting on a rug of her own, in front of the couch.

Hildie yawned, stretched and went back to sleep.

"Guess that's a 'no,'" Libby said.

The pups were always ready to go when they heard the car keys jingle, and she almost tripped over them twice crossing the kitchen to the back door.

After loading the adoptees into the back seat of the rust-mobile, parked in her tilting one-car garage on the alley, she slid behind the wheel, closed her eyes to offer a silent prayer that the engine would start, stuck the key into the ignition and turned it.

The Impala's motor caught with a huffy roar, the exhaust belching smoke.

Libby backed up slowly and drove with her headlights off until she'd passed Chief of Police Brent Brogan's house at the end of the block. The chief had already warned her once about emissions standards—she was clearly in violation of said standards—and she'd made an appointment at the auto shop to get the problem fixed, twice. The trouble was, she'd had to cancel both times, once because Marva was acting up and neither Julie nor Paige was anywhere to be found, and once because a water pipe at the shop had burst and she'd been forced to call in a plumber, thereby blowing the budget.

All she needed now was a ticket.

She caught a glimpse of the chief through his living-room window as she pulled onto the street. His back was to her, and it looked as though he were playing cards or a board game with his children.

Still, Libby didn't flip on her headlights until she reached the main street. Only when she'd passed the city limits did she give the Impala a shot of gas, and she kept glancing at the rearview mirror. Brent took his job seriously.

He was also one of Tate McKettrick's best friends. If by some chance he'd seen her sneaking out of the alley in a cloud of illegal exhaust fumes, she would simply explain that she was delivering these two dogs to the Silver Spur because Tate wanted them *tonight*.

She bit her lower lip. Tate had said he owed her big-time. Well, then, he could just get her out of trouble with Brent, if she got into any.

But Libby made it all the way out to the Silver Spur without incident, and Tate must have been watching for her, because he was standing in the big circular driveway, with its hotel-size fountain, when she pulled in.

The dogs went wild in the back seat, scrabbling at the doors and rear windows, yipping to be set free.

Tate's grin lit up the night.

He came to the car, opened the back door on the driver's side and greeted the pair with ear-rufflings and the promise of sirloin for breakfast.

The dogs leaped to the paving stones and carried on like a pair of groupies finding themselves backstage at a rock concert.

Frankly, Libby had expected a little more pathos when it came time to part, since she'd been caring for these rascals for over two months, but evidently, the reluctance was all on her side.

"Hey, Lib," Tate said, just when she'd figured he was planning to ignore her completely. "You saved my life. Want to come inside for some birthday cake?"

Lib. It wasn't the first time he'd called her by the old nickname, even recently. He'd used it over the phone earlier, conning her into bringing the dogs out to his ranch that very night. Hearing it now, though, in person instead of over a wire, caused a deep emotional ache in her, a sort of yearning, as though she'd missed the last train or bus or airplane of a lifetime, and would now live out her days wandering forsaken in some wilderness.

"I shouldn't," Libby said.

Tate crouched to give the dogs the attention they continued to clamor for, but his face was turned upward, toward Libby, who was still sitting in her wreck of a car. Lights from the enormous portico over the front doors played in his hair. "Why not?" he asked.

"It's late and Hildie's home alone."

"Hildie?"

"My dog," she said.

"Is she sick?"

Libby shook her head.

"Old?"

Again, a shake.

That deadly grin of his—it should have been registered somewhere, like an assault weapon—crooked up the corner of his mouth. "Will she eat the curtains in your absence? Order pizza and smoke cigars? Log onto the Internet and cruise X-rated Web sites?"

Libby laughed. "No," she said. Once, they'd been so close, she and Tate. She'd known his dog, Crockett, well enough to grieve almost as much over not seeing him anymore as she had over losing his master. It seemed odd, and somehow wrong, that Tate had never made Hildie's acquaintance. "She's a good dog. She'll behave."

"Then come in and have some birthday cake."

Libby looked up at the front of that great house, and she remembered stolen afternoons in Tate's bed, the summer after high school especially. Traveling further back in time, she recalled the night his parents came home early from a weekend trip and caught them swimming naked in the pool.

Mrs. McKettrick had calmly produced a bath sheet for Libby, bundled her into a pink terrycloth bathrobe, and driven her home with Libby, shivering, though the weather was hot and humid at the time.

Mr. McKettrick had ordered Tate to the study as she was leaving with Tate's mom. "We're going to have ourselves a *talk,* boy," the rancher had said.

So much had changed since then.

Tate's mom and dad were gone.

Her own father had long since died of cancer, after a lingering and painful decline.

Tate had married Cheryl, and they'd had twins together.

On the one hand, Libby really wanted to go inside and join the party.

On the other, she knew there would be too many other memories waiting to ambush her—mostly simple, ordinary ones, as it happened, like her and Tate doing their homework together, playing pool in the family room, watching movies and sharing bowls of popcorn. But it was the ordinary memories, she'd learned after losing her dad, that had the most power, the most poignancy.

With all her other problems, Libby figured she couldn't handle so much poignancy just then.

"Not this time," she said quietly, and shifted the Impala into Reverse.

"You need to get that exhaust fixed," Tate told her. The smile was gone; his expression was serious. Moments before, she'd been convinced he'd only invited her inside to be polite, wanted to repay her in some small way for bringing the dogs to him on such short notice. Now she wondered if it actually *mattered* to him, that she accept his invitation. Was it possible that he was disappointed by her refusal?

She nodded. "It's on the agenda. Good night, Tate."

He looked down at the dogs, still frolicking around him as eagerly as if he'd stuffed raw T-bone steaks into each of his jeans pockets. "What are their names?"

"They don't have any," Libby said. "I call them 'the dogs.'"

Tate chuckled. "That's creative," he replied. His body was half turned, as though the house and the people inside it were drawing him back, and she supposed they were. Garrett and Austin were both wild, in their different ways, but Tate had been born to be a family man, like his father. "You're sure you won't come in?"

"I'm sure."

One of the big main doors opened, and the twins bounded out, dressed in identical pink cotton pajamas.

Libby's heart lurched at the sight of them, and she put the Impala back in Park.

"Puppies!" they cried in unison, rushing forward.

Libby sat watching as the pups and the little girls immediately bonded, knowing all the while that she had to go.

"Happy birthday," Tate told his daughters, with a tenderness Libby had never heard in his voice before. He glanced back at her, mouthed the word, "Thanks."

Libby's vision was blurred. She blinked rapidly and was about to suck it up, back out of that spectacular driveway and head on home, where she belonged, when suddenly one of the children, the one with glasses, ran to the side of her car and peered inside.

"Hi," she said. "We have a castle. Would you like to see it?"

Libby looked up at the front of the house. "Not tonight, sweetheart, but thank you."

"My name is Ava. You're Libby Remington, aren't you? You own the Perk Up Coffee Shop."

Although Libby couldn't recall actually meeting the girls, Blue River wasn't a big place, and practically everybody knew everybody else. "Yes, I'm Libby. I hope you're having a happy birthday."

"We *are,*" the child said. "Uncle Garrett bought us our very own castle from Neiman-Marcus, and Uncle Austin sent us ponies. But *Dad* gave us what we *really* wanted—puppies!"

"Take these rascals inside and give them some water," Tate told his daughters. He lingered, while the "rascals" followed the twins into the house without so much as a backward glance at Libby.

Libby's throat tightened, partly because this was goodbye for her and the dogs, partly because of the little girls' obvious joy and partly for reasons she could not have identified to save her life.

"I actually bought them a croquet set," Tate confessed.

Libby frowned. In the old days, she and Julie and Paige had played a lot of backyard croquet with their dad, and she cherished the recollection. She'd been proud that when other daddies were on the golf course with their friends and business associates, hers had chosen to spend the time with her and her sisters. "What's wrong with that?"

He sighed, stood with his arms folded, his head tilted back. He'd always loved looking at the stars, said that was why he'd never be happy in a big city. "Nothing," he admitted. "But I kind of lost my head after the castle and the ponies were delivered. Call it male ego."

"You're not going to change your mind about the dogs, are you?" Libby asked, worried all over again.

Tate gripped the edge of her open window and bent to look in at her. His face was mere inches from hers, and for one terrible, wonderful, wildly confusing moment, she thought he was going to kiss her.

He didn't, though.

"I'm not going to change my mind, Lib," he said. "The mutts will have a home as long as I do."

"You wouldn't send them to town to live with your wife?"

"*Ex*-wife," Tate said. "No, Cheryl's not a dog person. Like the ponies, they'll live right here on the Silver Spur for the duration."

"Okay," Libby said, now almost desperate to be gone.

And oddly, *equally* desperate to stay.

Tate straightened, smiled down at her. Half turned again, toward the house. Toward his daughters and the dogs that were already loved and would soon be named, toward his brother Garrett and Esperanza, the housekeeper.

But then he turned back.

"I don't suppose you'd like to have dinner with me some night?" he asked, sounding as shy as he had that long-ago day when he'd asked her to the junior prom. "Soon?"

CHAPTER THREE

"I CAN'T PAY YOU," Libby warned, the next morning, when
her sister Julie showed up at the shop, all set to bake scones
and chocolate-chip cookies, her four-year-old son Calvin in
tow. Clad in swim trunks and flip-flops, with a plastic ring
around his waist, Libby's favorite—and *only*—nephew had
clearly made up his mind to take advantage of the first body
of water to present itself.

He adjusted his horn-rimmed glasses, with the chunk of
none-too-clean tape holding the bridge together, and climbed
onto one of three stools lining the short counter.

Libby ruffled his hair. "Hey, buddy," she said. "Want an
orange smoothie?"

"No, thanks," Calvin replied glumly.

Julie, twenty-nine, with long, naturally auburn hair that
fell to the middle of her back in spiral curls—also natural—
and a figure that would do any exercise maven proud, wore
jeans and a royal blue long-sleeved T-shirt. Thus her hazel
eyes, which tended to reflect whatever color she was wearing that day, were the pure azure of a clear spring sky. She

grinned at Libby and headed for the tiny kitchen in the back of the shop.

"You could take my week troubleshooting with Marva," she sang. "Instead of paying me wages, I mean."

"Not a chance," Libby said, but the refusal was rhetorical, and Julie knew that as well as she did. The three sisters rotated, week by week, taking responsibility for their mother, which meant visiting regularly, settling the problems Marva invariably caused with neighbors and hunting her down when she decided to take off on one of her hikes into the countryside and got lost. Marva was always up to something.

"Mom doesn't have anything better to do anyway," Calvin confided solemnly. He was precocious for his age, and he'd already been reading for a year. Julie, a high school English and drama teacher, was off for the summer, and her usual fill-in job at the insurance agency had fallen through for some unspecified reason. "You might as well let her make scones."

Libby chuckled and couldn't resist planting a smacking kiss on Calvin's cheek. "The community pool is closed for maintenance this week," she reminded him. "So what's with the trunks and the plastic inner tube?"

Calvin's eyes were a pale, crystalline blue, like those of his long-gone father, a man Julie had met while she was student teaching in Galveston, after college. As close as she and Julie were, Libby knew very little about Gordon Pruett, except that he'd owned a fishing boat and was a lot better at going away than coming back. He'd stayed around long enough to pass his unique eye color on to his son and name him Calvin, for his favorite uncle, but soon enough he'd felt compelled to move on.

Gordon didn't visit, but he wasn't completely worthless. He remembered birthdays, mailed his son a box of awkwardly wrapped presents every Christmas, and sent Julie a few hundred dollars in child support each month.

Most of the time, the checks even cleared the bank.

Calvin pushed his everyday glasses up his nose—he had better ones for important occasions. "I *know* the pool is closed for maintenance, Aunt Libby," he said, "but the kid next door to us—Justin?—well, his mom and dad bought him a swimming pool, the kind you blow up with a bicycle pump. His dad filled it with a garden hose this morning, but Justin's mom said we can't swim until the sun heats the water up. I just want to be ready."

Julie chuckled as she came out of the kitchen. She'd already managed to get flour all over the front of her fresh apron. "Hey, Mark Spitz," she said to her son, "how about going next door for a five-pound bag of sugar? Give you a nickel for your trouble."

Almsted's, probably one of the last surviving mom-and-pop grocery stores in that part of Texas, was something of a local institution, as much a museum as a place of business.

"You can't buy anything for a nickel," Calvin scoffed, but he climbed down from the stool and held out one palm, reporting for duty.

Libby gave him a few dollars from the till to pay for the sugar, and Calvin marched himself out onto the sidewalk, headed next door.

Julie immediately stationed herself at a side window, in order to keep an eye on him. No child had ever gone missing from Blue River, but a person couldn't be too careful.

"We've already *got* plenty of sugar," Libby said.

"I know," Julie answered, watching as her son went into Almsted's, with its peeling, green-painted wooden screen door. "I have something to tell you, and I don't want Calvin to hear."

Libby, busy getting ready for the Monday-morning latte rush, went still. "Is something wrong?"

"Gordon e-mailed me," Julie said, still keeping her careful vigil. "He's married and he and his wife pass through town often, on the way to visit his parents in Tulsa, and now Gordon and the little woman want to stop by sometime soon, and get acquainted with Calvin."

"That sounds harmless," Libby observed, though she felt a prickle of uneasiness at the news.

"I don't like it," Julie replied firmly. She smiled, which meant Calvin had reappeared, lugging the bag of sugar, and stepped back so he wouldn't see her. "What if Gordon decides to be an actual, step-up father, now that he's married?"

"Julie, he *is* Calvin's father—"

Julie made a throat-slashing motion with one hand, and Calvin struggled through the front door, might have been squashed by it if he hadn't been wearing the miniature inner tube with the goggle-eyed frog-head on the front.

"Here," he said, holding the bag out to his mother. "Where's my nickel?"

Julie paid up, casting a warning glance in Libby's direction as she did so. There was to be no more talk of Gordon Pruett's impending visit while Calvin was around.

"I'm bored," Calvin soon announced. "I want to go to playschool over at the community center."

"You should have thought of that when you insisted on wearing swimming trunks and the floaty thing with the frog-head," Julie responded lightly, heading back toward the kitchen with the unnecessary bag of sugar. "You're not dressed for playschool, kiddo."

"There's a dress code?" Libby asked. She generally took Calvin's side when there was a difference of opinion.

"No," Julie conceded brightly, "but I'd be willing to bet nobody else is wearing a bathing suit."

Two secretaries came in then, for their double nonfat lattes, following by Jubal Tabor, a lineman for the power company. In his midforties, with a receding hairline and a needy personality, Jubal always ordered the Rocket, a high-caffeine concoction with ginseng and a lot of sugar. Said it got him through the morning.

"Expectin' a flood, kid?" he asked Calvin, who was back on his stool, shoulders hunched, frog-head slightly askew.

Calvin rolled his eyes.

Hiding a smile, Libby served the secretaries' drinks, took their money and thanked them.

Meanwhile, Julie made sure she stayed in the kitchen. Jubal asked her to the movies nearly every time their paths crossed, and even now he was standing on tiptoe trying to catch a glimpse of her while the espresso for his Rocket steamed out of the steel spigot.

"He's not so bad," Libby had said once, when Julie had sent Jubal away with another carefully worded rejection.

"Julie and Jubal?" her sister had said, her eyes green that day because she was wearing a mint-colored blouse. "Our names alone are reason enough to steer clear—we'd sound like second cousins to the Bobbsey twins. Besides, he's too old for me, he wears white socks and he always calls Calvin 'kid.'"

The admittedly comical ring of their names, Jubal's age and the white socks might have been overlooked, in Libby's opinion, but the gruff way he said "kid" whenever he spoke to Calvin bugged her, too. So she'd stopped reminding her sister that there was a shortage of marriageable men in Blue River.

"Scones aren't ready yet?" Jubal asked, casting a disapproving eye toward the virtually empty plastic bakery display case beside the cash register. "Out at Starbucks, they've *always* got scones."

Libby refrained from pointing out to Jubal that he never bought scones anyway, no matter how good the selection was, and set his drink on the counter. "You been cheating on me, Jubal?" she teased. "Buying your jet fuel from the competition?"

Jubal looked at her and blinked once, hard, as though he'd never seen her before. "You want to go to the movies with me tonight?" he asked.

Calvin made a rude sound, which Jubal either missed or pretended not to hear.

"I'm sorry," Libby said, with a note of kind regret in her voice. "I promised Tate McKettrick I'd have dinner with him."

Julie dropped something in the kitchen, causing a great clatter, and out of the corner of her eye, Libby saw Calvin watching her with renewed interest. Since he'd been born long after the breakup, he couldn't have registered the implications of his aunt's statement, but that well-known surname had a cachet all its own.

Even among four-year-olds, it seemed.

"Well," Jubal groused, "far be it from me to compete with a *McKettrick*."

Libby merely smiled. "Thanks for the business, Jubal," she told him. "You have yourself a good day, now."

Jubal paid up, took his Rocket and left.

The instant his utility van pulled away from the curb, Julie peeked out of the kitchen. "Did I hear you say you're going to dinner with Tate?" she asked.

Libby tried to act casual. "He asked me last night. I said maybe."

"That isn't what you told Mr. Tabor," Calvin piped up. "You lied."

"I didn't lie," Libby lied. First, she'd driven her car without the emissions repair, single-handedly destroying the environment, to hear her conscience tell it, and now *this*. She was setting a really bad example for her nephew.

"Yes, you did," Calvin insisted.

"Sometimes," Julie said carefully, resting a hand on Calvin's small, bare shoulder, "we say things that aren't *precisely* true so we don't hurt other people's feelings."

Calvin held his ground. "If it's not the truth, then it's a lie. That's what you always tell *me,* Mom."

Libby sighed. "If Tate asks me out again," she told Calvin, "I'll say yes. That way, I won't have fibbed to anybody."

"I can't believe you didn't say 'yes' in the first place," Julie marveled. "Elisabeth Remington, are you *crazy?*"

Libby cleared her throat, slanted a glance in Calvin's direction to remind her sister that the conversation would have to wait.

"Can I go to playschool if I put on clothes?" Calvin asked, looking so woeful that Julie mussed his hair and ducked out of her floury apron.

"Sure," she said. "Let's run home so you can change." She turned to Libby. "I put the first batch of scones in the oven a couple of minutes ago," she added. "When you hear the timer ding, take them out."

"Are you coming back?" Libby asked, as equally invested in a "no" as she was in a "yes." Once she and her sister were alone again, between customers, Julie would grill her about Tate. If Julie *didn't* return, the first batch of scones would sell out in a heartbeat, as always, and there wouldn't be any more for the rest of the day, because Libby always burned everything she baked, no matter how careful she was.

"Only if you promise to take my turn babysitting Marva so I can—" Julie paused, cleared her throat "—leave town for a few days."

"We're going somewhere?" Calvin asked, immediately excited. On a teacher's salary, with the child support going into a college account, he and Julie didn't take vacations.

"Yes," Julie answered, passing Libby an arch look. "If your aunt Libby will agree to look after Gramma while we're gone, that is."

Calvin sagged with disappointment. "Nobody," he said, "wants to spend any more time with *Gramma* than they have to."

"Calvin Remington," Julie replied, without much sternness to her tone, "that was a terrible thing to say."

"You say it all the time."

"It's still terrible, all right?" Julie turned to Libby. "Deal or no deal?"

Agreeing would mean two weeks in a row on Marvawatch. But Libby needed those scones, if she didn't want all her customers heading for Starbucks. "Deal," she said, in dismal resignation.

Julie grinned. "Great. See you in twenty minutes."

"Crap," Libby muttered, when her sister and nephew had reached the sidewalk and she knew Calvin wouldn't hear.

Julie took half an hour to get back, not twenty minutes, and in the meantime there was a run on iced coffee, so Libby nearly missed the "ding" of the timer on the oven. She rescued the scones in the nick of time and sold the last one just as Julie waltzed in, all pleased with herself.

"You're going, aren't you?" she asked, as soon as the customer and the scone were gone. "If Tate asks you out to dinner again, you'll say 'yes,' not 'maybe'?"

"Maybe," Libby said, annoyed. "And thanks a heap for sticking me with Marva for an extra week. I covered for you *last* month, remember, when you wanted to take your twelfth-grade drama class on that field trip to Dallas."

"They learned so much about Shakespeare," Julie said.

"And I came to understand the mysteries of matricide," Libby said, cleaning the spigots on the espresso machine with a paper towel. "Are you seriously planning to leave town so you can avoid Gordon and the new bride?"

"Yes," Julie answered. "According to his e-mail, he sold his boat, or it sank or both and it went for salvage—I forget. That means good old Gordon is thinking of settling down, and I don't want him asking for joint custody or something, just because he's got a wife now."

"I understand where you're coming from, Julie," Libby

said, after taking a few moments to prepare, "but you won't be able to hide from Gordon forever—if he really wants to be part of Calvin's life, he'll find a way. And he has a right to at least *see* the little guy once in a while."

"Gordon Pruett is the most irresponsible man on the planet," Julie reminded Libby, her eyes suspiciously bright and her voice shaking a little. "I can't turn Calvin over to him every other weekend, or for whole summers or for holidays. For one thing, there's the asthma."

A silence fell between them.

Libby hadn't witnessed one of Calvin's asthma attacks recently, but when they happened, they were terrifying. Once, when he was still in diapers, he'd all but stopped breathing. Libby's youngest sister, Paige, an RN, had jumped up and made sure he wasn't choking, then grabbed him from his high chair at the Thanksgiving dinner table at a neighbor's house, yelled for someone to call 911 and rushed to the shower, where she'd thrust the by-then-blue baby under an icy spray, drenching herself in the process, holding him there until his lungs were shocked into action.

Libby could still hear his affronted, frightened shrieks, see him soaked and struggling to get to Julie, who bundled him in a towel and held him close, once he'd gotten his breath again, whispering to him, singing softly, desperate to calm him down.

Paige had calmly turned on the hot water spigot in the shower then, and filled the bathroom with steam, and Julie had sat on the lid of the toilet, rocking a whimpering Calvin in her arms until the paramedics arrived.

The toddler had spent nearly a week in the pediatric ward of a San Antonio hospital, Julie at his bedside around the clock, and it had taken Paige months to win back his trust. He was simply too little to understand that she'd saved his life.

Now, he used an inhaler and Julie kept oxygen on hand, in their small cottage two blocks from the high school. Paige, living across the street from them in an old mansion converted to apartments, was on call 24/7 in case Calvin needed emergency intubation. Given that she usually worked four ten-hour shifts at a private clinic fifty miles from Blue River and the fire department EMTs were all volunteers, with little formal training, Paige had tried to show both Julie and Libby how to insert an oxygen tube, using a borrowed dummy.

While Libby supposed she could do it if Calvin's life were hanging in the balance, she was far from confident. It was the same with Julie.

In frustration, Paige had finally recruited one of Blue River's EMTs, a former Marine medic named Dennis Evans, and instructed her sisters to call him if Calvin had a serious asthma attack while she was too far away to help.

Julie kept Dennis's number on the front of her refrigerator, seven bright red, six-inch plastic digits with magnets on the back.

So far, Calvin's medications kept his condition under control, but Libby could certainly understand Julie's vigilance. Whenever he went through a bad spell, Julie didn't sleep, and dark circles formed under her eyes.

"So," Julie said now, returning to the main part of the shop after another batch of scones had been baked, and another rush of business had whisked the goodies out the door before they'd even cooled, "let's talk about Tate."

"Let's not," Libby replied. She'd been a codependent fool to even *think* about accepting a date with him, considering that he'd probably begun the process of forgetting all about her as soon as she'd been forced to leave the university and come home to help look after her ailing father. She'd taken what courses she could at Blue River Junior College, which was really just a satellite of another school in San Antonio and had since closed due to lack of funding, but she'd only been marking time, and she knew it.

"You really loved him, Lib," Julie said gently, taking

Calvin's stool at the counter and studying Libby with thoughtful eyes.

"That's the whole point. I loved Tate McKettrick. He, on the other hand, loved a good time." Libby sighed. She hated self-pity, and she was teetering on the precipice of it just then. She tried to smile and partly succeeded. "I guess it made sense that he'd be attracted to someone like Cheryl. She's an attorney, and she was raised the way Tate and his brothers were—with every possible advantage. I didn't even finish college. Tate and I don't have a whole lot in common, when you think about it."

Julie frowned, bracing her elbows on the countertop, resting her chin in her palms. Her eyes took on a stormy, steel-blue color, edged in gray. "I really hope you're not saying you aren't good enough for Tate or anybody else, because I'm going to have to raise a fuss about it if you are."

Libby chuckled. "Julie Remington, making a scene," she joked. "Why, I can't even *imagine* such a thing."

Julie grinned, raised her beautiful hair off her neck with both hands to cool her neck, then let it fall again. "OK, so I might have been a bit of a drama queen in high school and college," she confessed. "You're just trying to distract me from the fact that I'm right. You think—you *actually think*— Tate threw you over for Cheryl because she fit into his world better than you would have."

Libby raised one eyebrow. "Isn't that what happened?"

"What *happened*," Julie argued, "is this—Cheryl seduced Tate. Oil wells and big Texas ranches can be aphrodisiacs, you know. Maybe she intended all along to get pregnant and live like a Ewing out there on the Silver Spur."

"Oh, come *on*," Libby retorted. "I might not admire the woman all that much, but it isn't fair to put all the blame on her, and you damn well know it, Jules. It isn't as if she used a date drug and had her way with Tate while he was unconscious. He could have stopped the whole thing if he'd wanted to—which he obviously didn't."

"That was a while ago, Lib," Julie said mildly, examining her manicure.

"All right, so he was young," Libby responded. "He was old enough to know better."

The front door of the shop swung open then, and Chief Brogan strolled in, sweating in his usually crisp tan uniform. He nodded to Julie, then swung his dark brown gaze to Libby.

"Do I smell scones?" he asked.

"Blueberry," Julie confirmed, smiling.

Brent Brogan, a fairly recent widower, was six feet tall with broad, powerful shoulders and a narrow waist. Tate had long ago dubbed him "Denzel," since he bore such a strong resemblance to the actor, back in Denzel Washington's younger years.

His gaze swung in Julie's direction, then back to Libby. "The usual," he said. "Please."

"Sure, Chief," Libby said, with nervous good cheer, and started the mocha with a triple shot of espresso he ordered every day at about the same time.

Brent approached the counter, braced his big hands against it, and watched Libby with unnerving thoroughness as she worked. "I would have sworn I saw that Impala of yours rolling down the alley last night," he said affably, "with the headlights out. Did you get the exhaust fixed yet?"

"That was my car you saw," Julie hastened to say.

It was a good thing Calvin wasn't around, because that was a whopper and he'd have been sure to point that out right away. Julie's car was a pink Cadillac that had been somebody's Mary Kay prize back in the mid-'80s. Even in a dark alley, it wouldn't be mistaken for an Impala, especially not by a trained observer like Brent Brogan.

Libby gave her sister a look. Sighed and rubbed her suddenly sweaty palms down her jean-covered thighs. "I had an appointment at the auto-repair shop," she told Brent, "but then a pipe blew in the kitchen and I had to call a plumber and, well, you know what plumbers cost."

Brent slanted a glance at Julie, who blushed that freckles-on-pink way only true redheads can, and once again turned his attention back to Libby. "So it *was* you?"

"Yes," Libby said, straightening her shoulders. "And if you give me a ticket, I won't be able to afford to have the repairs done for *another* month."

The timer bell chimed.

Julie rushed to take the latest batch of scones out of the oven.

"I'm going to give you one more warning, Libby," Brent said quietly, raising an index finger. "Count it. *One.* If I catch you driving that environmental disaster again, without a sticker proving it meets the legal standards, I am so going to throw the book at you. Is—that—understood?"

Libby set his drink on the counter with a thump. "Yes, sir," she said tightly. *"That is understood."* She raised her chin a notch. "How am I supposed to get the car to the shop if I can't drive it?"

Brent smiled. "I'd make an exception in that case, I guess."

Libby made up her mind to put the repair charges on the credit card she'd just paid off, though it would set her back.

Julie looked toward the street, smiled and consulted an imaginary watch. "Well, will you look at that," she said. "It's time to pick Calvin up at playschool."

The pit of Libby's stomach jittered. She followed her sister's gaze and saw Tate walking toward the door, looking beyond good in worn jeans, scuffed boots and a white T-shirt that showed off his biceps and tanned forearms.

Scanning the street, she saw no sign of his truck, the sleek luxury car he sometimes drove or his twin daughters.

Libby felt as though she'd been forced, scrambling for balance, onto a drooping piano wire stretched across Niagara

Falls. It was barely noon—Tate had suggested *dinner,* hadn't he, not lunch?

Either way, she reflected, trying to calm her nerves with common sense, she'd said "Maybe," not "Yes."

Tate reached the door, opened it and walked in. His grin was as white as his shirt, and even from behind the register, Libby could see the comb ridges in his hair.

He greeted Brent with a half salute. "Denzel," he said.

Brent smiled. "Throw those blueberry scones into a bag for me," he said, though whether he was addressing Julia or Libby was unclear, because he was watching Tate. "I'd better buy them up before McKettrick beats me to the draw."

Tate was looking at Libby. His blue gaze smoldered that day, but she knew from experience that fire could turn to ice in a heartbeat.

"You had any more trouble with those rustlers?" Brent asked.

Libby ducked into the kitchen, nearly causing a sister-jam in the doorway because Julie had the same idea at the same time.

"Rustlers?" Libby asked, troubled.

"Not recently," Tate told his friend. Looking down into Libby's face, he added, "Rustling's a now-and-again kind of thing. Not as dangerous as it looks in the old movies."

Julie squirmed to get past Libby and leave to pick Calvin up at the community center.

"If you don't come straight back here," Libby warned her sister, momentarily distracted and keeping her voice low, "I'm only taking over with Marva for *half* of next week."

"Relax," Julie answered, turning back and grabbing a paper bag and tongs to fill the chief's scone order. "I'll bake all afternoon, and bring you a big batch of scones and dough-nuts in the morning. My oven is better than this one, and I really do have to fetch Calvin."

Libby blocked Julie's way out of the kitchen and leaned in

close. "What am I supposed to do if Brent leaves and Tate is still here?" she demanded.

Julie raised both eyebrows. "*Talk* to the man? Maybe offer him coffee—or a quickie in the storeroom?" She grinned, full of mischief. "That's about the only thing I miss about Gordon Pruett. Stand-up sex with a thirty-three percent chance of getting caught."

Libby blushed, but then she had to laugh. "I am *not* offering Tate McKettrick stand-up sex in the storeroom!" she said.

"Now, that's a damn pity," Tate said.

Libby whirled around, saw him standing in the doorway leading into the main part of the shop, arms folded, grin wicked, one muscular shoulder braced against the framework. Color suffused Libby's face, so hot it hurt.

Julie fled, giggling, with the bag of scones in one hand, forcing Tate to step aside, though he resumed his damnably sexy stance as soon as she'd passed.

"Well," he remarked, after giving a philosophical sigh, "I stopped by to repeat my offer to buy you dinner, since the girls are over at the vet's with Ambrose and Buford and therefore temporarily occupied, but if you want to have sex in a storeroom or anyplace else, Lib, I'm game."

"Ambrose and Buford?" Libby asked numbly.

"The dogs," Tate explained, his eyes twinkling. "They're getting checkups—'wellness exams,' they call them now—and shots."

"Oh," Libby said, at a loss.

"Could we get back to the subject of sex?" Tate teased.

"No," she said, half laughing. "We most certainly can't."

He straightened, walked toward her, in that ambling, easy way he had, cupped her face in his hands. She loved the warmth of his touch, the restrained strength, the roughness of work-calloused flesh.

His were the hands of a rancher.

"Dinner?" he asked.

"Are you going to kiss me?" she countered.

He smiled. "Depends on your answer."

"If I say 'no,' what happens?"

"You wouldn't do a darn fool thing like that, now would you?" he asked, in a honeyed drawl. Although his body shifted, his hands remained where they were. "Turn down a free meal, and a tour of a plastic castle? Miss out on a perfectly good chance to see how Ambrose and Buford are adjusting to ranch life?"

He meant to "buy" dinner at his place, then. The knowledge was both a relief and a whole new reason to panic.

"Will Audrey and Ava be there?"

"Yes."

"Garrett?"

"No. Sorry. He had to get back to Austin."

"Pressing political business?"

Tate chuckled. "Probably a hot date," he said. "Plus, he's afraid I'm going to kill him in his sleep for giving my kids a goddamn castle for their sixth birthday."

"Hmm," Libby mused.

"Well?" Tate prompted.

"I have a question," Libby said.

"What's that?"

"Why now? Why ask me out now, Tate—after all this time?"

He looked thoughtful, and a few moments passed before he answered, his voice quiet. "I guess it took me this long to work up my courage." He swallowed hard, met her gaze in a deliberate way. "Nobody would blame you if you told me to go straight to hell, Libby. Not after what I did."

She took that in. Finally, she said, "Okay."

"Is that an okay-yes, or an okay-go-take-a-flying-leap?"

Libby had to smile. "I guess it's an okay-one-dinner-is-no-big-deal," she answered. "We *are* still talking about dinner, right?"

Tate chuckled. God, he smelled good, like fresh air and newly cut grass distilled to their essences. And she'd missed bantering with him like this. "Yes, we're still talking about dinner."

"Then, yes," Libby said, feeling dizzy. After all, she'd promised Calvin she'd undo her lie if she got the chance, and here it was.

"Right answer," Tate murmured, and then he kissed her.

The world, perhaps even the whole universe, rocked wildly and dissolved, leaving Libby drifting in the aftermath, not standing in her shabby little coffee-shop kitchen.

Tate deepened the kiss, used his tongue. Oh, he was an expert tongue man, all right. Another thing she'd forgotten— or *tried* to forget.

Libby moaned a little, swayed on her feet.

Tate drew back. His hands dropped from her cheeks to her shoulders, steadying her.

"Pick you up at six?" It was more a statement than a question, but Libby didn't care. She was taking a terrible risk, and she didn't care about that, either.

"Six," she confirmed. "What shall I wear?"

He grinned. "The twins are dining in shorts, tank tops and pointed princess hats with glitter and tassels," he said. "Feel free to skip the hat."

"Guess that leaves shorts and a tank top," she said. "Which means you should pick me up at six-thirty, because I'm going to need to shave my legs."

Mentally, Libby slapped a hand over her mouth. She'd just given this hot man a mental picture of her running a razor along *hairy legs?*

"Here or at your place?" Tate asked, apparently unfazed by the visual.

"My place," Libby said. "I'd drive out on my own, but your friend the chief of police will arrest me if I so much as turn a wheel."

"Therein lies a tale," Tate said. "One I'd love to hear. Later."

"Later," Libby echoed, and then he was gone.

And she just stood there, long after he'd left her, the kiss still pulsing on her lips and rumbling through her like the seismic echoes of an earthquake.

CHAPTER FOUR

LIBBY CLOSED THE SHOP at five that day—no big sacrifice, since she'd only had one customer after lunch, a loan officer from First Cattleman's who'd left, disgruntled, without buying anything once he learned there were no more of Julie's scones to be had.

After cleaning up the various machines, stowing the day's modest take in her zippered deposit bag and finally locking up, she crossed the alley—trying not to hurry—and let a grateful Hildie out into the backyard.

The place seemed a little lonely without the formerly nameless dogs, but she'd see them that night, at Tate's. Given the way they'd thrown her under the proverbial bus when she'd dropped them off at the Silver Spur the night before, there was a good chance they'd ignore her completely.

"Now, you're being silly," she told herself, refreshing Hildie's water bowl at the sink, then rinsing out and refilling the food dish with kibble.

While Hildie gobbled down her meal, Libby showered, taking care to shave her legs, but instead of the prescribed shorts and tank top, she chose a pink sundress with spaghetti straps and smocking at the bodice. She painted her toenails to match, spritzed herself with cologne and dried her freshly shampooed, shoulder-length hair until it fluffed out around her face.

Libby owned exactly two cosmetic products—a tube of mascara and some lip gloss—and she applied both with a little more care than usual.

The phone rang at five minutes to six, and she was instantly certain that Tate had changed his mind and meant to rescind the invitation to have supper at the Silver Spur. The wave of disappointment that washed over her was out of all proportion to the situation.

But it wasn't Tate, as things turned out, calling with some lame excuse.

It was Gerbera Jackson, who cleaned for Marva three days a week, over at Poplar Bend.

"Libby? That you?"

"Hello, Gerbera," Libby responded.

"I know it isn't your week," Gerbera went on apologetically, "but I couldn't reach Miss Paige, or Miss Julia, either."

Gerbera, an old-fashioned black woman, well into her sixties, still adhered to the mercifully outdated convention of addressing her white counterparts as "Miss."

"That's okay," Libby said, hiding her disappointment. A problem with Marva meant the evening at the Silver Spur was history, the great event that never happened. "What's up?"

"Well, it's your mama, of course," Gerbera said sadly.

Who else? Libby thought uncharitably.

"I'm worried about her," the softhearted woman continued. "I recorded her stories for her, just like always, since her favorites are on while she's out taking those longs walks of hers, but Miss Marva, she doesn't want to look at them tonight. Told me not to bother putting a chicken potpie into the oven for her before I left, too. That's one of her favorites, you know."

Libby closed her eyes briefly, breathed deeply and slowly. Marva's "stories" were soap operas, and she hadn't missed an episode of *As the World Turns,* or so she claimed, since 1972, when, recovering from a twisted ankle, she'd gotten hooked.

"Not good," Libby admitted. When Marva didn't want to watch her soaps or eat chicken potpie, she was depressed. And when Marva was depressed, bad things happened.

"She hasn't been herself since they eighty-sixed her from the bingo hall for lighting up a cigarette," Gerbera added.

Just then, a rap sounded at the front door. Tate had arrived, probably looking cowboy-sexy, and now Libby was going to have to tell him she couldn't go to the Silver Spur for supper.

"I hate to bother you," Gerbera said, and she sounded like she meant it, but she also sounded relieved. If she had a fault, it was caring too much about the various ladies she cleaned and cooked for, whether they were crotchety or sweet-tempered. Until her nephew, Brent Brogan, had moved back to Blue River, with his children, after his wife's death, Gerbera had managed Poplar Bend full-time, living in an apartment there.

She spent more time with her family now, cooking and mending and helping out wherever she could. Brent claimed her chicken-and-dumplings alone had put ten pounds on him.

"No bother," Libby said, brightening her voice and stretching the kitchen phone cord far enough to see Tate standing on the other side of the front door. She gestured for him to come in. "She's my mother."

Some mother Marva had been, though. She'd left her husband and small, bewildered children years before, with a lot of noise and drama, and suddenly returned more than two decades later, after what she described as a personal epiphany, to install herself at Poplar Bend and demand regular visits from her daughters.

She had, for some reason, decided it was time to bond.

Better late than never—that seemed to be the theory.

Marva had money, that much was clear, and she was used to giving orders, but any attempt to discuss her long and largely silent absence brought some offhanded response like, "That was then and this is now."

For all Libby and her sisters knew, Marva could have been living on another planet or in a parallel dimension all those years.

Libby wanted to love Marva; she truly did. But it was hard, remembering how heartbroken their dad had been at his wife's defection—she'd run away with a man who rode a motorcycle and earned a sketchy living as a tattoo artist.

Clearly, the tattoo man had been out of the picture for a long time.

For their father's sake, Libby, Julie and Paige took turns visiting and handling problems Marva herself had created. They fetched and carried and ran errands, but Marva wasn't grateful for anything. *I am your mother,* she'd told Libby, in one of her cranky moments, *and I am entitled to your respect.*

Respect, Libby had retorted hotly, unable to hold her tongue, *is not a right. It's something you have to earn.*

Tate let himself in, at Libby's signal, and Hildie started playing up to him as though he were some kind of cowboy messiah.

"Thanks, Gerbera," Libby said, realizing she'd missed a chunk of the conversation. "I'll head over there right away and make sure she's okay."

Gerbera apologized again, said goodbye and hung up.

Libby replaced the receiver on the hook in the kitchen and went back to greet her breathtakingly handsome guest.

"Problem?" Tate asked mildly. He filled Libby's small

living room, made it feel crowded and, at the same time, utterly safe.

"My mother," Libby said. "I need to check on her."

"Okay," Tate replied. "Let's go check on her, then."

"You don't understand. It could take hours, if she's in one of her—moods."

Tate's shoulders moved in an easy shrug. "Only one way to find out," he said.

Libby couldn't let him throw away his evening just because her own was ruined. "You should just go home. Forget about supper." She swallowed. "About my joining you, I mean."

He was crouching by then, fussing over the adoring Hildie. She probably wanted to go home with him and be *his* dog. *Libby? That name seems vaguely familiar.*

"Nope," he said, straightening. "You and I and—what's this dog's name again?"

"Hildie," Libby answered, her throat tight.

"You and Hildie and I are having supper on the Silver Spur, just like we planned. I'll just call Esperanza and ask her to feed the girls early."

"But—"

Tate took in Libby's sundress, her strappy sandals, her semi-big hair. "You look better than fantastic," he said. Then he took Libby by the arm and squired her toward the front door, Hildie happily trotting alongside.

His truck was parked at the curb, and he hoisted Hildie into the back seat, then opened the passenger-side door for Libby. Helped her onto the running board, from which point she was able to come in for a landing on the leather seat with something at least *resembling* dignity.

"You don't have to do this," she said.

Tate didn't answer until he'd rounded the front of the truck and climbed behind the wheel. "I don't have to do anything but die and pay taxes," he replied, with a grin. "I'm here because I *want* to be here, Lib. No other reason."

Within five minutes, they were pulling into one of the parking lots at Poplar Bend, behind Building B. Marva lived off the central courtyard, and as they approached, she stepped out onto her small patio, smiling cheerfully. A glass of white wine in one hand, she wore white linen slacks and a matching shirt, tasteful sandals and earrings.

Libby stared at her.

"Well, *this* is a nice surprise," Marva said, her eyes gliding over Tate McKettrick briefly before shifting back to her daughter. "To what do I owe the pleasure?"

"Gerbera Jackson called me," Libby said, struggling to keep her tone even. "She was very concerned because you didn't want to watch your soap operas or eat supper."

Marva sighed charitably and shook her head. "I was just having a little blue spell, that's all," she said. She raised the wineglass, its contents shimmering in the late-afternoon light. "Care for a drink?"

Inwardly, Libby seethed. Gerbera was a sensible woman, and if she'd been concerned about Marva's behavior, then Marva had given her good reason for it.

Bottom line, Marva had decided she wanted a little attention. Instead of just saying so, she'd manipulated Gerbera into raising an unnecessary alarm.

"No, thanks," Tate said, nodding affably at Marva. "Is there anything you need, ma'am?"

Libby wanted to jab him with her elbow, but she couldn't, because Marva would see.

"Well," Marva said, almost purring, "there is that light in the kitchen. It's been burned out for weeks and I'm afraid I'll break my neck if I get up on a ladder and try to replace the bulb."

Tate rolled up his sleeves. "Glad to help," he said.

Libby's smile felt fixed; she could only hope it *looked* more genuine than it felt, quivering on her mouth.

Tate replaced the bulb in Marva's kitchen.

"It's good to have a man around the house," Marva said.

Libby all but rolled her eyes. *You had one,* she thought. *You had Dad. And he wasn't exciting enough for you.*

"I guess Libby and I ought to get going," Tate told Marva. "Esperanza will be holding supper for us."

Marva patted his arm, giving Libby a sly wink, probably in reference to Tate's well-developed biceps. "You young people run along and have a nice evening," she said, setting aside her now-empty wineglass to wave them out of the condo. "It's nice to know you're dating, Libby," she added, her tone sunny. "You and your sisters need to have more fun."

Libby's cheeks burned.

Tate took her by the elbow, nodded a good evening to Marva, and they were out of the condo, headed down the walk.

When they reached the truck, Tate lifted Libby bodily into the cab, paused to reach back and pet Hildie reassuringly before sprinting around to the driver's-side door, climbing in and taking the wheel again.

As soon as he turned the key in the ignition, the air-conditioning kicked in, cooling Libby's flesh, if not her temper.

She leaned back in the seat, then closed her eyes. Stopping by Marva's place had been no big deal, as it turned out, and Tate certainly hadn't minded changing the lightbulb.

But of course, those things weren't at the heart of the problem, anyway, were they?

All this emotional churning was about Marva's leaving, so many years ago.

It was about her and Julie and Paige, not to mention their dad, missing her so much.

Marva had departed with a lot of fanfare. Now that she was back, she expected to be treated like any normal mother. Not.

"I guess your mom still gets under your hide," Tate commented quietly, once they were moving again.

Libby turned her head, looked at him. "Yes," she admitted. He knew the story—everyone around Blue River did. Several times, when they were younger, he'd held her while she cried over Marva.

Tate was thoughtful, and silent for a long time. "She's probably doing the best she can," he said, when they were past the town limits and rolling down the open road. "Like the rest of us."

Libby nodded. Marva's "best" wasn't all that good, as it happened, but she didn't want the subject of her mother to ruin the evening. She raised and lowered her shoulders, releasing tension, and focused on the scenery. "I guess so," she said.

The conversational lull that followed was peaceful, easy.

Hildie got things going again by suddenly popping her big head forward from the back seat and giving Tate an impromptu lick on the ear.

He laughed, and so did Libby.

"Do you ever think about getting another dog?" she asked, thinking of Crockett. That old hound had been Tate's constant companion. He'd even taken him to college with him.

"Got two," Tate reminded Libby, grinning.

"I mean, one of your own," Libby said.

Tate swallowed, shook his head. "I keep thinking I'll be ready," he replied, keeping his gaze fixed on the winding road ahead. "But it hasn't happened yet. Crockett and I, we were pretty tight."

Libby watched him, took in his strong profile and the proud way he held his head up high. It was a McKettrick thing, that quiet dignity.

"Your folks were such nice people," she told Tate.

He smiled. "Yeah," he agreed. "They were."

They'd passed mile after mile of grassy rangeland by then, dotted with cattle and horses, all of it part of the Silver Spur. Once, there had been oil wells, too, pumping night and day for fifty years or better, though Tate's father had shut them down years before.

A few rusty relics remained, hulking and rounded at the top; in the fading, purplish light of early evening, they reminded Libby of the dinosaurs that must have shaken the ground with their footsteps and dwarfed the primordial trees with their bulk.

"You're pretty far away," Tate said, as they turned in at the towering wrought-iron gates with the name *McKettrick* scrolled across them. Those gates had been standing open the night before; Libby, relieved not to have to stop, push the button on the intercom and identify herself to someone inside, had breezed right in. "What are you thinking about, Lib?"

She smiled. "Oil derricks and dinosaurs," she replied.

Tate pushed a button on his visor, and the gates swung wide, then whispered closed again as soon as they passed through. Hildie, quiet for most of the ride, began to get restless, pacing from one end of the back seat to the other.

Once again, Libby dared hope her dog wasn't planning to move in with Tate and forget all about her, the way Ambrose and Buford apparently had.

"Derricks and dinosaurs," Tate reflected.

"You might say there's a crude connection," Libby said.

Tate groaned at the bad pun, but then he laughed.

When they reached the ranch house, he drove around back instead of parking under the portico or in the garage, and Libby gasped with pleasure when she caught sight of the castle.

It was enchanting. Even magical.

"Wow," she said.

Tate shut off the truck, cast a rueful glance over the ornate structure and got out to help Hildie out of the back seat.

Set free, Hildie ran in circles, as excited as a pup, and when Ambrose and Buford dashed out of the castle and raced toward her, all former grudges were forgotten. She wagtailed it over to meet them like they were long-lost friends.

The twins waved from separate windows in the castle, one at ground level and one in a turret.

"I've never seen anything like this," Libby said, shading her eyes from the presunset glare as she admired the oversized playhouse.

"Me, either," Tate said.

"Cometh thou in!" one of the little girls called from the tower.

Libby laughed. Tate shook his head and grinned.

Took Libby's hand just before he stooped to enter the castle, then pulled her in after him. The three dogs crowded in behind them, thick as thieves now that they weren't roommates anymore.

The inside was even more remarkable than the outside, with its fireplace and overhead beams and a stairway leading to the upper floor.

Libby wondered what Calvin would think of the place.

"It's so—big," she said slowly.

Ava nodded eagerly. "Dad says Audrey and I need to think about giving it to the community center, so other kids can play with it, too."

Libby glanced at Tate, saw that he was looking away.

"That's a very generous idea," she said, impressed.

"We haven't decided yet, though," Audrey put in, descending the stairs. "All Dad said was to *think* about it. He didn't say we actually had to *do* it."

Tate gestured toward the door. "I'm pretty sure supper is ready by now, ladies," he said. "Shall we?"

Audrey and Ava curtseyed grandly, spreading the sides of their cotton shorts like skirts.

"Yes, my lord," Ava said.

Tate laughed. *"Go,"* he said.

Both girls hurried out of the castle, the canine trio chasing after them, barking like dog-maniacs.

"'Yes, my lord'?" Libby teased, grinning, when the din subsided a little. "Now where would a pair of six-year-olds pick up an antiquated term like that?"

"Garrett probably taught them," Tate answered. "He likes to get under my skin any way he can."

Esperanza stood beside the patio table, laughing as she shooed the dogs out from underfoot and ordered the twins inside to wash their hands and faces.

Ambrose and Buford followed them, but Hildie paused, turned and scanned the yard, then trotted toward Libby with something like relief when she spotted her.

Touched, Libby bent to pat the dog's head.

Esperanza had outdone herself, preparing supper. There were tacos and enchiladas, seasoned rice and salad.

Libby enjoyed the food almost as much as the company, and she was sorry when the meal ended and Esperanza herded the twins into the house for their baths.

Overhead, the first stars popped out like diamonds studding a length of dark blue velvet, and the moon, a mere sliver of transparent light, looked as though it had come to rest on the roof of the barn.

Libby was totally content in those moments, with Tate at her side and Hildie lying at her feet, probably enjoying the warmth of the paving stones.

When Tate squeezed her hand, Libby squeezed back.

And then they drew apart.

Libby stood and began to gather and stack the dishes.

Tate got to his feet and helped.

Libby had forgotten how big the kitchen was, and as they

stepped inside, she did her best not to stare as she and Tate loaded one of several dishwashers and cleaned up. The pool was visible on the other side of a thick glass wall, a brilliant turquoise, and looking at it, Libby couldn't help remembering the skinny-dipping episode.

She smiled. They'd been so innocent then, she and Tate. So young.

And such passionate lovers.

Tate took her gently by the elbows and turned her to face him. Kissed her lightly on the forehead. "Thanks for saying 'yes' to tonight, Lib," he said. "It's good to have you back here."

Libby's throat tightened with sudden, searing emotion.

Tate cupped her chin his hand and tilted her face upward, looked into her eyes. "What?" he asked, very gently.

She shook her head.

He drew her close, held her tightly, his chin propped on the top of her head.

They were still standing there, minutes later, not a word having passed between them, when Esperanza returned, the front of her dress soaked, her lustrous, gray-streaked hair coming down from its pins. Barking and the laughter of little girls sounded in the distance.

"The dogs," Esperanza told Tate breathlessly, "they are in the bathtub, with the children."

Tate sighed in benign exasperation, then stepped away from Libby. "I'll be back in a few minutes," he said. As he passed Esperanza, he laid a hand on her shoulder, squeezed.

"These children," Esperanza fretted. "I am too old—"

Libby hurried over to help the other woman into a chair at the table. Brought her a glass of water.

"Are you all right?"

Esperanza hid her face in her hands, and her shoulders began to shake.

It took Libby a moment to realize the woman was laughing, not crying.

Relieved, Libby laughed, too.

Tears of mirth gleamed on Esperanza's smooth brown cheeks, and she used the hem of her apron to wipe them away.

Then, crossing herself, she said, "It is just like the old days, when the boys were young. Always in trouble, the three of them."

Tate returned, pausing in the doorway to take in the scene. Like most men, he was probably wary of female emotion unleashed.

Libby took in every inch of him.

Tate McKettrick, all grown up, was *still* trouble.

The kind it was impossible to resist.

CHAPTER FIVE

LIBBY WAS UP EARLY the next morning, feeling rested even though she'd only had a few hours' sleep. After driving her home and walking her to her front door the night before, like the gentleman he could be but sometimes wasn't, Tate had kissed her again, and the effects of that tender, tentative touch of their mouths still tingled on her lips.

The sun was just peeking over the eastern horizon when she took Hildie for the first walk the poor dog had enjoyed since Ambrose and Buford had come to stay with them weeks before. It was good to get back into their old routine.

All up and down Libby's quiet, tree-lined street, lawn sprinklers turned, making that reassuring *chucka-chuck* sound, spraying diamonds over emerald-green grass. Hildie stopped for the occasional sniff at a fence post or a light pole or a patch of weeds—Julie, joint owner, along with Calvin, of a surprisingly active three-legged beagle named Harry, would have said the dog was reading her p-mail.

As Libby and Hildie passed Brent Brogan's house, a small split-level rancher with a flower-filled yard and a picket fence, Gerbera stepped out of the front door, bundled in a summery blue-print bathrobe, and hiked along the walk to get the newspaper.

Seeing Libby, Gerbera paused and grinned broadly. "Land sakes," she said, "I thought you'd given up on walking that old dog. Never see you go by here anymore."

Libby paused, holding Hildie's leash loosely. "I was fostering two puppies," she explained, "and walking the three of them at once was too much. I did manage to get the little buggers housebroken, though."

Gerbera cocked a thumb toward the white-shingled house behind her. "I've been after that nephew of mine to go on down to the shelter and get his kids a pet. Give them some responsibility and get them to unplug those earphones and wires from their heads once in a while. But Brent always says it would be him or me that wound up looking after any cat or dog we took in, once the kids lost interest."

"Well, if you manage to change his mind," Libby said, always ready to promote adoption when she knew a good home was a sure thing, "the kennels are usually full."

Gerbera got the rolled-up newspaper out of its box and tucked it under her arm. "You want to come in and have coffee? Nobody around but me. Kenda and V.J. are still sleeping, like kids do in the summertime, and Brent's been gone most of the night—that's why I stayed over."

Ironically, since she owned the Perk Up and java was her stock-in-trade, Libby drank very little coffee. It made her way too hyper. "We've got a ways to go to finish our walk," she said, with a nod toward the Lab. "Hildie and I both need all the exercise we can get. Another time?"

Gerbera smiled. "Sure enough," she agreed, before launching into a good-natured report. "Your mama called me last night and fussed at me something fierce for getting you all worked up, but I could tell she was pleased to get a visit from you and a good-lookin' McKettrick man."

Libby might have been annoyed with someone else, but Gerbera's intentions were always good. Hildie began to tug determinedly at the leash then, ready to go on, follow the route they always took, through several side streets, around the city park with its pretty gazebo-style bandstand, back home by way of the old movie house and the community center. "I think it was the good-lookin' McKettrick man that cheered her up, not me."

Something changed in Gerbera's face, something that went beyond the sparkle fading from her eyes and the way her mouth suddenly turned down a little at the corners. "Lordy," she said. "I swear, I get more forgetful every day!" She paused, drew in a breath. Her eyes were worried. "You don't *know,* do you? And how *would* you know?"

"Know what?" Libby asked, suddenly jittery, tightening her grip on Hildie's leash when the dog rounded the corner of the Brogans' fence ahead of her, pulling even harder now.

"Brent's been out there on the Silver Spur most of the night," Gerbera said slowly, "doing whatever he can to help. Libby, Pablo Ruiz is dead."

Libby gasped. Pablo was a friend, an institution in Blue River. He *couldn't* be dead. "What happened?" she managed to ask.

"There was an accident of some kind," Gerbera said, touching Libby's upper arm. "That's all I know."

An accident. Libby nodded, numbed by the news, thinking of Isabel, Pablo's wife, of Nico and Mercedes, their son and daughter, and the two nephews they'd brought to the United States, several years before, after Isabel's younger sister, Maria, had died of what turned out to be peritonitis.

Ricardo and Juan were teenagers now; honor students, well-mannered youths who stayed out of trouble; the kind of kids a community like Blue River was proud to call its own.

Nico, a close friend of Tate's, had once confided that when word of his aunt's death had reached them, he and Pablo had immediately set out for Mexico, expecting to find the boys living with neighbors in Maria's small village, or perhaps with their late father's family.

Instead, they'd been told that Ricardo and Juan had vanished, soon after Maria's death, and no one had seen them since.

There had been several more trips, Nico had said, each one a failure, before he and his father had finally tracked the children down to a nearby landfill. Both boys were filthy and half-starved, foraging for scraps of food, stealing and sleeping wherever they could find a safe place to lie down.

With a lot of help from Tate's cousin, Meg, a top executive with McKettrickCo at the time, Pablo had finally arranged for the boys to enter the country legally.

They had been almost feral in the beginning, those children, constantly afraid, stealing food, snarling and nipping when Pablo wrestled them into a tub and scrubbed them down on their first night in the United States. Eventually, Pablo and Isabel had won their trust, as well as their love.

What would happen to them now? What would happen to Isabel?

Libby's stomach did a slow, backward roll. "Oh, Gerbera," she whispered. "This is awful."

Gerbera nodded sadly. "I guess they look out for their own, though," she said. "Those McKettricks, I mean. And all the folks who work for them."

The reminder comforted Libby a little. It was true. Tate and his brothers would make sure Isabel and the boys lacked for nothing—that was the McKettrick way. And the long-term employees were like kin to each other.

Libby knew most of the dozen or so men who worked on the Spur year-round—everyone did. The married men lived with their wives and children in well-maintained trailers alongside one of the creeks, while the bachelors occupied a comfortable bunkhouse nearby. All of them got their mail

MCKETTRICKS OF TEXAS: TATE 317

and their groceries in Blue River, had their hair cut at the barber's or Valdeen's House of Beauty, came into the Perk Up on windy winter days for hot, strong coffee.

Gerbera shook her head, looking somber now. "I don't know what Isabel will do without that man. The kids, either. And now I wish I hadn't been the one to tell you, Libby. Brent specifically asked me not to 'broadcast' this until he was sure all the family had been informed."

Wanting to reassure her friend, Libby tried to smile. "Just about everybody in town owns a police scanner, so if Brent used his radio even once, the word's out." She spoke distractedly; half her mind had strayed to the Silver Spur; she couldn't help wondering how Tate and the children and Esperanza had taken the news. The other half was on Hildie, who was hunkered down and putting her full weight into the effort to drag her mistress back into motion.

"You'd better go on and I'd better get my old self ready for work," Gerbera said, noting the dog's antics with a sad smile.

Libby nodded, and she and Hildie were off again.

By the time they'd finished their walk almost an hour later, three different people had come to their front gates in bathrobes to ask if Libby had heard about Pablo Ruiz. They'd all gleaned the information from their police scanners, just as Libby had expected.

Nobody knew the exact cause; Chief Brogan had been closedmouthed about it, when he'd called in the coroner. All they'd been able to gather was that there had been an accident on the ranch, a fatal one.

Most likely, the chief had made calls he didn't want half the county listening in on, over his cell phone.

Back home, Libby took a hasty shower—her breakfast was half a banana, since she didn't have much of an appetite—dressed in jeans and a sleeveless cotton top, bound her hair back in the usual no-fuss ponytail, and skipped the mascara and lip gloss.

While Hildie napped in a patch of sunlight in the kitchen, Libby let herself out the back door, crossed the yard and the alley, unlocked the rear entrance to the Perk Up and nearly jumped out of her skin when Calvin leaped out at her from behind a box of pop-on cup lids and yelled, "Boo!"

The fight-or-flight response stopped Libby in her tracks, one hand pressed to her pounding heart.

Julie peeked out of the kitchen, wearing an apron and holding a mixing bowl in the curve of one arm and a batter-coated spoon in the other. "For Pete's sake, Calvin," she scolded merrily, "how many times have I told you that you shouldn't scare the elderly?"

"You are just *too* funny," Libby said, directing the terse remark to her sister and a warm smile to her nephew.

Calvin had left his swim trunks and frog-floater at home that day, and he looked very handsome in his miniature chinos and short-sleeved plaid shirt. He was even wearing his good glasses, the ones with no adhesive tape spanning the bridge.

"Something big going on at playschool today?" Libby asked, setting her purse on a high shelf and reaching for an apron.

Calvin nodded eagerly. "We're getting a castle!" he crowed. "With turrets and everything!"

So, Libby thought, Tate's girls *had* decided to donate their birthday present to the community center. That was quick.

"You're getting a castle today?" she asked Calvin, wondering if Tate had intended to give away the massive toy all along; perhaps called to make the arrangements almost as soon as it arrived on the Silver Spur.

Calvin swelled out his chest. "No," he said. "Justin's mom is best friends with my teacher, Mrs. Oakland, and she told Justin's mom that it would take time and sweat and a lot of heavy equipment to move the thing."

Having seen the castle, Libby agreed. "Then why are you so dressed up?" she asked.

Calvin gave a long-suffering sigh. In his oft-expressed opinion, adults could be remarkably obtuse at times. "Because we're going to have a meeting at recess and elect a king," he said, very slowly, so his elderly aunt could follow. "I'm on the committee."

Libby and Julie exchanged looks. Julie smiled and shrugged as if to say, "That's what you get for asking a dumb question," but her eyes—pale violet that day because her T-shirt was purple—were solemn. She raised her eyebrows.

"Yes," Libby told Julie, an expert at sister-telepathy, "I heard."

"Heard what?" Calvin wanted to know, following as Libby headed for the front of the shop to fire up the various gadgets and switch the "Closed" sign to "Open."

"That you're campaigning to be king," Libby hedged. "Do you have your speech ready? Buttons and bumper stickers to pass out to the voters?"

"If nobody else is going to point out that kings are not elected officials," Julie said, still stirring the batter, "I will."

Calvin looked worried. "Buttons and bumper stickers?" he repeated.

Libby's heart melted. She bent to kiss the top of her nephew's blond head. "I was just teasing, big guy," she said. "And your mom is right. To my knowledge, there is not now and never has been one single king of Texas."

Calvin beamed. "Then I could be the first one!" he cried, delighted. Since he wasn't even in kindergarten yet and was already serving on committees, Libby figured he might just pull it off.

She smiled again, went to unlock the cash register and see if she had enough change on hand for the day.

"Calvin," Julie said, pointing, "sit down at that table in

the corner, please, and watch for customers. If you see one approaching, let us know."

Calvin obeyed readily, and he sat up so straight and looked so vigilant that a whole new wave of tenderness washed over Libby.

Julie immediately maneuvered her toward the kitchen, where they could talk with some semblance of privacy.

"Gordon followed up his e-mail with a phone call," she said, in a desperate whisper. "He's willing to take things slowly, but he *definitely* wants to get to know Calvin."

"Okay," Libby said. "What are you going to do?"

"Hide," Julie responded. "Calvin and Harry and I are going to hit the road. We'll be gone for as long as we have to—"

Libby held up both hands. "Julie! Are you *listening* to yourself? This is not something you can run away from. Besides, you have a house and a job and friends and—" she paused to clear her throat "—*family* in Blue River. Shouldn't you at least hear Gordon out?"

"Did Gordon hear *me* out when I told him I was expecting his baby?" Julie demanded, though she was careful to keep her voice down so Calvin wouldn't hear.

Libby knew there was no way to win this argument. Julie was just venting, anyway. "Did you hear about Pablo Ruiz?" Libby asked.

Julie's eyes widened. "No. What—?"

"He's dead, Jules. There was some kind of accident, yesterday or last night, on the Silver Spur—"

Julie gasped. "Not Pablo," she said, splaying the fingers of her right hand and pressing the palm to her heart.

Libby nodded sadly. "He was so proud of Mercedes," she whispered. Pablo and Isabel's only daughter would graduate from medical school in Boston in just a few weeks. She'd already been accepted into the internship program at Johns Hopkins: eventually, Mercedes wanted to become a surgeon.

Julie nodded, dashed at her wet eyes with the back of one

floury hand, leaving white, sticky smudges on her cheek. "Do you remember how Pablo came and mowed our lawn every week, after Dad got too sick to leave the house?"

Libby did remember, of course, and she might have broken down and cried herself, if Calvin hadn't yelled, at that precise moment, "I see one! I see a customer!"

Pablo's smiling face lingered in Libby's mind. She'd tried to pay him once, for taking care of the yard, and he'd refused with a shake of his head and a quiet, heavily accented, "Friends help friends. Mr. Remington, he helped our Mercedes with her schoolwork. Nico, too, when he was applying for scholarships. It is a privilege to do what little I can. "

"The scones!" Julie blurted out, suddenly remembering that they were done, and rushed to pull a baking sheet from the oven.

Despite an almost overwhelming sense of loss, there was work to be done. Libby straightened her shoulders and headed for the espresso machine again.

The customer Calvin had announced turned out to be Tate McKettrick, and he looked, as the old-timers liked to say, as if he'd been dragged backward through a knothole in the outhouse wall.

"I'm so sorry about Pablo," Libby said, wanting to go to him, take him in her arms, but uncertain of the reception she'd get if she did. The old sparks were definitely back, but she and Tate were older now and things were different. They had adult responsibilities—the shop for her, the children for Tate.

He was pale, he hadn't shaved—which only made him *more* attractive, in Libby's opinion—and his clothes, the same ones he'd worn the night before at supper, looked rumpled. What was he doing here, in the Perk Up, on the morning after he'd lost a dear friend and long-time employee?

He acknowledged her words of condolence with a nod. Shoved a hand through his hair. "It's either strong coffee," he said, "or a fifth of Jack Daniels. I figured the coffee would be a better choice."

"Sit down," Libby said, indicating the stools in front of the counter. "Where are the girls, Tate?"

He sat. Rested his forearms on the countertop. "With Esperanza. I haven't told them about Pablo yet—but of course they know something's going on…"

Calvin hurried over. "We're getting a *castle* at the community center, Mr. McKettrick," he announced exuberantly. "And I'm running for king."

"I heard about the castle," Tate said, with a wan smile. For a moment, his weary gaze connected with Libby's. "I didn't know there was going to be a special election, though."

"Only kids can vote," Calvin said importantly. "*Little* kids, who go to playschool. The big ones don't even know we're going to elect a king."

"Ah," Tate said, "a coup. I'm impressed."

"What's a koo?" Calvin asked.

Tate sighed.

"Never mind, Calvin," Libby interceded gently. "Go back to your table and watch for customers."

"Why?" He pointed to Tate. "We've already *got* one."

Tate chuckled at that, but it was a raw, broken sound, and hearing it made the backs of Libby's eyes burn.

"Calvin," she said evenly, but with affection, "I *said* never mind."

"Jeez," Calvin protested, flinging his arms out from his sides and then letting them fall back with a slight slapping sound. "People talk to me like I'm a *baby* or something, and I'm *four years old*."

"Go figure," Tate said, with appropriate sympathy.

Libby set a cup of black coffee in front of Tate.

Calvin stalked back to his post to keep watch, clearly disgusted and probably still wondering what a coup was.

"That kid," Tate remarked, after taking an appreciative sip

of the coffee, "is way too smart. Is he really only four—or is he forty, and short for his age?"

The way Tate said "kid," reflected Libby, was a 180 from the way Jubal Tabor did. Why was that?

"Tell me about it," Julie interjected before Libby could respond, as she came out of the kitchen and set a plate of fresh scones in front of Tate, along with a little bowl of butter pats in foil wrapping. She'd wiped the flour smears from her face at some point, and even with the pallor of shock replacing the usual pink in her cheeks, she was radiantly lovely. "Eat these, McKettrick. You look like hell warmed over. Twice."

"You always had a way with words, Jules," he replied. But, his big hands shaking almost but not quite imperceptibly, he opened two pats of butter, sliced a steaming scone in two, and smeared it on. "And with cooking."

Libby was seized by a sudden, fiercely irrational jealousy, gone as quickly as it came, fortunately. No matter how many new recipes she tried, how many chef shows and demonstrations she watched on satellite TV, taking notes and doing her best to follow instructions, when it came to cooking, she was doomed to be below average.

She was, she supposed, painfully ordinary.

Julie was the gypsy sister, with many and varied talents, of which baking was only one. She could sing, dance and act. Her scones were already drawing in customers, and if she ever made her float-away biscuits, folks would break down the door to get at them. She was great with kids—*all* kids, from her students to Calvin.

On top of all that, Julie had the kind of looks that made men stop and stare, even when they'd known her all their lives.

Paige, the baby of the family, was the smart one, the cool, competent one. And she was just as beautiful as Julie, though in a different way.

Libby bit her lower lip. As for her—well—she was just the *oldest*.

She was passably pretty, but she couldn't carry a tune, let alone perform in professional theater companies, singing and dancing in shows people paid money to see—spectacular productions of *Cats* and *Phantom of the Opera* and *Kiss Me, Kate,* as Julie had done periodically, during her college years.

She didn't shine in a life-and-death emergency, like Paige.

And why was she even thinking thoughts like this, when Pablo Ruiz, a man she'd liked and deeply respected, had just died—and long before his time, too?

"I don't see a single customer!" Calvin reported, his voice ringing across the shop.

"Keep looking," Julie counseled. "There's got to be one out there somewhere."

Libby was still watching Tate. Even wan and worn, with his dark beard growing in and his hair furrowed because he'd probably been raking his fingers through it all night, as all the ramifications of Pablo's death unfolded, he was a sight to stop her breath and make her heart skitter.

Here was *her* claim to fame, she thought gloomily.

She'd been dumped by Tate McKettrick.

For six months after the breakup, people had sent her cheery little cards and notes, most acting out of kindness, a few taking a passive-aggressive pleasure in her downfall. Her father had been diagnosed with pancreatic cancer by then—the dying by inches part would come later—but no one had mentioned her dad, in person or on paper. They'd written or said things like, "You'll find someone else when the time is right" and "It wasn't meant to be" and "What doesn't kill you makes you stronger."

Like hell. She'd been blindsided by Tate's betrayal. Fractured by it.

And here she was, letting him back in her life when she knew—*knew* what he could do to her.

While Libby was reconciling herself to reality, Julie collected her purse, jingled her car keys to attract Calvin's attention. "Time for playschool, buddy," she said. She squeezed Tate's shoulder as she passed him and promised Libby she'd be back in no time. If she needed scones for the midmorning rush—*if* she needed scones?—there were four dozen in the kitchen; Julie had baked them at home the night before, as promised.

As soon as Julie and Calvin had gone, Tate got off his stool, walked to the door, turned the "Open" sign to "Closed," and twisted the knob to engage the dead bolt.

Libby didn't utter a word of protest. She took the stool next to his, once he'd come back to the counter, and leaned his way a little so their upper arms just barely touched.

"Want to tell me what happened, cowboy?" she asked, very softly.

"Yeah," Tate said, pushing away his plate, now that he'd eaten the scones. He didn't meet her gaze, though. He just stared off into the void for a long time, saying nothing, though Libby saw his throat work a couple of times, while he struggled to control his emotions.

Libby simply waited.

"The dogs started raising hell, about half an hour after I went to bed," he told her, when he was ready. "They woke up Audrey and Ava, of course, since all four of them were bunking together. I went to see what was going on—I thought there was an intruder in the house or something, the way those mutts carried on. As soon as I opened the door to the girls' room, the pups shot past me, baying like bloodhounds picking up a strong scent. They ran down the stairs and straight to the kitchen—by the time I got there, they were hurling themselves at the back door like they'd bust it down to get out if they had to." He paused, drank the dregs of his coffee, but stopped Libby with a touch to her arm when she started to get up and go around the counter to get the pot and pour him a refill. After a long time, he continued. "Esperanza was awake by then, too, of course, and she kept the kids and the dogs inside while I went out to have a look around. I saw that the lights were on in the barn, and I'd turned them off after I checked on the horses an hour earlier, but I figured one of the ranch hands was out there, meaning to bunk in the hayloft. The younger ones do that sometimes, when they've had a fight with a wife or a girlfriend or gotten a little too drunk to go home."

He paused again then, swallowed hard, gazed bleak-eyed into that same invisible distance.

Once more, Libby bided her time. For Tate, not a talkative man, this wasn't just an accounting of what had taken place, it was a verbal epic, a virtual diatribe. Normally, he probably didn't say that much in half a day, never mind a few short minutes.

"I was pretty sure the dogs were just skittish because they're pups, and in a new place with new people," Tate went on presently. "They'd probably heard a rig drive in, I figured, and felt called upon to bark their damn fool heads off. I went outside, and I saw Pablo's company truck parked between the barn and that copse of oak trees."

Libby waited, seeing the scene Tate described as vividly as if she'd been there herself.

"It wasn't unusual for Pablo to turn up at the barn, even late at night—he didn't need much sleep and since he always had some project going on at his place, he stopped by often to borrow tools, equipment, things like that." Tate sighed. "I checked the barn, and Pablo wasn't inside, though all the horses were jumpy as hell, and, like I said, the lights were on. I headed for the truck, and I was nearly run down by a big paint stallion—that horse came out of nowhere.

"Pablo and I had talked about buying the stud if it went

up for sale. We were going to turn him loose on the range, let him breed and see if any of the mares threw color—"

Libby touched Tate's arm, felt a shudder go through him. "Take your time," she said, very quietly.

"Pablo *had* bought that stallion," he went on, after swallowing a couple of times. "He picked him up from the buyer and brought him over, probably planning on leaving him in the holding pen until morning, when we could have the vet come and look the paint over before—"

Libby closed her eyes for a moment. By then, she'd guessed what was coming next.

Tate looked tormented. It seemed like a long time passed before he went on. "I found Pablo on the ground, behind the trailer, trampled to death."

Sorrow swelled in Libby's throat, aching there. Such accidents weren't uncommon, even among experienced men like Pablo Ruiz. Horses—especially stallions—were powerful animals, easily spooked and always unpredictable.

"I'm sorry, Tate," Libby said. "I'm so sorry."

He nodded, made a visible effort to center himself in the present moment.

The blue of his eyes deepened to the color of new denim and, very briefly, Libby pondered the mystery of why a loving God would give dark, thick lashes like that to a man instead of some deserving woman who would have appreciated them.

Like her, for instance.

Tate rose from the stool, stood so close to Libby that she could feel the heat of his skin, even through his clothes. She felt an irrational and almost overwhelming need to lead Tate to some private place, where the two of them could lie down, hold each other until things made sense again.

"How's Isabel?" Libby asked.

Tate had his truck keys out, but he hadn't moved toward the door. His concern for Pablo's widow was almost palpable. "She'll be all right in time, I guess," he said. "Esperanza checks on her every so often. Nico's been out of the country on business, but he'll be here as soon as he can."

Libby nodded.

Tate hesitated, then touched her face lightly with the backs of the fingers of his right hand. "Wish I could hold you," he said.

Talk about that old-time feelin'.

Libby choked up, and her eyes burned. "Probably not the best idea," she said, when she could manage the words. "You need to get some rest, and I have a business to run."

Tate dropped his hand to his side. "Yeah," he said. "I'd better get out of here. Esperanza's wonderful with the kids, but she can't say no to them. By now, they may have conscripted her and half the ranch hands to dig a moat around the castle."

Libby smiled slightly at the picture his words brought to mind, followed him to the door, and then outside, into the hot, dry sunshine beating down on the sidewalk and buckling the asphalt in the road.

"You'll call if you need anything?" she said, when Tate opened the door of his dusty truck to get behind the wheel.

He arched an eyebrow, and one corner of his mouth quirked upward, so briefly that Libby knew she might have imagined it. "You walked right into that one," he said. Then he leaned forward, kissed her briefly on the mouth, and got into his truck. "See you soon," he said.

See you soon.

"Come over and have supper with me tonight," she said, because she'd had to let go of Tate McKettrick one too many times in her life, and this time she couldn't. "Six o'clock," she hastened to add. "Bring the kids."

Idiot, Libby thought. *Why don't you just jump up onto the running board of that truck like some bimbo with hay in her hair and invite him to join you in an appearance on the* Jerry Springer *show?*

Maybe the episode could be called, "Women who chase after men who stomped on their hearts."

Tate flashed that legendary grin, the one folks claimed had been passed down through his family since the original patriarch, old Angus McKettrick, had broken his first heart back in the 1800s.

"Six o'clock," he confirmed. "We'll see about the kids."

Still ridiculously flustered, Libby finally registered that a number of her regular customers had gathered inside the Perk Up since she'd stepped outside with Tate, and they were peering out through the window as he drove away.

Embarrassed to be part of a spectacle, she hurried inside.

She could close up at five, she was thinking, hit the deli counter next door at Almsted's for cold chicken and potato salad and—whatever. She would improvise.

In the meantime, there were orders to fill.

What did kids like to eat? Libby wondered, her mind busy planning supper while her hands made lattes and frappes and iced mochas by rote. Hot dogs? Hamburgers?

The regulars had barely left when a tour bus full of senior citizens pulled up. They were on their way to San Antonio, Libby learned, to see the Alamo.

It was hectic, juggling all those orders, but Libby managed it, and stood waving in the doorway as the bus pulled away.

Long before Julie got back, sans King Calvin, the scones plus four bags of cookies hastily purchased at Almsted's were gone.

"What took you so long?" Libby asked, but she smiled a little as she waggled a handful of cash just plucked from the register.

"I had to walk Harry and put a load of towels in the

washer," Julie answered, her eyes widening at the sight of all that loot. "What did you do, jimmy open an ATM?"

BONE-TIRED AND SICK to his soul, but looking forward to seeing Libby again just the same, Tate made a point of passing Brent's office on the way out of town.

Beth Anne Spales, the dispatcher/secretary the chief had inherited from a long succession of predecessors, stood in the small parking lot, watering droopy pink flowers in terracotta pots. She wore a floppy sun hat and gardening gloves, and waved when she recognized Tate's truck.

His mind tripped back to last night.

He'd called Brent as soon as he'd found Pablo's body, then he'd concentrated on rounding up the agitated stallion, shutting it up in the corral. The chief had arrived quickly, as had the county coroner, whose regular job was running the Blue River Funeral Home.

The task of telling Isabel what had happened to Pablo fell to Tate.

He'd driven over to the house by the creek, unsurprised to find lights burning in the windows, late as it was. Isabel would have waited up for Pablo; by then, she'd know something was wrong.

Except for telling Garrett and Austin about the car accident that had taken their parents' lives, and telling Libby that he'd gotten another woman pregnant and meant to marry her, relaying to Isabel the news that Pablo was dead was probably the hardest thing Tate had ever had to do. Tiny, quiet, dignified Isabel had *yowled* when he told her, like an animal caught in the steel teeth of a trap.

Now, in the bright light of a new day, Tate pulled up to the only stoplight in town, which happened to be red and would be for a while, since the timing device had quit working on New Year's Eve of 1999, thus convincing the nervous types that Y2K, with cataclysmic results, was indeed upon them.

He rested his forehead against the steering wheel while he waited, breathing slowly and deeply.

He felt sick.

Someone honked a horn behind him, and Tate sat up straight, frowning when he saw that the light was still red. Glancing in the rearview mirror, he spotted Brent, driving the squad car.

"Pull over," Brent instructed, through that damn bullhorn of his.

Tate cursed under his breath and maneuvered the truck into the bank parking lot to his right. Buzzed down his window.

"I don't know what my crime was," he said, as Brent approached the driver's side door, "but it sure as hell wasn't speeding."

Brent flashed him the Denzel grin, though he looked even worse than Tate felt. "You shouldn't be on the road in the condition you're in," the chief said. "You're wiped."

"You shouldn't, either," Tate replied.

Brent sighed. Tucked his thumbs into that honking service belt of his. His badge looked dull in the bright light of day. Resting one foot on Tate's running board, he took off his sunglasses and squinted at his friend, looking worried. "You doin' okay, here, McKettrick?" he asked. "I know you were close to all the Ruizes, *especially* Pablo. You must be pretty broken up."

"I'll be all right," Tate said. *Eventually.*

"Isabel's in a big hurry to hold the funeral and move herself and those boys in with her sister, out in L.A.," Brent said. "Did she tell you that?"

"No," Tate answered. Thinking of the Ruiz house standing empty left him feeling as though he'd been punched in the gut. The place had been a second home to him and his brothers while they were growing up. Along with Nico, they'd fished and splashed in the cold water of the creek, stuffed themselves with apricots from Pablo's fruit trees, "camped out" in the Ruiz living room in sleeping bags. "No," he said again. "She didn't say anything about that. Seems like a pretty sudden decision."

Brent nodded. "It's her life," he said. "I just hope she's not being too hasty."

Tate agreed, and the two men parted ways.

Tate pondered Isabel's plans to move off the ranch as he drove toward home, navigating the familiar country roads by instinct. He nearly stopped off on the way to remind the woman that there was no hurry to clear out. He'd been planning on deeding the place over to Pablo anyhow, as soon as the old man retired.

In the end, though, Tate decided it was Isabel's own business if she wanted to live elsewhere. For all he knew, she'd hated living in the country all along, and here was her chance to live in a city.

When he pulled in next to the barn at home, Audrey and Ava and both dogs rushed him, were on him as soon as he stepped down out of the rig.

"Hey," he said.

"Can we ride our birthday ponies?" Audrey asked.

"Please?" Ava added.

Tate considered, decided a ride would be a good thing for everybody. He'd have to keep an eye on the pups, make sure they didn't try to weave back and forth between the horses' legs.

He'd planned on a few hours of shut-eye before going to supper at Libby's, but if they weren't out on the range too long, he and the kids, they could still make it.

"All right," he said, "saddle up."

The twins saddled their ponies with minimal help, having had lots of practice tacking up Bamboozle, while Tate threw a saddle on an old gelding named Bluejack.

Audrey and Ava were already outside, mounted on their

matching "birthday" ponies, when Tate ducked his head to ride out through the barn door.

It was only then that he remembered the paint stallion, still in the holding pen at the back of the barn.

"Stay clear of the pen," he called to the girls. The steel fence surrounding the holding pen was twelve feet high, the poles set in concrete, and there wasn't more than six inches between the slats, though Ambrose or Buford might be able to dig their way under, he supposed. It didn't seem likely that they would.

Over the years, that pen had held bulls and many another stallion—some of them pretty determined critters. The steel surround had always held.

Still, *this* stallion was hell-born, a killer.

The huge animal tossed his head back and forth, snorted and pawed at the ground with his right front hoof. He looked ready to charge that fence, steel or no steel, concrete fittings or none.

A shudder ran down Tate's spine as he caught up to his daughters and rode on the side nearest the stallion.

"Is that the horse that stomped on Mr. Ruiz and crushed his heart?" Audrey asked, her blue eyes huge as she looked up at Tate. Her golden pony pranced fitfully beneath her, and no wonder—the poor little filly was a fifth the size of that stallion, if not less.

"That's the horse," Tate confirmed, his voice grating past his throat, fit to draw blood in the process. "Who told you Mr. Ruiz's heart was crushed?"

"I heard Esperanza telling somebody on the phone," Audrey said. "She didn't know I was listening."

"I see," Tate replied.

Ava looked back as they moved farther and farther from the pen and the pacing, whinnying stud, churning up clouds of dust.

"Why is he still on the Silver Spur," Ava asked reasonably, "if he hurt Mr. Ruiz?"

"Some of the ranch hands say he ought to be shot," Audrey observed worriedly. "Because he's a demon and won't ever be any different."

Tate knew, of course, about the talk going around the bunkhouse and the trailers along the creek, but he also knew Pablo wouldn't have wanted the horse destroyed. No, Pablo would have said the stud was wild and ought to be let out to run the range, siring foals and making a legend of himself.

The decision wasn't Tate's alone—the paint had killed a man, and the authorities would have a say in whether the animal lived or died. If the choice was his to make, Tate would have agreed with Pablo.

Some horses weren't meant to be tamed, just like some people.

"For now," Tate told his daughters solemnly, "here's all you need to know about that stud. Stay away from him, and keep your dogs away, too."

Ava looked back over one shoulder. "He doesn't look very happy," she said.

"I don't imagine he is," Tate agreed. "Do I have your word? You'll both stay as far from that stud as you can, no matter what?"

Both girls lifted their right hand, as though giving a oath.

"Unless we don't have any other choice, of course," Audrey said, after Tate had bent to open the wire-and-post gate so the three of them could ride through, headed for the range.

"Audrey," Tate said sternly, "I want your word—as a McKettrick."

Audrey rolled her eyes, then nodded.

Ava said, "You have my word."

Tate put the stallion from his mind then, rode with his

girls and found that it cleared his head and his soul, just like always.

An hour later, back at the house, he dragged himself up to his bedroom, kicked off his boots and collapsed facedown on the bed, hoping to catch a little sleep before going back to town to have supper with Libby.

The twins joined him, and so did the dogs.

And just the same, he slept like a dead man.

CHAPTER SIX

DURING THE NEXT LULL, Libby locked up the shop for an hour and drove her car to the auto shop for the exhaust system repair, Julie following in her pink bomb to provide feminine moral support and a ride back.

Libby left the Impala with a mechanic and joined Julie in the Mary-Kay-mobile. She'd paid the cost in advance, using the profits from the coffee, scone and cookie sales she'd made to the people from the tour bus, but if the car needed extra work, especially something critical, she would have to use a credit card after all.

Julie reached over and patted her arm. "Don't worry," she said. "Gordon's check cleared this month. I can help you out if you need it."

"Thanks," Libby murmured, feeling like a charity case. "But doesn't that money go into Calvin's college account?"

"Most of the time," Julie said, checking all the mirrors before she backed out of her parking space. "It's no big deal, Lib. Pay me back when you can."

Relief coursed through Libby, but it didn't soothe all the places that ached. Things had seemed so wonderfully ordinary that morning when she'd taken Hildie out for her walk. Two kisses from Tate McKettrick the night before and she'd been walking on air.

The grass had been greener, the sky bluer.

Impossible things had begun to seem possible.

And then Gerbera had told her about Pablo Ruiz's death.

"Do you ever feel," she began, "as though no matter what you do, it's never going to be enough?"

Julie pulled right back into the parking space she'd just left, popped the elderly Cadillac into Park and shut off the engine. "Was that the voice of a depressed woman I just heard?" she asked. She spoke quietly, but at the same time she clearly meant to get a straight answer.

"I'm not exactly *depressed*," Libby said, thinking of Calvin getting out of playschool soon, and the shop closed for business and Hildie needing to be let out into the backyard for a little while. "*Overwhelmed* is more like it."

"Oh," Julie said. "Well, yeah, I know all about overwhelmed."

"I don't know how you do it," Libby said, with true admiration. "Raising Calvin alone, holding down a teaching job—"

"We all do what we have to," Julie replied when Libby fell silent, out of steam. "And I've wondered the same thing about you now and again, sister dear. You run the Perk Up by yourself most of the time, robbing Peter to pay Paul, and then there's Marva giving a grandstand performance every couple of weeks. Add on the way you always foster the overflow from the animal shelter and, hello, you make Wonder Woman look like an underachiever."

Libby blinked, surprised. "Wonder Woman?" she echoed, with an effort at a smile.

"You're too hard on yourself, Lib," Julie went on, after nodding once, with conviction. "No matter what comes at

you, you just keep on trucking. I happen to admire that quality in a sister, or anybody else."

"Well," Libby responded, honestly puzzled, "what *else*
can I do?"

Julie snapped her fingers. "See?" she said. "It doesn't
even *occur* to you to quit. Do you think everybody's like
that? My God, Lib, when Dad was sick, you were always
there for him and for Paige and me, too. You were unstop-
pable, even after a body blow that would have dropped a
lesser woman to her knees."

The body blow, of course, was Tate's defection to the
Cheryl camp.

"That was pretty bad," Libby admitted, remembering.
Bad? She'd lost fifteen pounds and a lot of sleep, developing
dark circles under her eyes. She'd dated a string of losers,
too, ready to settle for Mr. Wrong if only to spite Tate, because there was only one Mr. Right and he was taken.

Fortunately, Julie and Paige had intervened, threatening to
lock her up in a closet, bound with duct tape, so she wouldn't
be able to ruin her life before she came to her senses. For
good measure, they'd planned to spoon Ben & Jerry's into
her until she regained every pound she'd lost and ten besides.

Julie leaned far enough to tap lightly on Libby's temple
with an index finger and ask, "What's really going on in
there?"

Back when he was healthy, their dad had done that whenever one of his daughters got too introspective, or came
down with a case of what he called "the sullens."

"Tate's coming to dinner tonight, at my place," Libby said.
"And that pretty much cinches it: it's time to book a suite
at the Home for Stupid Women and learn the secret hand-
shake."

Julie erupted with laughter. "Forget it," she said. "The
waiting list is probably way too long."

Libby laughed, too—as she wiped away tears with the

heel of one palm. "Just my luck," she said, sniffling. She straightened her shoulders, raised her chin. "We'd better get going. Calvin will be through soon."

Julie started up the car again, and they were on their way. "There's one bright spot in all this," she told Libby.

"Oh, yeah? What would that be?"

"You'll get to have sex."

"Sex?"

"You know," Julie said, with a sly grin. "That fun, sweaty, noisy, slippery thing men and women do together, usually but not always in a bed?"

"Tonight isn't about sex, it's about *dinner,*" Libby said, turning red. "He's bringing the kids, the dogs and maybe even the housekeeper."

"You know damn well you're going to end up in bed with Tate McKettrick, sooner or later," Julie insisted. "And my money's on 'sooner.' Whenever the two of you are together, the air crackles."

"And you think I should just *go for it,* after all that happened?"

"That's exactly what I think. A lot of men aren't worth a second chance, but Jim and Sally McKettrick's boy? Definitely the one to bet on."

"The sisterly thing to say would be, 'Stay away from him. He hurt you once, and he'll hurt you again,'" Libby admonished.

"If that sister happened to be a cynic, maybe."

They reached the community center, and Julie parked the car. Calvin was on the playground, with a flock of other kids, engaged in a game of tag. Mrs. Oakland supervised, carrying a clipboard and wearing a whistle on a string around her neck.

"You're telling me you're not a cynic?" Libby countered. "You, the woman who's about to skip town to avoid a confrontation with her son's father?"

Julie sighed deeply, her hands tight on the steering wheel,

watching Calvin with her heart in her eyes. "I'm not going anywhere," she said, very quietly. "Time to face the music." Then she turned to look at Libby. "And how was my plan 'cynical'?"

"Think about it," Libby said. "You didn't even consider the fact that Gordon might have turned over a new leaf, now that he's married and maybe even ready to settle down for real. You cared enough once to make a baby with him, but now you just assume he'll be nothing but trouble. If that isn't cynical, I don't know what is."

Julie smiled smugly. "Well, listen to you, Libby Remington," she said, as Calvin spotted them, spoke to Mrs. Oakland and, when the woman nodded her permission, ran toward the car. "Admitting it's possible for a man to *change*. Even one like, say, *Tate McKettrick*."

"Shut up," Libby said.

"No possible way," Julie retorted. "And watch how you talk to me, or I won't help you cook a gourmet dinner that will have a certain dark-haired cowboy begging for your hand in marriage."

Libby's eyes widened. "You'd do that? *Prepare a gourmet dinner just to make me look good?*"

Calvin reached the car and lugged open the back door to scramble onto the seat.

"Of course I would," Julie said, before turning to smile at Calvin and ask him how his day went.

"I'm ahead in the polls!" he exulted.

"That's it," Julie answered. "No more *Meet the Press* for you, buddy."

Libby laughed. "Here he is now," she quipped, looking over her shoulder at Calvin, who was busy buckling himself into his car seat. "The man who would be king."

"WHAT WOULD YOU SAY to a partnership?" Libby asked Julie, later that afternoon, the two of them practically lost in the wilderness of pots, pans and bowls that was Libby's kitchen. Instead of reopening the shop, they'd raided Julie's cupboards and freezer for the makings of dinner, stopping at the supermarket for the few things she didn't already have.

"A partnership?" Julie echoed, dipping a spoon into a kettle of pesto sauce to do a taste test. "What kind of partnership?"

"At the Perk Up," Libby said, realizing too late what she was asking of her sister and wishing she hadn't brought the subject up at all. It wasn't as if the place were a runaway moneymaker—now that she had to compete with the famous franchise, she was operating in the red, for the most part.

Calvin's laugh, accompanied by a lot of happy barking from Hildie, came through the screen door.

"Never mind," Libby backpedaled, embarrassed. "It was just a thought."

"How about sharing that thought with me?" Julie inquired. She'd changed into shorts and a pink top while they were at her place, and her eyes were a silvery gray.

"It seems silly now."

"I can do silly," Julie grinned. "In fact, it's a way of life. Keeps me sane. Talk to me, Lib."

"I was just thinking—well, your scones are so popular, and you're not working at the insurance agency this summer, so…"

"Oh," Julie said, getting it. She puffed out her cheeks, the way she always did when something surprised her and she needed to stall for a few seconds so she could think.

"I told you it was silly."

"We could sell lots of other things besides scones," Julie mused, as if Libby hadn't spoken. "Soup and sandwiches and salads. Change the name of the place, serve high tea—"

"What's wrong with the Perk Up?" Libby interrupted, thrown off. She'd done a lot of brainstorming to come up with that moniker.

"Well," Julie said, with kind forbearance, "it's not very original, now, is it?"

Libby sagged a little, around the shoulders. "I guess not," she admitted. Then, "Wait a second. You're actually considering my offer?"

"Of course I'd go back to teaching in the fall," Julie said. "That will mean cutting back to part-time here, doing the baking at night and on weekends. But, yes. I think the idea has merit."

"You do?"

Julie grinned, glanced at the stove clock. Wiped her hands on her apron before taking it off. "Yep," she said. "Calvin and I are out of here. My, how time flies when you're making pesto."

"You're going to *leave?*"

Julie widened her eyes and mugged a little. "Uh, *yeah,*" she said. "The salad is in the refrigerator. There are hot dogs, in case the kids don't like pasta. You do know how to heat hot dogs, don't you?" After Libby tossed her a look, she went on, undaunted. "All you have to do is boil the noodles and zap the pesto in the microwave and *voilà!* Pasta à la Julie."

"Stay," Libby pleaded.

Julie ignored her, walking to the back door and whistling through her teeth. "Yo, Calvin!" she called. "Time to boogie!"

"Julie—"

Julie turned, her arms folded. "You can do this, Lib," she said firmly. "Go change your clothes. And—hey—why don't you go wild and wear some lip gloss?"

AROUND FIVE O'CLOCK, showered, semi-rested and shaved, Tate studied his reflection in his bathroom mirror. "What the hell are you doing, McKettrick?" he asked himself, resting his hands on the countertop and leaning in.

There was no time to come up with an answer—a light rap sounded at his door. "Are you decent?" Audrey called, from the other side.

Tate chuckled. Was he decent? Well, that depended on who you asked.

He adjusted the collar of his cotton shirt. He'd almost gone with a suit, one of the tailored numbers left over from his days with McKettrickCo, but in the end, he'd opted for his usual jeans and plain shirt. He didn't want to seem too eager, and besides, he'd be going to a good friend's funeral in a couple of days. One suit in a week was plenty.

"Who wants to know?" he teased.

"Audrey McKettrick, that's who!" his daughter yelled in reply.

"*And* Ava McKettrick!" cried the other daughter, not to be outdone.

"Come in," he said.

The door flew open and the twins and their dogs crowded through the gap.

"Uncle Garrett is on his way," Audrey reported.

"Uncle Austin, too," Ava added.

"I know," Tate answered, steering the pair and their faithful animal companions into the larger space that was his room. He sat down on the side of the bed to pull on his boots.

"Are they coming because they want to go to Mr. Ruiz's funeral?" Audrey asked.

"Yes," Tate said simply. He'd called them both, late the night before, to tell them what had happened. Pablo had been like a member of the family, and he'd really stepped up when their folks were killed. For a while, he'd functioned as a sort of surrogate father, and Isabel had mothered them as much as they'd allow.

Ava hiked herself up to perch on the bed beside him, and Audrey took the other side. "It's sad when somebody dies," Ava said solemnly.

"Yeah," Tate agreed. "It's real sad." Since the twins hadn't been born yet when their McKettrick grandparents passed away, he wondered what, if anything, they knew about death.

"Our goldfish died," Audrey confided. "Mom flushed them."

"Things like that happen," Tate said.

"They don't flush *people,* do they?" Ava asked, clearly concerned. "When they die, I mean?"

Tate wrapped an arm around both his girls, held them close for a moment. "No," he said gently. "They don't flush people."

"People are too *big* to flush, ninny," Audrey told her sister, leaning around Tate to look at Ava.

"No name calling," Tate ordered. Then he noticed that the girls were still in their playclothes. "Better clean up your acts," he said, "if you want to go to Libby's with me."

"Esperanza is cooking," Ava told him. "She says Mrs. Ruiz will need to have lots of food on hand, with so many people coming to visit."

"I imagine that's so," Tate said. "But what does it have to do with supper at Libby's?"

"We want to stay here and help Esperanza," Audrey replied.

"She keeps crying," Ava added. "I bet she's used a *million* tissues today."

"Plus," Audrey said, "Uncle Garrett and Uncle Austin will be here."

"Right," Tate acknowledged, giving the pair another simultaneous squeeze and clearing his throat before standing up. "It's possible, you know, that Esperanza might want to be alone for a while. And your uncles probably won't show up for hours yet."

"Esperanza needs us," Ava insisted, her eyes huge with a sorrow she felt but didn't understand, even though Tate had explained as best he could.

"We'll see," Tate said.

When they'd all trooped down to the kitchen, he saw that Esperanza was indeed cooking—with a vengeance. Fresh vegetables and stacks of her homemade tortillas, among other things, all but covered the center island, and lard smoked in a skillet on the stove.

Esperanza sniffled once, approached and straightened his shirt collar. "You look much better," she said.

He grinned. "Thanks," he replied, well aware of the girls crowding in behind him. "How about you, Esperanza? Are you doing all right?"

"When I am busy," she responded, "then I am also all right."

He nodded; he understood that particular tactic well.

"The girls," the housekeeper said. "You will let them stay?"

Tate raised one eyebrow. "If that's what you really want, sure."

Esperanza nodded. "It *is* what I really want," she confirmed.

Tate believed her. "All this food is for the Ruizes?" he asked, indicating the mountains of produce and other edibles. "They won't have room for all this—their house is pretty small."

Esperanza smiled moistly. "Isabel and her children will have much company," she said, "and anyway, Garrett and Austin are coming. They are always hungry when they've been away from home."

He leaned a little, placed a kiss on the top of Esperanza's head. "I won't be late," he said. As he passed the stove, he pushed the skillet back off the flames.

Ambrose and Buford would have gone along for the ride— they got hair all over the legs of his jeans letting him know they were more than willing—but he decided to leave them at home, since the girls were staying behind with Esperanza.

Before heading for the garage, he raided Esperanza's flower garden for a handful of pink daisies and a few sprigs of that white stuff florists always added to bouquets.

Instead of driving the truck, as he almost always did, he took his green Jaguar—the thing had been sitting in the garage for months, gathering dust. Maybe he'd blow out the carburetor on the last straight stretch before town.

And maybe not.

Brent Brogan—aka Denzel—was an equal-opportunity lawman. Best friends or not, he wouldn't hesitate to pull Tate over and write him a whopping ticket if he caught him speeding.

Especially in a Jag.

Tate thought of his daughters, and how they'd grow up with one parent—Cheryl—if he got killed being stupid on the empty road.

He stayed within the speed limit, all the way to Libby's place.

The flowers were starting to wilt, lying there on the passenger seat; he picked them up carefully, wishing he'd taken the time to stick them in a fruit jar full of water or something.

You're stalling, McKettrick, he told himself, sitting there in his too-fancy car in front of Libby's *not*-so-fancy house.

Libby appeared on the porch, wearing another sundress, this one pale yellow. The light was just right, and he could see through the fabric. She'd be embarrassed if she knew, so he wouldn't tell her. Anyhow, he enjoyed the view.

"Where are Esperanza and the girls?" she called, taking a few steps forward and shielding her eyes from the sun with one hand.

"They're busy tonight," Tate answered. "I like your dress." *And what's under it.*

"Are those flowers?" she asked, and then blushed.

"I believe so," Tate joked, checking out the yard as he came through the gate. He didn't give a rat's ass about the overgrown lawn, but if he kept staring at Libby the way he had been, she might realize her dress was transparent and put on something else, thus ruining his whole night. "When was the last time somebody mowed the grass?"

"I keep meaning to get to it—"

Tate climbed the steps, bent his head to kiss her lightly on the mouth and handed over the flowers. "The lawn looks fine, and so do you," he murmured.

She laid a hand on his chest. "The neighbors might be watching," she whispered.

"Well, if they have that much free time," Tate replied, "one of them should have mowed your lawn by now."

Libby took his hand, pulled him inside.

"I'll just put these flowers in a vase and warm up the pesto sauce," she said, walking away.

His gaze fell to her delectable backside and got riveted there.

His groin tightened, and he wished he'd worn a hat so he'd have something to hold in front of his crotch until his hard-on went down.

Better yet, he thought, he could peel that see-through dress off over Libby's head, lay her down on a bed or ease her up against a wall and lick every golden inch of her and put the hard-on where it belonged.

This is not helping, said the voice of reason.

But Tate was well beyond reason by then.

And furthermore, he wasn't hungry. Not for pesto sauce, anyhow.

Light poured through the kitchen window as Libby stood at the sink, filling a vase from the faucet for the flowers. She might as well have been stark naked.

Hildie, her dog, gave him a sleepy look from the hooked rug in front of the refrigerator and then sighed and closed her eyes to get some more shut-eye.

Tate stepped behind a high-backed chair and pulled it in

front of him. He just got harder, though, when Libby turned, smiling, and approached to set the flowers in the center of the table.

Her smile lost a little of its sparkle. She ducked her head a little, to look up into his face. "Is something wrong?"

Lots of things were wrong.

There was a damn plastic castle in his yard, and it might be weeks before he could get it moved to the community center.

Cheryl would be back in a few days, full of fresh poison, and she'd make a point of whisking Audrey and Ava back to town ASAP, because she knew it twisted his insides into a knot when they left the Silver Spur.

And Pablo Ruiz was dead.

He lowered his gaze, not trusting himself to speak, not wanting Libby to see what was in his eyes.

She rounded the table, pushed the chair aside, and put her arms around him.

Her eyes widened when she felt his erection, and fetching pink color bloomed in her cheeks. "Yikes," she said.

Tate chuckled. "'Yikes'?"

"I'd forgotten how—big you get. When you're—when—oh, God, why do I even *try* to talk?" Her face was on fire now.

So was his body.

He placed his hands on either side of her waist. "It's okay, Lib," he said, grinning in spite of all the sadness and hopeless need inside him. "We're both adults, here. And *big* isn't a word most men are offended by—not in that context, anyway."

Libby was wearing her hair down that night, instead of in a ponytail, and she swept it back off her shoulders—a gesture so inherently feminine that Tate's condition immediately got worse.

Or better.

Her eyes misted over. "What are we doing?" she asked, in a near whisper.

"Getting ready to make love?" Tate suggested hopefully.

"It scares me."

"Making love?"

"No," she said, slipping her arms around his neck and giving a little sigh as she let herself lean against him. "How much I want it. How much I want you."

He put his hands to her cheeks, eased her head back for the kiss he planned to give her. "Far be it from me," he murmured, as their breaths mingled, "to deny a lady what she wants."

Libby made a little moaning sound then, part need and part frustration, as he read it, and pulled back out of his arms before he could kiss her.

"Julie's wrong," she said, near tears. "I *am* stupid."

"Never," Tate said, and he meant it. Libby had every reason not to trust him, with her body or anything else, but she was one of the smartest and most resourceful people he knew. "I'm the stupid one, Lib. I had a chance to wake up every morning until the day I die with you beside me, and I blew it. If it's any comfort to you, I'll never stop regretting that."

He turned then, fully intending to leave her house and her life and stay gone.

"Wait," she said, just as he reached the doorway that lead into the living room.

Tate stopped, but he didn't turn around.

Libby didn't speak again for so long that he thought she might have sneaked out the back door, leaving him standing there in the doorway like the fool he was.

"Tate." The way she said his name—it caught at his heart, and a few other vital organs, too. When they were together before, that tone had meant only one thing: that she wanted him.

He made himself turn back to her, even though every shred of good sense he possessed advised against it.

Libby was standing a few feet away, holding out one hand.

Confused, Tate just stood there, drinking in the sight of her and wishing he could thank whoever it was who'd skimped on the cloth for that dress. It might as well have been made of yellow cellophane.

She seemed shy, unaware of how beautiful she was. And very uncertain.

Tate felt as though he'd been underwater too long, and blood thundered in his ears. He was a man poised on the precipice of something big, something life-changing, and as much as he wanted Libby Remington, he was scared. They'd had great sex as kids. But they weren't kids anymore.

What if it was too soon?

What if it was too late?

What if it wasn't as good as before?

Good God, what if it was *better?*

Tate knew these renegade thoughts made no real sense, but he couldn't seem to rein them in.

Libby smiled, almost sadly. "Is something wrong, Tate?"

His boot soles might have been nailed to the floor, he stood so still.

Finally, he shook his head. Libby was the hometown-sweetheart type, the kind of woman a man was proud to take home to the folks, but she'd been a passionate lover, too.

He took a step toward her, closed his hand around hers. Pulled her against him, so that their torsos collided. And he kissed her. Gently at first, then, slowly and carefully, he turned up the heat.

Libby trembled—he knew she was torn between pulling away and giving herself to him then and there—and put her arms around his neck again.

Tate kissed her harder, cupped her perfect little rear end in his hands—he'd have sworn under oath that she was naked under that dress—and hoisted her up a little, her cue to wrap her legs around him.

She did.

Tate moaned, tore his mouth from hers, breathless. "Where?" he rasped.

"Right here, if you don't hurry," Libby replied, with a little laugh, a nervous mingling of desire and reticence, kissing him again.

Too preoccupied to see where he was going, Tate pushed open three different doors before he finally found her bedroom. Walking wasn't that easy, with a woman wound around him and their mouths welded together, but it was a challenge he meant to meet.

"Stop," Libby said with obvious reluctance, just as he was about to lower her sideways onto the bed, push the dress up around her waist and do what came naturally. "Tate, *stop*. Please."

He stopped.

She unclenched her legs and stood on her feet again, her face flushed, her conflict naked in her eyes.

"It's too soon," she told him miserably. "What if the time isn't right and we're not ready?"

Tate McKettrick was a Texas boy, raised right. If Libby didn't want to make love, that would be a disappointment, but of course he wasn't going to force the issue. Waiting would be hard, but Libby was worth it.

Anyhow, he hadn't brought condoms, and she probably wasn't on the pill. They'd been apart for a long time, and a lot had happened in between then and now.

Libby raised her hands to his face, and just that was almost his undoing. "Time," she said. "We need a little time first, that's all."

"How *much* time?" Tate rasped.

She laughed softly, but her eyes—her beautiful, expressive eyes—were awash in tears. "Enough to make sure we're not making a mistake," she said. "There's a lot to think about."

With a sigh, he sat down on the edge of Libby's bed, took her hand and pulled her onto his lap. Putting his arms around her, he rested his forehead against her right ear. "Did you wear that dress to torture me?" he asked, partly sighing the words, and partly grinding them out. His breath was still fast and shallow.

"What?" Was that surprise he heard in her tone, or mischief?

"Come on, Lib," Tate said. "I've seen toilet paper with more substance than that dress."

She laughed. "*Toilet paper?* Well, that's romantic, McKettrick."

He raised his eyes then, looked into hers, and the realization hit him like a whisky barrel rolling downhill.

God help him, *he loved her.*

She sobered a little, still content, it appeared, to sit on his lap in a dress made out of spun nothing and stitched together with a short length of zilch. "You okay, cowboy?" she asked quietly.

"No," he said, because lying to Libby Remington had always been impossible, and that was still so. "Not really."

Libby ran the pad of one thumb over his mouth, lightly. "When was the last time somebody held you just because you needed holding, Tate McKettrick?" she asked.

The question made his throat cinch up tight and his eyes sting. Even if he'd had the voice to answer, he wouldn't have known what to say.

She slipped off his lap to sit beside him on the mattress, kicked away her sandals and then scooted to the middle, to lie down. And she waited, without a word.

Tate hesitated, but the pull of her was too strong. He took off his boots and stretched out beside her, confused by all the things she made him feel.

Libby had made it clear that she wasn't ready to make love, yet she took him in her arms and rested her forehead against his chest.

He was lost in the softness of her body, the scent of her hair and the silken feel of her skin, the solace she seemed to radiate from somewhere in the core of her being.

I love you, he wanted to say.

But it was too soon for that, too.

So he simply lay there and let Libby hold him. Just because.

CHAPTER SEVEN

THE SHIFT HAPPENED between one heartbeat and the next.

Lying there on her bed, facing Tate, Libby felt her heart soar and then plummet, as though she were riding some cosmic roller coaster. She'd loved this man since he was a boy and she was a little girl, barely older than Audrey and Ava were now.

Over the years, that love had changed, always finding its level. Like a river, it had sometimes overflowed its banks, and she'd been swept away by its force. After Cheryl arrived on the scene, it had gone underground, leaving only cracks and debris on the surface.

Now, the river was rising rapidly, springing up from some elemental and seemingly inexhaustible source of devotion, not only within Libby, but *beyond* her, bubbling and churning, swirling into violent eddies. This time, there would be no stopping it, no changing its course, no stemming the tide.

It would be what it was, and what it was becoming, and that was that.

Powerless before the enormity of it, Libby wept in stricken silence.

Tate must have felt her tears through his shirt, because he turned her gently onto her back, so he could look down into her face.

"What?" he asked, breathing the word, rather than saying it.

Libby shook her head. Even if she hadn't been afraid to tell him what she was feeling, she wouldn't have known how to put it into words. It was as though she'd died, and then been resurrected as a different woman, with a new soul.

Tate kissed her cheekbones, her eyelids. "Lib," he persisted, his voice husky. "What is it?"

A sob tore itself from her throat, raw and hurting, and, shaking her head again, she tried to roll onto her other side, turn her back to him. But he didn't allow it.

The former Libby, practical and wary, emotionally bruised and battered, had stopped him from making love to her for a lot of very good reasons.

The new one wanted him with an incomprehensible ferocity, an instinctual craving that would not be refused, delayed or modified.

Libby took Tate's hand, brought it to her mouth, and flicked at his palm with the tip of her tongue.

He made a low sound in his throat, but he never closed his eyes. He consumed her with them, drew her into that boundless blue, where all but her most primitive instincts faded away.

She moved his hand again, this time to cup her right breast, crooned when he used the side of one thumb to caress her nipple through the gossamer cloth of her dress and the thin silk bra beneath. Her back arched, of its own accord, and her heart thrummed so loudly that the sound of it seemed to fill the room, push at the walls.

Libby knew, in those moments, only one word—his name.

It came out of her, that name, on a long, low groan, and she struggled to get free of the dress, would have ripped it away as though it were burning, if Tate hadn't pulled the garment up and then off over her head.

She felt her bra go next, her bare breasts spilling free.

Tate closed his mouth over one aching nipple, then the other, and at the same time slipped his hand inside her panties to part her, tease her with gentle plucking motions of his fingers.

Libby cried out, flailing and whimpering, desperate to be naked, to be utterly vulnerable to him in every way. When the panties were gone, first dragged down over her thighs and knees and ankles so she could kick free of them, he parted her legs and, with the heel of his palm, made slow circles at her center until she was wet with the need of him.

To his credit, Tate tried to reason with her, his voice low and ragged, reminding her that only minutes before, she'd wanted to wait, take things slowly. But he couldn't have known about the river flowing within her, flowing *through* her from some other world, with all the force of an ocean surging behind it.

At some point, he must have realized there would be no turning back, because he knelt astraddle of her thighs, pulling his shirt out of his jeans, working the buttons, tossing the shirt aside.

When he leaned over to kiss her, Libby ran her hands over his chest, his shoulders, up and down his arms and his sides, frantic to touch him, to chart the once-familiar terrain of his body.

The kiss was devastating, a thorough taking in its own right, and Libby struggled to breathe when Tate broke away from her, nibbled his way down the length of her neck, suckled at one breast and then the other.

And still Libby spoke a language composed of a single word.

"Tate." She reveled in the sound of it. "Tate."

He moved down then, slid his hands under her, squeezing, hoisting her high off the bed. When he nuzzled through and took her into his mouth, she instantly splintered, shouting now, riding a ghost horse made of fire.

The long climax convulsed her, time and again, drove the breath from her lungs and melted her very bones, leaving her limp in its aftermath. She couldn't see or hear or speak—she could only feel.

And Tate wasn't through with her.

He draped her legs over his shoulders, squeezing her buttocks slightly as he continued to use his mouth on her, now nibbling, now sucking, now flicking at her with his tongue.

The next release was cataclysmic; and it, too, went on and on, something eternal.

Transported, Libby gave one continuous, straining moan as her body buckled and seized, rose and fell, quivered and went still.

Tate was relentless, feasting on her, summoning up every sensation she was capable of feeling.

She flung her head from side to side, pleaded and threatened and coaxed, all by uttering his name alone.

He sucked on her until she'd given him everything, and then he demanded even more.

Aware of him viscerally, in every fiber and cell, though he might have been an invisible lover for all she could see through the haze of near-desperate satisfaction that had settled over her after that last orgasm, she knew when he moved to take off his jeans.

She moaned and parted her legs for him when he covered her again, an act that took all the strength she had left.

"Libby," she heard him say, through the blissful void, "if you want me to stop, say so now, because once I'm inside you, I'm not going to pull out until it's over."

She managed only the slightest demur, still floating in

a warm sea of sweet ambrosia. She wanted him inside her, deep, deep inside her, but not because she expected another climax. She'd come so many times, with so much intensity, that she was soft and moist and peaceful inside.

Until he took her in earnest, that is.

With the first powerful thrust, he opened a whole new well of need, a blazing lake of fire. Libby's eyes flew open, and she gasped in wanting and alarm.

He drove into her, nearly withdrew, drove again.

Libby went wild beneath him, digging her heels into the bed to thrust herself upward to meet him, stroke for stroke, clawing at his back and his shoulders and any part of him she could get hold of, calling to him, raging at him in her one-word litany.

They shattered simultaneously, Tate holding her high and driving into her with short, rapid thrusts. Through a storm of dazzling light, as her own body convulsed in helpless ecstasy, she saw him throw back his head, as majestic and powerful as a stallion claiming a mare. She saw the muscles straining in his neck and chest and felt the warmth of his seed spilling into her.

When it was over, he collapsed beside her with a hoarse exclamation, still spanning her with one arm and one leg.

Libby drifted, seemingly outside her body, and it was a long time before she settled back into herself. The landing was soft, featherlight—at first. But as her scattered wits began to find their way home, flapping their wings and roosting in her heart and her brain and the pit of her stomach, her very spirit began to ache.

What had she done?

What if she was pregnant?

What if she wasn't?

Tears gathered inside her, filled her, but she could not shed them, even though she yearned for the relief crying would bring.

Tate held her, brushing her forehead with his lips, murmuring to her that everything would be all right. She'd see, he promised. *Everything would be all right.*

For him, it would be. After all, he was a man.

He would get up, shower, get dressed and go back to his regular life—to his beautiful children and his sprawling ranch and all the rest of it.

The lovemaking hadn't changed him; he knew who he was, who he had always been and always would be: Tate McKettrick.

Libby, on the other hand, had been permanently altered by the experience they'd just shared, and she was going to have to get to know herself all over again.

The task seemed so daunting, so huge, so *impossible,* that she didn't know where to start.

She slept, awakened, slept again.

When she woke up the next time, Tate was gone.

His absence blew cold and bitter through her soul, like a winter wind.

Except for the aftershocks still rocking her sated body at regular intervals, she might have dreamed the whole thing.

Now came reality.

AUSTIN AND GARRETT WERE sitting at the kitchen table when Tate got home that night, a little after midnight.

Seeing his brothers, he immediately tucked in his shirt, something he'd forgotten to do before he left Libby's house. He felt heat rise in his neck and pulse along his jawline as Austin gave him that familiar, knowing once-over.

"Been with a woman," Austin said to Garrett. Except that he was thinner, and his brownish hair was in even worse need of barbering than usual, Austin resembled his old, pre-Buzzsaw self.

Physically, Tate knew, Austin had largely recovered.

But something deeper had been injured that day in the

rodeo arena, and the jury was still out on whether or not he would come back from that.

"Yep," Garrett agreed sagely, shoving a hand through his dark blond hair. His fancy white politician's shirt was open to the middle of his chest, and, like Austin, he was nursing a glass of whiskey. Scotch on the rocks, unless Tate missed his guess. "He's definitely been with a woman."

Tate chose to skip the Scotch and have coffee instead. Since Esperanza had long since scrubbed out the pot and set it for the morning, he brewed a cup of instant, using the special spigot on the sink. "You can both shut up," he grumbled, "any old time now."

With all he'd felt making love to Libby Remington again, there was a lot of mental and emotional sorting to do. Dealing with his brothers was something he would have preferred to avoid, at least until morning.

Austin laughed, and something in the tone of that laugh brought home a previously unconsidered reality to Tate. His kid brother probably hadn't been in rehab all that long; more likely, he'd been shacked up someplace with a woman.

Maybe several.

"At least he didn't give *my* present to the twins to the community center," Austin told Garrett, more than slightly smug. No matter how much Tate protested, they both spoiled their only nieces extravagantly. Cheryl allowed it, but it galled Tate.

He didn't want Audrey and Ava growing up thinking they were entitled to everything they wanted.

Garrett scowled. "It's a perfectly good castle," he said, and belched unceremoniously.

Tate wondered how long the both of them had been swilling Scotch and swapping lies. "Maybe," he growled, "you two could stop talking about me as though I'm not even here."

"Would that be fun?" Austin asked Garrett. In Austin's

world, everything had to be fun. He was the Western version of Peter Pan; Tate had long since given up the hope that his kid brother would ever grow up. He had more money than sense, and his looks—fatal to women—worked against him, in Tate's opinion.

Austin was used to coasting. Everything came too easily to him, and the effect on his character was less than impressive.

"No," Garrett said, after due and bleary consideration. "It would not be fun."

Tate took a jar of freeze-dried coffee from the cupboard and set it on the counter with more force than the enterprise really called for. "Some things never change," he said. "You're both as dumb as you ever were."

"Well, *he's* in a mood," Garrett remarked, and, after belching again, poured himself another double shot.

"God," Tate said, stirring coffee crystals into hot water and then approaching the table, "I hope you never get elected president. Two-and-a-quarter-plus centuries down the swirler. Everything Washington, Lincoln and FDR accomplished, gone."

Garrett belched again. "Now that was just plain low," he said.

"Downright mean-spirited," Austin agreed.

"You're both sloshed," Tate accused.

"Of course we're sloshed," Garrett said, his eyes suddenly haunted. "Pablo is dead. Jesus, stomped to death by a horse."

Austin looked away, but not before Tate saw that his eyes were wet. Ever quick to compose himself, Austin soon met Tate's gaze. "You found him?"

Tate nodded.

"Christ," Austin commiserated, shoving the bottle in Tate's direction. "Here. Put some of that in your chamomile tea, or whatever it is you're drinking."

"Austin?" Tate said quietly.

"Yeah?"

"Fuck off."

"So who's the woman?" Austin asked, typically unfazed. It had taken a murderous bull named Buzzsaw to get to him.

"Not Cheryl, I hope," Garrett said.

"Watch it," Tate warned, before lowering his voice to add, "She might be a bitch, but she's also the mother of my children."

"Her one redeeming virtue," Austin said.

Tate studied his youngest sibling carefully. Previously, he would have dodged a conversation with his brothers, but suddenly he was in another mode entirely. "Were you telling the truth, outside the operating room the day you were hurt, when you said you never slept with Cheryl? Because she claims it happened."

Austin raised his glass, already nearly empty again, in a mocking salute. "Nobody lies when they know they might be facing their Maker," he said. He downed what remained of his Scotch. Sputtered a little. His McKettrick-blue eyes were both looking in the same direction, but not for long if he kept drinking like that. "Besides, Tate, you're *my brother*. Much as I'd like to punch your lights out most of the time, I wouldn't do *that* even if the opportunity came my way— which, regrettably, it did."

An uncomfortable silence ensued.

More Scotch was poured.

"I'm not letting *that one* drop," Tate said.

Austin sighed, glanced in Garrett's direction.

Evidently, no help was forthcoming from the future president of the United States, who was already three sheets to the wind. If he ever made it to the White House, the tabloids would have no trouble at all digging up dirt on him.

Resigned and even a little regretful, Austin said, "I was in Vegas, for the finals. Cheryl showed up, told the desk clerk at the hotel that we were married. She must have shown him ID—her last name was McKettrick at the time, remember.

Anyhow, when I got back to my room, after the ride and the buckle ceremony at South Point, Cheryl was waiting."

Tate and Garrett were both watching him, Tate with tight-jawed annoyance, Garrett with pity.

"And?" Tate prompted.

"And she was naked," Austin admitted.

"Good God," Garrett told his younger brother, "you *are* stupid, admitting a thing like that. Are you *trying* to get those perfect white teeth knocked out of your head?"

Austin flushed. "She was naked," he insisted.

"So you said," Tate observed.

"And crying," Austin added.

"Boo-hoo," Garrett said.

"God help America," Tate said, "if *you* ever get your name on the ballot."

"The press would make hash out of him," Austin remarked to Tate, cocking a thumb at Garrett, "before he ever got the nomination."

Garrett scowled, but said nothing. He could have bull-shitted a lot of people, but his brothers weren't among them. They knew him too well.

"Cheryl was naked and crying in your hotel room *and*—?" Tate prompted, glaring at Austin.

"And," Austin said, with drunken dignity, "she said you didn't even ask for a divorce, you just told her you were filing for one. Did I mention she was in my bed?"

There had been more to Tate's decision to end the marriage, of course, but Cheryl, indignant that he'd refused to overlook her one-night stand with a prominent judge in Dallas and go on as if nothing had happened, wouldn't have included that part of the story.

Nor did Austin and Garrett need to know it.

"No," Tate said evenly. "You skipped that part, but you did say she was naked, so I guess it figures."

"She was in his bed," Garrett said, with portent. Where the hell had he been for the last minute or so?

"Thank you, Mr. President," Tate said. "And shut the fuck up, will you?"

"Listen to him," Garrett remarked to Austin. "I think I'll establish a national committee on casual profanity. Too many people swear. We need to get to the bottom of this, nip it in the bud, cut it off at the pass—"

"One more word," Tate told Garrett, "and I'm stuffing that whiskey bottle down your throat."

Garrett belched again.

Tate turned back to Austin. "Cheryl was in your bed," he reminded him.

"She was?" Austin said.

Tate reached across the table and got his kid brother by the shirt collar. "She was," Tate agreed. "And the next thing you did was—?"

Austin grinned. "Well, first, I wished you weren't my brother, and her husband, because mega-bitch that she is, Cheryl is one hot woman. I didn't ask her what she was after, because that was pretty obvious. She wanted to pay you back for divorcing her, in spades. I told her she needed therapy, and then I picked up my gear, walked out and slept on the couch in my buddy Steve Miller's suite."

"The buckle guy?" Garrett asked, evidently determined to be part of the conversation, even though he'd long since lost track of it.

"Yeah," Tate said tightly, "the *buckle guy*."

Miller, a representative of the company responsible for designing and constructing the fancy silver belt buckles winning cowboys were awarded at various rodeos around the country, was familiar to all three of them.

"I think I'll go to bed now," Garrett announced.

"Hell of an idea," Tate agreed. "That will save me the trouble of kicking your ass."

Garrett got out of his chair and stumbled in the general direction of his part of the house. The place was Texas-big, which meant they each had their own private wing, and it was not only possible but common for them to live for months under the same roof and still keep pretty much to themselves.

"He's drunk," Austin confided drunkenly.

"Ya think?" Tate asked.

Suddenly, Austin was sober. His blue eyes were clear. "I didn't sleep with Cheryl," he said.

Tate gave a great sigh. "I believe you," he said. And it was true.

"Hallelujah," Austin said, with some bitterness.

"It wouldn't hurt you to hit the sack, either," Tate told him. "You're going to have one bitch of a hangover tomorrow, if there's any justice in this world."

Austin laughed. "Lucky for me there isn't," he said, and poured himself more Scotch. "You were with Libby Remington tonight, weren't you?"

"Officially none of your damn business," Tate proclaimed.

"Might as well admit it. Somebody turned you inside out tonight, big brother, and I'm betting it was Libby."

"Okay." Tate sighed, his energy flagging now that he and Austin had settled the Cheryl incident. "It was Libby."

Austin grinned. "You're a couple again? That's good."

Tate's jaw clamped, and he had to take a second or so to unstick the hinges. "It's not that simple," he said.

"Because—?"

"Because I sold her out," Tate rasped. Basically, he thought, he was no better than Cheryl. He hadn't been married to Libby when he'd gone swimming in the romantic equivalent of a shark tank, letting things go way too far with the wrong woman, but they'd had an understanding. She'd trusted him completely, and he'd betrayed that trust.

He'd wounded her on a deep level, and he wasn't naive

enough to think that had changed, just because Libby had wanted sex. Libby had always enjoyed sex, and unless he missed his guess, she'd been doing without for quite a while.

On the other hand, maybe that was just wishful thinking.

She was a beautiful, desirable woman, and he wasn't the first—or the last—man to notice.

"Sounds to me," Austin observed dryly, after taking a few moments to mull over Tate's grudging admission that he had indeed been with Libby that night, "like all must be forgiven. Lib's nobody's fool—none of the Remington women are. If she took you into her bed, big brother, she's willing to forget the past, and that's a rare thing, especially for a woman."

The summer after he'd graduated from high school, Tate recalled, Austin had dated Libby's youngest sister, Paige. For a while there, things had been hot and heavy, if any part of the rumors flying around town had been true, but in the end, Paige had had the good sense to throw Austin over when she'd enrolled in nursing school that September and he'd gone right on risking his neck at the rodeo.

"At what point," Tate rasped, irritated, "did I say that Libby and I went to bed together?"

Austin chuckled. The sound, like the expression in his eyes and the set of his shoulders, was different somehow. His little brother had changed in ways Tate couldn't quite put his finger on.

"You didn't need to say it," Austin replied. "Your shirt was still half out of your pants when you came through the door a little while ago, your hair's furrowed from her fingers, and I'd bet money you've got a few claw marks under your clothes, too." He paused, obviously savoring Tate's silent but furious reaction to his blunt observations. "Even without all that, I'd know by the look in your eyes."

"You're wasted on rodeo," Tate all but growled. "You ought to be with the CIA or something."

Austin smiled. "Is all this going somewhere?" he asked. "You and Libby, I mean?"

Tate sighed. "Damn if I know," he said. "It could have been just one of those things."

"Or not," Austin said.

"While we're reading each other's minds," Tate ventured, "I see by my crystal ball that you haven't been in rehab most of these long months, as you led the rest of us to believe. Who is she and how serious is it?"

Austin wore a muted version of his old devil's grin while he decided whether he wanted to answer or not. "She's a waitress in San Antonio," he revealed, after considerable pause, "and it's over."

"You still think about Paige Remington every once in a while?" Tate knew he was pushing his luck, but that was a McKettrick family tradition, so long established that it was probably hereditary by now.

Austin looked away. "Yeah, sometimes," he admitted, and Tate thought they were getting somewhere, for a moment or two. As if. "When that happens, I wear garlic around my neck and nail the doors and windows shut at night."

Tate decided to let the subject drop. Shoved a hand through his hair, pushed back his chair. "Guess I'll look in on the kids and then turn in for the night. You'd better do the same, because with Pablo's funeral coming up in a few days and people coming from half a dozen states to pay their respects, things are bound to get wild around here."

Austin nodded, stood up, ready to head for his wing of the house. "What about the stud, Tate? Why's he still on the place, after he trampled Pablo like that?"

Tate thought of his little girls, asleep upstairs, and wouldn't let himself imagine the things that could happen if the devil-stallion ever got out of that pen. "The state vet took blood samples. He'll decide whether the stallion ought to be put down or not when the paperwork comes back."

Austin huffed out a breath. "You know what Dad would have done," he said. "Taken a rifle out there and dropped that horse in his tracks with a single bullet to the brain."

"Granddad, maybe," Tate answered, shaking his head. "But not Dad. What happened to Pablo was an *accident,* Austin. Something spooked the stud, just as Pablo went to lead him down the ramp from the trailer and through the corral gate. Anyhow, you know Pablo wouldn't want him destroyed."

Austin reflected a few moments. "You know I hate to see any animal put down if there's a choice, Tate," he said, his eyes clear as he met his brother's gaze, "but sometimes it has to be done."

"I know that," Tate said, though maybe he sounded a little peevish.

Austin's grin flashed; mercurial changes were a way of life with him. "I could ride that paint," he said. "Settle him down a little."

"The hell you will," Tate snapped, because grin or no grin, he knew the chances were 80 percent or better that his brother wasn't kidding. "Buzzsaw damn near killed you, and now you want to give that crazy stud a shot at breaking your neck?"

"Good ole Buzzsaw," Austin replied. "If it's the last thing I ever do, I'll ride that son-of-a-bitch to the buzzer. I'll trail him from rodeo to rodeo if I have to, but I'll draw him and I'll ride him."

Tate went cold, through and through. "You can't be serious," he marveled. "You get on that bull again, and it *will* be the last thing you ever do."

"It's the principle of the thing," Austin said.

"Like hell it is," Tate argued, with more heat than he thought he had in him after all those go-rounds with Libby. "It's your dumb-ass McKettrick pride. You're a world champion, several times over, so there's nothing more to prove.

Every cowboy gets thrown sooner or later, and Buzzsaw isn't the first bull to pitch you into the dirt, so why not let well enough alone?"

"There *is* something to prove," Austin countered quietly. "To myself."

Tate shook his head. "What? That you're certifiable?"

Austin looked Tate directly in the eyes. "I've never been scared of anything much in my life," he said. "But I'm scared of that bull. And that's something I can't live with, Tate. You know what Dad always said—if you get thrown from a horse, you'd better get right back on, because if you don't, the chances are good you never will."

Tate's gut clenched. He was the eldest; he'd always been the protector. Austin had just announced that he planned to commit suicide, and short of using some kind of unlawful imprisonment, Tate wouldn't be able to stop him.

Still, he couldn't let it drop. "Dad was talking about cow ponies, Austin," he reasoned, "not devil-bulls with blood in their eye."

Austin shrugged one shoulder. "Buzzsaw will be in the finals in Vegas this December, and so will I. There's got to be a showdown. And I'll draw him for my ride, because it's meant to be that way."

"Unless you don't enter," Tate said, chilled. "And you're a damn fool if you do."

"I've been called a lot worse," Austin answered. And then he turned and walked away from Tate, on his way to the stairs leading to his private living space on the second floor.

For a long time, Tate just stood there, his jawline tight, his fists bunched at his sides. At the moment, unlawful imprisonment looked like a viable option.

Then he shut out the lights and went upstairs.

Audrey and Ava were asleep in their beds, with one dog each curled up at their feet.

Quietly, he approached, straightening Audrey's covers and

then Ava's, kissing each of them lightly on the forehead, so they wouldn't wake up.

Cheryl would be back in a few days, he thought, trying to resign himself to giving up his daughters again. Renewed by her time away from Blue River, she'd have rearmed herself, come up with new arguments for why the twins ought to compete in the Pixie Pageant. She'd work hard to wear him down; she probably knew the effort was destined for failure, but that would only inspire her to get sneaky.

And Cheryl was real good at sneaky.

Audrey stirred in the midst of some dream, gave a soft sigh.

Her mother's daughter, she'd been working on him over the past few days, angling for his permission to enter the pageant, just as Ava had warned that she would. *Was* he just being bull-headed, refusing to sign, as Cheryl said?

Little-girl pageants offended him—he hated the costumes and the emphasis on looks—but surely they weren't *all* bad. Otherwise-sensible people—he did not include Cheryl in that category—allowed their kids to participate. Seemed to view it as a confidence builder, like playing on a soccer team or something.

Sure, there were few winners and a lot of losers, but that was life, wasn't it?

On top of all that, this particular shindig was local, not a stopover on the pageant circuit. They were holding it at the Blue River Country Club, a place as familiar to him as the post office or the feed store.

Maybe he'd been wrong, made the decision too quickly.

Audrey opened her eyes just then, smiled up at him. "Hi, Daddy," she said sleepily.

"Hello, sweetheart," he said, his voice coming out hoarse. This fathering business, he reflected, was not for cowards. You made one hard decision and there was another one coming along right behind it.

"Did you have fun at Libby's house?" his daughter asked, stretching.

Ava, in the next bed, slept on, dead to the world.

"Sure did," Tate told her.

"Esperanza cried all night," Audrey confided, worried. "I don't think she's ever going to stop."

Tate's throat tightened, aching right along with his heart. He could only shield his daughters from the hard realities, like death, for so long. "She'll probably do that for a while," he said quietly, leaning to kiss her forehead again. "But things will get better in time, you'll see."

Audrey nodded, yawned and closed her eyes. "'Night," she murmured.

Tate made as little noise as he could, leaving the room and closing the door behind him, assailed by the knowledge that while things *would* eventually get better, they might just get a whole lot worse first.

CHAPTER EIGHT

WHEN SATURDAY AFTERNOON rolled around, every business in town was closed for Pablo's funeral. Esperanza, Tate and both his brothers were among the first to arrive at the small Catholic church that would soon be bulging with mourners from every walk of life.

Since Cheryl had arrived home that morning, a day early and in a weirdly tractable state of mind, Tate had reluctantly allowed her to take the kids back to her place ahead of time. An open-casket funeral was no place for a couple of six-year-olds; they wouldn't understand about Pablo lying there in a box, still and waxy in the suit he'd bought to wear to his daughter's graduation from medical school.

A furious ache grabbed at Tate's heart as he walked slowly up the center aisle to pay his respects before the service got started. He and his brothers, along with one of Pablo's nephews and two of Isabel's, would be the pallbearers when it was time to carry the coffin outside to the hearse parked squarely in front of the churchyard gate.

There would be no graveside ceremony. Pablo had long

ago arranged to be cremated, and despite church regulations he'd left written instructions with Isabel that he wanted his ashes spread on the Silver Spur, where he'd lived and worked and raised his children. When she'd shared that request with Tate, he'd called to make the arrangements.

Up close, Pablo fulfilled all the funereal clichés. He looked natural, as though he were merely sleeping, and his expression was strangely peaceful, but when Tate touched his friend's hand, he felt a chill so cold it burned like dry ice.

"We'll look after Isabel, Pablo," Tate said, in a ragged whisper. "We'll see that she and the kids have everything they need."

A hand landed on Tate's right shoulder, and he was startled, since he hadn't heard anyone approaching. He turned to see Brent standing behind him, Denzel-handsome in a freshly pressed uniform.

"This isn't your fault, old buddy," Brent said. His intuition was a force to be reckoned with; sometimes it seemed to Tate that his friend could read minds.

"If only I hadn't told Pablo I'd buy that stud if it went up for sale," Tate answered. Isabel had just arrived, a small, veiled figure, surrounded by sons and daughters and sisters and cousins and solicitous friends. "I should have been out there to help unload that horse. Would have been, if Pablo had just called to let me know he was bringing him in."

Brent dropped his hand to his side. "I've got some regrets myself," he said. "Sooner or later, you've got to let go of the if-onlys, Tate, because you'll go crazy if you don't."

Tate nodded; he was familiar with his friend's regrets, most of which centered around his young wife, who'd been shot in a scuffle on the concourse of an outdoor mall. He left Brent beside the casket and made his way to the front pew, where the Ruizes were settling in. Nico, the eldest son, lithe and dark and intense as a matador, put out his hand in greeting. Back when they were all kids, Nico had spent a lot of time at the main ranch house with Tate and his brothers, but over the years, they'd drifted apart.

"Thanks for being here, Tate," Nico said, swallowing hard to control his emotions.

Tate would have traveled from any part of the planet to say goodbye to Pablo Ruiz, and Nico knew that. Saying thanks was just a formality.

Tate nodded, too choked up to speak.

Isabel, already seated, her face nearly invisible behind the layers of black netting comprising her veil, put out her frail hands to Tate, and he squeezed them with his own, felt her trembling. He nodded to Mercedes, who was weeping silently, and the younger boys, Juan and Ricardo. They were still in high school, Tate knew, and the luminous sorrow in their nearly black eyes tore at him.

How well he remembered the ache of that bleak and fathomless loss of a parent—he still felt it sometimes, when he was riding alone on the range, along trails he'd traveled so many times with his dad, or when he saw women around his mother's age, dressed up for church or some luncheon out at the country club. Sally McKettrick had dearly loved any occasion that gave her an excuse to wear a splashy hat, a pastel suit and high heels.

Some change in the atmosphere made Tate scan the pews as he left the Ruizes, intending to take his place alongside Esperanza and his brothers and brace himself to get through all that was to come.

His gaze settled on Libby—he hadn't seen her since the night they'd skipped supper to make love—and even in those grim circumstances, she warmed something inside him. Her dress was navy blue and her hair swept away from her face, caught up in back with some kind of clip. Julie stood next to her, clad in dramatic black, and Paige was there, too, wearing a dark brown pantsuit, her short cap of glossy black hair catching colored light from the stained-glass windows.

Tate took a step toward the three sisters, his attention focused solely on Libby, but the aisle was already crowded, and he couldn't get through.

"Tate," he heard Esperanza whisper. "Here we are."

He looked to his right, saw the housekeeper sitting in a nearby pew, between Garrett and Austin, who appeared to be supporting her with the pressure of their shoulders. Garrett studied the Remington women as they found places and sat down, but Austin stared straight ahead, with determined disinterest, toward the altar and Pablo's gleaming casket.

Just before Tate joined the others in their pew, Libby's gaze found and connected with his. Nothing in her expression changed—he might have been a total stranger instead of the man who had so recently shared her bed—but an invisible cord seemed to stretch between them, drawing taut and then snapping back on Tate with an impact that made him blink.

He took a seat next to his family.

Other mourners crowded into the church, and it got so warm, even with the laboring air-conditioning system, that people began to sweat. The organist took her place and sonorous music joined with the oppressive heat, creating a humid stew of sound.

Tate longed to loosen his tie, but out of respect for Pablo and the Ruiz kin, he refrained.

Altar boys appeared, carrying lighted candles, followed by Father Rodriguez, a slight, trundling man who moved like one carrying an enormous weight on his narrow shoulders.

A pregnant woman toward the front fainted, and there was a brief flurry while she was revived with smelling salts and led out of the sanctuary by a side door. Esperanza, who had been weeping for days, sat dry-eyed now, all cried out except for the occasional sniffle. Although she had liked Pablo, as had everyone else for miles around, Tate knew the bulk of her grief was reserved for Isabel, left a widow with two children still at home.

Esperanza had lost a husband, too, before she left Mexico as a relatively young woman, but if she had kids of her own, she had never mentioned them to Tate. A woman of benevolent and unflagging faith, she believed both her own lost love and Pablo Ruiz were safe in heaven, and that those forced to go on alone were the ones to be pitied.

Although Tate wasn't sure there was such a place as heaven, he hoped so. Hoped his folks and Pablo and Crockett, his old dog, were all together somewhere, in some bright and painless place where there were horses to ride and plenty of green grass for their grazing.

Father Rodriguez conducted Mass in solemn Latin—no doubt Pablo, an old-fashioned Catholic, had wanted it that way—and then various people took their turns going up front to say a few words about Pablo. Tate was among them, as were Garrett and Austin. He was never able to remember, after that day, exactly what he'd said—only that he'd gotten through the brief speech without losing his composure.

It had been a close one, though.

After him, Libby rose, made her way to the microphone, and told the sweltering congregation, her voice trembling, how Pablo had come to the Remington house faithfully, every single week after her father got sick, how he'd mowed the lawn and weeded and raked the flower beds and fixed whatever needed repair, from the rain gutters to the washing machine. She honestly didn't know, she said, what they would have done without him.

The story stung Tate in some deep and tender place, one he'd never explored.

The townspeople had rallied to help the Remingtons in every possible way. Had *he* done anything?

His gut roiled with the guilt he'd never been able to shake.

Oh, yeah. He'd done something, all right. Far from home, overwhelmed by the demands of law school and, most of all, missing Libby, he'd gotten drunk at a party and wound up in bed with Cheryl. Gotten her pregnant, for good measure.

Tate lowered his head.

Garrett, sitting beside him, nudged him back to the here-and-now with a motion of one elbow.

Having completed her short eulogy, Libby returned to her pew and sat down, and someone else got up to speak.

The service ended after two full hours, and Tate, Garrett and Austin joined Pablo and Isabel's nephews up front.

The coffin's bright brass handles gleamed. The lid was lowered, and one of the Ruiz women cried out then, a piercing, anguished sound—and the organist began the recessional.

Red, yellow and blue light from the stained-glass windows played over the mounds of white flowers draped across the top of the casket as the six men carried it down the aisle, toward the dazzle of afternoon sunshine at the open doors.

The casket, surprisingly light, was loaded carefully into the back of the hearse. People streamed out of the church, milled in the yard and on the sidewalk, talking in quiet voices, some of them wiping their eyes with wadded handkerchiefs, others hugging, consoling each other. Some smiled through their tears, perhaps remembering how Pablo had loved to tell stupid jokes, or share the produce from his garden, or drop off a pan of Isabel's fine enchiladas when they were sick or out of a job or mourning the loss of a loved one.

Isabel, Nico and Mercedes and the boys accepted hugs and handshakes and exhortations to call if they needed anything at all, and looked profoundly relieved when the funeral director steered them toward a waiting limousine. They were settled quickly inside, and then gone.

Tate looked around for Libby, the way a man might look for water when his throat was parched, found her standing under an oak tree, dappled in sun and shadow, Paige and Julie close by as always. They spoke quietly to friends, and though they bore little resemblance to each other, Tate knew it would have been clear even to a stranger that they were related. Something indefinable bound them together, made them a unit.

The heat was oppressive, but somehow, Libby looked cool as a mountain spring in that dark blue dress. Once in a while, her gaze strayed to Tate, only to bounce away again when their eyes met.

By tacit agreement—because that was the way things were done in places like Blue River, Texas—folks waited and foot-shuffled and fanned themselves with their simply printed programs, giving Isabel and her brood plenty of time to get home and get settled before they began stopping by with the ritual salads and spiral-cut hams and bakery goods. Personal condolences would be offered and graciously received, along with sympathy cards containing checks of varying size.

However much Isabel and the others might have preferred to be alone with each other and their memories of Pablo, the gathering at the modest house beside the winding creek was as important as the funeral. There would be a guestbook, and sooner or later, when she'd emerged from the haze of bereavement, Isabel would examine it, page by page, taking in the names of all those who'd cared.

With the throng still clogging the path between himself and Libby, Tate saw no way to get to her without shouldering his way through. So he shook hands with neighboring ranchers, kissed the cheeks of his mother's friends, and waited.

Finally, when he'd decided that enough time had passed, Father Rodriguez got into his dusty compact car to drive out to the Ruiz house, with Esperanza to keep him company on the way.

Maybe, Tate thought, he'd get a chance to talk to Libby over postfuneral coffee and a paper plate heaped with food he didn't want. On the other hand, she might have written their encounter off as a lapse of judgment and decided to steer clear from there on out.

Nobody would have blamed her for that, least of all Tate himself.

JULIE TOOK THE WHEEL of the pink Cadillac, while Libby claimed the passenger seat and Paige slipped into the back.

"For God's sake," Paige said distractedly, "turn on the air-conditioning. It's hot as hell's kitchen in here."

Julie complied, casting a brief glance in Libby's direction.

An understanding passed between them, no words necessary.

Paige, as upset over Pablo Ruiz's death as any of them, had spent most of the service trying not to look at Austin McKettrick and failing visibly.

Libby rolled down her window and fluttered the church bulletin under her chin. "Austin looks good," she commented, keeping her voice light, "for somebody who tangled with a bull not all that long ago."

"He's an idiot," Paige said, with a dismissive tone that didn't fool either of her sisters. They well remembered that, although Paige had been the one to end things with Austin, she'd grieved for months afterward.

Libby and Julie exchanged glances again, but Julie had to navigate the after-funeral traffic, so she quickly turned her attention back to the road.

"If only all idiots were that good-looking," Julie contributed. "How many guys have a whole calendar devoted just to pictures of them?"

"Shallow," Paige retorted, though she owned the calendar in question. "A Year of Austin," it was titled—she kept it pinned to the laundry room wall at her place, even though it was out of date, open to July and the image of her favorite cowboy riding a wild bull and wearing a stars-and-stripes shirt. "Austin McKettrick is *shallow*. And he'll never grow up."

"He looks pretty grown up to me," Libby observed, with a slight smile.

Julie made an eloquent little sound, part growl and part purr.

"Shut up," Paige said, peevish. "Do we have to go out to the Ruizes' place? It will be jammed, and it's so hot. I'd rather go back to your house and keep Calvin and the dog company."

"Of *course* we have to go to the Ruizes'," Julie answered, in her big-sister voice, waving to people walking along the sidewalk. "How would it look if we didn't at least stop by? And it isn't as if Calvin and Harry are home alone. Mrs. Erskine is looking after them until we get back."

Paige sighed. She could be dramatic at times—especially when she knew she might come face-to-face with the man she'd dumped before starting nursing school. "I can't believe Pablo is gone," she said. "I just saw him at the post office a few days ago. He told me some silly knock-knock joke."

The caravan of cars and pickup trucks wound out of Blue River into the countryside; Libby imagined how it would look from high overhead—like a big metal snake.

She shifted in the seat, rolled her window back up when the AC finally kicked in. A sort of delicious unease stirred in her as she recalled making love with Tate—she both dreaded and anticipated seeing him again, up close and personal. Which meant she had no business remarking on Paige's reluctant fascination with Austin at the funeral.

"Why do things like this happen?" Libby asked, knowing there was no real answer.

"Good question," Julie said, with a little shudder. "What an awful way to die."

A silence fell, and a replay of their dad's lingering death flashed in Libby's mind. He'd been heavily sedated, in no physical pain to speak of, at least toward the end, but he'd suffered just the same, she'd seen that in his eyes. A proud man enduring the indignities of a failing body.

Her own eyes burned, though they were dry, and her throat tightened until it ached. Julie, who always seemed to know what she was thinking, reached over to pat her arm.

It wasn't far to the part of the Silver Spur where Pablo and Isabel had made their home for so many years, but the ride seemed interminable that day. Dust boiled up off the winding country roads, sometimes rendering the vehicles ahead all but invisible.

No more was said about Pablo's death, or about unfortunate romantic attachments to certain men. Of the three of them, Julie was the only one unscathed by the legendary McKettrick charm, though, of course, she had demons of her own.

Gordon Pruett, Calvin's biological father, for instance.

Julie and Libby talked about the pros and cons of going into business together, turning the Perk Up into a café, but the conversation was dispirited, stopping and starting at odd times, when one or the other of them remembered why they were driving to the Silver Spur.

They were neither the first nor the last to arrive—there were cars and trucks everywhere, parked at strange angles at the edges of the Ruizes' expansive lawn. Julie found a place for the Cadillac, wedged it in and thrust out a sigh of resignation.

"Here goes," she said, shutting off the engine and shoving open her door.

The engine went through the usual sequence of clicks and clatters as it wound down.

Libby unsnapped her seat belt and climbed out, too, teetering a little because the ground was uneven and she wasn't accustomed to wearing high heels—she owned exactly one pair, relics of her high school prom—but Paige didn't move at all.

Bending her knees slightly, Libby rapped on the car window.

"I'm coming," Paige called testily, but she remained still.

The yard was crowded with people, most of them helping themselves to bottles of water jutting from metal tubs full of ice or food set out on long, portable tables tended by ladies from Isabel and Pablo's church.

Libby followed her sister's gaze and spotted Austin at the center of things, shaggy-haired but clean-shaven, and spruced up in a suit he probably wore as seldom as possible.

"Come on, Paige," she urged, growing impatient. She wanted to get on with it, so she could go home, peel off her sweaty clothes and the pantyhose that were chafing the insides of her thighs and take a long, cool shower, and the only way to get there was *through* the next stage of the ordeal. "Austin isn't going to bite you."

"That," Julie remarked, just loudly enough for Paige to hear her through the car window, "might be the problem."

Paige's pale, perfect complexion pulsed with pink. She thrust open the door and got out, glaring at Julie, who was characteristically unfazed. She linked arms with Paige, Libby taking the other side, and the three of them forged ahead.

They found Isabel first, and offered their condolences.

They signed the guestbook, and then joined the crowd on the lawn, accepting plates brimming with food they would only nibble at.

They would *circulate,* like the well-mannered Texas women they were, and make their escape at the customary signal from Libby. She was and always had been constitutionally incapable of standing in green grass without taking off her shoes; when she slipped them back on, everyone would say their farewells and converge on the car.

Libby couldn't have missed Tate, even if she'd tried. He

towered over almost everyone else gathered in the Ruiz yard, his hair blue-black in the afternoon sunshine. Aware that he was making his way toward her, pausing to speak to this one and that one, Libby surrendered to the inevitable and waited, her shoes dangling by their narrow straps from her left index finger, her plate sagging in her right hand.

"Pretty good turnout," he said, when he reached her. Tate had never been good at small talk.

"Yes," Libby agreed simply, not inclined to make things easy for him.

Color flared up in his neck and under his jawline, then subsided. "About what happened—"

Libby raised both eyebrows, pretending confusion. As if she hadn't practically dragged the man to bed and then carried on like a she-wolf in heat while he did all the right things to her.

"Dammit, Libby," he muttered, onto the game, "knock off the deer-in-the-headlights routine. This is hard enough."

The phrase *hard enough* made an inappropriate giggle bubble into the back of her throat. She barely swallowed it in time.

"I assume," she said, with false ease, "you're referring to our having sex?"

"Will you keep your voice down?" Tate said, on a rush of breath.

"If I remember correctly," she continued, in an exaggerated whisper, having already made certain no one was close enough to overhear, "we *did* have sex."

"I'm not denying that," Tate snapped.

"Why bring it up?" Libby asked mildly, knowing full well why he'd mentioned the tryst. He wanted to make sure she understood that the encounter had been meaningless, a fling. She mustn't expect anything more.

"Because," Tate said, leaning in close, his forehead nearly touching hers, "things have changed."

The statement took Libby by surprise, and when she widened her eyes and raised her brows this time, she wasn't pretending. "Changed?" she echoed stupidly.

Tate took her by the elbow, the one on the left, with the shoes dangling from the corresponding finger, and hustled her away from the gathering to stand in the small orchard, under one of Pablo's cherished apricot trees. She looked around, spotted Julie arguing quietly with Garrett, and Paige and Austin standing with their backs to each other, not a dozen feet apart, both of them stiff-spined.

Clearly, neither of her sisters would ride to her rescue.

"Tate, what…?"

"Stop it," Tate rasped. "*Something happened,* Libby, and I'm not going to pretend it didn't."

Another giggle, this one hysterical, tried to escape Libby, but she dropped her shoes and put her hand over her mouth to keep it in.

Tate let out his breath, and his broad shoulders sagged a little under the fine fabric of the tailored suit he was sweltering in. Once again, Libby imagined a cold shower, but this time Tate joined her in the fantasy, and the resulting surge of heat nearly melted her knees.

"I want another chance with you," he said, stunning her so thoroughly that he might as well have aimed a Taser gun at her and pulled the trigger. Shoving a hand through his hair, he sighed again. "I know I don't deserve it," he went on. "But I'm asking for another shot."

The plate fell from Libby's hand, potato salad and cold chicken and something made with green gelatin and sliced bananas plopping at their feet. Both of them ignored it.

"*What?*" Libby sputtered, amazed.

An expression of proud misery moved in Tate's strong face, was gone again in an instant. "A simple 'no' would do," he said. Maybe the misery had gone, but the famous McKettrick pride was still there.

"You—you mean, it wasn't—well—just one of those things?" Libby managed.

"'Just one of those things'?" His tone was almost scathing. "Maybe you have that kind of sex all the time, Lib, but *I don't.*"

This round, the giggle got past all her defenses. It was a shaky sound, a little raspy. "You think I have sex all the time?" she asked, only too aware that she was prattling and completely unable to help herself. Whenever sex and Tate McKettrick occupied the same conversation, or even the same thought, her IQ seemed to plummet. Incensed by this sudden realization, she raised both hands, palms out, and shoved them hard into Tate's chest. *"You think I have sex all the time?"*

Through the haze surrounding her, Libby sensed that heads were turning.

She caught a glimpse of Julie hurrying in their direction. Paige was probably on the way, too.

"Dammit, Libby," Tate almost barked, "this is a *wake.*"

Libby shoved him again, and then again. Enjoyed a brief mental movie in which he tumbled backward and landed on his fine McKettrick ass under Pablo's apricot trees.

Tate proved immovable, though, since he was so much bigger than she was. Just as Julie reached them, he grasped Libby's wrists to stay the blows.

"Look," he ground out, "that didn't come out right. I meant—"

Libby felt dazed, literally beside herself. Her heart pounded, and she was sure she was hyperventilating.

Julie stooped to snatch up Libby's shoes. "Time to go," she chimed.

Slowly, Tate released his hold on Libby. "I'm sorry," he said.

Libby stared at him, nearly blinded by tears. Didn't resist

when Julie tugged her away, keeping to the edge of the crowd.

Paige caught up, double-stepping.

"What just happened here?" Julie asked moderately, when they were all in the car.

Before, the blast of cool hair from the vents on Julie's dashboard had been a blessed relief; now, it made Libby hug herself and shiver. Her lower lip wobbled, and she couldn't bring herself to look at her sister.

"I'm not sure," Libby said brokenly, but only after Julie had put the Cadillac into Reverse, stepped on the gas and negotiated a series of complicated maneuvers, involving a lot of backing up, inching forward and backing up again. "Things just—got out of hand."

"I'll say," Paige commented, from the back seat.

Fresh mortification washed over Libby. "Please tell me we weren't yelling."

"You weren't yelling," Julie said.

"Really? Or are you just saying that?"

Julie chuckled. "Honey, neither of you *had* to yell. The air crackled like it does before a good ole Texas lightning storm. From the looks of things, the two of you were either going to kill each other or make a baby on the spot."

Libby slid down in the seat, horrified. "Oh, my God," she moaned.

"McKettrick men," Paige offered calmly, "can turn a sane woman crazy."

Tate's words came back to Libby. *This is a wake.*

"Isabel will never forgive me," she said.

"Isabel," Julie soothed, in her practical way, "was inside the house by the time hostilities broke out, lying down with a cold cloth over her eyes. And don't look now, but sparks flying between you and the McKettricks' number one son aren't exactly breaking news around these parts."

Libby's embarrassment was now total. How would

she face people after making such a scene? What had come over her?

She tried to retrace the conversation in her mind, to pinpoint exactly where she'd stepped on a land mine, but it was all a nonsensical jumble of he said/she said.

Except that Tate had basically accused her of being promiscuous.

Hadn't he?

"This is it," Libby decided aloud, as they bumped over the rutted dirt road leading back toward the highway. "I'm leaving town forever. I'll change my name, dye my hair—"

Paige unhooked her seat belt and poked her head between the front seats. "Don't be silly," she said. "Everybody makes a complete and utter fool of themselves now and then."

"Gee," Libby nearly snarled, "*that* was a comforting thing to say."

"If it's any consolation," Paige pressed on, undaunted, "Tate looked as if he wished the ground would open up and swallow him."

"It isn't," Libby replied.

"Let's not bicker," Julie interjected.

"We're *not* bickering," Paige bickered. "I was merely stating a fact. Playing the fool once in a while is only human."

"Paige?" Julie said sweetly.

"What?"

"Shut the hell up."

Paige sagged backward, fastened her seat belt back with a metallic snap, grumbling something under her breath.

"*You* never made a fool of yourself," Libby accused her youngest sister, her gaze colliding with Paige's in the rearview mirror. "Miss Perfect."

Paige rolled her eyes. "You've got a short memory," she shot back. "I tried to run Austin McKettrick over with a golf cart once, if you'll recall."

"Chased him right down Main Street," Julie reminisced fondly. "Good thing he was so quick on his feet."

"Shut up," Paige said.

"That was my line," Julie answered.

Libby began to laugh. Like the giggles she'd battled earlier, this laughter was more a release of tension than amusement Still, it *had* been funny, watching Austin sprint down the white line, sometimes backward, laughing at Paige as she swerved behind him at lawn-mower speed.

Austin had finally taken refuge on the courthouse steps, gasping for breath, and Paige had plainly intended to drive right up after him. Fortunately, she'd commandeered a golf cart instead of an army tank—the front wheels bumped hard against the bottom stair and then the engine died. *Un*fortunately, she'd nearly been arrested and would probably have gone to jail for attempted assault if Austin hadn't refused to press charges.

"Okay," Libby admitted, turning to look back at Paige, "there was that one lapse. But I've never seen you lose your temper, before or since, which makes me wonder if you're an alien or something."

"Some of us," Julie remarked loftily, "have sense enough not to get involved with a McKettrick in the first place."

"Oh, for Pete's sake," Paige scoffed. "I saw you shaking your finger beneath Garrett's nose back there. If he wanted to get under your skin, he could—it's a gift. They all have it."

"Please," Julie said, gliding up to a Stop sign pocked with bulletholes, a common sight in that part of Texas, and signaling a left turn before swinging that big pink boat out onto the asphalt to head for town. "Me and *Garrett McKettrick?* The man is a *politician.* You know what I think of *that* species."

"He's also good-looking in the extreme," Libby pointed out.

"Not to mention McKettrick-rich," Paige added.

"He's a player," Julie went on. "God knows how many women he's stringing along."

Again, Libby's gaze connected with Paige's in the rear-view mirror.

"Uh-oh," Paige said.

"I don't care about looks," Julie insisted. "*Or* money. Garrett McKettrick is definitely not my type."

"What *is* your type?" Libby asked, glad to be talking about something besides the debacle with Tate, back there in the Ruizes' orchard.

"I don't have one," Julie said. "I've resigned myself to being single. In fact, I *like* being single. Calvin and I are doing just fine on our own, thank you very much. The last thing we need is a man complicating our lives."

"What about sex?" Paige asked. "Don't you miss that?"

Libby began to feel overheated again. Why did *sex* have to come up in every conversation? She went months without thinking about the subject at all—much—and now it seemed to be in her face every time she turned around. What was up with that?

"You don't have to be married," Julie reminded her sisters, "to enjoy sex."

"No," Paige agreed, "but a *man* helps."

Libby's face flamed as her flesh prickled with remembered sensations: Tate's mouth on her neck, on the insides of her elbows and the backs of her knees, on her—well, *everywhere.*

"Don't tell me you're using a vibrator," Paige said, like it was a crime or something. "You're still young, Julie. You need a man."

Julie's neck was bright red. "Who said anything about a vibrator?" she snapped. "And how do you know I'm not having a wild, passionate affair? I do have *some* secrets from you two, after all."

"No, you don't," Paige replied smugly. "If you were seeing

someone, I'd know it, and so would everybody else in Blue River."

Here it comes. Libby bit down on her lower lip, closed her eyes.

But Paige was on a roll. "That's the problem with small towns," she went on mercilessly. "When somebody goes to bed with somebody else—" here, she paused for effect "—word gets around in no time. Take Libby and Tate, for instance."

Libby winced.

"Libby," Julie said, sounding intrigued, as well as shocked, *"you didn't."*

"Oh, yes, she did," Paige trilled, the triumphant little sister avenging a multitude of childhood slights.

Libby covered her face with both hands and groaned.

"Is this true?" Julie asked slowly.

Libby would gladly have violated a lifetime of principles just then and lied like a pro, but she knew both her sisters would see right through it. They knew each other too well.

"Yes," she said, after a very long time. "Yes, I slept with Tate McKettrick. Are you satisfied?"

"No," Julie said succinctly. "But I'll bet *you* were."

CHAPTER NINE

As far as Tate was concerned, the house was just too damn big.

He knew Garrett and Austin were around, but they were keeping to themselves, and with the kids back at Cheryl's place and Esperanza helping with the clean-up over at the Ruizes', Tate might as well have been alone on the planet.

Except, of course, for Ambrose and Buford.

Most likely missing the twins, the pups had found his best work boots next to the back door and systematically chewed them to pieces.

With a pang, he thought of Crockett. As a pup, his old dog had had a penchant for chewing boots, too. And Charlie, one of Crockett's many predecessors, had reduced a custom-made pair, Tate's dad's pride and joy, to shreds.

Tate recalled how scared he'd been. Another kid's father had shot a dog for a far lesser crime, and even though Jim McKettrick, a strict but fair father, had never raised a hand to any of his sons or their mother, Tate had been sure his beloved dog was facing immediate execution.

Eight years old at the time, he'd left home with Charlie, the two of them headed overland in the general direction of Oklahoma, going by the compass he'd gotten for Christmas. He was lugging the dog's plastic food bowl and a rolled-up sleeping bag and not much else, with no specific destination in mind.

His dad caught up to them on horseback about an hour into the journey, probably tipped off by one of the ranch hands. On a busy spread like the Silver Spur, it was hard for a kid to get away with much of anything since somebody was always watching, ready to run off at the mouth at the first opportunity.

"Where you headed?" Jim had asked, almost casually, pulling his well-worn hat down low over his eyes and shifting easily in the saddle. His big chestnut gelding snorted, peeved at being reined in when he'd rather be punching cattle.

Tears had welled up in Tate's eyes; all those years later, he could feel the burn of them, a sort of dry, scalding sensation. "Me and Charlie figured we ought to leave," he'd answered, dropping his head for a moment before meeting Jim's steady gaze. "Charlie went and chewed up your good boots—the ones Mom had made for your birthday, with our brand and the Alamo and the flag of the Republic on them."

Jim had taken off his hat then, run the sleeve of his sweat-stained chambray shirt across his face and leaned forward a little, resting one forearm on the saddle horn. "I see," he'd said quietly, before putting the hat back on. "And you reckoned that lighting out on your own was the best course of action?"

Tate had swallowed hard. Now, he was going to be in trouble for running away, he guessed, on top of Charlie taking a bullet in the head out behind the barn. Having no answer at hand, he'd simply looked up at his father and waited forlornly for the collapse of the known universe.

Jim had sighed, swung one leg over the gelding's neck, and jumped to the ground. Approaching Tate and the dog, he'd crouched to ruffle Charlie's mismatched ears, one a grayish-brown, one white. A stray who'd shown up at the ranch one day with his ribs showing and his multicolored coat full of burrs, Charlie wasn't much to look at, but except for boot-chewing, he pretty much behaved himself.

"Look at me, boy," Jim had said, his voice gentle.

Tate had met his father's fierce blue gaze. "You gonna shoot Charlie, Dad?" he'd asked.

"Now why in the devil would I do a thing like that?"

"That's what Ryan Williams's dad did when their dog wrecked the new carpet."

"Well, son," Jim had drawled reasonably, still sitting on his haunches, "I'm not Ryan Williams's dad, now am I? I'm yours."

Tate's heartbeat had quickened, and he'd almost flung himself into his father's arms before he remembered that he was eight years old and too big for that kind of stuff. "I guess I'm still in trouble, though?"

Jim had looked away, probably to hide a grin. "I guess you are," he'd answered presently. "Running away from home is a dangerous thing to do, Tate. Your mother is half frantic, calling all over the countryside looking for you."

"How about Charlie? Is he in any trouble?"

Jim had chuckled then. Stood up tall, with the sun behind him. "Charlie's in the clear. Dogs chew things up sometimes, because they don't know any better. You, on the other hand, don't have that excuse. You *do* know better. You're going to have to do extra chores for a month, and you can forget that school field trip to Six Flags next week, because you won't be going along."

Tate had merely nodded, too relieved that Charlie was going to be all right to care about staying behind when everybody else in the whole school went to Six Flags. He knew he'd care plenty when the time came, though.

His dad had laid a hand on his right shoulder. "Let's go on home now," he said, "before your mother calls in the FBI."

Tate had ridden back to the ranch house in front of Jim, clutching the dog bowl and the sleeping bag, Charlie trotting cheerfully alongside the horse.

Back in the present, Tate crouched the way his father had done that day. Ruffled one dog's ears, then the other's. "You're a pair to draw to," he said. "And this'll teach me to leave my boots by the back door when I come in from the range."

After that, he took the mutts outside.

They headed straight for the castle, sniffing the ground, probably trying to track Audrey and Ava.

Tate missed his daughters sorely as he watched their dogs searching for them. Even when he was a kid, broken homes were common, but he and his brothers had grown up under one roof, with parents who loved them and each other, and until the split with Cheryl, the concept had been foreign to him.

Now, he was all too familiar with it.

The dogs returned to him, tails wagging, taking their failure to scare up the twins in their stride. He wished he could accept the kids' absence as philosophically as the pups had.

When Garrett's black sports car zoomed backward out of the garage, Tate was so startled that he almost left his hide in a pool on the ground and stepped out of it like a pair of dirty jeans.

Seeing him, accurately reading the glower taking shape on his face like clouds gathering to dump a ground-pocking rain, Garrett winced. Rolled down his window.

"Sorry," he told Tate, with a sheepish grin.

Maybe if it hadn't been for Pablo's funeral and the way he'd blown things with Libby in the orchard and the kids being gone from home again, Tate would have held his temper. As things stood, though, his brother's careless mistake pushed him one step over the line.

Rounding the ridiculously expensive car, he slammed both fists down onto the shiny hood and glowered hard at Garrett through the bug-specked windshield.

"Hey!" Garrett protested, shoving open the driver's side door and piling out, face flushed, eyes flashing. "What the *hell*—"

Tate advanced on Garrett, seething. Gripped him by the front of his white dress shirt and hurled him back against the car. "Did you even glance in your rearview mirror before you shot out of that garage like a goddamm bullet?" he yelled. "What if one of the kids had been behind you, or one of these dogs?"

Garrett paled at the mention of possibilities he obviously hadn't considered.

Tate let his hands fall to his sides, stepped back out of his brother's space.

A few awkward beats of silence passed.

"You all right?" Garrett asked at last, his voice hoarse.

Tate looked away, didn't answer because anything he said would only make bad matters worse.

"Tate?" Garrett pressed, never one to leave well enough alone.

Tate met Garrett's gaze, held it steadily, still holding his tongue.

"Look," Garrett said, "I'll be more careful after this. It's been one hell of a day for all of us, and I guess I just wasn't thinking."

"You think this was a bad day?" Tate said, after grinding his back molars together for a second or so. "That wouldn't begin to cover it if you'd killed somebody just now."

Garrett surveyed him. "I said I was sorry, Tate," he replied evenly. "I said I wouldn't make the same mistake a second time. What more do you want—a strip of my ornery Mc-Kettrick hide?"

"I'll have a lot more than a *strip* of your hide if you ever do a damn fool thing like that again."

Garrett sighed and straightened his shoulders, and Tate could almost see the politician in him coming to the fore. Trouble was, Garrett *wasn't* a politician, he was a rancher, though it looked like he was going to be the last one to figure that out. "Can we start over, here? Before we wind up rolling around in the dirt the way we did when we were kids?"

Tate thrust out a breath. Allowed himself a semblance of a smile at the memory of all those barnyard brawls. Their mother had broken up more than one by spraying her three sons with a garden hose. Their dad's method had been more direct: he'd simply waded into the middle of the fray, got them by the scruff and sent them tumbling in three different directions.

"Okay," he said. "Let's start over."

Garrett grinned. Then he got into his car, drove it into the garage and backed out again, covering about an inch per hour.

Watching Tate, he raised both eyebrows as if to say, *Satisfied?*

"Where were you headed in such a hurry, anyhow?" Tate asked.

"The senator," Garrett said, the grin gone, "is having an emergency."

"The senator," Tate replied, "is *always* having an emergency. What is it now? Did the press catch him naked in a hot tub with three bimbos again?"

"That," Garrett replied, stiff with indignation, "is not what happened."

"Right," Tate scoffed. It was a wonder to him how Garrett's famously incompetent boss and so-called mentor kept getting reelected to the U.S. Senate.

"You know what you are, Tate?" Garrett countered, scowling. "You're a sore loser. You voted for the opposition, they lost by a landslide and now you're raking up muck. I'm surprised at you."

Tate gripped the edge of the open window and stooped a little to look directly into his brother's face. "Pull your head out of your ass, Garrett," he said. "*The senator,* as you so augustly refer to him, is a crook—and that's his *best* quality. When are you going to stop cleaning up his messes and set about making some kind of life for yourself?"

"A life like yours?" Garrett retorted, his eyes fairly crackling with blue fire. "Playing the gentleman cowboy while a bunch of ranch hands do the real work? Don't kid yourself, Tate. You might be all grown up on the outside, but inside, you're still the rich kid from the biggest ranch in four counties, feeling like you ought to apologize to folks who have to earn a living. When the kids are with Cheryl, you just mark time until they come back. Maybe that looks like a life to you, but I'd call it something else."

Physically, Tate didn't move. On the inside, though, he pulled back, stunned by Garrett's words—and the sickening knowledge that they were at least partly true.

"Oh, hell," Garrett said, sounding pained. "I didn't mean that—"

"Sure you did," Tate broke in gruffly. "And maybe I had it coming."

Garrett started to open the car door, waited pointedly until Tate got out of the way. "It wasn't your fault, what happened to Pablo," he said calmly, once he was on his feet again.

"Wasn't it?" Tate countered bitterly. "Pablo wasn't a young man. He shouldn't have been transporting that stallion on his own. *I'm* the one who thought it would be a good idea to breed ourselves some spotted ponies."

"And Pablo should have called you beforehand, let you know what was going on. You could have helped unload the horse, or arranged for someone else to make the delivery." Garrett paused, probably following the obvious mental trail, and frowned. "You might have been killed yourself, Tate."

Tate didn't reply. He was too busy imagining his girls with one parent—Cheryl. She'd have them in boarding school by puberty at the latest, and spend the bulk of her time trying to figure out how to get into their trust funds.

Garrett started to get back into the car. "I'd better get back to the capital," he said. "The senator has been under a lot of stress lately."

A sour taste filled Tate's mouth at the mention of the politician his brother revered so much, and he spat.

Garrett reddened. "His enemies are trying to discredit him," he said hotly. "The press dogs his every step and his older brother is dying of prostate cancer. Maybe you could cut the senator just a *little* slack."

"I'm sorry about his brother," Tate allowed. By his reckoning, the senator's other problems were his own doing.

Garrett glared. "The senator," he said, "is a truly great man."

Tate shook his head, resisted the need to spit again. "You've definitely got a blind spot where Morgan Cox is concerned, Garrett, whether you'll admit as much or not. What has to happen before you *get* it? You're climbing the ladder to success, all right, but it's up against the wrong wall."

"What you need," Garrett retorted furiously, after maybe thirty seconds of internal struggle, "is a woman. Maybe you'd have a better temperament than a grizzly with a bad toothache if you got laid. Why don't you go find yourself a lady again, and bang her, and get the burrs out from under your hide?"

Tate folded his arms. "I really hope," he said, "that that wasn't a reference to Libby Remington. Because if it was, I'm going to have to kick your ass from here to Houston and back."

A grin crooked up one corner of Garrett's mouth. The man, Tate reflected, was tired of living, egging him on like that. "Wait a second," Garrett said. "That little set-to the two of you had in the Ruizes' orchard this afternoon—"

"That was nothing," Tate said flatly, and without a hope in hell that Garrett would believe him.

"Damn," his brother went on, in the tone of the man enjoying a sudden revelation, "you could do a lot worse than Libby Remington. Come to think of it, you *did* do a lot worse than Libby Remington. Did I mention that I ran into Cheryl at a party in Austin the weekend before the twins' birthday?"

"No," Tate said. "Maybe you didn't mention it because you know I don't give a rat's ass what Cheryl does, as long as she takes good care of my kids when they're with her."

Garrett snapped his fingers. "Maybe that was it," he said, clearly delighted to be nettling Tate.

"In about another second," Tate replied, "I'm going to wipe up the ground with you, little brother."

Garrett removed his cuff links, rolled up his sleeves. "Bring it on," he said.

That was when the spray struck them, ice cold and shining like liquid crystal in the last light of a long, difficult day.

Both of them roared in surprised protest and whirled around to find Austin standing a few yards away, holding the garden hose and grinning like an idiot with a winning lottery ticket in his pocket.

"Peace, brothers," he said, and drenched them completely with another pass of the hose.

Water shot through the open window of Garrett's car and made a sound like fire on the fancy leather seats, then sluiced down the inside of the windshield.

Tate laughed out loud, but Garrett bellowed with rage and advanced on Austin, dripping wet, ready to fight.

Tate went after their kid brother, too, but for a different reason.

Water fights were something of a McKettrick tradition, and it had been way too long since the last one.

JULIE SEEMED A LITTLE TROUBLED when she and Paige dropped Libby off in the alley behind the house they'd all grown up in.

"Are you sure you won't come home with us for supper?" she asked. "My special spaghetti casserole has been simmering in the slow cooker all day and Calvin would love to see you."

Libby, standing by her back gate with the straps of her high heels in one hand and her clutch purse tucked under the opposite arm, shook her head and smiled. "I'd love to see Calvin," she said sincerely, "but Hildie needs a walk, and I plan on getting to bed early tonight. The sooner I fall asleep, the sooner this day will be over."

Paige, out of the back seat and about to climb in up front, rose onto her tiptoes to peer at Libby over the roof of the car. "No hard feelings, Lib?" she asked hopefully.

Libby shook her head again. "No hard feelings," she replied.

"I could bring over some spaghetti casserole," Julie fretted. "Leave it on the porch if you and Hildie are still out walking when I get here—"

Libby cut her off. "Julie," she said, *"I'm fine."*

Paige got into the passenger seat and shut the door.

Libby waved. *"Goodbye."*

Still, Julie waited until Libby had fished her keys out of her bag, unlocked the back door and stepped inside to greet an overjoyed Hildie.

Behind her, Libby hear the Cadillac drive off.

After receiving a royal welcome from her favorite canine, Libby opened the door again, and Hildie trundled out into the yard. By the time the dog returned, Libby had washed out and filled the usual bowls with kibble and water.

While Hildie ate and drank, Libby exchanged her dress for tan cotton shorts and a T-shirt. The hateful pantyhose went into the bathroom trash can, and she flung the shoes to the back of her closet. Short socks and a pair of sneakers completed the ensemble.

The walk was pleasant, restoring Libby a little, and by the time she and Hildie got home, she was getting hungry. Wishing she hadn't been quite so quick to turn down Julie's offer to drop off some of her famous spaghetti casserole, Libby was taking a mental inventory of the contents of her refrigerator as she stepped through the front gate, and didn't immediately notice the figure huddled on the porch steps.

Hildie gave a half-hearted little bark—she wasn't much of a guard dog—and Libby stopped in her tracks, fighting an urge to pretend she had the wrong house, turn around and flee.

"Marva?" she asked, instead.

Her mother wore a black and gold, zebra-striped caftan from her extensive collection of leisure garments, along with plenty of makeup. "It's about time you got home," Marva accused, making a petulant face. "I don't have a house key anymore, you know."

Libby considered the distance between the condominium complex and her place, and frowned. Marva often took long walks, but never without her prized athletic shoes, and to-night she was wearing metallic-gold flats with pointed toes. "How did you get here?" Libby asked.

Marva jutted out her chin, still angling for a welcome, evidently. "I took a cab," she said. "It's not as if I could count on any of my *children* for a ride, after all."

Libby remembered to latch the gate, leaned down to unhook Hildie's leash. There was precisely one taxi in Blue River, and it was often up on blocks in the high weeds behind

Chudley Wilkes's trailer-house, though he'd been known to fire it up when someone called, wanting a ride someplace and willing to pay the fare.

"Are you hungry?" Libby asked, sitting down beside her mother on the step. Up close, she could see that Marva's red lipstick had gone on crooked and was mostly chewed off. "I could make scrambled eggs—"

"The cabdriver was a hayseed," Marva went on, as though Libby hadn't spoken at all. "He claims he's related to John Wilkes Booth, on his mother's side. Booth's mother, not his."

"Chudley likes to spin a yarn, all right," Libby said. "Not many people call for a taxi in a town this size, so he has a lot of time to study the family tree. Over time, he's grafted on a few branches."

"Aren't you going to ask me in?" Marva asked. "I came all this way, and you just leave me sitting on the front porch like some beggar."

Libby figured there no use pointing out that she'd just offered to whip up some scrambled eggs and hadn't planned to serve them on the front porch. "Of course you can come in," she said, rising.

All this time, Hildie had been standing on the walk, head tilted to one side, studying Marva as though she had sprouted out of the ground only moments before.

"Whose dog is that?" Marva fussed, though she'd made Hildie's acquaintance at least once before. "I don't like dogs. It will have to stay outside." She made a go-away motion with the backs of her hands. "Scat! Go home."

"Hildie is my dog," Libby said carefully, a sick feeling congealing in the bottom of her stomach. "She *lives* here."

"Shoo," Marva said, paying no attention to Libby. Most of her conversations were one-sided; she did all the talking and none of the listening. "Go away."

Hildie hesitated, then backed up a few steps, confused.

"Mother," Libby said, annoyed, as well as alarmed, "*don't*. Please. You're scaring her."

But Marva had turned her head to stare at Libby. "Did you just call me 'Mother'?"

Libby wasn't sure how to answer. Years ago, before she'd packed a suitcase and left, Marva had hated being addressed by that term, or any of its more affectionate variations.

"It doesn't matter," she finally said. "Let's go in and I'll start the scrambled eggs." Then, more firmly, she called her dog. "Come on, Hildie."

Hildie hesitated, uncertain, then lumbered toward Libby, full of trust.

"I won't be in the same house with that horrible creature," Marva warned.

"Then you'll have to eat your supper out here," Libby replied, very quietly, "because Hildie is coming inside with me." *And, furthermore, she is not a "horrible creature."*

Marva began to cry, sniffling at first, then wailing. "You hate me! I'm all alone in the world!"

The truth was, Libby didn't hate Marva—she'd shut that part of herself down a long, long time ago—but she couldn't have said she loved her, either.

"Come inside," Libby urged gently. "I'll brew some tea. Would you like a nice cup of tea?"

Marva stepped over the threshold, stood in the small, modestly furnished living room, looking around. She didn't seem to notice when Hildie slunk in behind her and took refuge behind the couch.

"I lived here once," Marva said, as though she'd just recalled the fact.

"Yes," Libby confirmed, at once suspicious and sympathetic. "You lived here once."

And then you left. Even though Paige and Julie and I begged you not to go.

"Where did he die?" Marva asked. Her mascara had run,

404 LINDA LAEL MILLER

and her hair was starting to droop around her face, but the expression in her eyes was lucid. "Show me where he died."

Libby moved to stand where her father's rented hospital bed had been, during the last months of his life. "Here," she said. "Right here."

I was holding his hand. Paige and Julie were here, too. And the last word he said was your name.

"On the living-room floor?"

"In a hospital bed."

"Well, I'm not surprised. The man had no imagination."

Libby struggled to hold on to her temper. She'd lost it once already today, and she wasn't about to let it go again. Moments before, she'd considered the possibility that Marva was genuinely ill. Now, she suspected she was being played, manipulated—again. "Dying doesn't require much imagination," she remarked, with no inflection whatsoever. "A lot of courage, perhaps."

Dad raised us, provided for us, sacrificed for us. He loved us and we knew it. That's more than you ever did.

"Courage!" Marva huffed. "Will Remington was a small-town schoolteacher, content to plod along, living in this rat-trap of a house and calling it home. Driving a secondhand car and buying day-old bread and clipping coupons out of the Wednesday paper. How much courage does that take?"

"A lot, I think," Libby said calmly. *He washed our hair. He told us bedtime stories and listened to our prayers before we went to sleep. Maybe it took some courage to hear his children asking God to send their mother home, night after night. Maybe, damn you, it took courage just to keep getting up in the morning.*

Marva whirled on her. "You do, do you?" she challenged hotly. "You think your father was such a hero? Well, let me tell you something, missy—Will was dead his whole life. *I'm* the one who did all the living!"

Hildie peered around the end of the couch and growled pitiably.

Libby left the room, trembling, and came as far as the inside doorway with her car keys in one hand. She jangled them at her mother. "It's time for you to go," she said.

Marva frowned. "What about the scrambled eggs?"

"I'm fresh out," Libby replied. "Of eggs, I mean."

"But I'm hungry!"

"Then we'll get you a hamburger on the way over. Let's go."

"This is a fine how-do-you-do," Marva ranted. "I come to visit my own daughter, in my own home, and I get the bum's rush!"

"This isn't your home," Libby said. *And I wish to God I wasn't your daughter.* "Things have changed. You moved out years ago."

Hildie whimpered. She wasn't used to stress.

"Please," Marva pleaded, with such pathos that, yet again, Libby wasn't sure if the woman was mentally ill or had simply changed her tactics. "Let me stay here. Just for tonight."

"Let's go," Libby said, hardening her heart a little against the inevitable guilt. What if Marva actually was sick? What if she was having a breakdown or something?

"I'm your mother," Marva reminded her.

Yes, God help me. You are. But I don't have to love you. I don't even have to like *you.*

"And I'm lonely," Marva persisted, when Libby didn't speak. "None of you girls are willing to make room in your lives for me."

Libby closed her eyes. *Don't go there*, she warned herself.

"Suppose I die? You'll be sorry you treated me this way when I die."

A year after you left, I started telling people you were dead. They all knew better, because they remembered you.

They remembered the scandal. But they pretended to believe me, just to be kind.

"Dad loved you so much," Libby blurted out. Or was it the little girl she'd once been, not the woman she was, doing the talking? "He never stopped believing you'd come back."

"I couldn't take you with me," Marva said, true to form. Libby might not have spoken at all. "You were practically babies, the three of you. And we lived like gypsies, Lance and me." She paused, and a dreamy expression crossed her face, all the more disturbing because of her smeared makeup. "Like gypsies," she repeated softly.

Lance. Libby had never known Marva's lover's name.

Not that it mattered now.

She bit her lower lip, tried to think what to say or do, to get through to Marva, and jumped when a light knock sounded at the front door.

Hildie retreated behind the couch.

"Libby?" Paige let herself in, a small, lidded dish in her hands. "I brought you some of Julie's casserole—she insisted—" Seeing Marva, Paige's brown eyes widened. "Oh," she said.

"Yeah, oh," Libby confirmed. She could have hugged her little sister, she was so glad to see her. As a nurse, Paige would know if Marva needed medical help. "She's acting strangely," she added, gesturing toward their mother.

"Don't talk about me as though I weren't even here," Marva huffed.

The lid on Julie's dish rattled a little as Paige set it aside on the small table beside the door.

"I love casserole," Marva said, smiling happily.

Paige marched right over, confident as a prison matron taking charge of a new arrival, grasped their mother firmly by the arm and hustled her toward the door. "Some other time, maybe," she said cheerfully, casting a reassuring look at Libby. "Right now, Marva, you and I are going to take a little spin in my car."

"Thank you," Libby mouthed.

"You owe me," Paige said.

And just like that, the latest Marva episode was over.

For now, anyway.

Libby locked the front door, leaving the casserole dish right where it was, and turned to Hildie.

It took fifteen minutes to persuade the poor dog to come out from behind the couch.

THE WATER FIGHT TURNED out to be a dandy—even the dogs got involved. When it was over, Tate and Garrett and Austin all sat in the kitchen in their wet clothes, drinking beer and talking about the old days.

It was generally agreed that when it came to dousing people with a hose, their mother was still the all-around champ. She'd had an advantage, of course—raised Southern, none of them would have considered wresting the thing out of her hands and soaking her in retribution, the way they would have done with each other.

Sober and a little chilled, Tate was about to head upstairs to take a hot shower and hit the sack, the dogs set to follow on his heels, when his cell phone rang.

He picked it up off the table, checked the digital panel to see who was calling and flipped it open. "Cheryl? Are the kids all right?"

"Yes," Cheryl said. "They're fine. Sound asleep."

Tate glanced at the clock; it was after eleven. "And you're calling me at this hour because—?"

"Don't be mean," she purred.

Good God. Was she *drunk?* What if the house caught fire, or one of the kids got sick?

"Cheryl, are you all right?"

Austin scraped back his chair and rose from the kitchen

table, shaking his head. Garrett gave Tate a pitying look and headed for his own part of the house. Evidently, he'd forgotten the senator's "emergency," whatever it was.

"No," Cheryl burst out, sobbing all of the sudden. It still amazed Tate, the way she could change emotional gears so quickly. "I'm *not* all right. I'm divorced. I'm an attractive, educated woman, in the prime of my life, stuck in Blue River, Texas, for the next twelve years—"

"Have you been drinking?"

"Would you care if I had been?"

"Hell, yes, I'd care," Tate snapped. "You're alone with my children."

"I'm perfectly sober, and they're *my* children, too."

Tate drew in a long, deep breath, released it slowly. This was no time to needle her. "Yes," he said, in what he hoped was a reassuring tone of voice. "They're your children, too."

Cheryl was quiet for a few moments, so quiet that Tate began to wonder if she'd hung up. "We could try again, Tate," she said tremulously. "You and me. We could try again, make it work this time."

Tate closed his eyes. If she wasn't drunk, she must have snorted something. The subject of reconciliation had come up before, usually after she and some boyfriend had had a falling-out and gone their separate ways.

"No, Cheryl," he said, when he figured he could trust himself to speak. "You don't really want that, and neither do I."

"Because of Libby Remington," she said, with a trace of bitterness. "That's why you won't try to save our marriage. Did you think I wouldn't hear about you and Libby, Tate?"

Save their marriage? They'd been divorced for five years.

"We're not going to talk about Libby," Tate replied, silently commending himself for not reminding her that this marriage she wanted to save had long since died an acrimonious—and permanent—death. "Not tonight, anyway."

"I hate this town." Three-sixties were common with Cheryl when she was upset. There was no telling where she'd try to take the conversation next.

"The solution is simple, Cheryl," Tate reasoned. "Let Audrey and Ava live with me. You'd be free to do whatever you wanted, then. You could live anyplace, practice law again."

"You'd like that, wouldn't you?" The question, though softly put, was a loaded one, and Tate proceeded accordingly.

He was already on his feet, heedless of his damp clothes, rummaging for his truck keys. Austin lingered, leaning against one of the counters, sipping reheated coffee and not even bothering to pretend he wasn't eavesdropping. The dogs waited patiently to go upstairs, wagging their tails.

"I'll take care of the mutts," Austin said, between swallows of coffee.

Cheryl's rant continued, rising in volume and making less and less sense.

Tate nodded his thanks to his brother and stepped into the garage.

"Are you *listening,* Tate McKettrick?" Cheryl demanded.

"I'm listening," Tate said, climbing into his truck and pushing the button to open the garage door behind him. It rolled up silently, an electronic wonder. "Keep talking."

She started crying again. "It would have been so perfect!"

"What would have been perfect?" Tate asked, backing out into the moonlit Texas night, stars splattered from one horizon to the other.

"Our life together," Cheryl said, after a small, choked sob.

"How do you figure that?" There was a limit to Tate's ability to play games, and he'd almost reached it.

"We could have had it all, if only—"

Tate frowned, turning the truck around, pointing it toward town. "If only what?"

"If only you hadn't been in love with Libby Remington the whole time," Cheryl said. "She came between us, from the very beginning. You never got over her."

"That's crazy, Cheryl," he said, racing down the driveway to the main road.

She went off on another tangent, something about her lonely childhood, and how money didn't buy happiness, and she'd *always* wanted a real family of her own.

You could have fooled me, Tate thought.

But he listened, and when she ran down, he got her talking again.

Long minutes later, he braked in front of Cheryl's house, bolted from the truck, leaving the door open and the engine running, and strode to the front door.

"Let me in," he said, into his cell phone.

"Let you in? Where are you?"

Tate shoved his free hand through his hair and let out his breath. "On your porch," he said. "Open the damn door, Cheryl. *Now.*"

CHAPTER TEN

CHERYL SWUNG her front door open slowly, and Tate, just snapping his cell phone shut on their disturbing conversation, which had spanned the distance between the ranch and her house in town, was stunned. He'd expected to find his ex-wife an emotional train wreck, given the way she'd whined and fussed. Instead, her skin glowed with what looked like arousal, her makeup was perfect, her dark hair wound neatly into a single, glossy braid reaching nearly to her waist. And in her eyes, Tate saw a guarded glint of triumph.

"Come in," she said, her voice throaty and all Texased-up with heat and honey, a neat trick since she didn't have a drop of Southern blood in her.

And the keyword was *trick*.

Tate stood stiffly on the doormat. If he allowed his gaze to drop, even slightly, he knew he'd get the full impact of what she was wearing—a sexy nightgown that revealed a lot more than it covered up and barely breezed past her thighs. She held a glass of white wine in one hand.

"Want some?" she asked, ever the mistress of the double entendre, and took a sip.

"This was a *setup?*" The question was rhetorical, of course, and the situation wasn't all that surprising, but Tate seethed with indignation just the same. She'd cast her line into the water using the kids as the bait—something she often accused *him* of doing—knowing he'd have no choice but to take the hook.

In that moment, Tate's dislike for his former wife deepened to outright contempt.

Cheryl retreated a step, an oddly graceful move, almost dancelike, and then he couldn't help taking her in. He waited for a visceral response—though mad as a cornered rattler, he was as well-supplied with testosterone as any other man—and was a little surprised when it didn't come.

"A setup?" Cheryl replied softly, her lower lip jutting out in a pout. "I wouldn't exactly put it *that* way."

Tate swayed slightly on his feet, caught in a swift, spinning backwash of fury, averted his eyes and shoved a hand through his hair. "I need to see the kids," he said, on a long, raspy breath. "Then I'm leaving."

Even without looking directly at Cheryl, he knew when her face crumbled. He also knew the reaction didn't stem from the heartbreak of unrequited love. Cheryl had never loved him, any more than he'd loved her. They'd simply collided, at an unfortunate intersection of their two lives, both of them distracted by unrelated concerns, and two innocent and very precious children had been the result.

She stepped back again, gesturing with her left hand, still holding the wine, slopping some onto the spotless white carpet as she did so. "They're asleep. They won't even know you're here," she said wearily. "But suit yourself. You always do."

Tate turned sideways to pass her, headed straight for the stairs. The words *You always do* lodged between his shoulder blades like a knife, but he shook them off out of habit. All he wanted to do right then was gather his girls up, one in each arm, and carry them out of there, take them *home,* where they belonged. Audrey and Ava were McKettricks—they needed to grow up on the land.

Cheryl, however dysfunctional, was neither drunk nor high. Pissed off as he was, Tate had realized that the moment she'd opened the door. Under the terms of their custody agreement, this was Cheryl's week with the twins, and he couldn't rightly intervene.

At the same time, he wasn't about to leave that house without making sure Audrey and Ava were okay. If there were consequences, so be it.

He was halfway up the staircase when his daughters appeared at the top, barefoot and sleepy-eyed, wearing their matching pink pajamas, the ones with the teddy bears printed on the fabric. They huddled close to each other, their small shoulders touching.

Even as babies, they'd done that. They'd only begun to thrive, in fact, when some perceptive pediatric nurse had cornered their doctor and persuaded him to let them share an incubator.

Tate's heart did a slow, backward tumble at the memory.

The idea had made sense to him then, and it made sense to him now. Audrey and Ava had been together in Cheryl's womb, aware of each other on some level, possibly since conception. Born too early, each had still needed the proximity of the other.

"What's wrong, Daddy?" asked Audrey, always quick to read his expression and generally the first to speak her mind.

Tate turned his head to look back over one shoulder at Cheryl. By some devious magic, she'd donned a rumpled robe made of that bumpy cloth—he could never remember what it was called—pale lavender and worn thin in places. She was projecting Mommy vibes so effectively that, for one moment, he thought he must have imagined the sexy nightgown she'd had on when she'd answered the door, the glass of wine in her hand.

"Want some?"

It was the gotcha look in Cheryl's green eyes that convinced Tate he was still sane, though that probably wasn't the reaction she'd been going for. This whole thing was some kind of game to her; she got a weird satisfaction out of jacking him around, and when she felt thwarted, the next attempt was bound to be a real son-of-a-bitch.

"Daddy?" Ava prompted, clasping Audrey's hand tightly now, leaning into her sister a little more. "Is everything okay?"

Tate put Cheryl out of his mind, focused all his attention on his children. *We have to stop this,* he thought. *Somehow, Cheryl and I have got to call a truce.*

"Everything's fine," he said, with a lightness he hoped was convincing. "I was in town, so I came by to tuck you in and say good-night, that's all."

Both girls looked relieved.

"Did you bring Ambrose and Buford?" Audrey asked.

Tate shook his head. "No, sweetie," he answered. "They were headed off to bunk in with your uncle Austin when I left the house."

Behind him, Cheryl cleared her throat, an eloquent little sound. Tate made no attempt to decode it.

"I'd be happy to tuck both of you in," she told her daughters, her tone sunny. "Unless you'd really rather have your daddy kiss you good-night than me."

Tate closed his eyes, sickened. *Unless you'd really rather have your daddy kiss you goodnight than me.* With Cheryl, everything was a contest, a case of either/or—even the love of their children.

"Why can't you *both* kiss us good-night?" Ava asked, her voice fragile.

Tate gazed up at his daughters, full of love and despair and tremendous guilt. They were tearing these children apart, he and Cheryl, and whether he wanted to believe it or not, he was equally responsible.

It had to stop—no matter what.

"One at a time, though," Audrey said. "Because you always fight when you're in the same room."

God in heaven, Tate thought.

"Daddy first," Ava said.

"Certainly," Cheryl chimed, and Tate knew by her voice that she'd turned away. "Why consider *my* feelings? I'm only your mother."

"Cheryl," Tate ground out, not daring to face his ex-wife. "Don't. *Please,* don't."

Cheryl said nothing, but he could feel her bristling somewhere behind him, a little off to the side, a porcupine about to throw quills in every direction.

By deliberate effort, Tate unfroze his muscles and climbed the stairs, forcing a smile. Reaching the top, he herded the little girls, now giggling, in the direction of the large, pink and frilly room they shared.

He tucked them back into their matching canopy beds.

He kissed their foreheads.

He told them he loved them.

And he waited, perched on the cushioned seat set beneath the bay windows overlooking the street, until, at long last, they slept.

Tate dreaded going downstairs again, because it might mean another run-in with Cheryl. He wasn't sure how much self-restraint he had left, and while he'd never struck a woman in his life and didn't intend to start now, words could be used as effectively as fists, and the ones crowding the back of his throat in those moments were as hard and cold as steel.

Fortunately, there was no sign of Cheryl, although as soon as he'd stepped over the threshold onto the porch, he heard the dead bolt engage behind him with a resolute thump. She must have been lurking just inside the living room.

He started down the walk, wasn't even half surprised when Brent Brogan's cruiser pulled in behind his truck. While he'd been saying good-night to Audrey and Ava, waiting for them to drift off into peaceful, little-girl dreams, Cheryl had been summoning the police.

Another segment in the continuing drama.

Suppressing a sigh, Tate opened the gate in the picket fence and stepped through it, onto the sidewalk. "Evenin'," he said, with a half salute, when Brent rolled down his driver's side window to look him up and down. "Slow night, Chief?"

Brogan shook his head. "Not according to the former Mrs. McKettrick," he said, with a nod toward the house. "What are you doing here, Tate? It's pretty late, in case you haven't figured that out already."

Tate stayed where he was, shoved his thumbs into the waistband of his jeans, which were still a little damp from the water fight with Garrett and Austin, hours before. He found that strangely comforting. "She called you," he said flatly.

"She called me," Brent confirmed. "Cheryl said she felt threatened."

Tate gave a raspy chuckle. Thrust the splayed fingers of his right hand through his hair. "Did she? Well, Denzel, that's bullshit and you know it. About forty-five minutes ago, she called *me,* too, and I'd have sworn she was either high or drunk, going by the things she said and the way she sounded. I got here as fast as I could, because, as you may recall, my *kids* live here when they're not on the ranch."

Brent shut off the cruiser's engine, pushed open the door, got out to stand facing Tate there beside the quiet street. He was wearing civilian clothes, instead of his uniform, which meant he was off duty. "I've got to knock on that door, see Ms. Darbrey with my own eyes, and hear her say she's all right," he said. And when Tate started to speak, Brogan held up a hand to silence him. "It's procedure. She's a citizen, she called in a complaint, and whatever my personal opinion of the lady might be, it's my job to follow through. "

Tate understood, though it rubbed him a little raw in places that, even for professional reasons, Brent couldn't take him at his word. After all, they'd been buddies since second grade, when his friend's dad, Jock Brogan, had come to work on the Silver Spur as a wrangler and all-around handyman, glad to have a steady paycheck and a trailer to live in. Jock's seven-year-old son had arrived by bus a week later, right on time for the first day of school, sweating in the suit and bow tie he'd worn to his mother's funeral a month before, as it turned out, and scared shitless.

It had taken some time, but eventually Brent, a city boy, had loosened up a little, gotten used to ranch life, and asked Tate to teach him "something about horses." Within a couple of months, the new kid was riding like a Comanche warrior, keeping up with Tate and Garrett, Austin and Nico Ruiz as easily as if he'd been born in the saddle. Being in the same class at school, and with a lot of common interests, Tate and Brent had formed a special bond.

They'd competed in junior rodeos together.

Played on the same baseball and basketball teams in their teens.

On the day they graduated from high school, Brent announced that he was joining the Air Force instead of going on to the university with Tate, the way they'd always planned. Jock Brogan had scrimped and done without and worked overtime to save enough to cover the better part of his son's college expenses, Brent said, and he wasn't going to take a dime of that money. He'd always wanted to be a cop, he'd reminded Tate, and the military was willing to provide all the training he needed and pay him wages in the bargain.

He could be an asset to his dad from then on, instead of a liability.

Standing there in the night, waiting for Brent to satisfy himself that Cheryl was still in one piece, the words Garrett had thrown in his face earlier that night came back to Tate.

—inside, you're still the rich kid from the biggest ranch in four counties, feeling like you ought to apologize to folks who have to earn a living—

Tate tipped his head back, looked up at the blanket of stars spilling lavishly across the Texas sky. *Was* he "still that rich kid," always wishing he could make up somehow for having more, just by virtue of being born a McKettrick, than so many other people did?

People like Brent Brogan.

People like Libby.

Did he want a second chance with her because what she made him feel was real love—or was he just feeling guilty because she'd had a tough road from early childhood on, while he'd coasted blithely through life until a truck crossed the median one night and crashed into his parents' car, leaving both of them fatally injured?

Brent returned, slapped him companionably on the back. "Uh-oh," he joked. "You're looking introspective. And that's almost *always* a bad sign, old buddy."

Tate sighed. Managed a grin. He did have a tendency to think too damn much, there was no denying that.

"Did you find my ex-wife tied up in a closet? Swathed in duct tape?" he asked.

Brent grinned. "No."

"Damn the luck," Tate said.

"Let's get a cup of coffee," Brent suggested.

"Look, it's been one hell of a day and—" Tate began, but the protest fell away, half-finished. There was no reason to hurry home—the kids weren't there, and Austin, while not the most dependable person on earth, could be trusted to take care of two sleeping dogs.

"Don't I *know* it's been one hell of a day," Brent agreed wearily. "I was at the funeral, remember, and the wake, too. Had a long talk with Nico, in fact, once the leftovers had been stuffed into Isabel's fridge and most everybody else had gone home. Follow me to my place, and I'll brew up some java and tell you about it."

"If I don't get some sleep," Tate said, with a shake of his head, "I won't be good for much of anything tomorrow, so I'll pass on the java this time."

"All right," Brent replied, opening the door of the cruiser, keyring in hand. When he hesitated, Tate knew his friend had more to say. "I spoke to Isabel Ruiz," Brogan went on. "She's going to L.A., all right, moving in with her sister."

The decision seemed hasty, but in the final analysis, it wasn't his business what Isabel did. So Tate merely nodded, opened the door of his truck and climbed in. It hurt to imagine that sturdy but humble house, buzzing with life and laughter for as long as he could remember, standing empty, with just the whisper of the creek or a passing wind to break the silence.

Pablo was gone for good; that was something he had to come to terms with in much the same way he'd had to accept the loss of his mom and dad. Things changed, that was the one thing a man could count on, and folks came and went, and you never knew when the last thing you'd said to them, or failed to say, might really be the last chance you were ever going to get, one way or the other.

On the lonely drive back to the ranch, through a sultry summer night, Tate missed his old dog even more than usual. It would have been a fine thing to have Crockett riding shotgun, as he'd done before, a sympathetic listener with his ears perked up and his eyes warm with canine devotion.

Had Crockett been there, Tate would have told him how

worried he was about Audrey and Ava, and the way they were growing up, bouncing back and forth between two different houses. He'd have said what a hard thing it was knowing Pablo had died so senselessly, hard, too, wondering if he could have prevented what happened somehow, and if his friend had suffered or had had time to be afraid before the end came.

He might even have said that he loved Libby, not in the fevered, grasping way of a boy, as he had before, but hard and strong and steady, in the way of a man, but he'd rather do without her for the rest of his days than risk hurting her again.

Tate might have said a lot of things to Crockett that night, but all that actually came out of his mouth was a quiet, "I sure do miss you, old dog."

BY THE NEXT DAY, Libby was entirely recovered from her mother's unexpected visit the night before, and *mostly* over making such an idiot of herself out at the Ruizes' place after Pablo's funeral.

She rarely did anything impulsive—she couldn't afford the luxury—but that bright summer morning, after she and Hildie had taken their walk, Libby decided not to open the Perk Up for business at the usual time.

Today, she just felt like playing hooky.

So she scribbled a message on a piece of yellow-lined paper, crossed the alley and let herself into the shop by the back way, passed through the kitchen into the main area and taped the sign to the glass in the front door.

CLOSED FOR REPAIRS, the notice read. BACK BY NOON. PROBABLY.

The "repairs" Libby needed to make weren't the kind that required wrenches and screwdrivers, and while she fully intended to be serving coffee and smoothies and scones, if Julie had baked any, by midday, she wasn't sure that would happen. That was why she'd added the "probably"—to give herself an out if the need should arise.

Back home, Libby switched her shorts and tank top for her best jeans and a sleeveless blue cotton blouse, then put on a pair of comfortable sandals. Brushed her hair, leaving it loose instead of binding it back in the usual ponytail, and applied some lip gloss.

Hildie, munching kibble in the kitchen when her mistress jingled the car keys in invitation, looked up, cocked both ears as she considered her options and promptly went back to eating her breakfast.

Libby smiled at that. "I'll be back soon," she promised, stroking the dog's broad back with one hand before heading out the door.

Standing on the back porch, she looked around her yard and wished she hadn't let the shrubs and flower beds get so out of hand. She'd never been much of a gardener, mostly because she'd never had the time, but now she felt a new and strangely keen longing to get her hands dirty, to weed and water and plant things just to watch them grow.

First, of course, she'd have to prepare the ground, and that would be a big job, one that might take weeks. By the time she'd finished, folks around Blue River would probably be fertilizing and tilling their garden plots under, to lie fallow until spring, when the nursery section down at the feed store would be awash in starter plants and brightly colored seed packets.

Before getting into her car and backing it into the alley, she looked under dusty tarps in the detached garage until she found her dad's old push-mower. The blades were probably dull; maybe later, she'd heft the ancient apparatus into the trunk of the Impala and take it out to Chudley Wilkes for sharpening. When he wasn't running his one-taxi empire, Chudley fixed things.

Just *thinking* about mowing the lawn empowered Libby

a little, though she supposed she'd be whistling a different tune once she'd made a few swipes through the high grass. As kids, she and Julie and Paige had taken turns doing yard chores, and she remembered the blisters, the muscle aches and all the rest.

They'd begged their dad to invest in a gas-powered mower, but he'd said hard work and exercise were good for the character. Of course, he hadn't been able to afford fancy equipment, especially with three young daughters to raise.

With a pang, Libby paused to pat the dusty handle. Indeed, hard work and exercise *were* good for the character—and she'd get a sense of accomplishment, the incomparable scent of fresh-cut grass and a tighter backside out of the deal.

Chudley's place was in the opposite direction from where she was headed, and stopping there would delay the opening of her coffee shop by at least an hour, but Libby popped open the Impala's trunk and hoisted the mower inside anyway. It was heavier than it looked, that machine, and the handles stuck out, so the trunk wouldn't close again.

She'd just have to alter her plans slightly, Libby concluded, after standing there in the alley biting her lower lip for a few moments. She'd drop the mower off at Chudley's first, then go on about her business. If Wilkes happened to be going through one of his ambitious phases—these were famously rare—the machine might be ready to cut grass later in the day.

Libby got behind the wheel, cranked up the engine and jostled off down the alley, wincing every time she hit a bump, causing the lid of the trunk to slam down on the shaft of the mower.

The Wilkes's home, two trailers welded together sometime in the fifties and surrounded by what seemed like acres of rusted-out cars, treadless tires and miscellaneous parts of God-knew-what, had been an eyesore for so long that folks around Blue River had long since stopped getting up petitions to force Chudley and his wife, Minnie, to clean the place up.

Libby pulled into the gravel driveway and waited a few moments before pushing open her car door, since Chudley had been known to keep mean guard dogs and once, reportedly, even an ostrich that might have killed the UPS man if Minnie hadn't rushed outside and driven it off with a broom handle.

Outsiders might have scoffed at that tale, thinking the odds were in the big bird's favor. Anybody who thought that had never met Minnie Wilkes.

She stepped out onto the sagging porch, wiping her hands on a faded apron and squinting, probably trying to place the green Impala. Six feet tall, with shoulders like a linebacker's, Minnie was a formidable sight, even pushing eighty, as she must have been.

Libby got out of the car. Smiled and waved. "It's me, Mrs. Wilkes," she called. "Libby Remington."

A blinding smile broke across Minnie's face. In her youth, the story went, she'd been quite a looker. Nobody'd ever been able to work out what caused her to throw in her lot with a little banty-rooster like Chudley. "Will's girl? Well, now, you've turned out just fine, haven't you? You still smitten with Jim and Sally McKettrick's oldest boy?"

Libby felt a little pinch inside her heart. Was *smitten* the word? "I see him around town," she said, approaching the gate, with its rusted hinges and weathered wooden latch, then hesitating. "Is that ostrich still around?"

Minnie's laugh boomed out over the seemingly endless expanse of junk. "Now there's a yarn that got right out of hand," she said, still standing on the porch. "Started out with one cussed old rooster, too stringy for the stewpot. Stubby— that was the rooster—went after the UPS man, right enough. But by the time that driver got through spreadin' the story around Blue River and half the county, I'll be darned if poor old Stub wasn't seven feet tall and a whole different kind of bird."

Libby smiled, started to open the gate.

Minnie stopped her. "You just stay right there, honey. We got another rooster pecking around here somewheres, and he might come at you, spurs out and screechin' like a banshee, if he don't happen to like your looks or somethin'."

Libby shaded her eyes and waited for her heartbeat to slow down, so her words wouldn't come out sounding shaky. "I was hoping Chudley could sharpen my lawn-mower blades," she said.

"He'll do it," Minnie said, with a decisive nod. "He's out on a taxi run just now, takin' Mrs. Beale home from the supermarket—she bought more than she could carry in that little pushcart of hers again—but he ought to be back soon. *One Life to Live* is fixin' to come on any minute now, and Chud never misses it."

Libby went around to the back of the car to unload the mower. Minnie, who had a light step for such a big woman, appeared beside her, elbowed her aside and lifted the all-metal machine from the trunk as easily as if it were a child's toy, made of plastic.

"I'd invite you in for a neighborly chat," Minnie said, holding the mower off the ground with one hand, the way she might have held a rake or a hoe. "But Miss Priss had her kittens on the couch yesterday, and she ain't ready to move them just yet. What with Chudley's magazines and such, there's no other place to sit."

Libby smiled. "Thank you just the same," she said. "But I'd have had to say 'no' anyway, because I've got so much to do today."

Minnie, bless her, looked relieved. She was known as much for her pride as for her bad housekeeping, and Libby had always liked her. Wouldn't have hurt her feelings or embarrassed her for anything.

"I'll see that Chudley brings this here piece of machinery by your place later on," Minnie said. "Good as new."

Libby opened the car door, reached for her purse.

"Keep your money," Minnie huffed, already trundling back through the gate, taking the mower along with her. "I meant to send over one of my sugar pies when your daddy was sick, and I never got around to it. Always felt bad about that—Will Remington was a fine man—but if it ain't one thing around here, it's another. Anyhow, Chudley will fix this mower right and proper, and I'll feel a sight better about not buildin' that sugar pie."

Libby's eyes burned. She knew the Wilkeses could have used even the small amount of money Chudley probably charged for sharpening the blades of a push lawn mower, but she wouldn't have discounted Minnie's belated but heartfelt condolence gift on any account. It would have been kinder to slap the woman across the face.

"Thank you, Mrs. Wilkes," she said.

Minnie plunked the mower down next to the porch steps, which dipped visibly under her considerable weight. Her thick hair, dyed an unlikely shade of auburn and bobby-pinned into a messy knot on top of her head, bobbed a little when she spoke, as it might tumble down around her shoulders. "You're a woman grown now," she said, with firm good grace. "Old enough to call me Minnie, if it suits you."

"Minnie," Libby repeated. It *did* make her feel more like a mature adult, addressing an older woman of slight acquaintance by her given name.

By the time she added a "Goodbye" Minnie had already disappeared back inside the conjoined trailers. After all these years, the seam still showed, a brownish, welded ribbon wrapping the structure like a gift and stopping directly above the front door.

Libby got back into her car, backed slowly into the turn-around and pointed the Impala back down the driveway toward the county road.

There, she stopped and looked both ways. On the left was an old porcelain toilet, red flowers—possibly geraniums—billowing from the bowl, riotous with well-being.

She smiled.

And to think people considered this place a blight upon the landscape.

CHAPTER ELEVEN

A WEEK HAD PASSED since Pablo Ruiz's funeral, and during that time, Tate McKettrick hadn't called once. Maybe, Libby thought, watching as a rare and badly needed rain pelted the road out in front of the Perk Up, her dad had been right, in years past, when he used to moralize that there wasn't much point in buying the cow when you could get the milk for free.

Libby sighed. A few days ago, she'd bitten the bullet and called Doc Pollack to ask for a prescription for birth control pills, which she'd filled at Wal-Mart, her cheeks burning with mortification. She knew every single person in Blue River, and they knew her, and it was just her luck that Ellie Newton, her high school nemesis, happened to be clerking in the pharmacy that day.

A brief scenario unfolded on the screen of Libby's mind, in which Ellie switched on a microphone and announced to the whole store that, in case they hadn't heard, Libby Remington was catting around with Tate McKettrick again. And after he'd made a fool of her in front of the whole county, too, throwing her over for that fancy woman he'd met in Austin.

Yes, folks, the imaginary version of Ellie Newton proclaimed in triumph, she had the proof right here, a little packet of pills.

While none of that *actually* happened, Libby would have sworn she'd seen just the tiniest spark of smug judgment in Ellie's eyes as she rang up the purchase.

Ellie's husband, Joe, worked on the Silver Spur as a ranch hand, Libby reflected; alone in the Perk Up with all the chores caught up, she had way too much time for introspection. Suppose Ellie had driven straight out there to the nice single-wide trailer she and Joe shared and told Joe that Libby was on birth control pills? *Further* suppose, Libby thought, gnawing on her lower lip, that Joe, hearing this news, went straight to his boss, none other than Tate McKettrick, and told *him?*

Tate would think she was hot to trot, jumping right on the pill when they'd been to bed exactly once.

And maybe she *was* hot to trot. With Tate, anyway.

Libby pressed the fingertips of both hands to her temples. What was the big deal here? This wasn't 1872. Consenting adults *had sex,* preferably responsible sex, all the time. And it wasn't as if she planned to keep the pills a secret from Tate—she just wanted to be the one to tell him, that was all.

It didn't help that business was slow.

A lot of Libby's regular customers had gone on vacation—good Lord, did they travel in a *herd,* or something? Every year, it seemed they all left at once.

No tour buses passing through town en route to the Alamo or Six Flags or some art or music fest in Austin stopped at Libby's place.

Even her sisters weren't around much—Paige was working double shifts at the clinic, and Julie had been helping out at Calvin's playschool, since the venerable Mrs. Oakland was recovering from an impacted wisdom tooth.

The McKettrick twins' castle was due to be delivered soon—volunteer fathers had dug and poured a cement foundation for it, along with a well for a very shallow fishpond nearby. Unless Mrs. Oakland's swelling went down soon, Julie would be in charge of the dedication ceremony.

All by her lonesome in the Perk Up, Libby wished the place had a jukebox, so she could have dropped some coins into the slot and played a sad song.

Instead, she checked the clock—4:37 p.m.—and made an executive decision; she'd close up early. Go home and let Hildie out for a run in the backyard.

Chudley had returned her lawn mower, sharpened and rust-free and ready to go, the day before. If the rain let up soon enough, she'd cut the grass.

If it didn't, she'd clean out some of the flower beds. Maybe it was too late in the season to plant, but just pulling the weeds would be an improvement.

After locking up, Libby crossed the alley and let herself into her yard through the back gate. The dust-scented rain had slackened to a drizzle, and a cool breeze dissipated some of the humidity.

While Hildie was outside, Libby changed into shorts, a sleeveless sweatshirt and flip-flops. She poured kibble in the dog's empty bowl, refilled her water dish and pushed open the screen door.

Hildie crunched happily away while Libby went outside, set her hands on her hips, and looked up at the gray sky. Texas had been in the grip of a drought for more than a decade, so any kind of precipitation was welcome, but her spirits dipped a little lower just the same.

The only sure remedy for the blues, at least in Libby's experience, was physical work—if it brought out a sweat and left her with achy muscles, so much the better. She hauled the mower out of the garage, considered the fact that it was made almost entirely of steel and put it back.

Work therapy was one thing. *Shock* therapy, courtesy of a lightning bolt, was another.

Hildie, finished with her supper, then scratched politely at the screen door from the inside.

Libby smiled, mounted the porch steps and let the dog out.

She was on her knees, pulling up weeds, when Hildie, lying under her favorite tree, out of the misty rain, rose to her haunches and gave an uncertain woof, more greeting than challenge.

Something tickled Libby's nose, so she ran a gloved hand across her face before turning around, expecting to see Julie, or Paige or even Marva.

But it was Tate who stood watching her, a slight smile curving his mouth upward at one side. "Hey," he said.

Libby swallowed. *If I filled a prescription for birth control pills, it's my own business,* she thought. "Hey," she replied, feeling stupid.

Tate hadn't *mentioned* her prescription, had he? Most likely, Ellie hadn't told Joe and therefore Joe couldn't have told Tate. Ellie had been a mean gossip in high school, it was true, but that was years ago and besides, she'd found religion—and Joe—since then.

"I tried to call," he said, when the silence stretched. "But you didn't pick up."

Libby hadn't thought to check her voice mail when she came home from the Perk Up—she didn't get that many calls. Paige and Julie usually just stopped by when they wanted to talk to her.

"What can I do for you?" she asked, her face heated.

Tate, wearing comfortable jeans, a T-shirt and old boots, crossed the grass and crouched beside her. "Well," he drawled, "you can *relax,* for a start."

Libby fought an insane urge to weep, and that used up any

energy she might have employed in talking. Anyway, she was too afraid she'd say something even stupider than *What can I do for you?*

Gently, Tate used the backs of his fingers to wipe a smudge of dirt from Libby's cheek. "I've missed you, Lib," he said. "A lot."

She swallowed.

One of his powerful shoulders moved in a partial shrug. That ghost-of-a-grin touched down on his mouth again, and she noticed that his eyelashes were spiky from the moisture in the air. "The last time we were together," he reminded her, "things didn't go all that well."

Libby stood up, telling herself it was because her knees were starting to cramp, and dusted her hands off against the damp fabric of her shorts.

Tate stood, too. His dark hair curled a little in the light rain.

It was all Libby could do not to bury her fingers in that hair. The thought made her flesh tingle, all over.

She raised her chin a notch, remembering the minor spectacle the two of them had made, out there in Pablo's orchard after the funeral.

"I'll apologize if you will," she said.

Tate laughed. "Deal," he said. Then he sobered, and the blue of his eyes seemed to intensify. "I'm sorry."

Libby's breath caught, just looking into those eyes. "Me, too."

If black holes were that color, she thought, the entire universe would have been sucked into oblivion long ago.

"Maybe I could make it up to you with dinner," Tate said.

Libby blinked, pulled herself back from the blue precipice. Looked down at her muddy shorts and T-shirt. "I'd have to change clothes first," she heard some foolish woman say.

Tate grinned. "I was thinking of steaks at my place," he told her. The grin rose to dance, mischievous, in his eyes. "We suspended the dress code years ago. In fact, we never really had one, unless you count Mom's stubborn refusal to allow barn boots any farther than the back porch."

"I can't go like this," Libby said, still serious. "I'm all muddy and—and sweaty."

Tate chuckled. "All right," he said, "if you're going to insist, may I suggest that yellow dress? The one you wore the other night?"

Libby's cheeks burned again. Right. The yellow dress he'd said he could see through—the one she'd been so eager to get out of, after making such a big, damn deal about how it was too soon to make love.

And now she had a packet of birth control pills in her medicine cabinet.

Libby pretended she hadn't heard his suggestion and started for the house.

He chuckled.

Hildie, the traitor, hung back so she could walk with Tate.

While Tate waited in the kitchen with the dog, Libby headed for the bathroom. A glance at herself in the mirror over the sink made her shake her head.

A streak of good Texas garden dirt ran the length of her right cheek, and her hair, caught up in the customary pony-tail, would frizz like crazy when she turned it loose.

She started the shower running, adjusting the faucets until she got just the right temperature—tepid, with the merest hint of a chill. She used a lot of conditioner after shampooing, hoping her hair wouldn't do its fright-wig thing.

Finished with her shower in record time, Libby dried off, pulled on her faded pink cotton robe, and collected clean jeans, fresh underwear, and a long-sleeved black and white T-shirt from her room.

Although she felt strangely rushed, she took the time to blow-dry her hair and even applied some mascara, though she skipped the lip gloss.

Just because she had birth control pills in her medicine

cabinet didn't mean she wanted to go sending "Seduce me" messages to Tate McKettrick by making her mouth all shiny and inviting.

Of course, if Tate hadn't been in the picture, she wouldn't have called Doc Pollack and then endured Ellie Newton's studied indifference to get the prescription in the first place.

Gripping the edges of the sink, Libby looked at her steam-blurred image in the mirror.

"You're *asking* for trouble, Libby Remington," she told herself.

Then she opened the bathroom door and stepped into the hallway.

Mustn't keep trouble waiting.

TATE LOADED HILDIE INTO the back seat of his truck, but although he'd opened the front passenger-side door for Libby, he stood back instead of helping her aboard, just so he could watch that sweet little ass in action, under the perfectly fitted jeans, as she made the climb.

Hot damn. A silent groan reverberated through him.

"Are the girls at the ranch?" Libby asked, once she was settled and he was behind the wheel. Hildie leaned between the seats and licked Tate's right ear just as he turned the key in the ignition.

He laughed, not at the question but at the dog, and immediately drew a confused glance from Libby.

"No," he said, as Hildie rested her muzzle on his shoulder and gave a contented little sigh. If only *all* females were so docile. "Audrey and Ava are in New York with their mother for a couple of days. Cheryl's folks moved into an assisted-living place in Connecticut a few months back, and she's putting their apartment on the market."

Libby offered no comment, only a nod. She shifted uncomfortably in the seat—and Tate figured she'd probably been counting on having the kids around as a sort of buffer.

Esperanza, Garrett and Austin were all at the main house, as it happened, but Tate wasn't taking Libby to the mansion. Where they were going, it would be just the two of them—and the old dog drooling on his shirt as he drove toward the outskirts of town.

"Are we going to talk?" Tate asked, when they'd traveled several miles in silence.

She smiled softly. "Do we need to?"

Damn. He wanted to pull over to the side of the road, right then and there, take Libby Remington into his arms and kiss her senseless.

"Probably," he said hoarsely.

"About—?"

"Things," Tate said, thrown by the scent of her, the warmth of her, the softness he could sense from three feet away, no touching necessary. Highly desirable, but not necessary.

"Things like—?"

"Like where we're headed, you and I," Tate said.

Libby's smile was faint and a little saucy. "I assumed, since you're behind the wheel, that you had our destination all figured out."

"That isn't what I mean," Tate said, mildly irritated, "and you know it."

"Where are we going, Tate?" Libby asked, with exaggerated patience, of the smart-ass variety. There was an undercurrent of excitement there, too, unless he missed his guess.

"On one level," Tate replied, "I'd say we're on our way to a soft spot in some tall grass." Out of the corner of his eye, he saw her blush, and took some satisfaction in that. "On another level—the long-range one—everything depends on you, Libby."

Libby turned in her seat, her eyes flashing a little. He could see her nipples jutting against the inside of her blouse, so he figured she was up for the proposed tumble in the grass.

All right by him.

"Now, why would everything depend on me?" she asked, her eyes wide.

Tate didn't give her an answer until he'd brought the truck to a stop at the edge of the yard that had been Pablo and Isabel's for so long.

"You're the one with all the forgiving to do, Lib," he said, gripping the steering wheel and staring straight ahead through the windshield. The lumber and other building supplies he'd been buying and hauling out from town all week waited, moist from the drizzling rain.

Libby turned slightly in the seat, gently eased Hildie back, off his shoulder. "Tate McKettrick," she said, "look at me."

He did. A big lump rose in his throat. He wanted her physically, but there was so much more to it than that.

"If you're talking about that fling with Cheryl," Libby told him, "I forgave you for that a long time ago."

Tate raised his hand to her cheek, brushed it lightly with the backs of his knuckles. "Maybe you believe that," he said, "but I'm not sure I do."

Her eyes widened again, and patches of pale pink pulsed in her cheeks, then faded. "If you could go back in time," she asked, after several long moments, "what would you change, Tate? Can you even imagine a world without your children in it?"

Tate unhooked Libby's seat belt, laid his hands on either side of her face so she wouldn't look away before she heard him out. "No," he said gruffly, "but if I had the kind of power we're talking about here, *you and I* would have conceived the twins. They'd be ours, together."

She turned her head, and her lips moved, light as the flick of a moth's wings, against his palm.

Fire shot up Tate's arm, set his heart ablaze, spread to his groin and hit a flash point. He barely contained the groan that rose from somewhere in the very center of his being.

Libby met his gaze again. Held it. "Do you know what

would have made it impossible to forgive you, Tate? If you'd denied those little girls, or bought your way out of the situation somehow—a lot of men in your position would have done that—but you took all the fallout. You did right by your children, and I'm pretty sure you *tried* to do right by Cheryl—"

In the back, Hildie whimpered, wanting out.

Tate shut off the engine, but made no move to get out of the truck and lower Hildie to the ground. "What about *you,* Lib?" he asked miserably. "I sure as hell didn't do right by you, now did I?"

She reached across, touched his arm. "I'm a big girl now," she said. "I'm over it."

"Over it enough to trust me?"

She thought for a moment, then nodded. "Until you give me reason not to," she said.

Hildie began to carry on in earnest.

Tate got out of the truck, opened the back door and two-armed the chubby old dog out of the vehicle and onto the ground.

Libby got out, too, and stood at the edge of the Ruizes' lawn, looking toward the house. Tate watched as she shook her head in response to some private thought.

"I guess you heard," he ventured, after a while, "that Isabel decided to take the boys and go live with her sister." He was distracted, still thinking about how she'd said she'd trust him until he gave her a reason to stop.

Libby Remington was an amazing woman.

Libby turned her head to look at him again, nodded. "She didn't waste much time getting out of here," she observed, and there was a deliberately noncommittal note in her voice that diverted some of Tate's attention from the riot she'd caused in his senses.

He hooked his thumbs into the waistband of his jeans and tilted his head to one side. Hildie squatted a few feet away, then came back to stand between him and Libby, tail wagging, tongue lolling, eyes hopeful that a good time would be had by all, dogs included.

"I told Isabel she was welcome to stay here on the Spur for as long as she wanted," Tate said quietly, "but she decided to leave right away. Nico said she saw Pablo everywhere she looked, and that was too painful."

Libby considered that, nodded. Hildie went off, found a short, crooked stick in the grass, brought it to Libby, and dropped it at her feet.

With a smile, Libby bent, picked up the stick and tossed it a little way.

Hildie trundled awkwardly after it. Brought it back.

"Why the impromptu dinner invitation, Tate?" Libby asked mildly. "And what's with all the lumber and shingles and bags of cement?"

Tate bent, picked up Hildie's stick, and threw it a little farther than Libby had. While the dog searched through the wild grass that grew beyond the edge of the lawn, Tate held out a hand to Libby.

"Come on," he said. "I'll explain while I show you around."

Libby hesitated, then took his hand. Hildie had found the stick, clasping it between her teeth, but she seemed to be done playing fetch for the time being.

Tate took care not to crush Libby's fingers as he led her up the front steps and into the house. The sexual charge that had arced between them on the drive out of town had gone underground, though Tate knew it would reassert itself sooner rather than later.

He watched Libby as she looked around, waited for the dog to waddle in, then quietly shut the door.

Over the few days since Isabel and Pablo's relatively few possessions had been loaded into a rented truck and hauled away, Tate had removed the old flooring and knocked out several walls. Sheets of drywall waited to be nailed in place once the new framing was in.

Libby's expression was curious and a little pensive when she looked at him. "I still don't understand," she said. "All this—?"

Tate put a hand to the small of her back and steered her toward the kitchen. It was the only room in the house he hadn't torn apart—yet.

"I'm planning on living here, Libby," he said, and his heart beat a little faster, because her reaction to that news was vitally important to him. "Maybe not for good—but for a while."

"Why?" she asked reasonably, folding her arms. The last light of day flowed in through the window behind her, and to Tate, she looked almost luminous, like a figure in stained glass.

"I'm not sure I can explain," he answered, reaching out to flip a switch so the single bulb dangling from the middle of the ceiling illuminated the kitchen. "I want to see what it's like to live in a regular-size house. Drive to a job every day. Actually work for a living."

Libby smiled faintly at that. She *did* live in a "regular-size house," and she certainly made her own way in the world. "I wouldn't know about commuting," she quipped, "but working for a living is overrated, in my opinion."

Tate shoved a hand through his hair, more nervous than he'd expected to be. He'd planned this evening carefully, right down to the steaks marinating in the refrigerator and the coals heating in the portable barbecue grill out back and the good red wine tucked away in one of the cupboards. It had made so much sense during those night hours spent prying up carpeting and stripping walls to the insulation and framework.

Libby came to him, laid her palms to his chest.

The gesture was probably meant to be comforting, but

she might as well have hit him with a couple of defibulator paddles, given the effect her touch had on him.

"Tate?" Libby urged.

He sighed. He'd meant to ask Libby to move in with him, come and live in that modest house by the bend in the creek as soon as the remodeling was done; but now he realized what a half-assed, harebrained idea it was. Libby wasn't ready for that kind of constant intimacy, and he wasn't, either.

The twins barely knew Libby, and of course the reverse was true, as well. He would make any sacrifice for his children, but he couldn't expect Libby to feel the same way.

"Give me a minute," he finally said, his voice hoarse, "to pull my foot out of my mouth."

She moved closer, frowning, then slipped her arms loosely around his waist. "What are you talking about?" she asked.

A reasonable question, Tate thought. "I wish I knew," he said.

Libby rested her head against his chest for a few moments, as though she were listening to his heartbeat, and the smell of her hair made him feel light-headed—it was as though all the oxygen had suddenly been sucked out of the room.

Finally, she looked up at him, and her eyes were at once tender and curious. "You're serious about living here, aren't you?" she asked.

Tate nodded. Maybe she'd hate the idea—that would be a problem for sure. And maybe she wouldn't give a damn— which would be even worse.

"And for some reason," Libby went on, "my opinion matters to you."

"Yes," he ground out. "For some reason, it does."

"Why?" Libby seemed completely, honestly puzzled.

"Because—" Again, Tate's neck burned. "Well, because it *would* matter to some women—they'd think I was crazy, moving out of a place like the ranch house, into this one…"

Libby brought her chin up a notch and set her hands on her hips. "Would it matter to you, if I thought you were crazy?"

"No," he answered, after some thought. "If you *didn't* think that, I'd figure you hadn't been paying much attention."

She laughed, stood on tiptoe to kiss the cleft in his chin. Then she looked around. "Alone at last," she said. "Do you want me as much as I want you, Tate?"

"Yeah," he replied, "and I've got the hard-on to prove it."

"So I've noticed," Libby crooned, grinding into him again. This time, there was no mistaking things—the move was deliberate.

"You might want to watch it," Tate warned, his hands making their own way to where they wanted to be—cupping Libby's ass and lifting her closer so he could do a little grinding of his own. "This time, I'm prepared. I have condoms."

Libby moaned, her eyes half-closed, her head back. A fetching wash of pink played over her cheekbones.

When Libby was fifteen and Tate was seventeen, he'd taken her virginity in the back seat of his dad's car, and she'd looked just the way she did now—flushed, eager, unafraid.

"I'm prepared, too," she said, so softly that Tate barely heard her.

His knees weak, Tate dropped into one of the four folding chairs he'd bought to go with the card table, his temporary dining suite. Standing Libby between his knees, he unsnapped her jeans, undid the zipper, pulled them down, waited for her to protest.

She didn't.

In fact, she kicked off her shoes and shed her jeans, right there in the kitchen. She was wearing ice-blue panties, trimmed in lace.

He nipped at her through the moist crotch, and she groaned, entwining her fingers in his hair.

"What do you mean, you're prepared?" he murmured, hooking his thumbs under the elastic waistband.

"I'm—I'm on the p-pill—" she gasped.

Had the table been sturdier, Tate would have laid Libby down on it and eaten her thoroughly, but he knew the thing wouldn't support even her slight weight. So he lowered her panties and plied her with gentle motions of his fingers until she was good and wet. Then he opened his jeans and eased her down slowly, onto his shaft, giving her a little at a time.

She wanted to ride him, and hard—that was evident in the way she moved, or tried to move.

Tate grasped her hips and stopped her. "Easy," he murmured. "Slow and easy, Lib."

She made a strangled sound, her eyes sultry, but she let him set the pace. Let him strip off her lightweight T-shirt and open her bra, so her perfect breasts were there for the taking.

Tate enjoyed them at his leisure until Libby made another sound—this one exasperated—and drew him into a kiss so hot that he nearly lost control and came right then and there.

"Do it," she gasped, when the kiss finally ended, "damn you, Tate McKettrick, *do it!*"

He chuckled, a raspy sound, and took her in earnest then, raising and lowering her, fast and then faster, deep and then deeper.

The release was cataclysmic, blinding Tate, rending a long, hoarse shout from him, like that of a dying man. Through it, he heard Libby, calling his name over and over again.

And then they were both still.

Slowly, the world reassembled itself around them.

"*Damn,* woman," Tate growled. "That was good."

Libby giggled. "Yeah," she said, moving to disengage herself. "Is there a working shower in this place?"

Tate stopped her from rising off him by tightening his grasp on her hips. He was getting hard again, and she was in for another ride.

"No," he said, raising her and then lowering her again, until she'd taken all of him, until she gasped. "No shower."

"Tate—"

He bent his head, tongued her right nipple until she groaned and arched her back, offering him full access. "Ummm?" he asked, his mouth full of her then.

"I—oh, God—I'm already coming—I—"

Tate slid his hands up, supporting her with his palms so she could lean back, give herself up to the orgasm.

He watched, fighting his own release, as Libby arched away from him, golden-fleshed, nipples hard and moist from his mouth, her hair falling free, her beautiful body buckling and seizing with pleasure.

When she cried out his name, and a long, sweet shudder of full surrender went through her, Tate couldn't hold back anymore. He let himself go, with a raspy shout, and she rocked on him until he'd given her everything he had to give.

"I'm not sure I can survive a whole lot of that," she admitted, a long time later, when they'd helped each other, bumbling and fumbling, back into at least some of their clothes.

"We need to spend more time together," Tate said. "Get in some practice."

Libby sighed contentedly. "And we'd—*practice* a lot?"

Tate grinned. "Maybe not on the kitchen floor, though. I was sort of planning on buying a bed, but, yeah, there would be a lot of rowdy sex."

Libby made a comical move that might have meant her underpants were wedged in where they shouldn't be. "I like rowdy sex," she said.

He laughed. Padded over to the fridge for the steaks. "So I've noticed," he responded.

Suddenly, she looked sad, and some of the glow was gone. "What if sex is all we have together, Tate? All we've *ever* really had."

Tate, halfway to the back door with the package of steaks

in one hand by then, turned to look at her. "Then I'd say we were pretty damn lucky," he responded. "But there's more, and you know it."

"Not that I'm angling to get married," she blurted out. Then she blushed miserably and groaned. "But nobody said anything about marriage, did they?"

"You're not ready for that," Tate told her, setting the meat on the counter and going back to stand facing her, "and neither am I. I've got things to prove to you, Libby."

She blinked. "Like what?"

"Well, first of all, you need to be sure you can trust me. For a lifetime."

"What if I told you I trust you now?" Another pause. "Although you're perfectly right—we're not ready to get married. I hope I didn't seem—well—*pushy*."

He grinned. "Never that," he said.

The steaks turned out perfectly.

They went on to the main ranch house and took a shower together in his en suite bathroom and made love again.

They slept, arms and legs entangled after hours of love-making, in his bed.

He should have known it had all been too easy.

CHAPTER TWELVE

A PHONE SHRILLED in the night, jarring Libby, in lurching stages, out of a rest so profound that no shred or tatter of a dream could have reached her. She opened her eyes, blinking, to utter darkness, and knew only that she wasn't in her own bed—the mattress, the bedding, the angles were all wrong.

"Tate McKettrick," Tate said, his voice gravelly with sleep and the beginnings of alarm.

Libby sat up, drawing her knees to her chest and wrapping her arms around her shins.

"Calm down, Cheryl," Tate went on. "I can't understand you—"

Libby closed her eyes a nanosecond before she heard the click of a lamp switch. Light flared against her lids, a fiery orange-red. She looked at Tate, blinking.

He sat up. "Take a breath," he said, shifting the phone from his right ear to his left, so he could close his fingers around Libby's hand and squeeze once. He threw back the covers, got out of bed, began pulling opening drawers, dressing—jeans, a T-shirt, socks and boots.

"Okay," he said. "Okay."

Libby's heart thrummed. A call at that hour—3:17 a.m. by the digital clock on Tate's night table—could not be good.

Tate was listening again; the glance he tossed in Libby's direction bounced away without connecting.

For the briefest moment, she felt dismissed, invisible.

"Put her on, Cheryl," Tate said. A long pause. "Cheryl? I said *put Ava on the phone.*"

Libby scrambled off the bed, nearly fell because she was so entangled in the top sheet. Her clothes were on the far side of the room, and she tripped twice, hurrying to get to them.

"Yes, Ava," Tate said, "it's Dad. What's the problem, Shortstop? I thought you were excited about visiting New York."

Libby could hear the timbre of the child's voice, if not the words. Ava was practically hysterical.

She forgot about getting into her clothes and went back to the bed, carefully managing the train of bedsheet in the process, plunking down on the end of the mattress and watching Tate as he paced, listening, nodding.

"You'll be home in a few days, honey," he told his daughter gently, when there was a break in the conversation.

Tate sat down beside Libby, slipped his arm around her waist.

She felt a little less like an outsider.

"Ava?" Tate waited. "I love you. I'll be right here when you get back. You can ride your ponies, and we'll go fishing in the creek—"

More hysteria on the other end of the line.

Tate sighed, and his shoulders sagged a little. "Let me talk to your mother."

Again, Libby wanted to flee. She didn't know exactly what she was hearing, but she was sure she shouldn't be hearing it.

Tate's entire bearing seemed to change when his ex-wife

came back on the phone. "Yes," he said. "Yes—sometime to-morrow. I'll let you know. And, Cheryl? Don't call in twenty minutes and say you've changed your mind. We're not going to pretend this didn't happen."

Libby lowered her head, waited.

Finally, Tate snapped his phone shut.

For a long time, he just sat there beside Libby, looking down at the floor.

Libby shifted, ran a hand down his back. "Anything I can do to help, cowboy?" she asked quietly. She didn't want to interfere, but she couldn't just sit there, either.

"I have to head for New York," he said. "First thing in the morning."

Libby nodded. Waited. If Tate wanted to explain, he would. If he didn't, that was okay, too.

Tate shoved a hand through his hair. His eyes were bluer than usual, and bleak, even as he tried to smile. "This is what my life is like, Lib," he said, very quietly. "I have an ex-wife and two kids and executive control over a ranch the size of some counties. There's always some kind of crisis, and a lot of them seem to happen in the middle of the night."

Libby drew the sheet more closely around her. "Audrey and Ava—they're okay?"

Tate held her against his side, rested his chin on top of her head. She felt his nod. "I didn't get the whole story," he said, "but the gist of it seems to be that getting her parents' apartment ready to put on the market is more work than Cheryl expected it to be, and the girls aren't making it any easier because they're fussy and homesick. Apparently, Ava had a pretty bad dream tonight—Cheryl showed the twins around the school she went to and asked them how they'd like to go there when they start first grade in the fall, and that must have freaked Ava out." He paused, sighed. "According to our divorce agreement, neither Cheryl nor I can reside anywhere but Blue River, Texas, without forfeiting custody to the other—but knowing my ex-wife, I'd say she figures I might give ground if I thought the girls really wanted to grow up somewhere else."

"Cheryl wants to live in New York?"

"Who knows?" Tate asked, letting go of Libby, standing. "I've never been able to figure out what Cheryl wants. I'm not sure *she* knows, actually."

Libby watched as he took a leather carry-on bag from the enormous closet, threw in a change of clothes and some shaving gear. "So you're going to bring the twins back home?"

He turned, looked at her. "Yeah," he said. Sadness moved in his eyes. "Ava wants to be in Blue River, anyway. I'm not so sure about Audrey. She might choose to stay on and come back with Cheryl, after the apartment's ready to be sold."

Libby stood, still draped in the top sheet, and crossed the room to pick up her clothes. While she didn't know Tate's daughters very well, she *had* figured out that Audrey was the bolder of the two. Ava, with her glasses and hearing aid, while just as bright as her sister, was shy.

"Lib—would you like to come along? To New York, I mean?"

Libby hadn't expected that question. She'd just assumed Tate would want to travel fast and light—get to the city, collect his children, bring them back to Texas.

Excuses rushed through her mind. She had the Perk Up to run, there was Hildie to consider—and what about mowing the lawn and cleaning out the flower beds?

What she actually *said* was, "It could be pretty confusing for the twins—my just showing up like that." She dressed slowly, not looking at Tate. "They're not used to seeing us together, after all."

Tate sighed. "Point taken," he said. "But if we're going to keep seeing each other, they need to start getting used to our being together, Lib."

She was wearing all her clothes by then, but she still felt naked, stripped to the soul. "Maybe it's a little soon to spring that on them," she ventured. "Our spending time together, I mean."

He left off packing then, crossed the room, took her gently by the shoulders. "When I've finished the house," he said, "I plan on asking you to come and live with me. You might as well know that." Curving his fingers under her chin, he lifted her face so he could look directly into her eyes. "As for sex—I'll be granting no quarter, Libby. Whether we're sharing a house and a bed or not, I promise you, I'll seduce you every chance I get, any way I can, any*place* I can."

Libby blushed so hard it hurt. Tate knew what she liked, in and out of bed. He knew all the right words to say, all the secret, special places where she loved to be caressed, nibbled, teased.

But, then, Libby knew a few things herself.

Two could play that game.

"You'd better be real quick to make the first move, cowboy," she said, unfastening his jeans, pushing her hand inside, loving the way he groaned, the way he swelled when she closed her fingers around him. "Or you might just find *yourself* being seduced."

Tate swallowed hard. "Libby—"

"No quarter, Tate," she said, working him, enjoying the way he responded. "No prisoners. If I want you, I'll have you. On the spot."

A powerful shudder moved through him, even as he gave a strangled laugh, perhaps at her audacity.

"In fact," Libby murmured, "I'm pretty sure I want you right now."

"Libby—"

"Right—here—"

He moaned aloud as Libby proceeded to prove her point.

TATE CAUGHT AN EARLY flight out of Austin, and the landing at LaGuardia went without a hitch. Since he'd only brought a carry-on—he didn't plan on staying even overnight—he didn't have to wait with the crowds around the luggage carousels.

The cab line was long, as usual, but it moved quickly.

The drive into the city passed almost unnoticed—Tate's mind was back in Texas, for most of the ride, with Libby.

When the taxi stopped in front of Cheryl's parents' building, though, he made the necessary mental shift—time to think about the business at hand.

He paid the cabdriver and turned, bracing himself.

The doorman stood under a green-and-white awning, eyeing him warily.

"My name's Tate McKettrick," Tate said. "I'm here to see Ms. Darbrey."

The older man smiled fondly at the mention of Cheryl. "I'll buzz her," he said, stepping inside and pressing one of a series of brass buttons gleaming on a panel behind his desk.

Tate waited outside, taking in the sounds and sights of a great city just gearing up for a new day. He was a rancher—body, mind and spirit—but he liked New York, liked the energy and buzz of the place.

The doorman returned, holding the door open. "Go right up, Mr. McKettrick," he said. "Apartment 17B."

Tate merely nodded and, gripping the handle of his carry-on, passed the doorman and headed for the elevator.

Outside 17B, minutes later, Tate stopped to prepare himself for whatever he might have to deal with. Since he'd been announced, there wasn't much point in knocking or ringing the doorbell.

On the other side of the door, a sequence of sliding chains and turning bolts began. Then the door opened, and Ava, still wearing pajamas, launched herself into his arms.

Audrey was there, too, but she stood back a little way, and Tate felt dread pinch his heart as he studied her small face.

He kissed Ava's cheek as he closed the door, gathered Audrey against his side.

Cheryl appeared in the arched doorway leading into the gracious living room, with its gas fireplace, built-in bookcases, and high, ornately molded ceilings. She looked coolly elegant in white slacks—the tails of her red silk shirt were tied at her midriff, revealing a flat, tanned stomach, and her hair was plaited into a single braid.

"Come in," she said. "Breakfast is almost ready."

"Are we going home today?" Ava wanted to know. "Are we going back to Texas?"

Cheryl's face tightened a little, but her smile remained in place. Nobody would have guessed, to look at her, that she'd called Tate in the middle of the night complaining that the twins in general and Ava in particular were about to drive her out onto the nearest ledge.

"We're going home today," Tate confirmed quietly, setting Ava on her feet.

Then, to Cheryl, he said, "Is there coffee?"

She nodded. "You haven't shaved," she remarked, and her cat-green eyes narrowed a little. Wheels were turning behind that alabaster-smooth forehead. "Late night, maybe?"

"I was in a hurry," he said, galled that he'd explained even that much.

They were in the living room now, and he looked around. No moving boxes, he noted. No clutter, either. Gone were her father's teetering stacks of reference books, notes and file folders bulging with clippings.

Cheryl's parents had fallen on hard times—mostly of their own making—long before she and Tate were married, but they *had* managed to hold on to the apartment, mainly by mortgaging it repeatedly.

By the time the twins were born, the place had gone into

foreclosure and Cheryl was making noises about bringing Mom and Dad to live with her and Tate, in Blue River.

Tate, unable to get cell reception, had promptly called his lawyer from a hospital pay phone and instructed him to buy the Park Avenue place outright and put the deed in Cheryl's name.

Her folks had gone on living there until just a few months ago, when she'd finally made the decision to move them into an assisted-living place. He was picking up the tab for that, too, since they couldn't afford it on their own.

"I want to go home today," Ava said firmly.

Audrey made a face. "You're such a baby."

"Hush," Tate said.

In the kitchen, which was as spacious as the living room and also showed no evidence that anybody had been packing for a move, Cheryl set out four mismatched antique plates on the round table. The piece, Tate decided, was probably supposed to look antique and French—"distressed," his ex-wife termed it—meaning it had been falsely aged with things like sandpaper and rusty bicycle chain, swung hard.

He could identify.

In a classic *you-big-dumb-cowboy* moment, Tate realized that Cheryl had never had any intention of selling the apartment. She'd probably spent the girls' weeks with him right here, getting settled. Making new friends, or reconnecting with old ones, circulating her résumé.

"Mommy got a job offer," Audrey said, confirming his thoughts.

"Audrey Rose," Cheryl said, "*hush*. I wanted to tell your daddy about that myself."

Tate's blood seemed to buzz in his veins; the feeling was a combination of pissed off and thank God. Calmly, he washed his hands at the kitchen sink, sat down in the chair his ex-wife indicated. Although his glance sliced to Cheryl, he held his tongue and kept his face expressionless.

Avoiding his gaze, Cheryl served him hot, strong coffee, while the girls had orange juice. Bagels and smoked salmon, cream cheese and capers followed, and fresh strawberries finished off the meal.

"Go and get dressed, both of you," Cheryl told the kids when they'd obviously eaten all they intended to, for the time being at least.

They balked a little, especially Ava, who seemed reluctant to let Tate out of her sight for fear he'd vanish, but the pair finally hurried off to put on their clothes.

"It's a long commute between here and Blue River," Tate commented quietly.

Cheryl sighed, and her cup rattled in its saucer when she reached for it. "I could be there every other weekend," she said, avoiding his gaze. When she finally looked at him, though, he saw a different woman behind those green eyes, a woman he'd probably never known in the first place.

"The job—it's a good one, Tate."

"I'm happy for you," he said, without sarcasm.

"Don't ruin this for me," she whispered. *"Please."*

"I'm not out to ruin anything for you, Cheryl," Tate told her reasonably, and in all truth. "But we have a custody agreement, and I'm not willing to change it."

Tears brimmed in Cheryl's eyes. "Ava wants to live with you, on the Silver Spur. I thought Audrey could—"

Tate leaned forward in his chair, careful to keep his voice down. "You thought Audrey could *what?*" he asked.

"Stay here, with me," Cheryl said. "Just during the week. Tate, Audrey loves New York, just like I do. It would be so good for her—"

"You want to split them up?"

Cheryl's shoulders moved in a semblance of a shrug, but there was nothing nonchalant in her expression. She looked miserable. "I know it's not an ideal situation," she said. Then she bit down on her lower lip, and when she spoke again, her voice had dropped to a desperate whisper. "I can't stay in Blue River until our daughters are eighteen, Tate. I just can't. I'll lose my mind if I try!"

Tate felt sorry for Cheryl in that moment—she was a beautiful woman, with a law degree and a lot of ambition. She wasn't cut out for the kind of life she'd been living in Blue River; she needed a career. She needed the throb and hurry of a city around her, subway trains rumbling under her feet, traffic lights changing, horns honking 24/7.

"I understand that," he said, and he did. "But, as I said, we have an agreement, Cheryl. It would be wrong—*worse* than wrong—to separate the twins, have them grow up apart."

Cheryl put her hands over her face and began to cry.

Tate loved Libby Remington—the time he'd just spent with her had left him more convinced of that than ever—but as bitter as his and Cheryl's marriage and divorce had been, he didn't like seeing her hurting the way she was.

"I'm going home later today," he told his ex-wife quietly, even gently, "and I'm taking Audrey and Ava with me. If you really want to practice law again though, here in New York or anywhere else, you ought to do it."

She lowered her hands. Her eyes were wet, puffy and a little red around edges. "Do you mean that?"

In the near distance, Tate heard his daughters approaching, engaged in some little-girl exchange that was part giggle and part squabble.

"Yes," he said. "I mean it."

"You wouldn't hold it against me—think I was a bad mother—if I stayed here?"

Born and raised in the country, among old-fashioned folks, a mother willingly living apart from her children was a foreign thing to Tate. Times were changing, though—maybe not for the better—and Cheryl had worked hard to earn that law degree. Barely gotten to use it.

"I think," he replied carefully, "that what you do with your life is your own business."

Audrey and Ava burst into the kitchen, wearing jeans and short-sleeved cotton blouses with little red and white checks.

"All packed to go back to Blue River?" Tate asked.

Ava nodded.

Audrey looked less certain. That gave him a pang.

"I need to talk to your mom alone for a few more minutes," he said. "Ava, maybe you could help your sister get her things together."

Audrey glanced at Cheryl, then turned and followed Ava out of the room again.

Cheryl shifted in her chair, cupped her hands around her coffee mug, as though to warm them. "I know I was supposed to sell this apartment, Tate, but—"

"Let's worry about that later," Tate said, when her words fell away. "This is a big decision, Cheryl. It might be the right one, and it might be one you'll come to regret someday. Possibly, it's both those things, life being what it is."

She swallowed, nodded. "What will you tell them?" she asked, her voice small. "When you take Audrey and Ava back to Texas, what will you tell them?" She glanced anxiously at the doorway, then her gaze swung back to Tate's face and clung. "It isn't that I don't love the kids."

"I know you love them," Tate said gruffly, and he *did* know. Like most people, Cheryl was probably doing the best she could. The insight made him feel incredibly sad. "I won't try to convince them otherwise, I promise."

"Thank you, Tate."

He pushed back his chair, meaning to stand, but Cheryl stayed him by touching his arm.

"Have another cup of coffee," she said. "There's no big rush, is there?"

Tate sighed. He liked New York well enough, but the walls of that apartment seemed to be creeping in on him, an inch or two at a time. "How are your folks doing at the assisted-living place?" he asked, while Cheryl hurried to the counter for the coffeepot.

Cheryl looked sad as she refilled his cup, then her own. It felt strange, her pouring coffee for him. "Not so well," she said, setting the pot on the table and sinking into a chair. "Every time I call or visit, they beg to come back here. When begging doesn't work, they start accusing me of things, like *stealing* their home out from under them—"

Tate guessed it was a tough row to hoe, having aging parents, but from his point of view, it sure beat not having any at all. "That might pass, once they get used to the new place," he said. "And if it doesn't, well, you know they don't really mean any of those things."

Cheryl sniffled, nodded.

A silence descended on that kitchen. They'd never had much to say to each other, unless they were talking about the girls.

Half an hour later, Tate was in a cab with both his daughters, headed for LaGuardia. Ava fairly bounced on the seat, she was so happy to be going home, but Audrey was—subdued, he guessed he'd call it.

"You like the Big Apple, Shortstop?" he asked her, squeezing her small hand.

She looked up at him, nodded. "Mommy was going to let me audition for TV commercials," she said wistfully. "And take singing and dancing lessons, too."

"I see," Tate said seriously, because to his daughter, these *were* serious matters.

"She thought you might let us live in New York with her for a while," Audrey added. "So you'd have more time to get reacquainted with Libby."

An acid sting shot through Tate's stomach. "I do like spending time with Libby," he confirmed evenly. "But I'd miss you way too much if you lived here."

Audrey's remarkably blue eyes widened slightly. "Then you still want us around? Wouldn't we be underfoot?"

Tate turned in Audrey's direction, tightened his arm around Ava's shoulders at the same time. "Of course I want you around," he said. "And you can get underfoot all you want."

Audrey smiled. "Okay," she said, and with a little sigh, she rested the side of her head against his chest.

"She still wants to be in the Pixie Pageant," Ava said righteously, folding her arms. "You don't even know when you're being *played,* Dad."

Tate hugged Ava closer. "I'm smarter than I look," he told her, and kissed the top of her head. Then he squeezed Audrey again. "Is that true, monkey? You really want to take on this Pixie thing?"

Audrey nodded. "I just want to *try,* Daddy. I'll be okay if I don't win."

Sometimes the maturity of a six-year-old could take a man by surprise.

"Tell you what," Tate said, when he'd mulled the insight over for a few moments. "When we get home, I'll look into this pageant deal and see if it's something we can both live with. Sound fair to you?"

The little girl beamed. "Sounds fair to me," she said, putting up her right hand for Tate's high-five.

ONCE THEY'D CHECKED IN, gone through security and boarded a plane bound for Austin, where Tate's truck would be waiting in the airport parking garage, the twins, seated side by side across the aisle from him, flipped the pages of the catalogs and airline magazines like a pair of vertically challenged adults.

They were only six.

And they would be grown women long before he was ready for that to happen.

The girls each had a suitcase, so they had to wait in baggage claim for a while, but soon enough they were in the truck and on their way to the ranch.

Ambrose and Buford were waiting when they arrived, barking their fool heads off and jumping as if they'd swallowed a bucket of those Mexican beans, but they stayed well clear of the truck—which meant that, between the two of them, they might have a lick of sense.

There was a big, blank spot in the yard where that ridiculous castle had stood, but if Audrey and Ava noticed at all, they didn't react. They were too glad to see the pups again.

The feeling was certainly mutual.

Tate grinned and shook his head as he watched his daughters, in their expensive playclothes, kneeling in the grass to accept canine adoration in the form of face-licking and happy yips and impromptu wrestling matches on the ground.

Esperanza came out onto the patio, wearing yet another apron from her vast collection, waving.

Audrey and Ava and the dogs scrambled toward her, all but tumbling over each other, and as he watched, Tate's throat thickened and his eyes burned.

He belonged on that land, and so did his children.

After all, they were McKettricks.

CHAPTER THIRTEEN

LIBBY WAS MOWING her lawn, sweat-soaked and bug-bitten, even after the streetlights had come on, determined to finish the job come hell or high water. Hildie sat on the front porch, head tilted to one side, ears perked, watching her mistress with pitying curiosity.

A light rain began, a mist at first, then a sprinkle, cooling Libby's overheated flesh and at the same time causing her to grit her teeth. *Here's the high water,* she thought, *so hell can't be far behind.*

She stopped at the edge of the flower bed below the front porch, turned the mower grimly in the opposite direction, and saw Tate McKettrick pull up to the curb in his big truck.

The rain made his dark hair curl at the ends and dampened his white shirt.

At once embarrassed to be caught looking like the proverbial drowned rat and delighted to see Tate, no matter what, Libby froze.

Tate opened the gate, came through, shut it again.

Hildie gave a welcoming woof and started down the porch

steps, but Libby neither moved nor spoke. The rain came in fat droplets now, spiking her eyelashes and blurring her vision.

Tate bent to ruffle Hildie's ears in greeting, then straightened to face Libby. He pried the handle of the push-mower from her fingers and leaned in to land a kiss on her right temple.

Damn, but he smelled good.

"Hey," he said.

Libby waited, her heart pounding, full of both delicious relief because he'd come back from New York and potential misery because he might have brought his ex-wife home with him.

Nobody knew it better than Libby did: This man would do *anything* for his kids, including marry a woman he'd never claimed to love. He'd done that once already, and she had no doubt whatsoever that he'd do it again, if he thought it was best for Audrey and Ava.

Tate smoothed Libby's soggy bangs back off her forehead, his touch light and, at the same time, electric. "You do realize," he began, in that easy and oh-so-familiar drawl of his, "that lightning could strike at any time?"

Libby stared up at him, baffled. As far as she was concerned, lightning had *already* struck, way back in second grade, when she'd suddenly looked at Tate McKettrick, that pesky ranch kid with all the freckles and the lock of dark hair forever falling into his blue eyes, in a startling new—and *old*—way. Barely seven at the time, Libby wouldn't have been able to articulate the feeling then, except to say it was like remembering—without the actual memories.

Heck, she wasn't sure she could articulate it *now,* and she was all grown up. Love? Lust? Some combination of the two?

Who knew?

All grown up into a pesky ranch *man,* sans the freckles

but still with an impish glint in his too-blue-to-be-legal eyes, Tate chuckled and steered Libby up the porch steps, Hildie following.

Libby stood just out of the rain, watching as Tate went back down the steps, easily hoisted the heavy push-mower off the ground, carried it onto the porch and set it in a corner, where it would stay dry.

She finally found her voice. "Did you bring the twins home?"

Tate nodded, opened the screen door, laid his hand on the small of her back and gently pushed her into the lighted living room.

"They're sound asleep in their own beds, and Esperanza is looking after them," he said, his eyes traveling the length of her, from her sturdy hiking boots to her jean shorts to the blouse with the tie front. He frowned as he closed the door behind him. "What's with the all-weather yardwork?" he asked. "You didn't hear the thunder? See the flashes of lightning? On top of all that, it's *dark*."

Libby had been jumpy all day—and some of the night, too. She'd been so busy over the last five years, looking after her dad, starting the Perk Up, and now helping out with Marva, too. Her life had been hectic, yes, but now it seemed things happened at warp speed; one moment, she was in bed with Tate, the next, she was trying to mow the lawn in the rain.

"I guess I just have too much energy," she said. *I'm going crazy, and it's your fault. For so long I could pretend you didn't exist, that we didn't have a history. Now I can't pretend anymore, because you won't let me.*

Tate folded his arms, and she saw a muscle bunch in his jaw, then relax again. "You need to warm up, Lib; your lips are blue and your teeth are chattering a little. Take a hot shower, and while you're doing that, I'll warm up some milk for you."

Warm milk? Not what she would have expected from a

confirmed cowboy like Tate. And she got the clear impression that he wasn't planning to strip out of his own rain-dampened clothes and join her in the shower, either.

This was both a disappointment and a relief.

Libby swallowed, just to keep from sighing. She hated warm milk unless it was liberally disguised with chocolate.

"Okay," she said, and her voice sounded tinny in her ears, as though she were one of those old-fashioned talking dolls, and someone had just pulled the string in her belly.

Resigned, she headed for the bathroom.

Fifteen minutes later, Libby joined Tate in the kitchen; by then she was wearing cotton pajamas, her unsexiest robe, and furry slippers from the back of her closet. As hot and muggy as that Texas night was, she felt oddly chilled.

Tate sat at the table, ruminating as he sipped instant coffee from a mug, but he rose to his feet when he spotted Libby, the chair scraping back behind him as he stood. "Sit down," he said.

His serious tone, on top of all that thinking, worried Libby. *Had* Tate and Cheryl reconnected somehow, while he was in New York, as she had secretly feared they would? Decided to give their marriage another try, if only for the children's sake?

"Why are you here?" she asked, crumpling a little on the inside.

Tate drew back a chair for her, waited in silence until she sat. Then he poured hot milk for her, added a dollop of brandy from a dusty bottle stored on the shelf above the broom closet, brought it to the table.

"We need to talk," he said.

Libby's heart began to thrum. *Here it comes,* she thought, *the part where he says he still has feelings for Cheryl, or the kids need him 24/7 or we're just plain moving too fast and need to take a breather...*

"Okay," she replied hoarsely, glad he couldn't see her

hands knotted together in her lap because the tabletop was in the way. Then she squared her shoulders, raised her chin, looked him right in the eye, and waited.

"Drink the milk," Tate said. "It has to be hot to work."

Libby unknotted her hands, picked up the cup, took a sip.

It wasn't half bad—but it wasn't half *good,* either.

She made a face.

Tate grinned, reached across to smooth away her milk mustache with the pad of one thumb.

Libby set the cup down, felt some of the tension drain from her muscles.

Tate's expression changed; he leaned slightly forward, his dark brows lowered but not quite coming together. "What do you know about this Pixie thing?" he asked gravely.

Libby blinked, mystified. And almost dizzy with relief, because he hadn't said he and Cheryl were getting back together.

"'Pixie thing'?" she echoed.

Was he asking if she believed in fairies, little people?

Tate looked deep into her eyes and a grin broke over his face. "Sorry," he said. "I guess I should have laid a little groundwork before I threw that question at you. I'm talking about the Pixie Pageant. It's some kind of shindig they're holding at the country club, for charity. Like a beauty contest, but for little girls."

"Oh," Libby said, vaguely remembering a piece she'd skimmed in the *Blue River Clarion,* the town's weekly newspaper, "*that* Pixie Pageant."

Tate's jaw tightened. "Audrey is real set on signing up for the thing," he said.

Libby smiled. "What about Ava?"

"Ava thinks it's silly and wants no part of it. I happen to agree. But, like I said, Audrey is determined."

"A determined McKettrick," Libby mused, grinning. "Just *imagine* it."

Tate gave a wan grin at that, relaxed a little. "I've been dead set against this—Audrey joining up with this Pixie outfit, I mean—from the first. There are so many ways she could get hurt—"

Libby chuckled, took another sip of the milk-brandy mixture, and set her cup down. "As opposed to some *safe* activity, like rodeo?" she teased. Tate, Garrett and Austin had all been involved in the sport from earliest childhood.

Tate sighed, shoved a hand through his hair, leaving moist ridges where his fingers passed. "I get your point," he said, and sighed again. A pause followed, long and somehow comfortable. Tate finally ended it with, "What do you think I should do? Let Audrey sign up for this thing, or stand my ground?"

"I think," Libby said carefully, "that this is a conversation you should probably have with Cheryl, not me."

"I know what Cheryl thinks. I want to know what you think, Libby."

Her heart beat a little faster. She drew a fast, deep breath and huffed it out. "Why?" she asked.

"I need an unbiased opinion."

"Did you ask Esperanza?"

"Yes, as a matter of fact," Tate answered. "I did. And she's biased."

"For or against?"

"For," Tate admitted. "She thinks the whole thing is harmless and if Audrey gives it a try, she'll lose interest. Get it out of her system."

"Makes sense," Libby said, still careful. This was dangerous ground; Cheryl was the twins' mother, Esperanza had been the family housekeeper forever. But *she,* Libby, was what to them? Their father's girlfriend?

Not even that.

She was someone he slept with when they weren't around.

"Come on, Lib," Tate urged.

"What makes you so sure *I'm* unbiased?" Libby asked, more than a little hurt, now that she thought about it. The term merely meant "impartial," she knew that, but it sounded so indifferent in this context—she might have been someone stopped by a survey taker, on the way out of a supermarket, for heaven's sake. *Did she prefer laundry detergent with or without bleach?*

Tears scalded her eyes.

"I'm overreacting," she said. "I'm sorry."

Tate looked as though he wanted to touch her, rise from his chair and pull her into his arms, or tug her onto his lap.

But he did none of those things.

He cleared his throat. Looked away from Libby, then looked back. "Tell me something," he said.

Something tensed in the pit of Libby's stomach. "What?"

"If we get together, you and I," Tate ventured quietly, "you'll be around the kids a lot. Does that bother you?"

"*Bother* me?"

"If they hadn't been conceived—"

Adrenaline stung through Libby's system. "You're *not* suggesting that I blame *those precious children* for *our* breakup?"

"It would bother some women," Tate said, sounding a little defensive and a lot relieved.

"I'm not one of those women," Libby told him, her voice tight. While it was true that she didn't know Audrey and Ava very well, she had always loved them, albeit from afar, because they were Tate's.

"Good," Tate said. "Now, how about giving me an opinion on the Pixie Pageant?"

She laughed. "You never give up, do you?"

"Never," he answered, but he wasn't laughing, or even smiling.

Libby was quiet for a while, thinking. Finally, she said, "Okay, here's my opinion—you should check the pageant out, talk to the people putting it on, find out exactly what's involved. If it's something you can live with, let Audrey compete if she still wants to."

Tate sighed. "What if I miss something?" he asked.

Libby smiled uncertainly. "Miss something?"

"I'm a man, Lib. I don't know squat about this Pixie thing. They'll probably need tutus and stuff—"

Libby pictured Tate shopping for tutus and put a hand over her mouth to keep from laughing. Then, seeing that he was truly concerned, she sobered. "Can't Cheryl take care of that kind of thing?"

"Cheryl," Tate said, "is staying in New York for the time being. Right now, she plans on coming back here every other weekend, to be with the kids, but I don't suppose that will last long."

Libby stared at him. "Cheryl is staying in New York," she repeated stupidly.

"I didn't mention that before?"

"You didn't mention that before."

"Oh." Tate pushed back his chair, stood. "Well, she is. Will you help me, Lib? With the Pixie Pageant, I mean?"

Libby stood up, went to him, rested against his chest. "Yes," she said. "I'll help you."

He grinned down at her, sunshine bursting through a bank of dark clouds. "Do you have any idea how sexy you look in those pajamas and that worn-out bathrobe?"

Libby made the time-out sign, straightening the fingers of her left hand and pressing them into the palm of her right.

"What?" Tate asked, sounding innocent, though the twinkle in his eyes was anything *but* innocent.

"No sex," Libby was surprised to hear herself say. "Not tonight, anyway. I'm still recovering from last time."

"Recovering?" Tate asked, pretending to be hurt. The twinkle remained, though.

"Yes, *recovering*," Libby said, blushing. "It's not just sex when we're together, Tate. Not for me."

He raised a questioning eyebrow, looked intrigued.

Ran his hands down her back and cupped her bottom.

"Lib?" Tate prompted, when she didn't say anything else.

She caught her breath, found her voice, lost it again.

Sex wasn't just sex to Libby, not with Tate McKettrick. But how the hell was she supposed to explain that, without coming right out and saying that she still loved him? That, like a fool, she'd never *stopped* loving him, even while he was another woman's husband?

Even after his and Cheryl's divorce, Libby had been careful to stay away from Tate. She managed pretty well, too, until the day of the twins' birthday, when he'd walked into the Perk Up and the earth had shifted on its axis.

No, for Libby, sex with this one man was cosmic. It was a personal apocalypse, followed by the formation of new universes.

The one thing it would never be was *just sex*.

Libby didn't even have names for the things she felt when she and Tate were joined physically, and for hours or even days afterward.

"It's getting late," she said, avoiding Tate's eyes because she knew she'd get sucked into them like an unwary planetoid passing too near to a black hole if she let him catch her gaze just at that moment. "Maybe you should go."

He held her close again. She breathed in the scent of him, knew she would be powerless if he made the slightest move to seduce her.

"You're okay?" he asked, his voice hoarse, his breath moving through her hair like the faintest breeze. He propped his chin on top of her head, a sigh moving through his chest.

"I'm okay," she confirmed.

He moved back, curved a finger under her chin, and lifted. "Lib?"

She looked up at him.

Don't kiss me.

I'll die if you don't kiss me.

God help me, I've lost my mind.

"Everything's going to be okay," he told her.

She nodded. Tears threatened again, but she managed to hold them back.

He kissed her forehead.

And then he drew back, no longer holding her.

He bent to ruffle Hildie's ears in farewell.

Then he left.

Libby poured the remains of her milk—now cold—down the sink. She listened to Tate's retreating footsteps, fighting the urge to run after him, call him back, beg him to spend the night. She heard the front door open, close again. Then, distantly, the sound of his truck starting up.

Only then did she walk through the living room to lock up.

She switched off the lamps, went back to the kitchen, let Hildie out into the yard one last time.

Once the dog was inside again, Libby retreated to the bathroom, where she brushed her teeth and shed the robe, hanging it from the peg on the back of the door.

"What a pathetic life I lead," she said, looking at the robe, limp from so many washings, the once-vibrant color faded, the seams coming open in places.

Hildie, standing beside her, gave a concerned whimper, turned and padded into Libby's room.

The two of them settled down for the night, Libby expecting to toss and turn all night, sleepless, burning for the touch of Tate's lips and hands, the warm strength of his arms around her, the sound of his heart beating as she lay with her head on his chest.

Instead, sweet oblivion ambushed her.

She awakened to one of those washed-clean mornings that so often follow a rainstorm, sunlight streaming through her bedroom window.

DAWN HADN'T BROKEN WHEN Tate got out of bed, but a pink-ish-apricot light rimmed the hills to the east. He hauled on jeans, a T-shirt, socks and boots. He'd shower and change and have breakfast later, when the range work was done.

He looked in on his girls in their room, found them sleeping soundly, each with a plump yellow dog curled up at her feet. His heart swelled at the sight, but he was afraid to let himself get too happy.

Things were still delicate with Libby.

And Cheryl could change her mind about New York, the apartment, all of it, at any time—come back to the house in Blue River and start up the whole split-custody merry-go-round all over again.

The thought made his stomach burn.

Quietly, Tate closed the door to his daughters' room and made his way along the hallway, toward the back stairs leading down into the kitchen.

The aroma of brewing coffee rose to meet him halfway.

He smiled.

Esperanza was up, then. Maybe he'd have to reconsider his decision not to take time for breakfast, since she might not let him out of the house until he'd eaten something.

Tate paused when he stepped into the brightly lit kitchen.

Garrett stood at the stove, wearing jeans, boots and a long-sleeved work shirt, frying eggs. "Mornin'," he said affably.

Tate blinked, figuring he was seeing things.

Even when he was on the ranch, which wasn't all that often, Garrett never got up before sunrise, and he sure as *hell* never cooked.

"You're dead and I'm seeing your ghost," Tate said, only half kidding.

Garrett chuckled. There was something rueful in his eyes, something Tate knew he wouldn't share. "Nope," he replied. "It's me, Garrett McKettrick. Live and in person."

Tate fetched a mug from one of the cupboards, filled it from the still-chortling coffeemaker on the counter, watched his younger brother warily as he sipped. "What are you doing here?"

"I live here," Garrett said. "Remember?"

"Vaguely," Tate replied. "To be more specific, what are you doing *in the kitchen, at this hour, cooking,* for God's sake?"

"I'm hungry," Garrett answered quietly. "And if you never went to bed in the first place, it doesn't count as getting up early, does it?"

"Oh," Tate said. His brain was still cranking up, unsticking itself from sleep.

"Have some eggs," Garrett said, looking Tate over, noting his get-up. "Planning on playing cowboy today?"

Tate felt his neck and the underside of his jaw turn hot, recalling Garrett's earlier jibe about feeling guilty over the money and the land, making a show of working for a living. He took a plate from the long, slatted shelf and shoveled a couple of eggs—"cackleberries," their grandfather had called them—onto it.

They both sat down at the big table in the center of that massive room, and Tate took his time responding to Garrett.

"Yeah," he finally ground out. "I'm planning on 'playing cowboy' today." He let his gaze roll over Garrett's old shirt once, making his point. "Where did you get that rag? From wherever Esperanza stashes the cleaning supplies?"

Garrett chuckled, glancing down at his clothes. "Found them in the back of my closet," he said. "On the floor."

"Okay," Tate said, "I'll bite. What's with the getup?"

Garrett sighed. Possibly practicing his political skills, he didn't exactly answer the question. "The lights were on in the bunkhouse and all the trailers along the creek when I came home a little while ago," he explained, before a brief shadow of sadness fell over his face. He needed a shave, Tate noticed, and there were dark circles under his eyes. "Except the Ruizes', of course. That was dark."

Tate dealt with his own flash of sorrow in silence. He knew Garrett had more to say, so he just waited for him to go on.

"I knew the men were up and around, getting ready for a long day herding cattle or riding fence lines," Garrett eventually continued. "I decided to put on the gear, saddle up and see if I still have it in me—a day of real work."

Tate felt a surge of something—respect, pride? Brotherly love?

He didn't explore the emotion. "These eggs aren't half bad," he said.

"Well," Garrett answered, "don't get used to it. I don't cook, as a general rule."

Tate chuckled, though it was a dry, raspy sound, pushed back from the table, carried his plate to the sink, rinsed it and set it in the dishwasher. Leaned against the counter and folded his arms, watching as Garrett finished his meal and stood.

"Everything all right?" Tate asked, very quietly.

"Everything's *fine,* big brother," Garrett replied. He was lying, of course. From the time he was knee-high to a garden gnome, Garrett hadn't been able to lie and look Tate in the eye at the same time.

Now, he looked everywhere *but* into Tate's face.

"Let's go," Tate said, after a few moments, making for the door.

Just then, Austin came down his personal stairway, clad in work clothes himself, though his shirt was only half-buttoned and crooked at that, and he had a pretty bad case of bed-head. Wearing one boot and carrying the other, he hopped around at the bottom of the steps until he got into the second boot.

"Is there any grub left?" he asked.

"You're too late," Garrett told him.

"Shit," Austin said, finger-combing his hair. "Story of my life."

"Cry me a river," Tate said, with a grin and a roll of his eyes, pulling open the back door.

The predawn breeze felt like the kiss of heaven as it touched him.

He thought about Libby, sleeping warm and soft and deliciously curvy in her bed in town. Since about the last thing he needed right then was a hard-on, he shifted his mind to the day ahead, and the plans he'd made for it.

He strode toward the barn, Garrett and Austin arguing affably behind him, glanced back once to see Austin tucking his shirt into his jeans, none too neatly. It was like the old days, when they were boys, and their dad roused them out of their beds at the crack to do chores, not only in the summer but year-round. The Silver Spur was their ranch, too, Jim McKettrick had often said, and they had to learn how to look after it.

So they fed horses and herded cattle from one pasture to another.

They shoveled out stalls and drove tractors and milked cows and fed chickens.

The chickens and the dairy cows were long gone now, like the big vegetable garden. The quarter-acre plot had been his mother's province; she and Esperanza had spent hours out there, weeding and watering, hoeing and raking. Tate and his brothers had done their share, too, though usually under duress, grumbling that fussing with a lot of tomatoes and green beans and sweet corn was women's work.

"You eat, don't you?" Sally McKettrick had challenged,

more than once, shaking a finger under one of their noses. "You eat, you *weed,* bucko. That's the way the *real world* works."

Reaching the barn door, Tate smiled to himself, albeit sadly. Most of the bounty from that garden had gone to the ranch hands and their families and to the little food bank in town. And what he wouldn't give to be sweating under a summer sun again, with his mom just a few rows over, working like a field hand and enjoying every minute of it.

He switched on the overhead lights.

The good, earthy scents of horse and grass-hay and manure stirred as the animals moved in their stalls, nickering and shifting, snorting as they awakened.

Tending the horses wasn't new to Tate—he'd taken the job over from a couple of the ranch hands when he and Cheryl split and she moved into the house in town—though he rarely got to the barn this early in the day.

The work went quickly, divided between the three of them.

Austin turned his childhood mount, Bamboozle, out with the other, larger horses, since the little gelding was used to them and they were used to him, but Audrey's and Ava's golden ponies had to be kept in a special corral, for their own safety.

In the meantime, Tate saddled Stranger, the aging gelding, a strawberry roan, that had belonged to his father. Garrett chose Windwalker, a long-legged bay, while Austin tacked up a sorrel called Ambush.

In his heyday, Ambush had been a rodeo bronc, and he could still buck like the devil when he took the notion.

Austin, being Austin, probably hoped today was the day.

Tate grinned at the thought, shook his head.

His little brother was stone crazy, but you had to love him. Most of the time.

The paint stallion kicked and squealed in his holding pen, scenting the other horses, wanting to be turned loose.

"What are you planning on doing with that stud?" Garrett asked, as the three of them rode away from the barn, toward the range.

"Brent said we might have to put him down," Tate answered. He hated the idea, knew Pablo would have hated it, too, but there had been a death—and that meant the authorities had a say in the matter.

"And you're just going to go along with whatever he says?" Austin wanted to know.

Tate bristled. "The law's the law," he said. "I'd rather not shoot that horse, but I might not have a choice."

"You could just let him go," Garrett suggested. "Say he got out on his own somehow."

"And lie to Brent?" Tate asked. "Not only the chief of police, but my best friend?"

Garrett went quiet.

Austin didn't seem to have anything more to say, either.

So they rode on, the purple range slowly greening up ahead of them.

The herd bawled and raised dust in the dawn as cowboys converged from all directions, some coming from the bunkhouse, which had its own rustic but sturdy stables, and from the various trailers along the creek. Some of the men were on horseback, while others drove pickups with the Silver Spur brand painted on the doors.

Tate and his brothers fell in with the others as easily as if they had never been away from the work, driving cattle between different sections of land to conserve the sweet grass, rippling like waves under a rising wind.

Resting the roan, Stranger, at the creek's edge, Tate nodded as Harley Bates rode up alongside him. Harley had ridden for the McKettrick brand almost as long as Pablo had, though Tate didn't know him as well. Married when he signed on, Bates lived in one of the coveted trailers, although his wife had long since boarded a bus out of town, never to be seen again.

"It ain't the same without ole Pablo," Harley said, resettling his hat, which, like the rest of his gear, had seen better days.

"No," Tate agreed.

Bates shifted in his saddle, and the odor of unwashed flesh wafted Tate's way. "I see you've been fixing up that house by the bend in the creek."

A beat passed before Tate figured out what the man was talking about. He nodded again. "So I have," he said.

"Guess it'll go to the new foreman," Bates speculated. All the men were probably wondering who would replace Pablo Ruiz, and they'd either put Bates up to finding out, or he'd come up with the idea on his own, maybe hoping for a raise in pay and more spacious quarters than the one-bedroom single-wide he banked in now.

"Yep," Tate answered, standing in the stirrups to stretch his legs a little before turning to meet the other man's gaze. "You're looking at the new foreman," he said. "For the time being, anyway. I'll be moving into the Ruiz place myself, as soon as the renovations are finished."

Whatever Harley Bates had expected to hear, it wasn't that. His small eyes popped a little, and his jaws worked as though he were chewing on a mouthful of gristle. "*You're* the new foreman?"

Tate nodded. He couldn't blame the other man for being surprised, even skeptical. After all, the foreman did real work, especially on a spread the size of the Silver Spur. Although Tate could ride and brand and drive post holes with the best of them, he couldn't claim that he'd filled his dad's boots.

And that was why he'd decided to take on the job. If he was going to run the Silver Spur, he had to get serious about it. He had to learn all there was to know about every aspect of running the ranch.

Although it stung, he knew Garrett had been at least partly right, accusing him of playing at being a rancher.

Bates took off his hat, slammed it once against his thigh, and slapped it on again with such force that it bent the tops of his ears.

Tate suppressed a sigh. "Tell the men there'll be a meeting tonight," he said. "Six o'clock, at the new place."

"You mean, the Ruiz place?" Bates all but snarled.

"I mean, the new place," Tate answered evenly. "Six o'clock. I'll provide the chicken and the beer."

Bates scowled, nodded once, wheeled his horse around and rode away.

CHAPTER FOURTEEN

TATE APPEARED at the Perk Up at four-thirty that afternoon, with his daughters and their dogs, though Buford and Ambrose waited in the truck.

Julie stayed in the kitchen, but Calvin stood at Libby's side, watching as Audrey and Ava bounced into the shop. They were wearing jean shorts and matching cotton blouses, blue and white checked.

"It was nice of you to give us your castle," Calvin said, very solemnly. "Thanks." Although he had yet to be elected king, he apparently considered himself a spokesperson for the community.

And by *us,* of course, Calvin meant the town of Blue River—the wonder toy was now installed on the lawn at the community center, and according to Julie, so many kids wanted to play in and around the thing that parents had been recruited to supervise. A few people even wanted to sell tickets.

Audrey and Ava looked at each other, then up at Tate, then at Calvin.

"You're welcome," Ava said, with great formality. She

was definitely the more serious twin, Libby noted, though no less confident than her sister.

"Daddy made us do it," Audrey added forthrightly. "But we still have our ponies."

"You have *ponies?*" Calvin said, with wonder in his voice. Then, again, as though such a thing were almost beyond the outer reaches of credibility, *"You have ponies?"*

Audrey nodded at him. "Three, if you count Uncle Austin's. His horse is Bamboozle, but we call him Boozle for short, and he's really old, and we haven't named our ponies yet—they're twins, like we are, or at least they *look* like twins. They're not, really, but they're the same age and the same color and—" She paused, though not for very long, to haul in a breath. "Are you a friend of Libby's?"

Tate and Libby exchanged amused glances.

"She's my aunt," Calvin replied, with a note of pride that warmed Libby's heart.

Audrey smiled at him. "Maybe you can come out to our place sometime, and ride Boozle. He's old, like I said. Uncle Austin got him when he was ten. Uncle Austin was ten, I mean, not the pony."

"How come you weren't at our birthday party?" Ava asked. "We know you from daycare at the community center. Your name is Calvin."

Calvin was unfazed. "I don't think I was invited," he said reasonably.

"Oh," Ava said.

"How old are you?" Audrey wanted to know.

"Four," Calvin admitted, squaring his little shoulders.

"Well, that's probably why," Ava said matter-of-factly. "You're practically a baby."

"I am *not* a baby!" Calvin asserted indignantly.

Libby rested a hand on his shoulder.

"You talk like a grown-up," Audrey allowed, and after surveying Calvin thoughtfully for a moment or so, she graciously conferred her approval. "He's right, Ava. He's not a baby."

"Guess not," Ava agreed, with the barest hint of reluctance.

Calvin was clearly mollified. Grinning toothily and adjusting his glasses yet again with the poke of one slightly grubby finger, he said, "It was probably a real girly party, anyhow. Lots of pink stuff."

Tate chuckled, subtly steering the girls toward the stools at the short counter. Libby had noticed, and appreciated, the way he'd paid careful attention to the exchange between the three children but hadn't intervened.

"Of course it was girly," Ava said, looking back at Calvin over one shoulder. "We're *girls*."

"Orange smoothies all around?" Libby piped up, figuring it was time to change the subject.

"Yes, please," Ava said, speaking like a miniature adult.

"Please," Audrey echoed, scrambling up onto a stool.

"Me, too, Aunt Libby," Calvin chirped, getting into the spirit of the thing. "But I want strawberry, please."

Julie stuck her head out of the kitchen. Nothing wrong with her hearing, Libby thought, with an inward smile. It was probably a mother thing.

"No way, José," Julie told Calvin. "You'll spoil your supper."

"It's not even five o'clock yet," Calvin complained.

"Grandma's coming over for meat loaf," Julie reminded him, "and she likes to eat early, so she can get back to her condo in time to watch her TV shows. We're picking her up in a little while, and we have to run a few errands first."

Calvin sighed his weight-of-the-world sigh. It rarely worked with Julie, and this instance was no exception, but with Calvin, hope sprang eternal.

"You'd be welcome to come out to the Silver Spur sometime soon and ride Bamboozle," Tate told the little boy quietly, his gaze shifting to Julie's face. "If it's all right with your mom, that is."

Julie smiled. She liked Calvin to have new experiences, and riding horses on the McKettrick ranch certainly qualified. As kids, Julie, Paige and Libby had been to lots of parties on the Silver Spur, but those days seemed long ago and far away.

In fact, Libby hadn't been on a horse since before she and Tate broke up over Cheryl.

"That would be nice," Julie told Tate. "Thank you."

He nodded. He looked ridiculously good in his dark blue T-shirt and battered jeans, and the shadow of a beard growing in only added to the testosterone-rich effect. "My pleasure," he drawled.

The timbre of his voice found a place inside Libby and tingled there.

She shook off the sensation and finished brewing up the orange smoothies, setting them in front of Audrey and Ava and smiling.

"There you go," she said.

They smiled back at her.

Several moments of silence passed.

"Audrey needs a tutu," Ava announced, without preamble, after poking a straw into her smoothie and slurping some up. She rolled her lovely blue eyes at Libby and giggled. "She's pixilated."

Tate took the third stool, next to the cash register. Rested his muscular forearms on the countertop and intertwined his fingers loosely. He had an easy way about him, as if it were no trouble to wait around.

Not every man was that patient, Libby thought.

"Pixilated?" she asked, to get her mind off Tate's patience and his muscular forearms and his five-o'clock shadow.

She was only partly successful.

"Ava's talking about the Pixie Pageant," Tate said easily.

Libby liked the way he could just sit there, not needing to fiddle with something to keep his fingers busy. There was a great *quietness* in Tate McKettrick, a safety and serenity that reached beyond the boundaries of his skin, big enough to take in his daughters, the old dog, Crockett, his family and the whole of the Silver Spur Ranch.

And maybe her, too.

Libby met his eyes, an effort because she felt shaken now, as though something profound had just happened between her and Tate. Which was silly, because the situation couldn't have been more ordinary, nor could the conversation.

"I guess things checked out okay, then? The Pixie Pageant is a go?"

Tate nodded, looking beleaguered but mildly amused. *Females,* his manner seemed to say: *Sometimes there's no figuring them out.*

"Yeah," he said. "It checked out, and it's a go. A lot depends on your definition of *okay,* though."

She smiled, resisting an impulse to pat Tate's shoulder, and poured him a cup of coffee. "On the house," she said.

Libby realized she'd lost track of her sister and her nephew, shifted her focus.

"Julie?"

Julie, it turned out, was ready to leave; she'd gathered her belongings and her son and was standing almost at Libby's elbow, a knowing and slightly bemused smile resting prettily on her mouth.

Of course Libby knew what was going through her sister's mind; Julie and Paige could stop worrying about their big sister if Libby and Tate got back together.

"See you tomorrow?" Libby asked, wishing Julie would stay just a little longer.

"Sure," Julie replied hastily, barely looking back. "To-morrow."

"Bring scones," Libby called after her.

Julie laughed, gave a comical half salute and left the shop. The bell jingled over the door, and Calvin looked back, one hand smudging the glass, his eyes full of yearning.

The sight gave Libby a pang. She knew the feeling: on the outside, looking in. It grieved her to see the knowledge in Calvin—he was so young, and she loved him so much.

"We just came from the country club," Tate told Libby, when Julie and Calvin had left, and she'd snapped out of the ache over her nephew's little-boy loneliness. He watched with an expression of mystified fondness as his daughters giggled over their drinks. "The pageant is a one-day thing. As far as I can tell, it's no big deal."

"You have to have a talent to win," Ava interjected.

Audrey elbowed her. "I *have* a talent," she said.

"Oh, yeah?" Ava countered. "*What* talent?"

"That's enough," Tate said, though he seemed as still and as calm as ever. "Both of you."

"I *do too* have a talent," Audrey insisted, as though he hadn't spoken. What were these two going to be like as *teenagers?* "I can sing. Mom says so."

Tate tried again. "Girls," he said.

"If you call that singing," Ava said, with a little shrug and a flip of her ebony hair. "I think you sound awful. Anyhow, you know how Mom is about this pageant thing. Her eyes get all funny when she talks about it."

Although the reference to Cheryl made her mildly uncomfortable, Tate's expression made Libby want to smile. But since that might have undermined his parental authority, she didn't.

For all his calm, he was obviously at a loss, too. What to do?

The answer, Libby could have told him, was nothing at

all. This was simply the way sisters related—twins or not. She and Paige and Julie still bickered, but it didn't mean they didn't love each other. There was nothing Libby wouldn't have done for Paige and Julie, and she knew the reverse was true, as well.

Libby opened her mouth to make a stab at explaining, realized she didn't have the words, and closed it again.

"One more word," Tate told the children, "and nobody rides horseback, swims in the pool, goes to the library or plays a video game for a whole month."

Two sets of cornflower blue eyes widened.

"Okay," Ava breathed, looking and sounding put-upon. She adjusted her glasses, though not by shoving them upward at the bridge of her nose, the way Calvin did.

"That's a word," Audrey pointed out triumphantly. "*Okay* is a word!"

"You just said a *whole bunch* of words!" Ava cried.

"Let's go pick up the fried chicken and beer," Tate said, shoving off his stool to stand, and the girls scrambled off their stools, too, orange smoothies in hand.

He paid for the drinks.

"Daddy's having a cowboy meeting at the house where Mr. and Mrs. Ruiz used to live," Ava said to Libby, her tone and expression serious. "He's going to tell them where the bear shit in the buckwheat."

Tate flushed, the color throbbing in his neck and then pulsing briefly above his jawline and darkening his ears a little. *"Ava."*

"That's what you told Uncle Austin," the little girl retorted. "I *heard* you."

"Esperanza's going to take care of us while Daddy's at the cowboy meeting," Audrey explained, rapid-fire. "Because cowboys cuss and we shouldn't be around to hear things like that. So we get to have tacos for supper and make popcorn and spend the whole night in Esperanza's suite and watch as many movies as we want to, even if it's a hundred!"

"Wow," Libby said, very seriously, widening her eyes a little for emphasis, "a hundred movies?"

"More like one movie, a hundred times," Tate said dryly. Libby laughed.

Ava spoke up again. "I don't see why it takes a whole meeting just to tell people where a bear—"

Tate cupped a hand around the child's mouth. "Maybe I could stop by your place later, so we could talk about the tutu and stuff?" he said, his eyes practically pleading with Libby to agree.

The image of Tate McKettrick shopping for a tutu was beyond funny. She could hold back another burst of laughter, but not the twinkle she knew was sparkling in her eyes as she enjoyed the mind-picture.

"What time does the buckwheat meeting get over?" Libby asked sweetly, resting her hands on her hips and heartily enjoying Tate's obvious discomfort. At the same time, it touched her heart, the way he cared so much about being a good father, getting things right.

Even to the extent of shopping for tutus, when it came to that.

Her throat ached. Her dad had been the same way.

She missed him so much.

"Eight o'clock, maybe," Tate said, looking hopeful. "Is that too late?"

"Not for me," Libby answered, "but *you* look a little tired, cowboy."

He flashed her a grin, maybe to prove he wasn't all *that* tired.

The twins were at the shop door by then, still squabbling.

Tate bent his head, spoke quietly into Libby's ear. "I'll save you some chicken and beer," he said. "Meet me at the new place later, and bring the dog if you want to."

"Maybe," Libby said firmly, unsettled now. "Last time—"

The patented McKettrick grin came again, even more dazzling than before. "Yes," Tate said. "I remember."

Libby was wavering, and she didn't want him to know that.

She all but pushed Tate to the door, and that made the girls laugh.

"Later?" he asked. His voice was a sexy rumble.

"Don't count on it," Libby said, but she was rattled and planning on showing up at his place for sure and they both knew it.

Tate smiled and left, shepherding his daughters across the street, hoisting them into the back seat of the truck, assisting with buckles and belts affixed to safety seats while gently fending off a pair of overjoyed pups.

Libby watched, resting her forehead against the glass in the front door of the Perk Up.

When she sensed that Tate was about to turn in her direction, she pulled back quickly and turned the "Open" sign to "Closed."

She locked the door.

Shut down all the machines and cleaned them.

Tucked the day's profits into a deposit bag, and the bag into her purse. Although the Perk Up had been doing a lot better financially since Julie had started baking scones and other goodies, Libby had been giving most of the money to her sister.

Which meant she was still just breaking even, most days.

At home, she let Hildie out into the backyard, as usual, and went back inside when she heard the phone ringing.

"Have you seen Marva?" Julie blurted anxiously.

"No," Libby said. "Isn't she at the condo?"

"No, she's not at the condo!" Julie almost screamed. "Libby, she stole my car!"

Libby sagged against the counter. "Oh, my God, Julie, Calvin wasn't—?"

"Calvin wasn't in the car, thank heaven," Julie answered, only moderately less hysterical than before.

Libby echoed that sentiment, letting out her breath, then asked, "Have you called Chief Brogan?"

Julie was beside herself. "Are you kidding? Call the cops on my own mother? Libby, I can't do that!"

"Calm down," Libby said firmly. "Julie, *calm down*. Take a slow, deep breath."

"But my car—my mother—oh, my *God*—"

"I'll be right over," Libby said. "If I see Marva along the way, I'll do my best to flag her down."

The words were disturbingly prophetic, as it turned out.

Libby had no more than uttered them when she heard an odd noise, looked through the window over the sink, and saw Julie's pink Cadillac speeding down the alley, bouncing over the ruts, tailpipe dragging and throwing off blue and orange sparks.

It all happened quickly, and yet Libby took in the scene in vivid and minute detail.

Marva was at the wheel, the windows rolled down. She was smoking a long brown cigarette jutting from a holder and singing along with the Grateful Dead at the top of her lungs.

"I don't believe this!" Libby gasped into the phone, one hand pressed to her heart. "I just saw her go by!"

"Try to catch her," Julie pleaded. "Go! Now!"

"Oh, right," Libby said, feeling pretty frantic herself, now. "Maybe I could sprint to the corner and just leap onto the hood and pound on the windshield with my fists. Julie, I know you're upset, but will you get real?"

"Libby, you've got to *do* something!"

"I'll go after her, but she's driving so fast the wheels are barely touching the ground. Get here as quickly as you can, and call Paige, too."

"Get *where* as quickly as I can?"

"To wherever I am, of course." With that, Libby hung up with a bang, raced out the back door and down the steps, passing Hildie, who had settled herself comfortably in her favorite shady spot under the big tree.

"Stay!" Libby told the dog.

Hildie hadn't shown any signs of moving so much as a muscle, but a person couldn't be too careful.

"Marva!" Libby yelled, running for the alley.

Dust roiled, but there was no sign of the Caddie.

"Marva," Libby repeated, this time as a plea.

She was about to go back inside the house, since she'd forgotten the keys to the Impala and it wouldn't be much use giving chase on foot when she heard the crash.

It was deafening, so loud it seemed to shake the earth and the fillings in Libby's teeth.

Glass tinkled.

A horn tooted and then honked steadily, a long, terrifying drone.

A cloud of dust billowed far above the roof of Libby's shop, and except for the horn everything was silent, for one quivering moment.

And then the roof of the Perk Up collapsed.

Libby stood staring, unable to move.

A siren blared somewhere.

"Oh, no," Libby whispered. *"Oh, no."*

Running full out, Libby dashed through the narrow space between Almsted's Grocery and her coffee shop. More dust and plaster showered down on her.

The horn continued to blow.

Libby finally reached the sidewalk, and there was the pink Cadillac—or part of it, at least—taillights still shining bright red, half buried under the rubble of the Perk Up.

A crowd, probably driven from Almsted's by prudence, clustered on the sidewalk.

Brent had already arrived; his cruiser was parked at the curb, lights flashing dizzily, siren shrieking fit to wake all the corpses in the Blue River Cemetery. Along with several passersby and members of the volunteer fire department, the chief dug frantically through fallen timbers and old drywall and shards of glass with his bare hands.

Where she got the strength, Libby did not know. But somehow she pushed through until she was shoulder to shoulder with Brent, and dug hard.

The roof of the car appeared, and the driver's-side window. Unbroken, thank God. The windshield had held, too.

"Marva?" Libby whispered.

Marva turned and looked at her dreamily, both hands still resting on the steering wheel. Except for a small cut above her right eyebrow, she seemed to be all right, but there was no way of knowing that until she'd been examined by a doctor, of course.

Marva rolled down the car window. "Oops," she said.

"Is she drunk?" Chief Brogan demanded of Libby. He was sweating, like everybody except Marva, who looked cool as could be.

"I doubt it," Libby said, as wave after wave of residual shock washed over her. She had to grip the edge of the open window to steady herself. "Are you all right, Marva?" she asked, in someone else's voice.

Marva nodded. "I'm fine," she said calmly.

The Perk Up was a complete shambles, but Marva was alive and, it appeared, unhurt. For the moment, nothing else really mattered.

It would be a short moment.

"I forgot how to stop," Marva said, amazed. "I can't believe I forgot how to stop."

"Does anything hurt anywhere?" Brent asked.

Marva shook her head. Her gaze meandered slowly from Libby's face to Brent's. "Am I under arrest?" she asked. "I'm stone sober, you know. And I didn't actually *steal* this car, either. It belongs to my daughter, and I'm sure Julie will vouch for everything I say."

Libby, dizzy, put a hand to her own forehead.

"Let's not worry about the legal implications right this minute, ma'am," Brent answered, very politely. "For now, we're just going to concentrate on making sure you're all right."

"I demand a lawyer," Marva said.

"You don't need a lawyer," Libby said.

"She might," Brent countered, in a whisper.

"Winston," Marva said, tilting her head back and closing her eyes, "will kill me."

"Winston?" Libby asked, puzzled.

"My husband," Marva answered, without opening her eyes. "Winston Alexander Vandergant the Third."

Libby blinked. "Your—?"

"Husband." Marva sighed.

"Would you mind spelling that?" Brent asked, taking a little notebook from his shirt pocket and clicking a pen with his thumb.

Marva calmly spelled out the entire name.

Brent wrote it down.

"You have a husband?" Libby echoed.

"Call him," Marva told Brent. "He'll straighten out this whole situation. Winston is just a whiz when it comes to problem solving."

Brent merely nodded.

Two EMTs politely elbowed Libby and Brent aside so they could remove Marva from the car.

Libby was standing on the sidewalk when Paige roared up to the curb in her subcompact car, Julie in the passenger seat.

By then, the paramedics had put a neck brace on Marva

and placed her carefully on a stretcher. She was loaded into the ambulance; according to protocol, she would be examined at the Blue River Clinic, and if her injuries were serious, transported from there to a trauma center.

Julie, standing on the littered sidewalk, assessed Marva, the collapsed roof of the Perk Up and her nearly buried car. *"What happened?"*

"I think that's obvious," Paige said dryly, but she ran over and climbed into the ambulance just as the doors were about to be closed, scrambling inside to take Marva's hand. The vehicle raced away.

Libby ran home, retrieved the keys to her Impala from the kitchen, backed the car out of the garage, and stopped for a still-stunned Julie in front of what was left of the Perk Up.

They headed for the clinic.

"Where's Calvin?" Libby asked, as she navigated the familiar streets. By then, her brain was clearing; she was starting to think in practical terms again.

"With Marva's neighbor, Mrs. Kingston," Julie answered.

Libby nodded, reassured. Mrs. Kingston, unlike their mother, was quite sane. A responsible human being.

"She could have killed herself," Julie fretted. "Marva, I mean."

"Right," Libby agreed tensely. "And a lot of other people, too."

Her mind raced. Julie's Cadillac might be salvageable, but the Perk Up was a total loss. What was she going to do now? How was she going to earn a living?

She'd barely been getting by as it was.

Ashamed of worrying about herself when Marva might be lapsing into a coma in the back of the ambulance at that very moment—she doubted it, but anything was possible—Libby blinked a couple of times and bit down hard on her lower lip. "Julie, how did Marva manage to swipe your car?"

Julie closed her eyes tightly, hugged herself. "I left the

keys in the ignition. I was talking to that nice Mrs. Kingston, Marva's neighbor—she has the loveliest climbing roses and I wanted to know how often she pruned and fertilized because I'm thinking of putting in a garden next spring myself and—"

Libby broke into the nervous flow of her sister's conversation. "Do you know how lucky we are that Calvin wasn't in the car? Or behind it, or *in front* of it—"

"Do *you* have to remind me of what *could* have happened?" Julie snapped. "It seems to me that what *did* happen is bad enough!"

"I'm sorry," Libby said, to keep the peace.

Julie reached over, squeezed her hand. "Me, too," she said. "I shouldn't have snapped at you."

Less than a minute later, they reached the clinic, a small brick building on the eastern edge of town. Thanks to the generous support of the McKettricks and other oil-and-cattle-rich families in that part of Texas, the facility was well-staffed, with four different doctors working in rotation, several nurses, a full office staff and assorted technicians.

The equipment was state-of-the-art, and there were two spacious four-bed wards for overnight patients.

Paige was waiting in the parking lot looking fidgety, when Libby and Julie wheeled in.

The three of them hurried past the parked ambulance, its rear door still standing open. Brent's cruiser stood beside it, empty.

The receptionist explained that Dr. Burt was examining Marva, and they might as well sit down because it would be a while.

Paige led the way into the small waiting room, plunked some coins into a vending machine, and watched as a cup dropped down a chute and began to fill with steaming coffee.

"She has a husband," Libby said, apropos of nothing. "Marva, I mean."

"A husband?" her sisters chorused.

"Winston Alexander Vandergort the Third, or something like that."

"Who?" Julie asked.

"That's all I know," Libby insisted, defensive.

Julie began to pace. "A husband," she muttered.

"Do you both have insurance?" Paige asked, ever practical, her gaze traveling between Libby and Julie.

"Yes," Julie said. "But that Cadillac was a classic. Irreplaceable."

"So was my business," Libby said. "Irreplaceable, I mean."

"Let's not panic here," Paige said.

"That's easy for you to say," Libby said.

"Yeah," Julie agreed.

"Everything will work out," Paige insisted.

Again, easy for *her* to say. She had a good job, with benefits, and she definitely didn't live from paycheck to paycheck, either. *Her* car hadn't been wrecked. *Her* coffee shop hadn't been reduced to a pile of broken boards and bits of plaster.

"We'll *manage,*" Paige said, putting one arm around Libby's shoulders and one around Julie's and squeezing. "I promise."

"We?" Libby challenged.

"We," Paige confirmed. "I have savings. I can help—"

"I won't take your money," Libby said.

"Neither will I," Julie agreed.

Brent came out of one of the exam rooms and approached them.

"Well," he said, "we won't be charging your mother with driving under the influence, anyway. Which is not to say her sanity isn't in question."

"But is she going to be all right?" Julie asked anxiously, staring up at Brent.

"She seems to be," Brent replied patiently. "The doctor

wants to run a CT scan and take some x-rays. Could be a long wait."

Julie glanced down at her watch. "Calvin is probably worried," she said, pale with anxiety.

"Let's pick him up and bring him here," Paige suggested. She looked up at Brent. "Would you mind giving us a ride back to my car, Chief? I left it at the Perk Up to ride in the ambulance with Marva."

"Sure thing," Brent replied, cocking a thumb toward the cruiser. "Hop in."

Julie nodded, then shook her head. Gave a despairing little giggle at her own contradictory response. "I mean, I don't have a car seat now—"

"I do," Paige reminded Julie. She'd purchased the seat at a garage sale two summers before, because she and Calvin spent a lot of time together when her schedule clicked with Julie's. "I'm beginning to think you're in worse shape than Marva is. Are you all right?"

"My car is buried under tons of rubble," Julie answered, almost snappishly. "Why wouldn't I be all right?"

They both climbed into the back seat of Brent's cruiser, still bickering.

Yep, Libby thought sadly, Julie's car was under tons of rubble. And that rubble had once been her business. Her livelihood.

Not that it had ever been all that lively.

Paige got out of the cruiser, came back to Libby and brought her cell phone out of her purse, handing it over. "Just in case," she explained.

Libby stared down at the device. It was a moment before she remembered Brent was still there.

Looking up at him, she calmly asked for Tate's cell number.

Brent gave it to her, and Libby nodded her thanks and

keyed in the digits as she walked around the corner of the clinic to stand in the side parking lot, out of earshot.

She watched as the cruiser pulled out onto the highway, then looked up, surprised to see that the moon was already visible, even though the sun hadn't fully set. The sky blazed crimson and lavender and apricot.

He answered after two rings. "Tate McKettrick," he said, a puzzled note in his voice.

Of course, Libby realized, Paige's number would have come up in the caller ID panel, since she was calling on her sister's phone.

Libby leaned back against the brick face of the Blue River Clinic, suddenly exhausted. "It's me," she said. "Libby."

"Lib? Are you all right?"

She had to swallow a throatful of tears before answering. "I'm okay," she said, and then it all came tumbling out, in a crazy rush. "But Marva—my mother—drove my sister's Cadillac through the front of the Perk Up, so we're all down here at the clinic so I can't make it to your place for leftover chicken and beer—and I don't suppose it even matters that much but I—"

"Libby," Tate said, firmly but with kindness. "Honey, take a breath."

Honey.

Libby fell silent. Honey. What an ordinary, beautiful word.

"Was anybody hurt?" Tate asked. His voice was level.

Libby's chest ached and her eyes burned and she still didn't trust herself to stand up straight, even though the bricks comprising the clinic's outer wall were digging right through her blouse into the flesh of her back. "Marva's being examined right now," she said.

"I'll be there as soon as I can," Tate said.

"Tate, no, I—I'm fine, really."

"I'm on my way."

"But—"

He hung up.

Slowly, Libby closed Paige's phone.

She hadn't expected Tate to drop everything and come to her—had she? If not, why had she called him in the first place, going to the trouble to borrow a phone and ask Brent Brogan for the number?

Damn. She didn't want to wind up like Marva, needy and manipulative.

Doing numbers on people.

Her eyes stung.

The automatic doors swung open, and one of the nurses stepped out, looked around. Seeing Libby, the woman smiled.

She was fortyish, and Libby remembered her vaguely from the Perk Up. Yes. Double mocha with extra espresso and chocolate shavings.

"Your mother would like to see you," she said. "And maybe a doctor should have a look at those scratches on your hands."

Libby nodded, then shook her head. "I'm okay," she said. "I just need to wash up." Dropping Paige's phone into her purse, she followed the nurse into the clinic, through the lobby and back to one of the exam rooms.

Going straight to the sink, Libby washed her hands, saw that the scratches weren't deep.

Marva was alone, lying on a gurney. She wore a hospital gown, and a plain white blanket covered her legs.

She was so still that, for one terrible moment, Libby thought her mother was dead.

"Marva?"

Marva turned her head, smiled. Stretched out a hand to Libby.

"I don't know what came over me," Marva confided, her voice croaky and miserable. "Suddenly, I just *had* to drive again, and there was Julie's car—"

"Shh," Libby said. "We can talk about it later, when we're sure you're all right."

Tears filled Marva's eyes, rolled over her temples into her mussed-up hair. "I'm sorry, Libby," she said. "I'm so sorry."

Libby just stood there, with no idea how to respond, willing herself not to cry.

Marva gazed up at her, squeezed her hand once, and let go. There was, it seemed, nothing more to say.

CHAPTER FIFTEEN

TATE MUST HAVE HAD the pedal to the metal all the way in from the ranch, because he was waiting in the lobby when Libby left Marva's exam room. Just seeing him was like a deep draught of cold well water after a long spell of thirst.

Libby walked into his arms. He embraced her loosely, and she rested her forehead against the hard wall of his chest.

"She's sorry," Libby told him, her voice muffled. "My mother is *sorry*."

Tate rocked her slightly, from side to side. "It's okay, Lib," he murmured. "Everything will be okay."

Why did people keep *saying* that? Everything would be okay for Paige, with her top-notch nursing skills and high-paying job. Everything would be okay for Julie, too, because she had Calvin and a career she loved. And everything would *certainly* be okay for Tate and all the other McKettricks, if only because they *were* McKettricks.

Libby loved her sisters and was proud of their accomplishments.

But she was tired of false reassurances.

Her shop was gone.

She had virtually no savings.

And jobs weren't exactly plentiful in Blue River.

There had been lower points in her life, of course—when Marva left, so long ago, when her dad died, when, with no warning at all, she'd lost Tate.

The pain of that most recent and totally unexpected loss seared through her, as fresh as if it had just happened. Libby knotted her fists and pushed pack from Tate.

He paled slightly, under his rancher's tan. "I drove by the shop on my way here," he told her, his voice gravelly. "Libby, I can help—"

"Stop," Libby said. Realizing her hands were still bunched against Tate's chest—she could feel the strong, steady *thud-thud-thud* of his heart—she splayed her fingers for a moment, drawing in the substance of him like a breath of the soul. And then she let both hands fall to her sides. "Don't say what I think you're about to say, Tate. I can't take money from you."

Julie and Paige had returned, along with Calvin; Libby was aware of them, on the periphery of the haze that seemed to surround her and Tate.

"Libby," he said. "Listen to me. Please."

She shook her head. Stepped back a little farther.

Both Paige and Julie had worked their way through college with the aid of scholarships and loans. They'd made something of themselves.

Paige saved lives.

Julie shaped young minds.

What had *she* done? Started a doomed coffee shop—one that had barely brought in survival wages even in the best of times—right there in the old hometown.

She'd loved one man her whole life—Tate McKettrick—and he'd betrayed her. While she'd forgiven Tate, she knew she'd never forgive *herself* if the same thing happened all over again.

Tate's hands still rested lightly on her shoulders.

He couldn't have known what she was thinking—that maybe it was time for her to leave Blue River, leave Texas. Go someplace entirely new, where she might be able to get some perspective. Come up with some goals.

No, he couldn't have known, but he looked as though he did.

The truth? Libby Remington had had only one goal, one dream, ever, and it was hopelessly old-fashioned. Politically incorrect to the nth degree.

All Libby had ever wanted was to marry Tate, love him and be loved in return, to bear and raise his children. To get old with him, and have flocks of grandbabies.

It would all be easier, she supposed, if Tate weren't rich—if he really were just a foreman on a big ranch, a hired hand with a steady paycheck, a simple three-bedroom house beside a creek and a good truck to drive. Instead, he was a multi-*multi*-millionaire, with his choice of beautiful women—supermodels, movie stars and professional women of all sorts. Doctors. Lawyers. Indian chiefs.

What did he want with her?

Sex?

Their lovemaking had been transcendental for Libby, but Tate was a man—to him, sex was sex. He probably took it where he could get it—and God knew, she had no compunction about giving it to him.

"Is Marva all right?" Julie asked, hovering a few feet away and wringing her hands.

Libby saw herself and Tate through Julie's eyes, standing almost toe-to-toe, as though he'd been comforting her in the aftermath of bad news.

"We haven't heard anything yet, Jules," Libby said, hugging her sister.

Julie hugged her back, sniffled.

Libby's eyes roamed, stopped on her nephew. Calvin was on the other side of the lobby, admiring the colorful fish in the clinic's fish tank. Paige stood beside the little boy, but she was watching her sisters and Tate, not the bright, flashing population of the large saltwater tank.

"Look, Aunt Paige," Calvin crowed, pointing a chubby finger at one of the fish and almost certainly leaving a smudge on the glass. "That one is transparent—I can see his guts!" He bent closer, and even though his back was to Libby, she knew when he adjusted his glasses. "And *that* one has a red line inside it, like a thermometer."

The mood lightened a little.

Julie stepped back out of Libby's embrace, and her gaze moved between Libby and Tate. She smiled slightly, turned and joined Calvin next to the fish tank.

Paige approached Libby. "May I have my cell phone back, please?" she asked. "It might be a long night, and I think the time has come to order pizza."

"Pizza!" Calvin whooped, overjoyed.

In spite of the stress and frustration and a host of other emotions, Libby laughed. She dug through her purse, found Paige's phone and handed it to her sister.

"Just tell me what kind of pizza you want," Tate said. "I'll go pick it up."

Calvin materialized immediately. It was almost as if he'd teleported himself from the fish tank across the lobby to where they stood. "Are you going to the Pizza Shack, Mr. McKettrick? Can I go with you? Where are your kids? Do you have any boys, or just girls?"

Tate crouched, so he could look Calvin straight in the eye. "Your mom and your aunts are kind of worried right now," he said seriously. "I think they need a man around, so maybe you ought to stay here."

Calvin's glasses had wriggled down his freckled nose, and

he replaced them with the usual thrust of his right index finger. He threw his shoulders back a little, and raised his chin. "They're all pretty good at taking care of themselves," he told Tate. "And you didn't answer my other questions."

Tate's mouth quirked up at one corner. "My daughters—Audrey and Ava—are at home. And, no, I don't have any boys." As he stood up again, he caught Libby's gaze. "Yet," he added quietly.

She felt the usual achy heat, and rose above it as best she could.

The man was an addiction, and she was thoroughly hooked.

Ready to leave town to get away from him one moment, charmed out of her socks the next.

As if getting charmed out of her *socks* was any part of the problem.

"I have the regulation car seats in my truck," Tate told Julie. "And we wouldn't be gone long."

"*Please,* Mom," Calvin pleaded. "I need a male role model. I spend way too much time around women. Mrs. Oakland said so."

Julie flushed to her ears. "Mrs. Oakland said that, did she?"

"Maybe it was Justin's mom," Calvin faltered.

"You're sure he wouldn't be any trouble?" Julie asked Tate.

"I'm sure," Tate said. This time, he didn't look at Libby. She might have vaporized, for all the notice he seemed to take of her.

"I'll call in the order," Paige put in, cell phone in hand. "The usual?" she asked her sisters.

Libby merely nodded, wanting Tate McKettrick out of her space so she could think straight, but Julie, the thoughtful one, had the good manners to ask if he'd prefer something other than thick-crust Hawaiian with extra cheese.

He said he'd already eaten.

"Do I get to go or not, Mom?" Calvin demanded.

"Go," Julie relented, and though she was smiling, Libby glimpsed pain in her sister's eyes.

Calvin let out a yippee that made the receptionist look up from her desk behind the glass window and smile.

The little boy fairly skipped out of the clinic, but he stayed close to Tate, as if to prove to anyone concerned that he meant to behave himself and follow all the rules.

Paige finished placing the pizza order, closed her phone, and dropped it into her purse. "You really ought to grab that one," she said, nodding in Tate's direction and simultaneously elbowing Libby lightly in the ribs. "He's obviously a good father."

Before Libby had to reply, Dr. Burt Renton appeared, a weary smile creasing his familiar face. The physician, a widower with no children, had been born and raised in Blue River, and returned home as soon as his training was finished to open an office on Main Street. After thirty years in practice, he'd tried to retire, but all that idleness, as he called it, "wasn't good for my character." He'd been working part time at the clinic since it had opened for business nearly a decade before.

Julie, Paige and Libby all hurried toward him, stood in a tight little semicircle at the edge of his personal space, waiting.

"I ran a CT scan, the usual blood tests and took x-rays," Dr. Burt told them kindly. "Your mother is shaken up, but with a few days of rest and some pampering, she'll be fine."

Libby backed up a step. Maybe it was the word *pampering*.

Julie and Paige looked at her curiously.

Julie was the first to get the message. Her face softened,

and Libby could have hugged her for the understanding in her eyes.

"Marva can stay with Calvin and me," Julie volunteered.

Guilt nudged Libby back into the half circle of sisters. She was the firstborn, and, as such, she had certain responsibilities. Marva was, for all her shortcomings, *her* mother, too.

She opened her mouth to say she'd look after Marva for as long as necessary, but the words wouldn't come out.

"I'd like Marva to stay here overnight," Dr. Burt was saying, "just to be on the safe side. That way, the nurses can keep an eye on her."

"Tell them to hide their car keys," Paige quipped, but she was watching Libby, still curious, maybe even a little worried.

Dr. Burt chuckled at that, but his eyes were solemn. "She feels very bad about that. Says she doesn't know what came over her."

In her mind, Libby saw her mother's tear-filled eyes again, heard her voice.

I'm so sorry.

"No one was hurt," Julie said. "That's the important thing."

"You can look in on Marva if you'd like. She's been sedated, though, so she'll probably drift off to sleep pretty soon." Dr. Burt pointed toward the corridor on the right, where the two large in-patient rooms were. "She has Unit B all to herself."

Julie and Paige started for the corridor immediately.

Libby remained where she was.

"I saw her earlier," she said when Dr. Burt glanced at her.

A few minutes later, Tate and Calvin returned with several huge pizza boxes and, with Libby's help, arranged the feast on the low-slung coffee table in the small waiting room. Calvin had scored a stack of paper napkins six inches high.

The child's face was luminous with delight. "Tate said we

could get cold drinks out of the vending machine here," he said importantly. "And I get to ride horses on the Silver Spur whenever I want and go fishing in the creek as long as my mom approves and there's at least one grown-up with me."

"Wow," Libby said softly, ruffling her nephew's sweaty hair.

Over the pile of pizza boxes, her gaze connected with Tate's.

"That's a lot of food," she said.

Calvin jumped right in with an answer. "Tate said the people who work here might want to eat, too," he said, before helping himself to a slice, breaking off a long strand of cheese with a karate chop.

Tate grinned, watching him.

"Tate used to have a dog named Crockett," Calvin went on, with his mouth partially full. "Crockett rode with him everywhere—they were buddies."

Libby's throat tightened. "Crockett was a good dog," she said, remembering.

She heard Julie and Paige approaching the waiting room, talking in low, hurried voices.

Tate didn't look at Libby; his gaze had turned toward the doorway, and he stood as her sisters entered.

"I *thought* I smelled pizza!" Julie said, leaning down to give her son a quick squeeze.

"Do you think Grandma would like some?" Calvin asked. His face was smeared with tomato sauce by then, and what was probably a piece of pineapple had gotten stuck in his hair.

"She's asleep," Paige told her nephew brightly.

Julie and Paige used a bottle of hand sanitizer from Julie's purse, helped themselves to napkins and pizza, and began to eat.

Tate didn't touch the food, and neither did Libby, until

Paige finally plopped a slice onto a napkin and forced it into her hands.

Tate got up and left the room to let the staff know there was pizza aplenty and they were welcome to join the party. The invitation brought a fairly steady stream of hungry people in scrubs, but Tate didn't come back.

Having eaten all she could get down—a little less than half of the portion Paige had given her—Libby excused herself and left the waiting room.

She could see Tate through the plate glass door at the front of the clinic, talking on his cell phone. His expression was serious, he was pacing and he kept thrusting a hand through his hair.

Libby hurried away, headed for the restroom, not wanting him to see her and think she'd been looking for him. Even though that was exactly what she'd been doing.

Once she'd washed her hands, stinging mildly now, from the scratches she'd gotten digging Marva out, splashed her face with cold water and grinned humorlessly into the mirror, to make sure there was no pizza detritus stuck between her teeth, she straightened her spine and marched back to the lobby.

Now that Marva had been examined and was resting comfortably, according to Dr. Burt, there was no point in sticking around. She'd go home, attend to the ever-patient Hildie, and then she'd switch on the TV set and stare mindlessly at the screen until she couldn't keep her eyes open anymore.

She could start thinking about the rest of her life tomorrow—or the day after that.

Or she could just pack a bag, gas up the Impala, load Hildie and her kibble and bowls into the back seat and strike out for parts unknown.

Yes, sir, she could go out there and *accomplish something*.

What that something would be, she had no idea.

Which was why she didn't want to think just yet.

"I guess I'll go on home now," she announced to her sisters and nephew and a couple of x-ray technicians, from the doorway of the waiting room. "Hildie will be waiting for me."

"Sure," Julie said uncertainly, leaning a little, to look past Libby. "Did Tate leave? I didn't get a chance to repay him for the pizza, or even say thank you."

Libby shrugged one shoulder. "He was outside a little while ago," she answered as casually as she could. "Talking to someone on his cell phone. Maybe something came up out at the ranch."

"Marva will be at our place after she's released," Julie told Libby. "In case you want to stop by and see her or anything."

Libby merely nodded, promising nothing.

She wanted to get away from the clinic.

She wanted this day to be over.

She waved a farewell to her family and the x-ray guys, turned and ran directly into Tate.

He steadied her by gripping her upper arms. If he hadn't, she would have fallen.

Libby pulled free, went around him.

He followed her through the automatic door and outside without speaking, or touching her.

It was dark and sultry, and the sky was splattered from horizon to horizon with enormous stars. Like the sunset earlier, the sight made Libby's breath catch.

Texas.

It was fine and dandy to think about starting over someplace far away.

But could she *really* call anywhere else "home"? Would she even be able to breathe properly outside the Lone Star State?

"Come home with me, Libby," Tate said, somehow steering her away from her car and toward his truck without laying a hand on her.

"Tate, I have a dog to feed and walk, and you have children—"

"We'll pick Hildie up on our way out of town. Along with your toothbrush and whatever else you figure you need to get you through till morning." He cleared his throat. "The twins are okay. They're with Esperanza."

Libby stopped, looked up at him. "Look, I know I agreed to come out to the Ruiz—to *your* place for chicken and beer, but—" She spread her arms wide, let her hands slap against her sides.

A slight and damnably sexy grin tugged at his mouth, was gone again. "But?" he prompted, his right hand resting lightly on the small of her back, ready to turn her gently, the way he'd turn a mare if she started off in the wrong direction.

"But what?" she challenged.

Tate chuckled. "I was waiting for an excuse. And you're going to have to do better than that poor old dog. She'd love a road trip to anywhere, and you know it."

She should have told him right then.

Speaking of road trips…she could have said, *I'm thinking of leaving Blue River for a while. You might say I have to find myself. No, that's too corny. Nobody worries about finding themselves anymore. Which just goes to show how out of touch I am, when it comes to the world outside central Texas.*

Libby choked up again. "Tate, what do you *want?*"

"Not what you think I want," he told her, opening the driver's-side door of the Impala so she could get in. "Not *just* that, anyhow."

Libby didn't know which was making her crazier, the conversation she was carrying on with Tate, or the one in her own head. "Good night," she said. "And thank you for the pizza."

She reached into her purse, closed her fingers around her

keys, took a couple of stabs at the ignition before she managed to start the engine.

"You're not getting rid of me that easily," Tate said affably, before closing her door and turning to walk away.

Libby watched him climb into his truck, blinked when his headlights came on, bright. He dimmed them, but she was still dazzled.

Almost a minute passed before Libby could see well enough to drive. Tate drove to the parking lot exit, but waited until she pulled in behind him.

She followed *him* to *her* house.

What was wrong with this picture?

Libby parked in the garage, off the alley, careful not to look toward the late, great Perk Up Coffee Shop. Wondered if Julie's car had been pulled from the rubble yet, and whether or not the vehicle could be salvaged.

Tate parked in front of the house.

By the time Libby had unlocked the back door and nearly been run over as Hildie shot from the house like a popcorn kernel from hot oil, Tate was there and ready to follow her up the porch steps and into the kitchen.

"You know," Libby said to Tate, leaving the door open for Hildie but wishing she could slam it for the sake of emphasis, "some people would consider this stalking. Your walking in here like this, I mean."

"If you want me to leave," Tate replied reasonably, "all you have to do is ask." He opened her refrigerator, scanned the contents, sighed with what might have been resignation, helped himself to a soda, popped the top and raised the can briefly, as though toasting her.

Libby opened her mouth, closed it again.

Tate drank deeply of the soda, swallowed audibly. At least he didn't belch.

"That Calvin," he said, "is one cute kid. And a fair hand to have along on a pizza run."

Libby couldn't help softening, thinking of her nephew and how glad he'd been to spend some time in Tate's company. "He's so smart, it's scary," she said.

Hildie, having completed her tour of the yard, scratched at the screen door. Libby opened it to let her in, filled her kibble dish and freshened her water.

"Calvin wants to get to know his dad," Tate said.

The statement fell between them like a flaming meteor.

Libby stood utterly still. Even though she'd encouraged Julie to work out some kind of visitation agreement with Gordon Pruett, she understood her sister's reluctance. Gordon might be a good man—or he might be a jerk.

Julie would be taking a big chance by letting Gordon into her life and Calvin's, but if he chose to force the issue legally, she wouldn't have a choice

"Calvin said that?" Libby nearly whispered, after a heartbeat or two.

Tate nodded. "Is this a problem?"

"It could be," Libby said simply. She wasn't comfortable discussing Julie's private business, and Tate seemed to know that, didn't press.

Libby shut and locked the back door. Hildie stood looking back and forth between Tate and her mistress instead of curling up on her dog bed, as she normally would have done.

"You have to promise we won't have sex," Libby blurted out. Tate was like some big, hard, human magnet, standing there in her kitchen. She felt the pull of him in every cell in her body—any second now, she'd go *splat,* like a bug on a windshield.

Tate indulged in a rather obvious struggle to hold back a grin, and one of his eyebrows rose into an ironic arch. "Forever?" he asked. "Or just for tonight?"

"Just for tonight," Libby said. "Forever seems unreasonable."

He chuckled. "Forever," he said, "is downright *impossible.*

But I won't make love to you tonight, Lib. I promise you that much." He paused. "Not even if you tear my clothes off in an insane fit of unbridled desire."

"Don't hold your breath waiting for *that* to happen, cowboy," she said, with a lofty sniff.

Please God, don't let me tear off his clothes in an insane fit of unbridled desire.

"If I have to promise," Tate said, "so do you."

"Oh, for Pete's sake," Libby said. "All right."

With that, she went into her bathroom and got her hairbrush and her packet of birth control pills. There was no need to take pajamas along, because she intended to sleep in her clothes.

If she slept at all.

They went to the main ranch house, instead of Tate's "new" place by the creek, and except for a single light burning under the portico, the massive structure was completely dark.

Libby panicked a little. "Tate, Audrey and Ava—"

"It's a big house," Tate said. "And besides, we're not going to have sex anyway, so I don't see the problem."

"I don't want to confuse them," Libby said.

"Neither do I," Tate answered, and another grin twitched at his mouth.

"You don't think it will be confusing when they wake up tomorrow morning and I'm in their house?"

"I think they need to get used to seeing you around," Tate said quietly.

Libby didn't dare go there. It was late, she'd been through a lot that day, and if she wasn't careful, she might say something she'd regret.

For the rest of eternity.

Tate pulled up to one of the garage doors, pushed a button on his visor, and drove in.

Once he'd parked and shut off the truck, he turned to Libby.

She looked neither left nor right. She *certainly* wasn't going to look in Tate's direction.

"Lib," Tate said, pulling the keys from the ignition, "don't look so worried. All I want to do is take care of you."

All I want to do is take care of you.

Libby could barely remember what it was like to be "taken care of" by anyone. Before her dad had gotten sick—long before—she'd felt safe, as though somebody always had her back.

But since then? Not so much.

She straightened her spine, found she still couldn't look directly at Tate.

He opened the door, rounded the truck, set Hildie gently on the cement floor, opened Libby's door and unbuckled her seat belt.

"Come on," he said.

He took her by the hand, led her through the darkened house, up the stairs, into his room. Hildie followed.

There, Tate stripped Libby bare, pulled one of his T-shirts over her head, and tucked her under the covers of his bed.

Then he lay down on top of those same covers, pulled her into his arms, and held her, his embrace strong and sure, until she slept.

CHAPTER SIXTEEN

LIBBY AWOKE WITH A START, sunlight burning through her lids.

She opened her eyes, found herself almost nose to nose with one of the twins—Ava, she realized. The child was wearing glasses.

"Good morning," Ava said, grinning.

Oh, dear God. She was in Tate McKettrick's bed—*with* Tate McKettrick.

And here was his six-year-old daughter.

Libby blinked, glanced wildly around, having no idea what to say or do, and saw that Tate was still sleeping. He was wearing all his clothes, boots included, and lying on top of the covers, though one leg and one arm sprawled across Libby's body.

"Good morning," Libby whispered back to Ava, embarrassed but trying hard to behave in a normal way.

Whatever that might be, in these circumstances.

Tate stretched, his powerful body lengthening as he rolled away from her. He yawned lustily and opened his eyes.

"Hey," he said to Ava, resting a hand on Libby's shoulder,

as if to console or reassure her. Or maybe because he knew she wanted to bolt.

"Hey, Daddy," Ava replied, still showing no overt signs of trauma at finding a woman in bed with her father. "Esperanza said to tell you breakfast is ready and Uncle Austin already fed the horses and did the chores and stuff."

Tate groaned, but it was a comfortable sound, good-natured. "So much for setting a good example as the new foreman," he said.

"That's all you're worried about?" Libby whispered.

He grinned down at her. "If you don't make a big deal out of this," he said casually, and there was a subtle singsong note to his tone, "nobody else will, either."

He was right, of course.

The child didn't seem curious, let alone traumatized, but making a fuss might change the easy flow of things.

New concerns assailed Libby. She put a hand over her mouth. How could the man wake up with *good breath?* He had—but she probably hadn't.

"Go and tell Esperanza we'll be right down," Tate told Ava. His voice was easy, as if he and Libby shared a bed *every* night. "Take Hildie with you—I imagine she'd like to go outside and then have a little of Ambrose and Buford's dog food."

Ava nodded importantly. "Come on, Hildie," she said, with cheerful authority. "Let's go."

Hildie got up, gave Libby one questioning glance, and then followed the little girl out of the master bedroom.

Libby tried to get out of bed the moment the door closed behind Ava and Hildie, but Tate pressed her back down with one hand splayed in the middle of her stomach and deliberately kissed her on the mouth.

Thoroughly.

Libby finally turned her face away, even though she'd liked the kiss.

"If you don't let me up," she said, "you're going to be sorry."

Tate chuckled at that—the threat was clearly an empty one—but he let Libby get up.

She found her way to the bathroom, which was roughly the size of her kitchen and living room combined, used the facilities, and rummaged through cupboards and drawers under the long marble countertop until she found a new toothbrush, still in its package.

She was standing at one of the antique brass sinks, scrubbing her teeth, when Tate ambled in, calm as you please, shedding clothes as he walked. The long mirror over the counter reflected his every move in exquisite detail.

He was completely, wickedly, *deliciously* naked by the time he reached the shower. In all that time, he hadn't so much as glanced in Libby's direction.

She, on the other hand, couldn't help staring.

From behind the glass door of the room-size shower, Tate grinned at her.

Libby tore her gaze away, flushing to the roots of her hair.

Stomped out of the bathroom and searched until she found her clothes, neatly folded and stacked on the seat of a sumptuous leather chair facing the cold fireplace.

Libby hauled them on, with the exception of her underpants; she wadded those into a ball and stuffed them into her purse.

Libby probably would have sneaked out of the house, sprinted down to the main road and *hitchhiked* into town, except that she couldn't abandon Hildie, not even knowing the dog was perfectly safe.

Besides, Ava had already seen her. In bed with Tate.

By now, the little girl had surely told her twin and Esperanza—and that was the *optimistic* count. Ava had mentioned Austin, saying he'd done the barn chores, so he might have heard, as well. And if Garrett happened to be around, he probably knew, too.

Dressed, but having no real idea what to do next, Libby plunked down on the edge of the bed. At least Tate had kept his word.

He'd slept on top of the covers, in all his clothes.

She'd been underneath them the whole night, clad in one of his T-shirts.

They hadn't made love. Libby figured she should have been happier about that than she was.

Because the shower was still running, indicating that she could expect a few more moments of privacy before Tate returned, she pressed the T-shirt to her face, drew in his scent. It seemed to seep into her cells and settle there, that lusciously distinctive smell, destined to remain a part of her forever, like her DNA.

Damn.

Just yesterday, at the clinic, despite a lot of misgivings, Libby had basically made up her mind to leave Blue River, start over somewhere else, make something of herself.

Like what? she wondered now.

Nothing occurred to her.

The sound of running water fell away into silence.

A minute or so later, Tate strolled out of the bathroom, barefoot, wearing button-front jeans and not much else. His hair was wet, though he'd towel-dried it and, from the looks of the ridges, he'd run his fingers through several times.

Could it be that he was as nervous as she was?

Surely not.

He crooked a grin at Libby. "Hungry?" he asked.

"I just want to go home," Libby said, blushing. Looking down at the floor.

What would she do at home?

Dig more weeds?

Cut more grass?

Get down on her knees on the sidewalk in front of her erstwhile shop and paw through the rubble looking for— what? A stray dream? A few tattered hopes?

"No problem," Tate said, his voice was quiet and so gentle that it made her want to cry. "If you want to go home, I'll take you there."

Libby didn't know what to say after that. Since Tate hadn't given her an argument, as she'd expected, she was stuck for a response.

The house in town was home—her dad had died there. She and her sisters had grown up under that roof, within those walls—but Julie and Paige had moved on.

She'd gotten stuck, somehow.

Tate disappeared into the massive walk-in closet, return- ing with one arm thrust into the sleeve of a light blue shirt, the other about to go in. His muscular chest was fully visible, lightly sprinkled with dark hair and tanned by occasional exposure to the sun.

He tossed Libby a pair of jeans and a yellow ruffled blouse; both garments were vaguely familiar.

Libby caught them, a funny little skitter dancing in her heart, let them rest in her lap, her head lowered. "Are these Cheryl's things?" she asked, thick-throated.

"No," Tate said gently. "They're yours."

Libby's gaze shot to his face. Her throat tightened even more, and her cheeks blazed. *Of course,* Tate wouldn't give her his ex-wife's clothes to wear. What had she been think- ing?

"You left them here once, a long time ago, when my folks were away," he reminded her, a grin resting on his mouth and twinkling in his eyes. He probably knew what was going through her mind, or pretty close to it, anyhow. "Esperanza was visiting her cousin, and Garrett and Austin were both gone, too, on the rodeo circuit. We spent the whole weekend pretending we were married—remember?"

Libby felt a bittersweet pang of mingled nostalgia and sorrow. Back then, marrying Tate McKettrick had seemed like a sure thing. They'd nearly eloped several times in their late teens and Libby sometimes wished they'd gone through with the plan.

Sometimes, and only until she came to her senses.

She and Tate had been so young. She'd had to drop out of college and come back to Blue River to take care of her dad after he got sick. Tate might have given up school, too, and eventually come to resent Libby and the demands she made on his time.

And Audrey and Ava wouldn't have been born.

Inconceivable.

The silence seemed to have weight.

"You don't really think I can still get into these jeans," Libby joked, to break the spell.

Tate laughed. "Can I stay and watch you try?"

Libby giggled, waved him away. "Get out," she said.

He smiled, buttoning his shirt to the middle of his breast-bone. "I was headed downstairs for coffee anyhow," he said. "Bring you some?"

She shook her head, stroking the yellow blouse. She'd loved the thing, saved her allowance and babysitting money to buy it. Felt so sexy with all those sun-colored ruffles floating around her. "No thanks," she said. "Maybe some tea?"

"You got it," Tate said.

With that, he left the huge room, closing the double doors behind him.

LIBBY HASTENED INTO THE bathroom, shut the door and wriggled into the jeans. They were a little tight, but they zipped up, and the blouse looked as good as it ever had.

Libby's raised spirits drooped a bit, though, as she considered the prospect of going downstairs and facing Esperanza and the twins.

She made up the bed, which was barely mussed, a stall tactic for sure.

Tate returned just as she was fluffing the pillows. Sipping from one cup, he carried a second. "The coast is clear," he said. "Audrey and Ava are out in the barn, with all three dogs and the ponies. Esperanza is with them, supervising."

Libby accepted the fragrant tea with a nod of thanks, took a sip, and felt better instantly. "Have they come up with names yet?" she asked. "For the horses, I mean."

"I don't think so." Tate grinned, touching Libby's hair lightly. His voice was low and throaty and he smelled so... clean. "It's a big decision."

"Maybe you could drive Hildie and me home, while they're busy?"

Not that she wanted to go.

Tate sighed. "Lib, they already know you're here."

She lowered her head, breathing in the steam rising off her tea.

Tate curved a finger under her chin and looked into her eyes. "Relax," he said. "We talked about this. Audrey and Ava need to get used to seeing you around."

"*You* talked about it," Libby said. "*I* didn't venture an opinion. Tate, they're children. And I'm not their mother. Letting them 'get used' to changes and their finding me in their father's bed first thing in the morning are not the same thing."

"You don't believe in total immersion?" Tate teased.

"Don't be a smart-ass," Libby countered.

"Sorry," he responded, after a long sip from his coffee. "I probably can't deliver on that one—not long term, anyhow."

"Be serious," she whispered angrily. "We're talking about your *children,* here."

Tate leaned in, touched his forehead to hers. "I'm aware of that," he whispered back, with exaggeration. "Lighten up a little, Libby. It's not as if Ava came in here and found us swinging naked from the curtain rods and yelling, 'Yahoo.' Yes, you were in my bed, but I was on top of the covers, wearing all my clothes." He backed up a little. Waggled his eyebrows. "Which, by the way, was a noble sacrifice on my part, and if ever there was a fine opportunity for a quickie, it's right now."

Libby laughed, in spite of herself. Gave him an affectionate push with her free hand, carefully balancing her tea in the other. "You really are impossible," she said.

"You'd forgotten that? That I'm impossible?" Tate asked. "I'm hurt."

"I should go home now."

"Why?"

"You know why."

"No, Libby. I don't know why. It's not as if you have to open the shop."

Her shoulders dropped a little. Of course she hadn't forgotten what Marva had done to the Perk Up, but she *had* managed to keep the full reality at a bearable distance.

Until now.

"Thanks," she said, terse now. It was a defense, not against Tate, but against a part of herself—the hoochy-mama part, born to boogie. She turned away, cup in hand, headed for the door.

Tate caught hold of her arm. "Let's take a breath here, Lib," he said. "Stay and have some breakfast. I'll saddle up some horses and we'll ride. I've already called the clinic, and your mother is doing fine. She wants to stay another day, in fact. Sounds to me like she's enjoying the attention."

"You talked to my mother?"

"No," Tate said. "To one of the nurses. I called her when I was downstairs."

Libby let out her breath, and Tate set his coffee aside, and her tea, and took a light hold on her shoulders.

"How long has it been since you've been on the back of a

horse?" Tate asked, his chin resting on top of her head. "You used to love it, remember?"

A tremor went through Libby. *I used to love so many things. And suddenly, they weren't part of my life anymore. You weren't part of my life anymore.*

"Scared?" Tate asked, without moving.

She saw no point in denying it; he obviously knew. She nodded, swallowed.

"Of me?"

"No," Libby said, letting herself be held, just as she had during the night. It felt so good. She'd never feared Tate, but she *was* afraid of what he could make her feel, and what she might be willing to risk because of that. "Of course not."

"Then, what?"

She shook her head, unable to answer.

Tate kissed the crown of her head. Sighed.

"You can call Julie and Paige," he said, after a long time. "Give them my cell number. If they need to reach you for any reason, they'll be able to do that."

"I don't know...."

Once again, he lifted her chin. "Just for once, never mind what you think you *should* do. Concentrate what you *want* to do. Do you even know what that is anymore, Libby?"

She swallowed, her throat suddenly full of tears, shoved back her bangs with one hand. "Of course I know what I want—"

"Okay. What?"

You and me, together for good. Kids and dogs and horses and a garden...

But there was another part of her, with other dreams.

She'd never seen the Eiffel Tower, or the Great Wall of China, that other Libby. And she wanted to.

Libby looked away from his face, looked back. Some of the anxiety she'd felt drained away, but another kind of charge sizzled in its place. "I want to go riding with you and your little girls," she admitted. "But what I *should* want—"

Tate interrupted, grinning and shaking his head. "Let's go downstairs and have breakfast," he said. "After that, we'll ride."

Libby considered that. "But my mother—my sisters—"

"Are all grown women," Tate said, taking her hand. "They don't need you with them to survive the day, Lib." He gave her a little pull. "Let's go."

She let him lead her downstairs.

To her relief, the big kitchen was empty.

Breakfast awaited in various chafing dishes, the kind Libby normally saw in buffet restaurants. There were blueberry pancakes, scrambled eggs, bacon and sausage to choose from, along with yogurt cups arranged in a bowl of ice.

Libby surveyed it in amazement.

"All this is for us and two six-year-olds?" she asked.

"And some of the guys from the bunkhouse," Tate said, handing her a plate before taking one of his own.

Libby felt her eyes go round. "You mean, a whole bunch of *cowboys* might come walking in here at any moment?" she asked, horrified. If that happened, the news that Libby Remington had spent the night in the main house on the Silver Spur—*again*—would circulate from the feed store to the post office to the Amble On Inn, where the old-timers hung out because "A man could still get a good beer for cheap."

"Maybe," Tate said. "Why does it matter?"

"You know damn well *why it matters!*"

Grinning, Tate took a step back and raised both his hands, palms out. "Okay, I know why it matters," he admitted. "You don't want the whole town of Blue River to hear that you showed up at breakfast."

Libby raised her chin a notch. "That's right."

"You can't possibly be that naive." He leaned in, whispered close to her ear, and even the warmth of his *breath* turned her on, for pity's sake. "We're old news, Libby. Everybody knows we're getting it on."

"'Getting it on'?" Libby jabbed two sausage links and plopped them onto her plate, moved on to the scrambled eggs. "Is that what you call it?"

Tate grinned down at her, speared four pancakes along with bacon and sausage. "What would *you* call it?" he countered, so obviously enjoying her heated discomfort that she wanted to spear him with a fork.

Libby decided to ignore the question, since she didn't want to say *making love*—that might sound sappy—and the f-word was out, too, because it was ugly. She turned her back on him, marched to the table with her plate and sat down.

Tate swung a leg over the back of a chair and sat across from her, setting his full plate down with a *plunk*. A mischievous—make that evil—grin danced at the corners of his mouth and sparked in his too-blue eyes.

"For somebody who could probably set the record for multiple orgasms," he observed, "you are pretty old-fashioned."

Libby blushed. "I consider that *your* fault," she said, poking at her eggs.

"Your orgasms are *my* fault?" He speared a sausage link and bit off the end, took his time chewing and swallowing.

"Well," Libby said, "I don't have them *by myself.*"

He laughed. "It's okay, Libby," he told her. "I don't mind taking the credit."

"You mean the blame."

"No. I mean the credit."

Color flared in Libby's cheeks. "Could we just eat?"

"See how testy you are? If you'd just let me have you against a wall before we came downstairs this morning, you'd be mellow right now, instead of wound up tight like an old pocket watch with the stem turned one too many times."

"Tate," Libby said, leaning toward him a little. "Shut up."

He sighed. "I'm just saying."

Fortunately, the back door opened just then, and Audrey and Ava bounded in, faces alight, with three dogs and a housekeeper in their wake.

"Can we go fishing in the creek?" Audrey asked.

"Not on your own," Tate answered.

"That spotted horse is trying to kick his way out of the pen," Ava added, looking worried. "He can't get out, can he?"

"He can't get out, honey," Tate assured his daughter.

Ava turned to Libby, her blue eyes serious behind smudged lenses. "That's the horse," she whispered, "that stepped on Mr. Ruiz and made him die."

Libby felt a maternal urge to gather the child in her arms and hug her. She glanced at Tate, wondering why a dangerous animal like the stallion was still on the place.

She quickly dismissed the concern. Tate was a rancher, descended from generations of ranchers; he certainly knew horses. He would do what needed to be done, when it needed to be done.

Tate calmly finished eating, stood, his gaze connecting with Libby's as he rose. "So how about that horseback ride?" he asked, and though his tone was easy, she knew by the expression in his eyes that her answer was important to him.

Audrey and Ava immediately began to jump up and down, eager to go along.

Ambrose, Buford and Hildie all barked, caught up in the excitement.

And Esperanza smiled serenely to herself.

The children—and the dogs—would have been too disappointed if she'd said "No." Or, at least, that was what Libby told herself.

In fact, Tate had been right earlier, reminding her how she'd once loved riding horses.

"Okay," she said. "But I need to call Julie and Paige first."

Mayhem broke out—dogs barking, little girls cheering and clapping.

Shaking her head benevolently, Esperanza picked up a laundry basket and started up one of the three sets of stairs that intersected on the far side of the McKettricks' kitchen.

"We can saddle our *own* ponies!" Ava cried jubilantly.

"Go and do it, then," Tate told the kids. "And take the dogs with you."

The big house seemed to let out its breath when it was just Tate and Libby again, alone in the room. He stood behind her, handed his cell phone past her right shoulder before moving away.

Libby dialed Julie's home number first, since it was still fairly early.

"Hello?" Julie answered sleepily, as Tate went out the back door.

"It's me, Libby," Libby whispered. It was silly to whisper, she decided, since she had the kitchen to herself, but whisper she did.

Julie sounded a lot more awake when she answered. "Are you with Tate?"

"Yes," Libby replied, since the only alternative was to lie. "We're—we're going horseback riding today, so Tate suggested that I give you his cell number, just in case you or Paige need to reach me for any reason—"

Julie giggled. "Wonderful," she said.

Libby bristled. "What do you mean, 'Wonderful'?" she snapped. "You do realize, don't you, that little elves didn't stop by and rebuild the Perk Up while we were sleeping, or bring the Pink Bomb back to its former glory?"

There was a pause.

Libby used it to rinse off her plate and stick it into the nearest dishwasher.

"This probably isn't a good time to tell you," Julie finally said, "that the tow-truck guy says the Cadillac can be repaired. It's going to take some major bodywork and a paint job, but the car is still structurally sound."

"Now why," Libby nearly snarled, "would this be a bad time to tell me anything?"

Hearing herself, she sucked in a hissy breath and squeezed her eyes shut for a moment. Exhaled.

"Let me try that again," she said, measuring out the words.

Julie gave a nervous laugh. "Libby, every—"

"Don't you dare say everything will be all right!"

At just that moment, Tate stuck his head inside the back door, assumed an expression of mock terror, ducked out as though he expected some missile to come hurtling his way and then stepped over the threshold.

"Horses are ready to ride," he said, just as Julie was speaking.

"Okay," Libby's sister said, very gently, "I won't say that. But it will be. You wait and see."

"Call me when the next disaster hits," Libby said, and she wasn't kidding. She held Tate's phone away with both hands and squinted at it, trying to find his phone number.

Standing close to her now, he fed it into her ear, digit by digit, while Libby repeated each new number to Julie. She felt silly, the whole time.

Everyone had a cell phone these days.

Except for her.

Why was that?

It wasn't just the money, although that was a factor in everything she did. Except for Paige and Julie, who were always either dropping by or calling her on either the shop phone or the one at home, she'd had no one to call or be called by.

Now she felt ridiculously behind-the-times.

Tate's hand rested on her shoulder, sending bolts of soft fire through her.

"Libby?" Julie prompted. "Are you still there?"

Libby nodded, swallowed, said, "Yes," in a frog-voice.

Tate's fingers began to work the taut muscles where her shoulders and neck met. She rolled her head, barely bit back a groan of pure pleasure.

For her, those particular muscles and the soles of her feet were erogenous zones. Thank God he wasn't massaging her feet—she might have reached a climax.

"I'm here," she said, croaking again and several beats late. "D-did you get the number?"

"Yes," Julie answered, and Libby could just see her smiling. "Are you all right?"

"Of course I'm all right!"

"Now, don't get your panties in a wad," Julie counseled. Then, wickedly, she added, "If you're wearing any, that is."

"Julie Remington, you have a dirty mind!"

"No," Julie said, "I'm just trying to think positively."

"Funny. Ha-ha, Julie, you are *so funny*."

"I'll call, or Paige will, if anything important happens," Julie went on, sounding so pleased with herself that Libby's back molars clamped together.

"Thanks," Libby said once she'd released her jaw, and shut the phone with a bang. Turned and fairly shoved it at Tate.

"You *really* need that quickie," he whispered.

She punched him.

But her heart wasn't in it.

TATE RODE STRANGER, the roan gelding, while Libby was mounted on a gentle—and equally aged—mare named Buttons. The twins followed on their golden, nameless ponies, with Ambrose and Buford frolicking alongside. Hildie brought up the rear, moving slowly, and Tate was keeping an eye on the old dog, same as Libby was.

The sun was hot and high, the sky a brassy blue that ached in the heart, as well as the eyes. Grass rippled and flowed around them like light on water, and clusters of cattle grazed here and there, while horses, some of them almost as wild as the stallion penned up back at the barn, lowered their heads for creek water.

Tate stood in the stirrups, stretching his legs, keeping an eye on his daughters bouncing happily along on their birthday ponies, a few dozen yards ahead of him and Libby, the dogs keeping up easily.

When Libby reined in, it was a moment before he noticed. Buttons wanted to keep up with the other horses, and kept turning around and around in a tight circle, tossing her head, resisting Libby's efforts to bring her to a full stop.

Half in the saddle and half out, Libby had one foot in a stirrup and no place to put the other one. Back a ways, Hildie sat in the high grass, panting hard, tongue lolling.

Tate rode back, got Libby's horse by the bridle strap, spoke firmly to the animal. It settled down right away.

The Ruiz place was close—less than a mile from the main house, traveling overland, as they were—and before setting out, Libby and Tate had agreed that Hildie could surely make it that far, since she and Libby took a long walk almost every day.

For whatever reason, Hildie obviously didn't plan on going another step.

Libby had shifted back into the saddle with an ease that did Tate proud, though he could not have said why.

When he was sure Buttons would behave, he got down off Stranger and walked back to Hildie, crouching when he reached her.

"Is she all right?" Libby called, anxious.

Up ahead, the girls had stopped to wait, turned their ponies around.

Tate and the dog were eye to eye. "Hey, girl," he said gently. "You get tired of walking?"

Hildie licked his right cheek and favored him with a dog

smile. Her tongue, long and pink, hung out of the side of her mouth.

"You better ride with me for a ways," Tate said, easing the animal to her feet, making sure she could stand. Her flanks quivered, but then she steadied, and he checked her paws for thorns or stones, the way he would have done with a horse.

Libby had ridden back to him by then, Stranger following, reins dragging along the ground.

"Is Hildie hurt?" Libby asked, sounding so worried that Tate looked up at her and felt his heart rush into his throat.

I love you, Libby, he wanted to say. *Trust me with your heart, the way you trust me with your dog.*

"Just tired, I think," he said. "A little overheated, too, maybe."

With that, Tate lifted the dog in both arms, careful to support her back, and managed to remount the gelding without dropping Hildie. The trick wasn't quite so easy to pull off as it had been when he was a kid, forever sharing a horse's back with one family dog or another.

Libby moved in close enough that their horses' sides touched, and her smile lodged somewhere deep in Tate's soul, a place beyond all reach until that day, and that woman.

"Thanks," she said. Her blue eyes shone with light.

Tate centered himself and Hildie, scooting farther back in the saddle so she wouldn't be jabbed by the horn and then reaching around to take hold of the reins again. "If I'd known all it would take for you to look at me like that was to ride double with your dog, Hildie and I would have been working the range together long before this."

Libby smiled tentatively, then made a dismissive motion with one hand.

The girls waited until Libby and Tate caught up.

"Did Hildie get tired?" Ava asked.

"She's not hurt, is she?" Audrey wanted to know.

Tate's pride in his daughters was a swelling in his chest

some of the time, a pinch in the wall of his heart or a catch in his breath—it varied. That day, it was a scalding sensation behind his eyes.

"No, Hildie's not hurt," he said, for Libby's benefit, as well as the children's. "She just needed a little help, that's all."

Audrey and Ava nodded sagely.

The Ruiz place—*his place*—was just ahead, gleaming in the curved embrace of the creek. The grass was green, and the round-topped oaks threw great patches of shade onto the ground.

Tate rode down to the creek and then right into the shallow part, making the girls shriek with delight.

Stranger bent his big head and drank, up to all four ankles in crystal-clear water, and Tate dismounted, set Hildie down gently on smooth pebbles that glittered like jewels.

Hildie shivered, gave a happy woof and drank thirstily before bounding up the creek bank like a pup, apparently refreshed and ready for adventure.

Tate slogged after the dog, pretending he was wetter than he was, and Hildie waited until he was within range to shake herself off with vigor, flinging water all over him.

Libby's laughter, and that of his little girls, rang in the pure light of that summer morning, weaving together, ribbons of sound.

CHAPTER SEVENTEEN

VARIOUS CONTRACTORS' trucks and vans encircled the former Ruiz house—painters, electricians, plumbers, drywallers and roofers plied their trades, swarming in and out. The ring of hammers and the shrill, devouring roar of power saws sliced the air, thick with summer heat.

Libby wondered how she could have failed to notice all that noise and activity. She'd been entirely transported, watching Tate ride his horse into the creek, balancing Hildie in his strong arms. Watching as he'd set the dog down in the water and grinned that one-of-a-kind patented grin of his as she drank—while, for the amusement of his small daughters, he'd pretended to be stunned and outraged when Hildie shook herself off and drenched him in the process.

The muscles on the insides of Libby's thighs throbbed from even that short time in the saddle as she climbed down, pausing a moment on shaky legs, the balls of her feet tingling. She left the mare to graze with Tate's horse and the two ponies.

"Looks like you've given up on landing a spot on the DIY

Network," Libby teased, nodding toward the house, wanting to touch Tate where sweat and creek water dampened the fabric of his shirt. *Lord knows, you've got the looks for TV, though. I can see you with a tool belt slung low around your hips, like an Old West gunslinger's gear, and breaking the hearts of female home-improvement enthusiasts everywhere.*

Tate's moist hair curled slightly around his ears and at the back of his neck. His smile was white, perfect and absolutely lethal, and the shadows of the leaves over their heads darkened his eyes, lightened them again.

"Yep," he drawled, with a shrug of shoulders made strong and broad first by heredity, and then by loading and unloading bales of hay and sacks of feed, by shoveling out stalls and carrying sweet old dogs who couldn't or wouldn't walk another step. "I admit it. I ran a white flag up the pole and sent for reinforcements. At the rate I was going, I figured the kids and I would be moving in here next year sometime, or the year after that. I want us to be living under this roof before Audrey and Ava start school in the fall."

"Can we go fishing, Daddy?" Ava asked, tugging at his sleeve. "Those poles you bought us are on the back porch, right?"

"Right," Tate said. "Dig the worms first."

The girls rushed off to do his bidding, and Ambrose and Buford followed, leaping and bounding through the grass. Hildie, bless her heart, was content to lie down in the shady grass under a nearby tree, keeping Libby in sight and staying clear of the grazing horses.

"Why?" Libby asked quietly.

"Why?" Tate echoed, eyes dancing. "Why should the kids dig worms before they go fishing?"

Libby smiled and shook her head. "Why do you want to live in this house when you have a perfectly good mega-mansion?"

Tate shoved a hand through his hair, turned to watch as

his daughters knelt in the middle of the large garden plot, between rows of cabbage, an old coffee can nearby, the pair of them digging for earthworms with their bare hands.

They'd be ring-in-the-bathtub filthy when they got back to the ranch house—the way little kids should be. When he and his brothers were small, their mother used to joke about hosing them down in the yard before letting them set foot on her clean floors.

He smiled at the recollection.

The pups, never far away from the twins, day or night, sniffed curiously at the ground, tails wagging, and Ambrose lifted his leg against a cornstalk.

"My reason for wanting to live here hasn't changed since we talked about it before," Tate answered, at some length.

Libby tilted her head to one side. Her expression was friendly, but skeptical, too. "You claim you want to see how 'regular' people live," she said. "I'm not convinced, Tate. Even if you moved into a tent, or a crate under a viaduct, you still wouldn't be an ordinary guy. You'd be a McKettrick."

"There's so much pride attached to that," Tate said, still watching his daughters and their dogs in the near distance. They were sun-splashed, and their chatter rang in the weighted air like the distant toll of country church bells. "Being a McKettrick, I mean. These days, it mostly means having money." He turned to face Libby, and because the light changed, she couldn't read his eyes. "Once, it meant something more, Lib. Something better."

She waited, listening with her heart, as well as with her ears.

"When Clay McKettrick took over the original hundred acres that became this ranch," he said huskily, "Blue River was a wide spot on a dusty cattle trail, and nobody had a clue there was oil here. Probably wouldn't have cared much if they *had* known—cars being few and far between, especially four hundred miles up the backside of no place." Tate paused, as if remembering. As if he'd been there, back in the early twentieth century. The McKettricks tended to know all about their kin, living and dead—it was just the way they were. "Clay started with the help of the woman he loved and the strength in his back. Part of the Arizona bunch—old Angus was his grandfather and Clay was the youngest of Jeb and Chloe's brood—he could have stayed right there on the Triple M and nobody would have thought the worse of him for it. But he wanted to do something on his own, and he did, Libby. He did."

Libby debated for a moment before moving closer to him. There were too many people around for any display of affection, so standing a little nearer and letting her upper arm touch his under the dappling shadows of the oak leaves overhead had to do.

"There are those who start things," she said, quietly, "and those who carry them on. Clay founded this ranch, and generations of McKettricks kept it going, made it grow. You're part of that, Tate—so are your brothers. How is that a bad thing?"

Tate watched the sparkling creek water, most likely pondering what she'd said, though he didn't reply.

Libby turned her eyes toward the garden—some of it had already been tilled under, and a lot of the produce had already been removed, probably given away. Ava and Audrey were high-stepping toward them, the partially rusted coffee can in hand, no doubt with worms squirming in the bottom. Ambrose and Buford kept pace, and the old house was a beehive of activity.

"Tate?" Libby prompted gently. "What's wrong with the other house? What do you hope to prove by moving into this one?"

He looked at her sharply, but then everything seemed to ease. His jaw and shoulders relaxed visibly. "There's nothing wrong with the main ranch house," he said quietly. "It has a long history. The memories are mostly happy ones. But it's *big,* Libby. Even when the kids are there, well, it's as if we were all staying in a hotel or something—on vacation all the time, and never just hanging out around home."

Libby nodded. She did understand.

Tate went on, his eyes fond and solemn as he watched his daughters, who'd stopped to argue over which one of them was going to carry the can of worms. His mouth crooked up in a semblance of a grin as they pulled it one way and then the other.

"Maybe we'll stay here for good," Tate went on, "and maybe we won't. But my daughters will at least have a sense of how normal people live."

"Would you ever leave the ranch, Tate?" Libby asked; for her, it was a bold question. "Would you ever leave and not come back?"

He looked at her closely then. "Nope," he said, with certainty. "I'm Texas born and bred. It's as if this dirt and this sky and these people are in my cells, Lib. What about you?"

Libby raised her shoulders, lowered them again. Sighed. "Sometimes I wonder who I'd be, away from here."

Tate squinted, as though to see her better, and he would surely have pursued the subject except that one of the twins let out a shrill shriek before he could say anything.

Shaking his head, Tate strode in their direction to settle the dispute over the worms.

"Hold it!" he said, holding up both hands.

Libby smiled, reminded of her dad. He'd been the peacemaker, the one who mediated little-girl arguments over whose barrette was whose, whose turn it was to bring in the newspaper or wash the dishes or weed the garden or sweep the kitchen floor.

Her dad had never raised his voice, as far back as she could remember. He'd certainly never lifted a hand to any one of them in anger, though he'd wiped away a great many tears and treated a million skinned elbows and scraped knees.

Who *was* Libby Remington, really?

Her father's daughter, and Marva's.

Julie and Paige's big sister, and Calvin's aunt.

Hildie's mistress, and a friend of animals everywhere.

The owner of the Perk Up Coffee Shop, now passed on into the realm of legend.

And most certainly the naive girl Tate McKettrick had dumped for somebody else.

She was over that last part—being dumped, anyway— she'd grown safely into a woman, and if there was one thing she'd learned in the process, it was that life was rarely easy, rarely simple, and often painful.

And it was worth all of that, to be here, now, doing nothing on a sunny summer day.

Libby watched as Tate dropped to his haunches, facing his daughters, after taking the can and peering inside.

Libby couldn't hear his words, but she saw the white flash of his grin, and knew he was working that McKettrick magic of his. She could imagine him saying what fine specimens those worms were, that he'd never seen better ones, that they were sure to catch the biggest trout in the creek.

The little girls listened with such earnest trust in their faces that Libby's eyes smarted. With a surreptitious swipe of one hand, she wiped them away, gave a delicate sniffle.

Straightening, Tate kept the rusty worm can, caught Libby's eye and winked, then gestured toward the house and said something more to the children. They raced around back, giggling again, the yellow dogs trotting behind them, baying like hounds on the hunt.

On his way back to where Libby stood, Tate stopped to speak with the plumber, and then the man loading a battered wooden tool chest, the old-fashioned kind, into the back of his van.

Libby knew all the men, of course, knew their wives and their children, their mothers and fathers, and in some cases, their grandparents, too. She realized, standing there, how silly it was to think she could have hidden her relationship with Tate, even briefly.

As he said, everybody knew they were "getting it on."

He came toward her now, grinning and carrying the worm can.

As she watched him moving nearer and nearer, Libby's heart swelled and then somersaulted in her chest, a big, slow and graceful motion, like that of some sea creature frolicking in deep waters.

Bold as you please, Tate leaned in and kissed her. It wasn't just a peck, either. There was tongue involved.

She gasped, breathless and unsteady on her feet, when he drew back. "Trout for supper," he said.

"I beg your pardon?" Libby asked, confused.

Tate held up the worm can. "Audrey and Ava are fetching the fishing poles even as we speak," he said. "Here's the agenda: we catch a few trout. The guys knock off early, gather up their gear and leave. There's a fish fry. We all stuff ourselves and I catch the horses and saddle them up again, and we all ride back to the main house. The dogs and the kids are exhausted—bound to sleep like rocks. Esperanza cleans them up and puts them to bed. I tend to the horses. Then you and I take a shower together—this time I remember to lock the bedroom door—and I make love to you until all the kinks are worked out of that perfect little body of yours."

Libby's knees went weak. "All the—?"

"Kinks," Tate finished for her. "It might take some doing," he added seriously.

She thought about it.

A sweet, hot shiver of anticipation went through her.

Then she grinned, rose onto her tiptoes and kissed the cleft in his chin. "Sounds good to me," she said.

Tate was happier than he'd been in a long time; it almost scared him.

Needing something physical to do, at least until his emotions settled down a little, he spoke to the contractors, asked them to take the rest of the day off.

Then he unsaddled the horses, took off their bridles, too.

They'd stay close, he knew, because the grass was sweet and plentiful, the creek was nearby and the trees provided shade.

After that, Tate just allowed himself to marvel at what a lucky bastard he really was, and forget the oil shares and the money. His kids were healthy, and they were *here,* with him, with Libby.

Sunlight gilded his baby girls like full-body halos. Their voices, their laughter, their concern for worms and fishes, as well as dogs and horses—all those things roosted in Tate's heart, flapped their wings and settled in to stay.

The land, the trees, the sky seemed to go on forever.

And in the center of all this magic was Libby, as sturdy and practical and down-home as a sunflower, sprung up in some unlikely place, but at the same time, as dazzling as crystals glittering on fresh snow.

She helped Audrey and Ava to bait their hooks and cast their lines into the creek—and made sure they didn't snag each other in the process. She laughed a lot, and they liked being close to her, leaning into her sides when she wrapped an arm around each of them and squeezed.

"You know how to *fish?*" Audrey had marveled at the beginning, obviously surprised. Her eyes glowed as she looked up at Libby, and so did Ava's. She seemed to fascinate them.

She certainly fascinated *him,* though in a different way.

As simply as Libby lived, as ordinary as she seemed to think she was, there was a sense of mystery about her, of depths and heights, an interior landscape, a planet, maybe even a *universe,* waiting to be explored.

That was Libby.

"You bet I know how to fish," she had beamed, answering Audrey's question. "My dad used to take my sisters and me camping whenever he could, and if we wanted trout or bass for supper, we had to catch it."

The afternoon progressed, slowed down with the heat. Tate and Libby wound up sitting side by side on the creek bank, their knees drawn up and their heels dug in and each of them with their arms around one of the twins, showing them when to let out the line, when to reel it in.

In the end, there was no fish fry, though.

They threw back everything they caught.

The kids wanted mac-and-cheese, anyway. The boxed kind was Tate's culinary specialty; when he felt like swanking it up, he added wieners.

He'd give Esperanza the night off, he decided—maybe she'd like to go to the movies or visit a friend.

By the time the mosquitoes were out and drilling for blood, Audrey and Ava were finally starting to run down. Hunger made them cranky, and they began to bicker.

"Seems like they've had all the fun they can stand," Tate told Libby.

She nodded, grinned up at him. Her eyes looked dreamy; the quiet afternoon had been good for her.

If Tate had his way, the night would be even better.

For a while, it looked as though that was actually going to happen.

Once the kids had stowed their fishing poles, everyone checked out the progress the contractors had made on the house. The twins' room was coming together, and so was the bathroom they would share. The kitchen and the master bedroom both had a ways to go.

Tate decided he might get back into the home-improvement groove after all. Delegate some of his duties as foreman—not that he was real clear yet on what those duties actually were.

He wished he'd spent more time riding with Pablo now, both on horseback and in the company truck. And not just because of the things he might have learned.

The man's absence was still a persistent ache in Tate's middle, a wind that sometimes abated and sometimes howled.

He saddled his horse and Libby's, checked to see that the girls had gotten their cinches tight enough and wouldn't be rolling off their ponies' backs onto the ground.

Not that they'd have far to go, he thought, with a smile.

The ponies were about the size of a large dog.

Once Libby was on Buttons's back and squared away, Tate handed Hildie up into her arms, made sure she had a good grip. That dog looked as easy in the saddle as if she played polo on weekends.

Letting the kids get a head start, Tate took his time swinging up into the saddle and turning Stranger in the direction of the main house.

Sometimes I wonder who I'd be, away from here.

Libby's remark had snagged in his mind, beneath all the sunshine and the fishing and the easy enjoyment of a sunny day.

If she thought he was going to let *that* one go, she should have damn well known better.

"So," Tate began, as they rode slowly onto the range again, the big house towering in the distance, like the castle it was. "Who do you think you'd be, Lib, away from Blue River?"

She nestled her chin onto the top of Hildie's head, her arms stretched around the dog's ample body, holding on to the saddle horn for balance and letting the reins rest loosely across the mare's neck.

After a long time, she replied sadly, "I don't know. Maybe someone who's accomplished things."

Tate nudged his horse a bit closer to Libby's, not to crowd her, but in case holding the dog got to be too much for her. He raised an eyebrow and shifted his gaze to the space between Stranger's ears, though he was still watching Lib out of the corner of one eye.

"Like what?" he asked, very carefully.

If Libby truly believed she had something to prove, well, as far as Tate was concerned, that was cause for concern. Especially if she thought she had to leave Blue River to do it.

She sighed. She shook her head.

Gently, he took Hildie from her.

Their horses moved apart again.

Hildie tilted her head back to lick the underside of Tate's chin.

He chuckled. The girls were too far ahead, almost to the fence, the pups weaving around them.

Tate gave a shrill whistle to get Audrey and Ava's attention, signaled them to wait for him and Libby.

"Will you do me a favor, Lib?" he asked, when she didn't say anything. "Before you decide to take off for parts unknown, so you can 'accomplish' things, will you give us a chance? You and me, I mean?"

Tears glistened in her eyes when she looked at him. "What kind of chance?"

"You know what kind of chance."

"What if it doesn't work?"

"What if it does?"

Libby bit down on her lower lip and looked away. "It didn't before."

"That was before. We weren't living in the same town. And that was a long time ago, Lib."

She met his eyes, with a visible effort. "Isn't that what we're doing now, Tate?" she asked quietly. "Giving things a chance?"

"I want to sleep with you every night, Libby. I want to shower with you and eat breakfast with you and do a whole lot of other things with you." He paused, looked back over his shoulder. "The house isn't finished, but it's livable. I'll rustle up some furniture, and we'll move in. You, me and the kids and the dogs."

She was quiet for a long time. So long that Tate started to get nervous.

"You're suggesting that we *live* together?" Libby finally asked. "In the same house with your children?"

The scandalized note in her voice made Tate chuckle. "Hello? The parents of half the kids in their kindergarten class 'cohabitate.'"

"There's cohabitation," Libby said, "and there's *shacking up.*"

"You know, for someone as sexually responsive as you are, Lib, you can really be prudish."

Her cheeks glowed with pink splotches. "You're not concerned that Audrey and Ava will be—confused?"

Tate huffed out a sigh. "No," he said. "Did Ava seem 'confused' this morning, when she found us in bed together? For better or worse, it's a different world, Libby." He watched her for a long moment, trying to gauge her reactions. They had almost caught up with the girls, so he lowered his voice. "If it really bothers you, though—*living in sin,* I mean—we could go ahead and get married."

"Married?"

"Well, wouldn't that be better than 'shacking up,' as you put it?"

"What about—" She stopped, swallowed so hard that Tate felt the dry ache in his own throat. "What about love?"

"Love isn't our problem," Tate replied quietly. "*Trust* is our problem."

Libby didn't affirm that assertion, but she didn't deny it, either. So he still had a fighting chance.

For now, though, the conversation was over.

Deftly, Ava reached, without dismounting, to work the gate latch.

In the distance, the stud kicked and squealed like he'd tear that pen apart, rail by rail and bolt by bolt. The sound of that animal's rage sent a shiver tripping down Tate's spine.

As soon as he'd ridden through the gate, Tate got down from the saddle, set Hildie on the ground and strode toward the pen, leaving Stranger to go into the barn on his own.

"Shut that gate," he called over one shoulder, "and go on into the barn."

Through the gaps between the steel rails, Tate saw the stallion bunch its hind quarters, put its head down and send both its back legs slamming into the pen's gate with enough force to shake the ground.

The gate held.

Tate swore under his breath. Fumbled for his cell phone and called Brent Brogan's direct line.

"Hey, Tate," Brent said, affably distracted, like he was doing paperwork or something. "Everything okay out there on the Ponderosa?"

Tate answered with a question of his own. "You heard a decision on what Animal Control wants to do with this stud?" he asked. "Because he's in a foul mood—fixing to kick his way out of the pen and kill somebody else."

Brent sighed. "I'll make a few calls," he said, "and get back to you."

"Thanks," Tate said. Call waiting clicked in his ear. "Later." Then, after pressing the appropriate button, "Tate McKettrick."

"It's Julie Remington, Tate. I need to speak with Libby."

So much, Tate thought, for loving the "kinks" out of Libby's delectable little body later on, when they would have been alone. He grabbed hold of the pen gate with his free hand and gave the thing a hard shake, making sure the stud hadn't sprung it.

"Sure," he said glumly. "Hold on a second."

Libby had gone into the barn, along with the twins, and when Tate reached the doorway, she and Audrey and Ava were all in separate stalls, unsaddling their horses and getting ready to brush them down. Stranger stood in the breezeway, waiting his turn, although Libby must have removed his saddle and blanket and bridle.

The old horse ambled toward Tate, nudged him good-naturedly in the chest.

Leaving Buttons's stall, Libby was smiling, dusting her hands together.

Job well done.

"For you." Tate held the cell out to her, and she took it.

"Julie," he added, opening the door to Stranger's stall and stepping aside so the animal could precede him.

Libby nodded, looking mildly troubled, and headed for the open door at the end of the breezeway.

Tate closed the stall door and began brushing down his horse.

"I'M *NOT* KIDDING," Julie said. "Marva is leaving. For good. The movers will come in a few days and clear out her apartment."

Libby rounded the corner of the barn, keeping to the shade, and gazed at the stallion in its big metal cage. The creature had quieted, but its flanks and sides were lathered as though it had run for miles and miles. It stood with its head hung low, its sides expanding, drawing in, expanding, drawing in again.

She thought about Pablo; how startled and afraid he must have been when he fell under the stallion's hooves. The pain, though probably brief, would have been horrendous.

"Julie, what do you want me to say?" Libby asked, backing away from the stallion now, resisting a strange and probably suicidal desire to reach between those steel slats and try to comfort it somehow. Speak softly and stroke its sweat-drenched neck. "If Marva wants to leave, she can leave. Hitting the road is her forte, after all, isn't it?"

"Nobody's denying that she left us, Lib," Julie said so quietly and so gently that Libby was ashamed of herself. "We were little girls. We needed her. She abandoned us and she abandoned Dad. But—"

"But?" Libby snapped.

On some level, she was still that terrified, heartbroken and *furious* kid who wanted her mother.

"Look," Julie went on, when Libby was silent for a long time, "she wants to see all three of us, tonight. At her place. She says it's important."

Libby wanted to scream, though of course she didn't. That would have alarmed the kids, and Hildie, who had followed her out of the barn and sat looking up at her now, pink tongue lolling.

"Why does it have to be tonight?"

"Because she's flying out of Austin tomorrow," Julie said. "Libby, I know you have issues with Marva—valid ones. We all do. But the woman *is* our mother, and I think we can do this much for her."

Libby's head began to throb. She dug into her right temple with three fingers and rubbed.

Returning to town meant she couldn't pretend the Perk Up was still standing.

It probably meant no sex with Tate.

And she'd been looking forward to that, to getting naked in the shower with him. To soaring outside herself.

Love isn't our problem, he'd said. Trust *is our problem.*

Did that mean he still loved her?

Dammit, she wanted to know. She *needed* to know.

"Just come," Julie said. "Please, Lib. Six-thirty, Marva's place."

Libby looked at her wrist, realized she wasn't wearing her watch, and asked, "What time is it now?"

"A little after five," Julie answered. "You're with Tate, aren't you?"

"Not for long, it would seem," Libby lamented. *We were starting to get somewhere, Tate and I.*

"I'm sure he'll understand."

"Of course he will. *I'm* the one having a hard time understanding."

"Well, *that* was certainly cryptic," Julie remarked. Then, barely missing a beat, "You'll be at Marva's, then?"

Libby nodded, glummer than glum. "Yes." She looked up, and Tate was standing maybe a dozen yards away, waiting, looking pensive.

And so deliciously hunky.

"See you at six-thirty," Julie said.

"See you," Libby answered, and closed the phone.

Walking up to Tate, she handed the device back to him.

"I have to go back to town," she said. "It seems my mother is leaving Blue River again—her work here is done now that my business is in ruins—and she wants to say goodbye. Tonight."

Tate sighed, took Libby's shoulders in his hands. "You're okay with this? Her leaving, I mean?"

"It's not as though she's been an integral part of my life, Tate." Libby spoke without bitterness; she was simply stating a fact she'd accepted long ago. Mostly.

He drew her close, as she'd hoped he would do, and held her, resting his chin on the top of her head. "Let me make sure Esperanza can look after the kids tonight, and then I'll drive you to town."

She nodded, wanting to cling to him, forcing herself not to clutch at the fabric of his shirt. "I don't want to go."

"Then don't."

"I *have* to, Tate."

She felt the motion of his jaw; knew he was smiling even before he held her a little way from his chest so he could look down into her face.

"This was a good day," he said.

"It was a good day," Libby agreed.

But the best part was over.

Fifteen minutes later, they were in Tate's truck, headed for Blue River. Hildie rode in the rear seat, but she wasn't any happier about leaving the Silver Spur than Libby was, evidently. The dog sat backward, looking out the window over the truckbed, and every few moments, she gave a small whimper.

Libby wanted to reassure Hildie that they'd be back, but she was strangely hesitant to make such a promise.

At home, she took a quick shower and put on a simple cotton sundress. She tracked Tate to the kitchen, where he was leaning calmly against the counter, arms folded, watching Hildie gobble up her kibble. He'd refilled her water dish, too, and even brought in the newspaper and the mail.

Libby, her hair still damp from the shower steam, searched for her car keys until she finally found them—hanging on their hook near the back door, where they were supposed to be.

"It always throws me," she admitted to Tate, "when things are where they're supposed to be."

He chuckled at that.

"You don't have to stay," she said, hoping he would.

Which was crazy, because he had children at home. He had a ranch, livestock. Responsibilities. It was just plain wrong to expect him to sit here in this house until she got back from Marva's at whatever time, in whatever emotional condition, just because she might need someone to talk to later on.

He crossed the room, opened her refrigerator, shook his head. The pickings were slim; she had to admit that.

"What do you live on?" he asked, and from the tone of his voice, he was only half kidding. "You have three green olives, a box of baking soda, and I don't even want to think about the expiration date on that cheese. It's not supposed to be blue-green at the corners, is it?"

Libby laughed. "I depend heavily on canned goods," she said.

"Yuck," Tate said.

The wall phone rang.

Libby grabbed the receiver, hoping for a reprieve. In a fraction of an instant, she came up with the perfect scenario: Julie was calling to say that Marva was still leaving, soon and for good, but tonight's visit had been postponed—better yet, canceled altogether.

"Good, you're home," Julie said. "Can you pick me up? Paige is still at work, so she's going to be a few minutes late, and—"

"Sure," Libby broke in, deflated. So much for perfect scenarios. "I'll swing by and get you. But chill out a little. This isn't a rocket launch, Julie. There's no second-by-second countdown."

Incredibly, Julie burst into tears. "Maybe you don't want to know *where the hell* our mother has been all these years," she blurted out, in a very unJulie-like way, "but I do! *By God,* that woman isn't going *anywhere* until she gives me *some* kind of explanation!"

"Julie," Libby said gently, her gaze connecting with Tate's, "where's Calvin?"

Julie sniffled inelegantly. "He's spending the night with Justin."

"All right. That's good. I'll be over in a few minutes."

Goodbyes were said, and both sisters hung up.

Tate jingled his keys at Libby. "Hildie and I are going out to pick up something decent for dinner," he said. "We'll be here waiting when you get back."

"It might be late," she warned.

He approached, kissed her lightly. "We'll be here," he repeated. "Hildie and me."

She nodded, too choked up, all of a sudden, to say more.

Since the Impala was parked in her garage, off the alley, Libby couldn't avoid getting a glimpse of the caved-in roof and tumbled-down walls of the Perk Up.

It wasn't enough that Marva had abandoned them all way back when, she reflected bitterly.

Six months ago, with no warning at all, she'd returned to Blue River, rented the condo, furnished it and begun trying to "make up for lost time" and get to know her daughters.

But an invasion of their lives wasn't enough for Marva. Oh, no. She had to destroy the one thing Libby had to show for her attempts to jerry-rig some kind of career for herself. She had to reduce the Perk Up to scrap metal and firewood.

Libby climbed into the Impala, started the engine, calmly backed into the alley, remembering those early days after Marva's sudden reentry into her and her sisters' lives.

She'd seemed genuinely baffled, Marva had, when they resisted her overtures—the phone calls, the unannounced visits, the gifts.

Julie had been the first to give ground.

She wanted Calvin to know his grandmother, she'd said.

Paige, to Libby's initial surprise, had fallen under the spell of Marva next. Of course, Paige was the baby; she'd still been wearing footed pajamas and sucking her thumb when their mother bailed.

She'd cried the longest and the hardest. Climbed into Libby's or Julie's bed at night, dragging her tattered "blankie" and whispering, "Do you know where Mommy is? When will she be back? Tomorrow? Will Mommy come home tomorrow?"

Remembering, still the big sister, Libby ached with the same helpless fury she'd felt back then.

Julie was waiting by her front gate when Libby pulled up, the diamond-paned windows of her pretty cottage alight behind her. Flowers climbed trellises, tumbled, riotous, over fences, and the fierce dazzle of the setting sun glowed around it all.

"I can't believe she's just going to take off again," Julie said, instead of hello.

"Believe it," Libby said grimly.

CHAPTER EIGHTEEN

AFTER A SHORT SPEECH, Marva produced three envelopes from her handbag and, with a flourish, presented one to each of her daughters.

To Libby, it seemed that the floor of the condo's living room pitched from side to side, like a swimming raft bobbing on choppy water. She squeezed the bridge of her nose between her thumb and forefinger, trying hard to stem the headache beating behind her eyes like a second heart.

The tick of the mantel clock was hypnotic—steady as a metronome—and it didn't help that Marva kept pacing back and forth in front of the cold fireplace, arms folded, the hem of her wildly colorful silk caftan billowing at her heels.

Julie, seated in the wingback chair, was the first to open her envelope, the first to speak. Staring down at the check inside, she whispered, "This is—this is *a lot* of money."

Paige, perched on the edge of a chintz-covered ottoman, couldn't seem to speak at all. She pressed one hand to the base of her throat, shaking, her eyes squeezed shut.

Libby didn't move so much as a muscle. She was too stunned.

Marva stopped pacing and stood still, sweeping Libby, Julie and Paige up in a single cheerfully magnanimous glance.

"Paige? Libby? Don't either of you have anything to say?" their mother demanded, her voice a touch too high.

Paige opened her eyes, swayed slightly. "Holy crap," she said.

Libby straightened her spine. The headache receded slightly, and the floor leveled itself out and stayed still. "Please, Marva," she said, in a near whisper, "sit down. You're making me dizzy."

Marva plunked down next to Libby, on the couch. Took one of Libby's hands between both her own, as though the two of them were as close as any mother and daughter, ever. "I added a little something to your share, dear," she said, in a whisper no one could have helped overhearing, even if they'd been in the next room. "Because I crashed into your little coffee shop and everything."

And everything.

Did I mention that Dad kept asking for you, right up until the day he couldn't talk anymore, because the hospice nurse and Doc Burt put him on a ventilator, and there was a tube in his throat, and even then *he asked with his eyes?*

That until the middle of first grade, Paige thought every ring of the doorbell, every car stopping out front, meant you were home?

Oh, yeah, and Julie saw you everywhere, for years—in the grocery store, in other cars at stoplights, on the River Walk in San Antonio.

Me, I just wanted to talk to you. I was so pathetic, I would have settled for a few more phone calls. Letters or postcards.

Hell, I'd have settled for smoke signals.

And everything, indeed.

"I can't accept your money," Libby said stiffly, after finding her voice and pulling free of Marva's grasp.

Julie glared at Libby from across the small room, fanning her flushed face with her check. "Lib," she said, "this is *no time* to let your pride do the talking."

Marva fluttered a hand, the gesture taking them all in. "It isn't *my* money, anyway," she said, in merry dismissal. "It's *yours.* I had a sizable insurance policy on your father's life—he and I took it out together, soon after you were born, Libby—and when he died, I collected. Winston—my present husband—is very good with money, and he invested the proceeds and—" She beamed, flinging her hands out wide. "*Voilà!* You are women of means!"

Women of means, Libby thought. Bile scalded the back of her throat.

"How—?" Paige paused, started again. "How could you leave us like that? We were *little kids,* Marva."

"I've never claimed to be perfect," Marva said, mildly indignant. The brilliant smile was gone.

A short, bristly silence followed. "I should have listened to Winston," Marva continued presently, frowning thoughtfully into the middle distance. "I thought if I came back to Blue River, well, we'd all get to know each other and bygones would be bygones. After all, we're all grown-ups, aren't we?" She sighed, causing her shoulders to rise and fall in an ebullient shrug. "Winston said you wouldn't react well, and he was right. I miss him terribly, and frankly I'm tired of being the only one around here who even *tries* to build a relationship. I want to get on with my life. I want to go home."

Home, Marva had explained earlier, before the ceremonious presentation of the envelopes, was a condominium overlooking a beach in Costa Rica. Winston was a retired proctologist and, apparently, a very indulgent husband—as well as a financial whiz.

Since responding to the things Marva had said would have

amounted to crossing a conversational minefield, none of the sisters said anything.

The evening was, for all practical intents and purposes, over.

Libby left her envelope, still unopened, on Marva's coffee table.

She said goodbye, travel safely, and other things she couldn't quite recall later, when she looked back on the experience.

She had almost reached the Impala when Julie caught up to her, shoved the envelope at her. Her name was neatly inscribed on the front, in flowing cursive.

"Don't be an idiot," she said. "Marva destroyed your business. And, anyway, Dad would have wanted you to have this money. He probably kept up the premiums the whole time Marva was away. *Take it.*"

Libby swallowed, snatched the envelope out of Julie's hand, shoved it into her purse as Paige joined them, shivering a little, hugging herself, even though the night was warm.

"I wouldn't make any investments or impulse purchases if I were you," Libby told both her sisters, as she opened her car door to get in and drive away. "Not before these checks clear the bank, anyway."

With that, she got into the Impala and started the engine.

"Are you coming with me?" Libby asked Julie, who was staring at her as though she'd turned into a total stranger.

"I'll go with Paige," Julie said, recovering enough to offer a thin smile. "She's a little shaken up."

Aren't we all? Libby thought wearily.

When she got back to the house, Tate was waiting for her, just as he'd promised he would be. He'd been to the store, too—supper was grilled chicken breast from the deli at the supermarket, along with potato salad and biscuits. Almsted's, which had abutted Libby's building, was closed until inspectors could determine whether or not there had been structural damage.

Hildie, resting contentedly in her usual place in front of the stove, rolled her eyes open in greeting, then closed them again. She'd had a big day, out there on the Silver Spur.

They all had.

Once Libby had washed her hands, dried them and sunk into the chair Tate held for her at the table, the day caught up with her, too. With an impact.

She was exhausted.

"So?" Tate asked, sitting down across from Libby. "Are you going to tell me what the big summons was all about?"

"Yes," Libby said, helping herself to a piece of chicken and some potato salad. "She's going back to her husband, Winston, the retired proctologist, in Costa Rica."

"I see," Tate said.

They ate in silence for a while.

"There's money," Libby said. "Sort of."

Tate raised an eyebrow. "Sort of?" he echoed. "How can there 'sort of' be money?"

Libby got up, rummaged through her purse for the envelope, handed it to Tate.

"See for yourself. There should be a check inside. I'm not getting excited until it clears the bank."

Tate chuckled at that, started to set the envelope aside, still sealed.

Libby's heart climbed into her throat. "Open it," she said, almost in a whisper. "Please?"

"It's yours, Lib. You should be the one to open it."

Libby shook her head. "I can't."

"Okay," Tate said. Slowly, probably giving her time to change her mind, he inserted the blade of a butter knife under the flap and slit the crease, pulled the check out without looking at it.

Libby closed her eyes. Waited.

"Tell me," she said.

Tate gave a long, low whistle of exclamation.

When he read off the amount, she gasped.

He handed it across the table. "Looks legitimate to me," he said quietly.

Libby briefly examined the check, groped for the envelope and shoved it back inside. Then she put the envelope on top of the fridge, under the cookie jar.

Out of sight, out of mind.

As if.

"I suppose it's too soon to ask if you have plans?" Tate ventured, when they'd both finished eating.

"Plans?" Libby echoed. He seemed to have withdrawn from her somehow, pulled ever so slightly back into a space she couldn't quite reach—but maybe she was imagining that.

Tate stood, began clearing the table, putting things in the fridge, scraping bones and other scraps into the trash bin. "Yeah," he said gently. "You could do a lot with that kind of money, Libby. You need to think about this." He sighed. "Without me distracting you."

"Distracting me?" She felt the floor tremble beneath her.

"Libby, you have some new options now, that's all I'm saying. You need to explore them."

To think *she'd* been hung up on Tate's earlier statement that he planned on asking her to move in with him, once the house was ready. She'd pretty much decided she'd say "yes," when and if the time came, but now—now Tate was talking about thinking and options and explorations.

For Libby, the money hadn't changed anything, really.

But maybe it had, for Tate. Maybe he'd liked her better when she was running a failing business, living on a shoe-string. Or maybe he'd just felt sorry for her—poor Libby—and now that she was a "woman of means," as Marva had put it, he could cut her loose, with no strain on his noble McKettrick conscience.

Dammit, was the man looking for an out?

She loved Tate.

She loved his daughters, too—that hadn't taken long. Two minutes, maybe.

Yes, there had been dreams. She'd wanted to travel a little, perhaps take some courses online, buy a decent car...

But all those were things she could have done without leaving Blue River, or at least without leaving Tate.

"I'm not even sure the check is good," Libby reiterated, after letting out a long breath. If Tate was having second thoughts, looking for an exit, she could deal with that. She could survive it—just as she had before. "Marva could be delusional—or even some kind of con artist, for all I know."

Tate leaned back against the counter, watching her. Sadness illuminated his eyes. "But if it is good?"

"I don't know, Tate. Do I have to decide tonight?"

He crossed the room, leaned down, kissed the top of her head, lightly, in a way that said, See you later. "No," he said hoarsely. "All you need to do tonight is get some sleep. We can talk tomorrow or—whenever."

Whenever? Libby thought. Her disappointment was out of all proportion to the situation. *Whenever?*

"Lock up behind me," Tate said.

He bent, patted Hildie on the head and started toward the front of the house.

Just like that, he was leaving.

Going back to the ranch—alone.

Libby waited until Tate was down the front steps, through the gate, on the sidewalk—until he'd actually driven away in his big-ass redneck truck—before she engaged the dead bolt on the front door and stormed back to the kitchen. Shot that dead bolt, too.

Hildie hoisted herself up off the floor, yawning.

Libby shut off the kitchen lights and led the way down the

hall toward her bedroom. By then, she was absolutely certain she'd been dumped again.

Slam, bam, thank you, ma'am.

"Never trust a man," she told the dog.

Hildie plopped down on the rug at the foot of Libby's bed, while Libby peeled off her clothes and flung them away. Shimmied into an oversized T-shirt and hauled back the covers on her bed.

"He's probably got you snowed," Libby said, heading for the bathroom, where she washed her face and brushed her teeth. On her return, she resumed the one-sided conversation. "All that McKettrick charm. 'You're too tired to walk? Poor old dog. Here. Let me carry you, on my horse—'"

Hildie sighed, dog-tired.

Libby climbed into bed. Switched out the lamp.

A tear trickled down over her right temple, tickling.

"What exactly did Tate do to make me so angry, you ask? As anyone would. He *left*. As soon as a challenge comes up—*poof!*—Tate McKettrick is out of here." She paused, pulled up a corner of the top sheet to dry her cheeks. "The thing is, Hildie," she finished, staring up at the darkened ceiling, "I'm in love with the man. What do you say to that?"

Hildie, of course, said nothing at all.

Somehow, against all odds, Libby slept.

He hadn't seen—or spoken to—Libby in four days.

Cheryl called on Friday morning—early, even taking the time difference between Texas and New York into account.

Tate, sleepless since leaving Libby's house the night of the meeting with her mother, had just started the coffee brewing. Having glanced at the caller ID panel, his usual greeting was gruffer than usual.

"Tate McKettrick. What do you want, Cheryl?"

"My," Cheryl said. "Aren't we testy?"

Tate drew in a breath, let it out slowly. "You don't know the half of it," he said.

"How are my babies?" The chirpy note in Cheryl's voice made him instantly suspicious. He hated it when she wheedled, and that chirp was the equivalent of a fire alarm.

"Audrey and Ava are fine," he said evenly. "Looking forward to seeing you tonight. A whole weekend with Mommy. Audrey wants to show you the routine she's been practicing for the Pixie Pageant. What time does your plane get in?"

Cheryl was silent for a few moments. "You're letting Audrey enter the Pixie Pageant?"

"Yeah," Tate said. "I might have been wrong, saying 'no' out of hand the way I did. She's giving it a shot."

"*You,* Tate McKettrick, were *wrong* about something?"

"I can think of several," Tate answered. A pause, during which he restrained himself from listing those things he'd been wrong about. It would surprise Cheryl to know she wasn't number one on that list—that slot went to screwing up what he'd had with Libby in the first place. "Can we cut to the chase now, Cheryl? You didn't call to shoot the breeze. It's not even four o'clock out here—the girls are sleeping."

A short, stormy silence, during which he could feel the bad mojo building. "Dammit, Tate," she finally burst out, "you *know* why I called, and you're *deliberately* making it all as difficult as possible!"

Since there was some truth in her accusation—he *had* known why she was calling—Tate decided to chill out a little. "Okay," he said. "I'll stop making things difficult for you. Go ahead and say it."

She sighed, and her voice sounded moist; either she was crying, or she wanted him to think she was. "It's the job— I'm new—low man on the totem pole—"

Tate suppressed a sigh. His knuckles tightened around the cell phone. God knew, he didn't give a rat's ass if Cheryl *ever* came back to Blue River, but the girls did. They were only six, and they loved and missed their mother.

"I'd suggest that Audrey and Ava come here," Cheryl went into her bravely-carrying-on routine. "But there wouldn't be much point in that, when I'll be at the office all weekend."

"No," Tate said. "There wouldn't be much point in that."

"I'll come *next* weekend," she promised, rallying. "And bring presents." A pause. "Will you tell them that? That I'll come next weekend and bring presents?"

"No," Tate replied. "They need to hear it from you."

Cheryl sounded pained. *"Why?"*

"Because this is between you and the kids."

He heard her draw in an angry breath. "You *love* making me look bad, don't you?"

Tate closed his eyes, held back the obvious retort.

"All right." He nearly growled the words. "I'll explain—this time. But you still need to call Audrey and Ava yourself, Cheryl. They're your daughters. They miss you, and they'll want to hear your voice."

"I'll call," Cheryl said, after a long time.

"Yeah," Tate said, and hung up without a goodbye.

Right about then, Austin meandered down his private stairway, wearing nothing but a pair of black boxers. Scars from two different rotator-cuff surgeries laced his right shoulder, front and back.

He ruffed up his already mussed hair and gave an expansive yawn.

"Tell me you stayed out all night," he drawled, "because nobody in his right mind gets up this early, even on a freakin' ranch."

Tate chuckled, but the sound was rueful. *"You're* up," he pointed out.

Austin all but staggered to the counter, took a mug from the cupboard and poured coffee into it, even though the stuff was still percolating in the fancy steel-and-steam apparatus

"That bull almost killed you before. Why give him a second chance?"

Austin's eyes were grave. "You know why."

"All you have to do is turn your back. All you have to do is walk away."

But Austin shook his head again, and Tate knew that particular conversation was over.

MARVA LEFT TOWN, ON SCHEDULE.

A day later, a moving van pulled up in front of her condominium, and her furniture and other household goods were removed.

Just like that, she was gone.

Again.

Libby, Julie and Paige drove all the way to Austin in Paige's car, just to deposit the checks Marva had given them. That way, they had each other for moral support, and it would be considerably less embarrassing than walking into First Cattleman's Bank in Blue River and finding out there was no money, carefully invested by a fiscally minded, retired proctologist.

The checks were good.

They plunked down on a bench in front of the bank, the three of them in a row, stunned.

"We're rich," Julie said.

"Not rich," Paige clarified. "Comfortable."

"I'm a teacher," Julie countered. "You're a registered nurse with state-of-the-art skills. Maybe this kind of money says 'comfortable' to you, but it says 'rich' to me."

Libby laughed. "Hot damn," she said.

She could go anywhere, do practically anything.

She had choices.

"What are you going to do with your share?" Julie asked, probably relieved that Libby hadn't torn the check into little pieces and tossed them into the breeze.

"Buy a new car," Libby said.

"That's all you want?"

"It's not all I want," Libby answered, smiling to herself. *And sometimes you have to go after what you want, and have confidence that you'll get it.*

The clarity was sudden, and it was glorious.

"Let's get lunch," she said. "I have things to do at home."

"Don't we all?" Paige agreed.

They had salads at a sunny sidewalk café.

Libby bought a cell phone and, between Paige and the salesman, figured out how to operate it.

And then they drove back to Blue River.

"You look like a woman with a purpose," Paige said, dropping Libby off at the back gate.

Inside the house, Hildie began to bark a relieved welcome.

Libby merely nodded; she knew her mysterious smile and wandering attention had been driving her curious sisters nuts all morning.

Waggling the fancy phone, which was probably capable of polishing the lenses of satellites deep in outer space, she smiled and unlatched the gate with her free hand.

"Call you later," she said.

Paige honked her horn in farewell and drove away.

Libby hurried up the walk and unlocked the back door.

Hildie spilled out gleefully, greeted her with a yip and squatted next to the flower bed.

While the dog enjoyed a few minutes of fresh air, Libby changed out of her go-to-the-bank-in-Austin dress and sandals and pulled on comfy jeans, a short-sleeved black T-shirt and tennis shoes. She brushed her hair and pulled it back from her face.

She put on lip gloss.

"Come on," she said to Hildie, grabbing up her purse and the new cell phone and the keys to the ratty old Impala. "We're on a mission."

During the drive, Libby rehearsed what she'd say when she reached her destination.

I love you, Tate McKettrick.

Let's give "us" a chance.

Now that we're all grown up, let's make it work.

She'd done a lot of thinking in the days since Tate had left her to consider her options. She'd realized he hadn't so much dumped her as assumed she was going to dump him. But she wasn't, and she trusted that he'd respond to her rehearsal speech just the way she wanted him to.

She stopped at the small house first; there were signs that Tate had been there, pounding nails and splashing paint onto the walls, but he wasn't around at the moment.

Libby called Hildie back from the creek where she'd been exploring, and they moved on to the main place.

There were trucks everywhere, parked at odd angles, but Libby didn't see anyone, either by the barn or in the spacious yard.

She was standing there, beside the Impala, trying to decide whether to knock on the kitchen door or check out the barn, when she heard the small, shrill scream.

Libby's heart actually seized in her chest.

For one terrible moment, she couldn't move.

Couldn't speak.

The scream came again, smaller now, more terrified.

And it was followed by the sound of the stallion trying to kick his way out of the pen again.

Libby broke into a run. "Tate!" she yelled. "Somebody—anybody—*help!*"

She rounded the corner of the barn.

The stallion was kicking in all directions now, raising dust, a whirling dervish.

And through that choking dust, Libby saw one of the twins—Ava, she thought—wriggle under the lowest rail and right into the stud pen.

Jesus, Libby prayed, *Jesus, Jesus, Jesus...*

She slammed against the side of the pen, grabbing the rails with both hands to steady herself.

Ava huddled within inches of the stallion's flying hooves, sheltering one of the pups with her little body.

Raising her eyes, the child spotted Libby.

Libby flopped to her belly in the dirt, but she clearly wasn't going to fit under that fence. She bolted back to her feet and started up the side, hand over hand, rail to rail.

"Tate!" she screamed, once more, as she reached the top.

And then she was over, landing in a two-footed crouch in the churned up dust and dried manure, Ava within reach.

The stallion froze, quivering all over, sizing her up.

Libby knew the respite was only temporary.

She could barely see for the dust, and her eyes scalded. Her heart pounded, and her throat felt scraped raw.

Moving slowly, she got Ava by one skinny upper arm, pulled.

Ava held on to the puppy.

The stallion snorted, laid back his ears.

A bad sign, Libby thought, strangely calm even though her body was stressed to the max. A very bad sign.

She pressed Ava and the pup behind her, against the rails. Pinned them with her back, spread her arms to shield them as best she could.

"Easy," she told the stallion, hardly recognizing her own voice. Her nose itched. She thought she might throw up. But she didn't dare move her arms. "Nobody wants to hurt you."

"Hold on, Lib." The voice was Tate's. He was just behind her.

Thank God he was there.

Thank God.

"Daddy," Ava whimpered. "I know I gave my word as a McKettrick, but Ambrose dug a hole under the stud-pen fence and got inside and I—"

"Hush," Tate said, very gently.

He started up the rails, making the same climb Libby had.

Libby became aware that Austin was there, too, fiddling with the padlock on the pen's door. A rifle rested easily in the crook of one of his arms as he worked.

Everything seemed to be happening in slow motion.

The stallion began to get agitated again, tossing his head, snorting. Pawing at the dirt with one front hoof, then the other.

Tate was over the fence, in front of Libby.

Shielding her and Ava and the little dog, he spoke to the stallion. His words were quiet, and their meaning innocuous—it was the tone of his voice, the energy Tate projected, a sort of calming authority, that made the difference.

The pen gate slowly creaked open.

The stallion turned his huge head in that direction, then back to Tate.

The danger was by no means past.

The pen was small, the stallion still riled. Sweat glistened on his hide, and his eyes rolled, all whites except for tiny slits of dark along the upper lids.

Libby let her forehead rest against the back of Tate's right shoulder.

Behind her, Ava and the puppy squirmed.

Austin moved away from the pen gate, wide-open now, and cocked the rifle.

Dear God, was he going to shoot the horse?

She must have wondered aloud, because Tate answered her. "Only if the stallion turns on us, Lib," he said.

Libby closed her eyes, clutched at Ava and the pup, holding them in a sort of backward hug, and waiting—waiting for the stallion to make up his mind.

Had Pablo's heart pounded like this?

Or had death come too swiftly for fear to take hold?

"Come on, now, horse," Austin said mildly, backing farther out of the path of freedom. "You come on now."

The stud took one step toward the gate, then another.

Quivered again, from behind his ears, laid sideways now, all the way to his flanks and down his haunches.

Then, with breath-stopping suddenness, the enormous and terrifyingly beautiful beast kicked out his hind legs, high and hard, missing Tate by inches.

And bolted and ran.

Cowboys stayed clear, though one rider opened a series of corral gates, clearing the way to the range beyond, the hills beyond that.

Tate finally let out his breath, turned around to look into Libby's eyes.

Ava set Ambrose on the ground, and he promptly fled.

"Daddy," she whispered, as Tate hooked an arm around her, lifted her and held her tightly against his side. She buried her face in his neck, sobbing.

Tate's gaze was riveted to Libby's.

"I love you," she said. "Maybe this isn't the right time to say so, but I do. I have choices. I can go away or I can stay here, and this is where I want to be. I really, truly, forever *love you,* Tate McKettrick."

The white flash of his grin made a dazzling contrast to his unshaven face and the stud-pen dust embedded in his skin and lightening his hair.

"I'll be damned," he said, throwing back his head, giving a whoop of joyous laughter.

"Hardly romantic," Libby said, pretending to be indignant.

"I'm saving the romantic stuff for when we're by ourselves," he answered.

Austin handed off the rifle to another cowboy and took Ava from Tate. She clung for a moment, then attached herself to her uncle.

"Where is Audrey?" Libby asked.

"Rehearsing for the Pixie Pageant," Tate answered, taking her hand.

Hildie was still shut up in the Impala, crazy to get out.

Tate opened the door for her, and promptly hoisted her into the back seat of his truck. He did the same with Libby.

"What about Ava?"

"She'll be fine with Austin and Esperanza," Tate answered, getting behind the wheel and starting up the big engine.

They drove to the other house.

Not a contractor in sight.

Tate lifted Hildie to the ground, and she immediately settled under a shade tree, the picture of canine contentment.

Progress had been made on the inside of the house—the kitchen was coming together, boasting granite countertops, glass-fronted cupboards and travertine tile floors.

There was still no furniture, but the shower in the master bath was working fine, and a sizable blow-up mattress stood in the center of the largest bedroom.

Tate opened the etched-glass shower door, reached in to turn the brass spigots.

Water shot, like a hard rain, from the matching showerhead, which looked as though it was roughly the same diameter as a manhole cover.

When Tate was satisfied with the temperature of the water, he tugged Libby closer, hooked a finger in the neckline of her T-shirt.

"I love you, Libby," he said gruffly. "I mean to spend the rest of my life proving that to you but, for now, it'll have to be sex."

"Oh, no," Libby joked, kicking off her shoes, unfastening her jeans, wriggling out of them.

Tate laughed, pulled her close.

They began to kiss.

And undress each other.

And the water from the big brass showerhead poured down over both of them, washing away the worst of the dust.

Washing away, it seemed, the mistakes and the heartbreaks and the disappointments of the past.

The foreplay was brief; they were both too desperate for contact to drag things out. Tate teased Libby to the absolute verge of a climax, then took her against the slick wall of the shower, the first thrust as hard and deep as the last.

Long minutes later, they both erupted, mouths locked together, tongues sparring, shouts of release ricocheting from one to the other.

They sank to the floor of the shower when it was over, leaning into each other for support.

"Will you marry me, Libby?" Tate asked, both of them kneeling under the fall of water. "Please?"

She nodded, traced his jaw with the tip of one finger, tasted his mouth. "Yes," she said. "I want a big wedding, on New Year's Eve." She nibbled at his lower lip. "In the meantime, though," she said, caressing him intimately, loving the way he groaned—and grew—in response, "let's keep working on sex until we get really, really good at it."

Tate gasped. "We're—pretty—good at it now."

Libby kissed him. "Practice makes perfect," she said.

September...

"YOU LOOK LIKE A PRINCESS in that sparkly blue dress," Ava said, a mite wistfully, as she and Libby made their way backstage at the Pixie Pageant, just a few steps behind Tate.

Libby smiled, squeezed the little girl against her side. "Thank you, sweetheart," she said. "You're not unlike royalty yourself, as it happens."

Up ahead, she saw Tate lean down to catch Audrey up in his arms. Libby's heart clenched with love as he straightened, this man she would marry on New Year's Eve.

They caught up, Libby and Ava; the four of them were together.

After tearful explanations over the phone, Cheryl had sent an impressive bouquet from New York; she was working on a big case and hadn't been able to get home for the pageant.

She and Libby e-mailed each other fairly regularly, always about the girls. Libby took a lot of pictures, uploaded them and sent them to Cheryl.

"I lost," Audrey announced cheerfully, as Tate set her back on her feet.

"Nobody wins all the time," Ava said consolingly.

Audrey shrugged. "It was fun," she said, "but I'm ready to move on."

Libby and Tate exchanged smiles at that.

"Could we get pizza?" Audrey asked her dad.

"Yep," Tate said. "We can get pizza."

They stopped on the way home, picked up the steamy, fragrant boxes—Hawaiian with extra cheese. Back at the house, Hildie, Ambrose and Buford greeted them with a lot of barking and jumping around.

The meal was happy cacophony, around their kitchen table. Audrey was still wearing her tutu, leotard and full stage makeup.

"So," Ava asked her twin, with real interest, "what are you going to do next, now that you're not into beauty pageants anymore?"

Audrey gave the question due consideration, even though it was clear to Libby that she'd already made up her mind. "Rodeo," she said.

"Rodeo?" Ava echoed.

Tate put down his second slice of pizza and opened his mouth to speak.

Libby laid a hand on his arm.

"Barrel racing, I think," Audrey went on.

"I want to do that, too!" Ava decided.

"Mom won't like it," Audrey warned. "Not unless we get to be rodeo queens."

Libby hid a smile behind a paper napkin.

"Barrel racing," Tate repeated, after clearing his throat.

"We'll need lessons," Ava said, ever practical.

Tate caught Libby's eye. *Help,* his expression said.

"You'll be fantastic," Libby told the girls. "You're McKettricks—rodeo is in your blood."

Tate gave her a *This isn't helping* look.

"Can we call Mom and tell her we're going to be barrel racers?" Audrey asked excitedly.

"Yeah, can we?" Ava chimed in.

"Go," Tate said.

They raced to the cordless phone on the kitchen counter, and Ava got there first.

"Don't you dare dial Mom's number," Audrey cried, "until I have the phone from Dad and Libby's bedroom!"

"Thanks for jumping right in there and taking my side," Tate told Libby, a wry grin tilting his mouth up on one side. But he took her hand, moved the big diamond in her engagement ring back and forth with the pad of his thumb a couple of times, and then kissed her palm, sending fire shooting through her.

"Don't do that," Libby whispered.

An impish twinkle lit Tate's wonderfully blue eyes. Where he'd been kissing, he flicked his tongue.

Libby groaned.

He laughed, tugged her onto his lap. Nibbled at her earring.

"You look hot in that dress," he murmured.

"Like a princess, I'm told," Libby said.

"You'll look even hotter when I get you out of it, of course."

She blushed. "Tate."

He slipped a finger under her low neckline, inside her bra,

found her nipple. Grinned. "Do we have to wait until New Year's to get married?" he asked, his voice a low rumble, his gaze fixed on her mouth.

Libby removed his hand, afraid the girls would come back. "Yes," she said. "We have to wait until New Year's. Why?"

"Because I want to make a baby with you."

He kissed her, long and deep.

She forgot they were in the kitchen.

"You'll want to get it right, naturally," she whispered.

"Absolutely," he responded. "And that means we need to keep right on practicing."

They kissed until the twins burst into the room again.

"Mom says we *cannot, under any circumstances,* take up barrel racing!" Audrey announced.

"Does she, now?" Tate asked. He didn't move Libby off his lap, or even stop kissing her, really.

Ava heaved a big sigh. "Come on, Audrey. Let's go watch TV."

"Yeah," Audrey agreed.

"They're practicing again," Ava said.

Audrey nodded. "And that's so boring," she replied.

They vanished into the living room.

"Boring?" Libby asked, against Tate's mouth. "I don't *think* so."

* * * * *

Mills & Boon® Online

Discover more romance at
www.millsandboon.co.uk

- 🌹 **FREE** online reads
- 🌹 **Books** up to one month before shops
- 🌹 **Browse our books** before you buy

...and much more!

For exclusive competitions and instant updates:

 Like us on **facebook.com/romancehq**

 Follow us on **twitter.com/millsandboonuk**

 Join us on **community.millsandboon.co.uk**

Visit us Online | Sign up for our FREE eNewsletter at **www.millsandboon.co.uk**

WEB/M&B/RTL4